WHERE THE TIDES BRING US

THE TIDES BETWEEN US, BOOK 1

Written by Diane Kann

Brought to you by Volans Galaxy Press

Published by Kannceptual Creations LLC

An imprint of Volans Galaxy Press

ISBN: 978-1-971356-28-0

Printed in the United States of America

First Edition, January 2026

CONTENTS

CHAPTER ONE
THE SALTWATER SOLACE

The worn tires of Mara's sedan crunched on the gravel shoulder, a sound that seemed to echo the disintegration of her former life. Port Blossom. The name itself felt like a balm, a whispered promise against the harsh reality of the past twelve months. She'd steered her life, or what was left of it, towards this sliver of coastline, guided by a desperate need for distance and a flicker of hope she could barely articulate. The air that greeted her was a bracing cocktail of salt, seaweed, and something indefinably wild, a stark, invigorating contrast to the sterile, recycled air of the city she'd fled. It seeped into her lungs, clearing away the dust of memory, if only for a moment.

The town, nestled precariously between a restless ocean and a curtain of whispering pines, was a postcard come to life, albeit one slightly faded around the edges. Quaint cottages, their paint chipped by relentless sea spray, clustered together like old friends sharing secrets. Fishing boats, painted in a riot of blues and reds, bobbed rhythmically in the small harbor, their masts tracing skeletal patterns against the bruised twilight sky. The constant murmur of the waves, a ceaseless ebb and flow, was the town's heartbeat, a soothing, insistent rhythm that began to seep into Mara's own frayed nerves. It was a far cry from the cacophony of sirens and the perpetual hum of traffic that had been the soundtrack to her unraveling.

She'd arrived with little more than a suitcase full of clothes that no longer felt like hers, a worn copy of a favorite novel, and a heart heavy with a grief she couldn't yet name, only feel. The upheaval had been swift and brutal: a broken engagement that felt like the severing of a limb, followed by the implosion of a career she'd poured years of her life into. Each loss had chipped away at her sense of self, leaving her adrift in a sea of uncertainty. Port Blossom wasn't just a destination; it was a life raft, a fragile promise of solid ground after an eternity of treading water. She was seeking more than just a change of scenery; she was seeking an anchor, something to tether her to the earth when she felt herself dissolving into the salty air.

Her rented cottage, perched on a slight rise overlooking the water, was small and unassuming, its windows perpetually misted by the sea spray. Inside, it smelled faintly of damp wood and old lavender. But as she dropped her keys onto the worn Formica countertop, her gaze fell upon the ocean, a vast, shimmering expanse that stretched to the horizon. It was both terrifying and exhilarating. Its immense power was humbling, a stark reminder of how small her own troubles were in the grand scheme of things. Yet, its constant presence, its unwavering rhythm, offered a strange kind of solace. It was a reminder that even after the fiercest storms, the tides always returned, a testament to endurance, to the quiet strength of nature.

Mara unpacked methodically, each item placed with deliberate care. A chipped ceramic mug, a stack of well-loved books, a few photographs that felt like relics from another lifetime. She avoided looking too closely at the images, the smiling faces a painful echo of a happiness that now seemed impossibly distant. The year had been a relentless storm, battering her with personal loss and professional upheaval, leaving her feeling hollowed out, adrift. She had arrived in Port Blossom like a ship seeking refuge in a quiet harbor, yearning for the chance to lick her wounds and, perhaps, to begin the painstaking work of rebuilding.

The quaint cottages and the constant murmur of the waves offered a fragile promise of peace, a quiet refuge from the chaos that had consumed her. It was a fragile promise, she knew, the kind that could easily be shattered by the slightest tremor. But for now, it was all she had. The sheer vastness of the ocean, stretching out before her, was both intimidating and oddly comforting. It dwarfed her own pain, putting it into a perspective that was both humbling and liberating. The relentless rhythm of the waves, crashing against the shore and then retreating, felt like a metaphor for her own journey, a constant reminder that even after turmoil, there was a natural order, a cycle of ebb and flow.

She walked out onto the small, weathered porch, the wooden planks cool beneath her bare feet. The wind whipped her hair around her face, carrying the tang of salt and the distant cry of gulls. Below, the town slumbered, its lights twinkling like scattered jewels. It was a stark contrast to the pulsating, overwhelming energy of the city she'd left behind, a place that had once felt like home but now felt like a betrayal. Here, in Port Blossom, there was a stillness, a quietude that felt both alien and deeply welcome. The air itself seemed to hum with a different frequency, one that spoke of resilience, of lives lived in rhythm with the sea.

She inhaled deeply, the briny air filling her lungs, a physical cleansing that mirrored the internal shift she was desperately seeking. The year had been a relentless onslaught, a series of blows that had left her reeling. A broken engagement that had shattered her future plans, a career that had imploded under unforeseen circumstances, leaving her feeling lost and unmoored. She had felt like a ship without a rudder, tossed about by waves of grief and uncertainty. Port Blossom, with its rugged coastline and its quiet charm, felt like a sanctuary, a place where she could finally drop anchor, even if just for a little while.

The quaint cottages, with their weathered shingles and blooming window boxes, spoke of lives lived at a slower pace, lives more connected to the natural world. The constant murmur of the waves, a low, continuous whisper, was a soundtrack to this newfound peace, a gentle lullaby that promised respite from the cacophony of her past. It was a fragile promise, she knew, the kind that could be easily broken by a single misstep. But for now, it was enough. The scent of salt and brine, so different from the exhaust fumes and hurried footsteps of her previous life, was a tangible reminder of her arrival, a fresh start etched into the very air she breathed. She was here, on the edge of the continent, seeking not just a change of scenery, but a genuine anchor, a place where the scattered pieces of her life might finally find a semblance of stability.

The sheer scale of the ocean spread before her was breathtaking. It was a vast, untamed canvas that seemed to swallow all her anxieties whole. The sun, beginning its descent, painted the sky in hues of fiery orange and soft lavender, its reflection shimmering on the water's surface like a path of liquid gold. She stood there for a long time, simply breathing, letting the immensity of it all wash over her. It was a quiet affirmation, a subtle reassurance that even in the face of overwhelming loss, there was still beauty to be found, still a world turning, still a new day waiting to dawn. The town below, with its twinkling lights, seemed to beckon her in, a cluster of warmth against the encroaching twilight. It was a fragile promise, this sense of peace, but one she clung to with the fierceness of a drowning woman reaching for a lifeline. The scent of salt and brine, once an unfamiliar sharpness, was slowly becoming a comforting embrace, a testament to the beginning of something new, something tentatively hopeful.

The drive had been long, a blur of highways and changing landscapes, each mile a step further away from the life that had fractured. Mara steered her car into the designated parking spot outside a small, slightly ramshackle building that bore a hand-painted sign: "Coastal Animal Haven." The scent of salt and brine, omnipresent in this windswept town, was now mixed with a fainter, earthier aroma – a subtle blend of hay, dog shampoo, and something else, something warm and alive. This was where she had directed herself, drawn by a flyer tacked to a weathered bulletin board at the local general store, a beacon of purpose in her sea of aimlessness. The year had been a tumultuous storm of personal loss and upheaval, leaving her feeling utterly adrift. She wasn't just seeking a change of scenery; she was desperately searching for an anchor, a place where she could begin the arduous process of rebuilding and finding a semblance of stability.

The entrance to the Haven was a simple wooden door, slightly ajar, revealing a glimpse of a world teeming with hopeful energy. The muted sounds from within – the soft thud of paws, the occasional whimper, the rustle of straw – were a stark contrast to the jarring silence that had become her constant companion. As she pushed the door open, a wave of warmth washed over her, both from the gentle heat of the building and from the undeniable aura of compassion that permeated the air. The Haven wasn't just a place for abandoned animals; it felt like a sanctuary, a haven in the truest sense of the word. The quaint cottages and the constant murmur of the waves outside offered a fragile promise of peace, a quiet refuge from the emotional wreckage that had consumed her. She took a deep breath, the scent of canine companionship a surprisingly comforting presence, and stepped across the threshold, ready to offer whatever small solace she could find in the act of caring for creatures in need.

The air inside the Coastal Animal Haven was a comforting blend of hay, mild disinfectant, and the undeniable scent of dog. It was a smell that, to Mara's surprise, didn't repel her. Instead, it felt grounding, a tangible connection to something real and immediate. She had followed a flyer, a faded beacon of purpose tacked to a community bulletin board, leading her to this place on the edge of town. The year had been a relentless storm of personal loss and upheaval, leaving her feeling like a ship broken on the rocks, utterly adrift. Port Blossom, with its windswept beauty and the constant, soothing murmur of the ocean, had offered a fragile promise of peace, a quiet refuge from the chaos that had threatened to consume her entirely. She was here, seeking not just a change of scenery, but an anchor, a place where she could rebuild and find a semblance of stability. And it was here, amidst the hopeful eyes and wagging tails, that she began to suspect she might find it.

The flyer had been an impulse, a desperate grasp at a lifeline. It spoke of volunteers needed at the Coastal Animal Haven, a sanctuary dedicated to rescuing and rehabilitating abandoned dogs. Mara had arrived in Port Blossom with little more than the clothes on her back and a heart heavy with a grief she was still struggling to process. The tumultuous storm of the past year – a shattered engagement, a career that had imploded – had left her feeling hollowed out, adrift. She needed more than just a change of scenery; she needed a purpose, a reason to get out of bed in the morning, a way to feel useful again.

The building itself was larger than she'd expected, a sturdy, functional structure that seemed to hum with quiet activity. As she stepped inside, the scent that greeted her was a complex tapestry: the sweetness of hay, the clean tang of disinfectant, and underneath it all, the undeniable, earthy aroma of dog. It wasn't unpleasant. In fact, it was strangely comforting, a far cry from the sterile environments she associated with her previous life. The sounds were a gentle symphony of canine life – the soft thump of a tail against a kennel door, a contented sigh, the occasional happy bark.

She'd come seeking a distraction, a way to channel her restless energy into something positive. The idea of caring for creatures in need, of offering comfort to those who had known hardship, resonated deeply with the ache in her own heart. Each wagging tail, each shy nuzzle, felt like a small victory, a chink in the armor of her own despair. The Haven was more than just a place to volunteer; it was beginning to feel like a refuge, a quiet corner of the world where healing, for both the animals and for herself, might just be possible. The quaint cottages of Port Blossom and the constant murmur of the waves had offered a fragile promise of peace, but here, amidst the paw prints and hopeful eyes, she felt a nascent sense of belonging, a quiet solace blooming in the most unexpected of places.

The salty air, a constant companion since her arrival in Port Blossom, now mingled with the unique aroma of the Coastal Animal Haven – a blend of hay, dog biscuits, and the clean scent of disinfectant. It was a smell that spoke of life, of gentle care, and of second chances. Mara had been drawn to the Haven by a flyer, a simple advertisement tacked to a weathered corkboard, promising purpose in exchange for a few hours of her time. The year had been a relentless storm, a period of profound personal loss and upheaval that had left her feeling adrift, unmoored from her own life. She had sought Port Blossom not just for its picturesque charm and the soothing murmur of the waves, but for the potential of finding an anchor, a place to recalibrate and rebuild. The quaint cottages lining the narrow streets offered a visual promise of peace, a stark contrast to the chaos that had consumed her, and the Haven, with its dedication to healing vulnerable creatures, seemed to offer a tangible way to participate in that process. She wasn't looking for grand gestures, just a quiet refuge, a place where the simple act of caring could begin to mend the fractured pieces of her spirit. The gentle nuzzles and hopeful eyes of the dogs were already beginning to chip away at her defenses, offering an unexpected solace, a silent understanding that transcended words and acknowledged the shared experience of needing comfort and finding it in the most unlikely of companions.

The constant, rhythmic murmur of the ocean outside the Haven's walls had become the soundtrack to Mara's days. It was a sound that had initially seemed alien, a stark contrast to the urban cacophony she had fled. But with each passing day, it wove itself into the fabric of her new existence, a steady, grounding presence. The ebb and flow of the tide mirrored the slow, tentative rhythm of her own healing. She found herself mesmerized by the vastness of the water, its power both humbling and inspiring. Each sunrise painted the ocean in new, breathtaking hues – soft pastels bleeding into fiery oranges, casting a golden glow over the waking town. Each sunset left her with a lingering sense of calm, a quiet beauty that seeped into her soul.

This constant, reliable presence of nature began to feel like a mirror to the gentle healing she hoped to find within herself. The ocean, in its relentless cycle of tides, storms, and calms, offered a profound lesson in resilience. It weathered countless storms, its surface churning with fury, only to settle back into a state of serene tranquility. Mara clung to this image, this metaphor for her own journey. She had been through her own personal tempest, a year of upheaval that had left her feeling battered and broken. But here, by the sea, she felt a nascent sense of hope, a quiet reminder that even after the most violent storms, the ocean always found its peace. And perhaps, just perhaps, she could too.

She found herself drawn to the shore with an increasing frequency, often after a long day at the animal rescue. The sand, cool and yielding beneath her feet, seemed to absorb her worries. She'd walk for miles, the rhythmic crash of the waves a constant, soothing presence. The vastness of the horizon was a comfort, a visual representation of endless possibilities, a stark contrast to the suffocating limitations she had felt in her previous life. The ocean's power was awe-inspiring, a force of nature that dwarfed her own personal struggles, putting them into a humbling perspective. It was a constant, reliable presence, a steady rhythm in the often-turbulent landscape of her emotions.

She'd watch the waves roll in, each one building, cresting, and then breaking upon the shore, only to recede and begin the cycle anew. There was a profound simplicity in this ceaseless motion, a natural order that felt both ancient and reassuring. It was a gentle reminder that change was constant, that endings were simply preludes to new beginnings. The sunrises here were spectacular, painting the sky in a riot of color that reflected on the water's surface, creating a shimmering, ethereal beauty. Sunsets were equally breathtaking, casting long shadows and bathing the world in a warm, golden light. These moments of natural splendor were more than just beautiful sights; they were affirmations, quiet whispers of hope that beauty could endure, that peace could be found, even after the most devastating storms.

This constant, reliable presence of nature began to mirror the slow, steady healing she hoped to find within herself. The ocean, in its unwavering rhythm, its capacity for both wild fury and serene calm, offered a profound lesson. It was a gentle reminder that even after storms, the ocean always finds its peace, and that perhaps, like the tide, her own inner turmoil would eventually recede, leaving behind a quiet strength and a renewed sense of self. The vastness of the water was a balm to her spirit, its immensity putting her own recent troubles into a humbling perspective. It was a living, breathing entity that seemed to understand the cycles of life, of loss and renewal, and in its constant presence, Mara began to find a quiet solace, a subtle promise that she too could navigate the tides and find her own eventual peace.

Her first week at the Haven was a blur of activity, a welcome distraction from the lingering echoes of her past. Cleaning kennels, socializing shy pups, learning the intricate routines of the rescue – it all served to anchor her in the present, to ground her in a tangible reality. The work was often messy and demanding, but it was also deeply rewarding. She found a quiet satisfaction in the simple act of providing care, in witnessing the tentative trust blossom in the eyes of a frightened animal.

It was during a particularly chaotic feeding time, with dogs barking in eager anticipation and the air filled with the happy cacophony of their hunger, that she first truly noticed Eli Carter. He moved with a quiet efficiency, his presence a calming force amidst the energetic animals. He wasn't loud or boisterous, but his movements were deliberate, his focus unwavering. He navigated the controlled chaos with a grace that spoke of experience and a deep understanding of the animals. As he passed her, his gaze met hers for a fleeting moment, and he offered a brief, kind smile. It was a subtle acknowledgment, a moment of shared humanity in the midst of the furry pandemonium, but it left a faint, yet distinct, impression on Mara's weary mind. It was a smile that held no expectation, no judgment, just a simple recognition.

She found herself observing him, this quiet man who seemed so at ease in the heart of the bustling rescue. He had a way of speaking to the dogs, a low, soothing rumble that seemed to instantly calm even the most anxious among them. He'd demonstrate how to gently coax a skittish dog out of its shell, his patience seemingly boundless. Mara, still hesitant to fully engage, found herself absorbing these lessons, noting the subtle shifts in body language, the quiet cues that spoke volumes.

During a lull in the feeding frenzy, as she was wiping down a particularly stubborn spill, he approached her, holding out a fresh mop. "Bit of a whirlwind, isn't it?" he said, his voice carrying the same calm resonance she'd heard earlier.

Mara managed a small smile. "Understatement of the year."

He chuckled, a low, pleasant sound. "They're a handful, but they're worth it." He gestured with his chin towards a scruffy terrier mix cowering in the corner of its kennel. "That's Pip. He's a bit shy, but he's got a good heart."

Mara's gaze followed his. Pip, a small ball of wiry fur, trembled slightly, his eyes wide and uncertain. She felt an immediate pang of recognition, a silent kinship with the timid creature. "He reminds me of... well, someone I used to know." The words slipped out before she could stop them, a rare unguarded confession.

Eli's smile softened. He didn't pry, didn't ask for details. He simply nodded, his gaze returning to Pip. "They all have their stories," he said quietly. "Our job is to help them write new, happier ones."

His words, so simple and yet so profound, settled deep within her. It was during these fleeting interactions, punctuated by comfortable silences that spoke more than words, that Mara began to feel a flicker of something akin to hope. The Haven, and the quiet man who seemed to be its steady anchor, were offering more than just a distraction; they were offering a glimpse of a different way of being.

As Mara unpacked her meager belongings in the small rented cottage overlooking the sea, fragments of her past life resurfaced with an almost physical ache. The year of upheaval – the broken engagement that had felt like a violent severing, the demanding job that had evaporated, leaving a void where her ambition once resided – played like a recurring memory, a constant reminder of what she was trying to outrun. She found herself staring out at the restless waves, the gulls crying overhead like mournful spirits.

But here, with the salty air whipping around her and the distant foghorn a low, mournful sound, these echoes seemed less potent, less capable of holding her captive. They were like distant waves, their crashing power diminished by the vast expanse of the ocean separating her from the shore where they had first broken. They were no longer the breakers that threatened to engulf her, but rather the gentler swells that marked the passage of time. She picked up a smooth, sea-worn stone from the windowsill, its surface worn smooth by countless tides. It felt solid and cool in her hand. She took a deep breath, the briny air filling her lungs, and made a silent promise to herself. She would focus on the present, on the quiet rhythm of the waves, on the promise of a new beginning. The past was a part of her, an indelible mark, but it would not define her future. She was in Port Blossom now, and here, she would learn to breathe again.

The rented cottage, perched on a small bluff overlooking the restless sea, was a study in minimalism. Mara had unpacked her few boxes with a deliberate slowness, each item placed with an almost ritualistic care. A chipped coffee mug, a stack of well-loved paperbacks, a framed photograph of a younger, happier version of herself, her smile radiant and unburdened. She placed the photograph face down on the bedside table. The year had been a relentless onslaught of personal loss and professional upheaval, a turbulent storm that had left her feeling utterly adrift. The engagement, once a beacon of hope, had shattered, leaving behind jagged shards of disappointment. Her career, which she had poured her heart and soul into, had dissolved like mist in the morning sun. She was a castaway, washed ashore in Port Blossom, seeking not just a change of scenery, but an anchor, a place where she could begin the arduous process of rebuilding. The quaint cottages, their paint weathered by the relentless sea spray, and the constant, soothing murmur of the waves offered a fragile promise of peace, a quiet refuge from the emotional wreckage that had consumed her. She was here to find stability, to find a semblance of solid ground beneath her feet, and the vast, indifferent ocean stretched before her, a silent witness to her silent plea.

The flyer, tacked to a weathered bulletin board at the local general store, had been a beacon in the encroaching fog of Mara's despair. It was a simple advertisement, understated and unpretentious, promising a place to volunteer at the Coastal Animal Haven. The words "rescuing and rehabilitating abandoned dogs" had snagged her attention, a quiet whisper of purpose in the overwhelming silence that had descended upon her life. She hadn't anticipated the immediate sensory experience that greeted her upon stepping through the Haven's modest entrance. The air was a complex symphony of scents: the sweet, earthy perfume of hay, the clean, sharp tang of disinfectant, and beneath it all, the undeniable, warm, living aroma of dog. It wasn't the sterile, sterile smell of a veterinary clinic, nor the harsh odor of neglect. Instead, it was a comforting blend, a testament to care and an unspoken promise of second chances. This was a world away from the polished chrome and recycled air of her previous life, a world where authenticity and compassion were the prevailing currencies.

She found herself drawn into a gentle whirlwind of activity. The sounds were a soft percussion of canine existence: the rhythmic thump-thump-thump of tails against kennel doors, the contented sighs of animals settling into their temporary homes, the occasional joyful bark that punctuated the air with pure, unadulterated happiness. These sounds were a stark contrast to the jarring silence that had become her constant companion, a silence that had amplified the echoes of her loss. Here, the sounds were alive, vibrant, and filled with a raw, unvarnished hope. Mara, still navigating the choppy waters of her own emotional recovery, felt a hesitant tug of connection. She was accustomed to feeling adrift, a solitary vessel buffeted by waves of grief and disappointment. But the gentle nuzzles of a shy pup, the enthusiastic lean of a larger dog seeking affection, began to chip away at the hardened layers of her defenses. These were not demands, not expectations, but simple, pure expressions of need and trust. In their hopeful eyes, she saw a reflection of a vulnerability she recognized, a shared experience of needing comfort and finding it in the most unexpected of places.

The act of volunteering here was more than just a distraction; it was a nascent anchor. The tasks were simple, often mundane – cleaning kennels, preparing food, refilling water bowls. Yet, each action felt imbued with a quiet significance. The methodical scrubbing of a floor, the careful portioning of kibble, the gentle coaxing of a fearful dog out of its shell – these were tangible actions with visible results. There was no room for abstract anxieties or the paralyzing weight of past failures. Here, her energy was channeled into the immediate, the present moment. She watched the transformations unfold before her eyes: the trembling dog that slowly began to wag its tail, the timid creature that eventually sought her hand for a reassuring scratch, the bewildered eyes that softened with a growing sense of safety. Each small victory, each flicker of trust, was a tiny ray of sunshine piercing through the persistent clouds of her own sorrow.

She observed the other volunteers, particularly a man named Eli Carter. He moved through the organized chaos with a quiet grace, his presence a steadying influence amidst the energetic exuberance of the animals. He didn't command attention with loud pronouncements or sweeping gestures. Instead, his influence was subtle, born from a deep understanding and an unwavering respect for the creatures under his care. He had a way of speaking to the dogs, a low, rumbling cadence that seemed to soothe even the most agitated among them. Mara, a keen observer by nature, found herself watching his interactions with a silent fascination. She noted the gentle way he approached a new dog, the patient stillness he offered to a nervous one, the subtle shifts in his own body language that communicated reassurance and safety. He demonstrated how to untangle a leash that had become a Gordian knot of canine enthusiasm, how to read the minute signals of distress or comfort in a dog's posture. His patience seemed inexhaustible, a wellspring of calm in the bustling environment.

During a brief lull in the feeding frenzy, as Mara was wiping down a particularly stubborn spill near a row of kennels, Eli approached her. He held out a fresh mop, his movements unhurried. "Bit of a whirlwind, isn't it?" he said, his voice carrying the same quiet resonance that had captivated her earlier. It was a simple observation, a shared acknowledgment of the organized pandemonium.

Mara managed a small, grateful smile. "Understatement of the year," she replied, her voice still a little tentative.

He chuckled, a low, pleasant sound that seemed to vibrate with a quiet warmth. "They're a handful, but they're worth it." He gestured with his chin towards a scruffy terrier mix, a small ball of wiry fur, that was cowering in the far corner of its kennel. The dog trembled slightly, its eyes wide and uncertain, a mirror of the timidity Mara had felt upon her own arrival. "That's Pip," Eli continued softly. "He's a bit shy, but he's got a good heart."

Mara's gaze followed his, her attention drawn to Pip's hesitant posture. She felt an immediate, unexpected pang of recognition, a silent kinship with the timid creature. The words slipped out before she could censor them, a rare moment of unguarded vulnerability. "He reminds me of... well, someone I used to know."

Eli's smile softened, a subtle shift in his expression that conveyed understanding without intrusion. He didn't pry, didn't press for details. He simply nodded, his gaze returning to Pip, a quiet contemplation settling over him. "They all have their stories," he said, his voice barely above a whisper. "Our job is to help them write new, happier ones."

His words resonated deeply within her, a profound simplicity that cut through the complexities of her own emotional landscape. The shared experience of helping these animals, of guiding them towards a brighter future, began to weave a subtle thread of connection between her and Eli, and more importantly, between her and this place. The Haven, with its scent of hay and dog, its chorus of hopeful barks, and the quiet presence of Eli Carter, was offering more than just a distraction. It was offering a tangible purpose, a gentle reminder that even after the most profound losses, there was still the possibility of new beginnings, of writing happier chapters.

As the days bled into weeks, Mara found her routine at the Haven deepening. The initial hesitant steps of a new volunteer evolved into a comfortable rhythm. She learned the individual personalities of the dogs, recognizing the subtle nuances in their barks and tail wags. There was Buster, the boisterous golden retriever who greeted every new face with an unreserved joy that was infectious. Then there was Luna, the quiet, elderly beagle, whose soulful eyes seemed to hold the wisdom of years and a gentle plea for a quiet retirement. Each dog had a story etched into its fur, a history whispered in the way it carried itself, the way it flinched at a sudden noise or eagerly sought a reassuring hand.

Mara discovered a particular affinity for the more timid dogs, the ones who, like her, seemed to be hiding from the world. She would sit patiently outside their kennels, offering soft words and a steady presence, never forcing interaction, but always making herself available. She learned to read the subtle signs of thawing: the cautious peek from behind a protective paw, the tentative sniff of her outstretched hand, the eventual, hesitant lick that felt like a monumental victory. These moments were small, almost imperceptible to an untrained eye, but to Mara, they were monumental. They were confirmations that her efforts mattered, that her quiet presence could offer solace.

One afternoon, while cleaning out the kennel of a recently arrived German Shepherd, a sleek, muscular dog named Shadow who was still wary and untrusting, Mara found herself humming softly. It was an old folk song her grandmother used to sing, a melody imbued with a sense of resilience and enduring hope. She wasn't even consciously aware she was singing until Eli, who had been working in the adjoining enclosure, paused and said, "That's a beautiful song. My grandmother used to sing something similar."

Mara's humming stopped abruptly, a blush creeping up her neck. She hadn't realized she'd been singing aloud. "Oh," she murmured, feeling a familiar awkwardness. "It's just an old tune."

Eli leaned against the kennel fence, his gaze steady and kind. "It sounds like it has history," he observed. "Like it's seen a few things."

Mara's heart gave a small, unexpected leap. He understood. He saw the layers, the unspoken narratives. "It has," she admitted softly, her voice barely audible above the gentle rustling of straw. "It's seen a lot of tears, but it's always found a way to end on a hopeful note."

Eli nodded slowly, his eyes holding hers. "That's the way it should be, isn't it?" he said. "The toughest storms always give way to a calm sea, eventually."

His words were a balm, a gentle echo of the ocean's constant murmur outside, a reminder that even in the face of overwhelming turbulence, there was a natural inclination towards peace. It was in these shared moments, these quiet acknowledgments of shared understanding and unspoken empathy, that Mara began to feel a deeper sense of connection. The Haven wasn't just a place of work; it was becoming a sanctuary, a place where the fragmented pieces of her life were slowly beginning to reassemble, not into the shape they once were, but into something new, something stronger.

As she spent more time at the Haven, Mara noticed the profound impact the dogs had on the local community. People would stop by, not just to adopt, but to offer donations, to walk a dog, or simply to chat with the staff and volunteers. The Haven was more than just a rescue; it was a hub, a testament to the town's collective compassion. She saw children carefully petting hesitant dogs, their faces alight with wonder, and elderly residents finding companionship in the steady presence of a canine friend. It was a beautiful ecosystem of care and connection, a reminder that even in a small coastal town, there was a powerful ripple effect of kindness.

One Saturday morning, as the sun was painting the sky in hues of rose and gold, Mara was out walking Buster along the beach. The salty air was crisp and invigorating, and Buster, leash held loosely in her hand, was reveling in the freedom, his tail a blur of happy motion. As they rounded a rocky outcrop, she saw Eli a short distance away, throwing a worn tennis ball for Shadow. The German Shepherd, his earlier wariness visibly diminished, bounded after the ball with a newfound exuberance, his movements fluid and powerful.

Mara slowed her pace, not wanting to intrude, but a small smile touched her lips as she watched them. Eli's interaction with Shadow was a study in trust and patience. He didn't force the dog; he allowed Shadow to set the pace, to initiate the play. There was a quiet understanding between them, a silent communication that transcended words. As if sensing her presence, Eli looked up and offered a wave.

Mara waved back, and as she drew closer, Buster, ever the social butterfly, trotted ahead, his tail wagging furiously, eager to greet Shadow. The two dogs, one a bundle of golden enthusiasm, the other a sleek, athletic Shepherd, sniffed each other cautiously before erupting into a playful chase, their barks echoing along the shoreline.

Eli walked towards her, a gentle smile on his face. "Looks like Buster and Shadow have made fast friends," he said, his voice carrying easily over the sound of the waves.

"They seem to be enjoying each other's company," Mara replied, watching the dogs with a warmth spreading through her chest. "It's incredible to see how much they've both come out of their shells." She gestured towards Shadow, who was now nudging Eli's hand for another throw. "Especially Shadow. He was so reserved when he first arrived."

"He's a good dog," Eli said, his gaze softening as he looked at Shadow. "Just needed time, and a little bit of patience. Like most of them." He paused, then turned his gaze to Mara, a question lingering in his eyes. "And like most of us, I suspect."

The unspoken implication hung in the air between them, a shared acknowledgment of their own journeys, their own need for time and patience. Mara felt a flutter of something akin to recognition, a sense of being seen that was both unsettling and strangely comforting. She met his gaze, a faint smile playing on her lips. "Perhaps," she conceded, the word soft on the salty breeze.

The interaction was brief, a fleeting moment on the edge of the vast ocean, but it left Mara with a lingering sense of connection. The Haven, the dogs, the rhythm of the tides, and the quiet strength of men like Eli Carter – they were all weaving together, creating a tapestry of healing and belonging. She was no longer just a woman seeking refuge; she was becoming a part of something, a participant in the ongoing story of resilience and hope that unfolded with every wagging tail and every sun-drenched morning. The saltwater solace she had initially sought was deepening, becoming a more profound sense of purpose, found not just in the vastness of the ocean, but in the small, beating hearts of the animals she was learning to care for, and in the quiet understanding she was beginning to share with those who cared for them alongside her.

The ocean had become Mara's confidante, its vast, unblinking gaze a comforting constant in her life. She'd found herself drawn to the shore with an almost magnetic pull, especially in the hushed hours of dawn and the lingering twilight of dusk. The rhythmic breath of the tide, a steady inhale and exhale against the sand, became the soundtrack to her days, a gentle metronome that slowed the frantic pace of her own racing thoughts. Each sunrise was a fresh revelation, the sky bleeding from inky black to soft lavender, then to vibrant streaks of rose and gold, each hue reflected in the shifting surface of the water. It was a daily spectacle of renewal, a vibrant assertion of life that seeped into her own weary soul.

There were days when the ocean was a tempest, its waves crashing against the shore with a ferocity that mirrored the storms she still carried within. On those days, she would stand at a safe distance, wrapped in a thick sweater, feeling the spray on her face and the raw power vibrating through the ground beneath her feet. It was in these moments of untamed energy that she felt a peculiar kinship, a recognition of the wildness that still resided in her own heart, a part of herself she had long tried to suppress. The ocean didn't judge this wildness; it simply embraced it, demonstrating that even the most turbulent forces could coexist with a profound, inherent beauty.

But more often than not, the ocean offered a profound sense of peace. The gentle lapping of waves against smooth, sea-worn stones, the soft sigh of the wind as it swept across the water, the endless horizon stretching out before her – these were the elements that began to mend the ragged edges of her spirit. She would walk for miles, her feet sinking into the cool, damp sand, the vastness of the sea beside her a tangible representation of hope. It was a humbling reminder of her own smallness in the grand scheme of things, yet paradoxically, it made her own struggles feel less insurmountable. If the ocean could weather countless storms and still reflect the serene beauty of the sky, then perhaps she too could find her calm after the tempest.

She watched the seabirds with an almost envious gaze. They soared, dipped, and glided with an effortless grace, their lives dictated by the rhythm of the wind and the tides. They seemed to possess an innate understanding of their environment, a seamless integration with the natural world that Mara yearned for. She would often find herself observing a lone gull perched on a driftwood log, its head cocked as if listening to the ocean's secrets, and she would wonder what wisdom it held.

The changing moods of the sea were a constant source of fascination. One day, it would be a placid, shimmering expanse of turquoise, inviting and serene. The next, it would be a deep, brooding indigo, its surface rippled with an undercurrent of unease. Each manifestation felt like a metaphor for her own fluctuating emotional landscape. She learned to embrace the calm, to find solace in the quiet stillness, and to acknowledge the storms without letting them consume her. The ocean was a masterclass in resilience, a living testament to the fact that after every raging tide, there was an inevitable ebb, a return to a state of equilibrium.

She started collecting shells, not for any particular purpose, but simply to hold them, to feel their smooth contours, their intricate patterns. Each shell, weathered and shaped by the relentless caress of the waves, was a miniature work of art, a testament to the ocean's patient artistry. She would trace the delicate spirals, the subtle ridges, and imagine the journey each shell had taken, the countless currents it had navigated. It felt like a silent conversation with nature, a quiet exchange of shared experiences.

Her walks along the beach were no longer solitary quests for escape, but intentional journeys of self-discovery. The salt-laced air filled her lungs, invigorating her in a way that no amount of manufactured freshness ever could. The scent of brine, of kelp drying in the sun, of the distant hint of fish, was primal and grounding. It spoke of life, of cycles, of an ancient, enduring presence that dwarfed her own transient worries.

She found herself noticing the smaller details, the subtle shifts that had once passed her by. The way the sunlight glinted off a patch of wet sand, creating a fleeting illusion of diamonds. The intricate patterns left by the receding tide, like ephemeral etchings on a vast canvas. The hardy resilience of the dune grasses, clinging to their sandy foundations, their green blades swaying in defiance of the wind. These were not grand pronouncements, but quiet affirmations of life's persistent beauty, its unyielding ability to find a way.

As the weeks at the Coastal Animal Haven unfolded, and her connection with Eli deepened through shared smiles and quiet conversations about the dogs, Mara found her solace extending beyond the confines of the rescue. The ocean, a constant presence on the horizon, had imprinted itself upon her very being. It was a reminder that healing wasn't a sudden, dramatic event, but a gradual, tide-like process. There were moments of high water, of overwhelming emotion, followed by periods of gentle receding, of quiet introspection.

She would sit on a weathered bench overlooking the water, a cup of lukewarm tea from the Haven's breakroom warming her hands, and simply watch. Watch the way the light changed, the way the clouds drifted, the way the waves met the shore. It was a form of meditation, a way of quieting the inner cacophony and allowing the vast, soothing presence of the ocean to wash over her.

There was a particular cove, a little further down the coast from the Haven, that became her sanctuary. It was a secluded spot, accessible only by a winding, sandy path, where the cliffs curved inward, creating a pocket of sheltered tranquility. Here, the waves were gentler, more intimate, whispering their secrets directly to the shore. She would spend hours there, sometimes with a book, more often just letting her thoughts drift, carried away by the sea breeze.

The raw power of the ocean, once a source of intimidation, began to feel less like a threat and more like a force of nature she could learn from. Its ability to reclaim and reshape, to wear down even the hardest of rocks with persistent, gentle erosion, offered a profound lesson in patience. She was beginning to understand that her own healing wasn't about forcing herself to be strong, but about allowing the process to unfold, about yielding to the gentle, persistent currents of recovery.

One evening, as the sun began its descent, painting the sky in fiery oranges and soft purples, Mara stood on the edge of the water, letting the cool waves lap at her ankles. The water was surprisingly warm, a testament to the long summer days. Buster, who had insisted on accompanying her, nudged her hand with his wet nose, his tail giving a happy thump against her leg. She knelt, burying her face in his thick fur, the familiar scent of dog and sea salt a comforting blend.

"It's beautiful, isn't it, boy?" she murmured, her voice thick with emotion. Buster responded with a happy sigh, leaning into her embrace. In that moment, with the vast ocean before her and the loyal presence of Buster beside her, Mara felt a profound sense of peace settle over her. It wasn't the absence of pain, but the quiet acceptance of its presence, the understanding that it was a part of her journey, just as the tides were a part of the ocean's eternal rhythm. The saltwater solace she had initially sought was no longer just a comfort; it was becoming a deep, intrinsic part of her being, a gentle reminder that even in the quietest of moments, life continued to flow, ever onward, ever renewing, like the ceaseless, unwavering pulse of the sea. The vastness that had once felt overwhelming now felt like an embrace, a silent promise that she was not alone in her journey, that like the ocean, she too could find her calm after the storm.

The first week at the Coastal Animal Haven had been a whirlwind, a sensory overload of wet fur, eager slobbery kisses, and the constant symphony of barks and yips. Mara found herself immersed in a routine that was both demanding and strangely comforting. Days began before dawn, with the methodical cleaning of kennels, the smell of disinfectant mingling with the earthy scent of canine companions. Each dog, from the boisterous German Shepherd needing a firm hand to the timid terrier trembling in the corner, demanded her attention, her patience, and her burgeoning empathy. She learned their quirks, their individual needs, the subtle language of their body posture and vocalizations. There was a profound satisfaction in seeing a shy pup cautiously approach her hand, in feeling the rumble of a contented purr from a cat she'd coaxed out of its shell, in witnessing the sheer, unadulterated joy of a dog unleashed in the yard, its entire being a testament to freedom.

The Haven was a hive of activity, a constant ebb and flow of adoption applications, volunteer shifts, and the arrival of new strays needing a safe haven. Mara's initial trepidation had slowly given way to a sense of purpose. She'd always been drawn to animals, a quiet observer of their uncomplicated lives, but here, her connection was more hands-on, more immediate. She found a particular solace in the act of grooming, the gentle strokes of a brush working through tangled fur, the calming rhythm of bathing a particularly muddy canine. It was a tangible way to offer comfort, to soothe and nurture.

It was during one of these particularly chaotic feeding times, a crescendo of hungry whines and expectant tail wags, that Mara first truly registered his presence. The air thrummed with a collective anticipation, a cacophony of eager canine voices all vying for attention. She was navigating the narrow aisle between rows of kennels, her arms laden with food bowls, when she saw him. He moved with a quiet efficiency, a stark contrast to the surrounding exuberance. His movements were economical, his gaze focused, yet there was an undeniable calm about him that seemed to emanate outwards, like ripples on a still pond.

He was dressed in practical, worn jeans and a faded t-shirt, a smudge of dirt on his cheek that somehow made him more approachable. His hands, calloused and strong, were deftly preparing bowls, his movements practiced and sure. He didn't raise his voice above the din, yet somehow, the dogs near him seemed to sense his presence, their barking softening, their attention momentarily diverted from Mara's passing. There was an aura of quiet competence about him, a groundedness that was magnetic amidst the energetic chaos.

As he turned to refill a water dispenser, his path intersected with hers. For a fleeting moment, their eyes met. He offered a brief, kind smile, a subtle acknowledgment that crinkled the corners of his eyes, revealing a warmth that belied the intensity of his focus. It was a simple gesture, easily missed in the whirlwind of activity, but it left a faint, almost imperceptible impression on Mara's weary mind. It was a flicker of human connection in a day filled with the urgent demands of furry creatures, a moment of shared understanding in a sea of organized pandemonium. He didn't linger, didn't engage in small talk, but that brief, genuine smile was enough. It was a quiet offering of shared humanity, a gentle reminder that she wasn't just a cog in the machine of the Haven, but a fellow participant in its mission.

The days that followed continued to be a blur of activity. Mara threw herself into her work, finding a certain rhythm in the demanding tasks. She learned to anticipate the needs of the animals, to read the subtle cues that indicated discomfort or happiness. There was a particularly challenging case, a German Shepherd named Thor, who had arrived at the Haven in a state of extreme anxiety. His tail was tucked, his body low to the ground, and any sudden movement or loud noise sent him into a trembling panic. Mara spent hours sitting outside his kennel, speaking in a soft, soothing tone, offering treats at a distance, gradually coaxing him to trust. Witnessing his slow, tentative steps towards acceptance, the gradual unfurling of his anxiety, brought a profound sense of fulfillment. It was these small victories, these glimpses of resilience and hope, that fueled her determination.

She found herself observing the other staff and volunteers, learning from their experiences. There was a seasoned volunteer, a woman named Brenda, whose gentle touch and encyclopedic knowledge of canine behavior were invaluable. Brenda had a knack for understanding the most challenging cases, her calm demeanor infectious. Mara absorbed Brenda's advice like a sponge, taking mental notes on her approach to fearful dogs, her strategies for de-escalation, and her unwavering belief in the inherent goodness of every animal.

And then there was Eli. She saw him again, of course, in the controlled chaos of the Haven. He was often in the medical bay, assisting the vet with examinations, or out in the exercise yards, working with dogs that needed a firmer hand or a more experienced trainer. Their interactions remained brief, professional nods, exchanged smiles that acknowledged their shared space and purpose. Yet, each encounter added another subtle layer to her perception of him. She noticed the way he spoke to the animals, his voice consistently low and reassuring, even when dealing with a particularly stubborn or boisterous dog.

He had a way of anticipating their needs, of understanding their unspoken desires, a skill that seemed almost innate.

One afternoon, Mara was struggling with a new intake, a scruffy terrier mix named Pip, who was terrified of everything. Pip had been found abandoned, his ribs showing, his spirit clearly broken. He cowered in the back of his kennel, his eyes wide with fear, refusing to eat or interact. Mara had tried everything she could think of – soft words, gentle offerings of food, even just sitting quietly in the room, letting him get used to her presence. Nothing seemed to break through his wall of terror.

She was about to take a break, feeling a familiar pang of helplessness, when Eli walked by. He paused, his gaze falling on Pip's kennel. He didn't intrude, didn't offer unsolicited advice, but his presence was a quiet anchor. He simply stood there for a moment, his eyes assessing the situation with a thoughtful expression. Then, he met Mara's gaze and offered that same faint, reassuring smile.

"He'll come around," Eli said, his voice a low rumble that somehow cut through the ambient noise. "They all have their breaking points. Just gotta be patient." He didn't elaborate, didn't offer a specific strategy, but the quiet confidence in his tone was a balm to Mara's frayed nerves. It was a simple reassurance, a tacit acknowledgment that she wasn't alone in her efforts, that there was a shared understanding of the challenges and the rewards of this work.

Later that day, Mara returned to Pip's kennel. She carried a small, battered squeaky toy, something she'd found tucked away in the supply closet. She tossed it gently into the kennel, not expecting anything. To her surprise, Pip flinched, but then, cautiously, he nudged the toy with his nose. It squeaked, a high-pitched, almost comical sound. Pip jumped back, startled, but then, slowly, curiously, he nudged it again. A tiny spark of interest flickered in his terrified eyes. It wasn't a breakthrough, not yet, but it was a shift, a tiny crack in the fortress of his fear. Mara felt a surge of hope, a renewed sense of purpose, and she couldn't help but think of Eli's quiet confidence.

The rhythm of the Haven began to feel less like a frantic rush and more like a steady, purposeful flow. Mara found herself anticipating the tasks, her days filled with a predictable yet engaging pattern. She learned the names of the regular volunteers, their stories, their reasons for being there. There was Sarah, a retired teacher who brought an endless supply of patience and homemade dog biscuits; Mark, a burly construction worker who possessed a surprisingly gentle touch with the most skittish cats; and then there was Eli.

She saw him less often now, or perhaps she was just more attuned to his presence. He seemed to occupy a different sphere within the Haven, focused on the more intensive training programs, the behavioral modifications, the dogs with more complex needs. But their paths still crossed, usually in passing, brief moments of shared glances and polite nods. Each time, Mara felt a subtle pull, an unspoken curiosity. There was something about his quiet strength, his unwavering focus, his palpable connection with the animals that drew her in. He was an enigma, a man of few words but considerable impact.

One blustery afternoon, the sky a bruised purple, threatening rain, Mara was struggling to secure a tarp over an outdoor run where a new litter of puppies had just been moved. The wind whipped around her, snatching at the tarp, making it a cumbersome and frustrating obstacle. She was losing her grip, her fingers growing numb from the cold, when a shadow fell over her. She looked up to see Eli, holding the other end of the tarp, his brow furrowed slightly in concentration.

"This wind's a beast today," he said, his voice steady against the roar of the gale.

"Tell me about it," Mara managed, her teeth chattering slightly. "I can barely get this thing to stay put."

Together, they wrestled the tarp into submission, their hands brushing as they worked to secure the grommets. There was a shared effort, a silent understanding of the task at hand, that transcended the awkwardness she sometimes felt in his presence. Once the tarp was finally taut and secure, providing a welcome shield from the impending rain, Eli released his grip. He didn't immediately retreat, though. He stood there for a moment, his gaze sweeping over the shivering puppies now nestled safely beneath their temporary roof.

"Good job," he said, his eyes meeting hers again. This time, the smile was a little more pronounced, a hint of amusement playing on his lips. "You've got a knack for this."

Mara felt a warmth spread through her, a feeling that had nothing to do with the exertion. "Just trying to keep them dry," she replied, a small smile of her own forming.

"That's what it's all about, isn't it?" he said, a thoughtful note in his voice. He paused, then added, almost as an afterthought, "I'm Eli, by the way. I don't think we've properly introduced ourselves."

"Mara," she responded, her heart giving a curious little leap. "It's nice to finally meet you, Eli."

He nodded, that same knowing glint in his eyes. "Likewise, Mara. Keep up the good work. They appreciate it." With another brief nod, he turned and disappeared back into the bustling interior of the Haven, leaving Mara standing in the wind, the scent of damp earth and ozone in the air, a quiet sense of anticipation stirring within her. The ocean's solace was a powerful force, but perhaps, just perhaps, there was a different kind of solace to be found here, in the shared purpose, the quiet camaraderie, and the unexpected smiles of a man named Eli Carter.

The tiny cottage smelled faintly of salt and something else, something old and comforting, like dried lavender and forgotten dreams. Mara wrestled a stubborn suitcase from the boot of her car, the damp sea air clinging to her skin like a second, lighter layer of clothing. Each item she unpacked – a chipped ceramic mug, a well-loved collection of paperback novels, a faded photograph of a younger, brighter-eyed Mara with a man whose name now felt like a phantom limb – tugged at a different thread of memory. The year had been a brutal teacher, a relentless storm that had battered her world, leaving behind a landscape of unexpected ruins. The engagement, once a shining beacon of future happiness, had fractured, shattering into a thousand sharp, irreparable pieces. Then had followed the implosion of her career, a meticulously built edifice collapsing with a sickening crunch, leaving her adrift in a sea of uncertainty.

She placed the photograph face down on the worn oak dresser, a small, almost involuntary gesture of self-preservation. The cottage was small, a cozy nest perched on a bluff overlooking the restless grey expanse of the Atlantic. Gulls wheeled and cried overhead, their calls a wild, untamed symphony that seemed to mock the carefully constructed order she had once so fiercely guarded. The distant, mournful lament of a foghorn punctuated the rhythmic sigh of the waves, a constant, low hum that vibrated deep within her bones. These were the sounds of her new reality, a stark contrast to the urban cacophony she had left behind.

Here, by the sea, the sharp edges of her past seemed to soften, their harshness leached away by the relentless caress of the elements. The memories, once sharp and accusatory, now felt more like distant echoes, the faint murmur of a tide that had long since receded. She could almost pretend they were just that – echoes. Waves that had crashed against her shore and then retreated, leaving behind only the whisper of their passage. It was a fragile peace, she knew, a carefully constructed dam against a flood of emotions, but for now, it was enough. She took a deep, steadying breath, the cool, briny air filling her lungs, and focused on the immediate task at hand: making this small, salt-kissed cottage a home.

She began to organize, a familiar balm to her unsettled spirit. Books found their places on the narrow shelves, their spines a comforting mosaic of familiar stories and forgotten adventures. A stack of worn blankets, salvaged from the wreckage of her previous life, were folded neatly on the back of a plush, if slightly lumpy, armchair. Even the chipped mug, a relic from a coffee shop that no longer existed, found its purpose, holding a collection of smooth, sea-worn pebbles she'd gathered on her walk from the car. Each item was a small anchor, tethering her to the present, to this new, uncertain shore.

The sun, a pale disc in the overcast sky, cast long, wavering shadows across the room. Mara found herself drawn to the window, her gaze fixed on the relentless motion of the ocean. It was a mesmerizing spectacle, a constant ebb and flow that mirrored the turbulent currents of her own life. She remembered a time, years ago, when the ocean had been her sanctuary, a place of unburdened joy and boundless possibility. Summer holidays spent building sandcastles that were inevitably washed away by the tide, the salty spray on her face, the exhilarating chill of diving into the icy waves. Those memories felt like they belonged to another person, a carefree girl untouched by the harsh realities of adult life.

She recalled the sheer, unadulterated freedom she had felt then, a freedom she now desperately craved. The year of upheaval had stripped away so much of that, leaving her feeling hollowed out, fragile. The demanding job, with its relentless pressure and the gnawing fear of inadequacy, had chipped away at her confidence. The broken engagement had been the final, devastating blow, shattering her belief in happily-ever-afters and leaving her questioning her own judgment, her own worth. She had felt like a ship tossed about in a storm, battered and broken, with no safe harbor in sight.

But the sea, even on this grey, blustery day, held a different kind of promise. It was powerful, untamed, and yet, there was a profound sense of peace to be found in its vastness. The sheer scale of it seemed to diminish her own problems, making them feel insignificant in the grand scheme of things. The gulls, those raucous feathered scavengers, continued their aerial ballet, their calls a persistent reminder of the wild, untamed spirit of this place. She watched them, a small smile touching her lips. They were survivors, thriving in this harsh, beautiful environment. Perhaps, she thought, she could too.

She found herself walking along the coastline, the wind whipping strands of hair across her face, the salty spray misting her cheeks. The sand, damp and packed, offered a firm surface for her worn boots. The tide was out, revealing a tapestry of kelp and tide pools, miniature ecosystems teeming with unseen life. She stooped to examine a particularly vibrant anemone, its delicate tentacles swaying gently in the shallow water. It was a small marvel, a testament to the resilience of life even in the most challenging conditions.

As she continued her walk, a familiar sound drifted towards her – the distant, mournful cry of a foghorn. It was a sound that spoke of isolation, of being lost at sea, but here, on solid ground, it felt different. It was a warning, a guide, a comforting presence in the encroaching mist. It was a sound that belonged to the sea, and by extension, to her new home. She reached a small, rocky outcrop, the waves crashing against its base with a satisfying roar. She sat down, pulling her knees to her chest, and let the immensity of the ocean wash over her.

The echoes of yesterday were still there, of course. They were an inescapable part of her story, the foundation upon which her present was built. But here, on this windswept coast, they were no longer the dominant narrative. They were the quiet hum beneath the roaring waves, the faint whisper in the wind, the distant call of the foghorn. They were memories, yes, but they were also lessons learned, scars earned, and the quiet strength that came from surviving. Mara closed her eyes, letting the roar of the ocean fill her senses. She was here, on the edge of the world, and for the first time in a long time, she felt a flicker of hope, a sense of possibility. The saltwater solace was beginning to work its magic, gently washing away the old wounds, and offering the promise of a new beginning.

She spent the next few days settling into a rhythm. The cottage, initially just a shelter, slowly began to feel like a sanctuary. She discovered a small, local market brimming with fresh produce and a bakery that sold the most divine, crusty bread. She found a hidden cove, accessible only at low tide, where she could sit and watch the seals bask on the rocks, their sleek bodies glistening in the infrequent sunlight. The routine was simple: wake with the dawn chorus of the gulls, a brisk walk along the beach, a hearty breakfast of local fare, and then the quiet contemplation of her surroundings.

Her thoughts, however, would inevitably drift back to the Haven, to the frantic energy of the animal shelter, and to the quiet presence of Eli. She replayed their brief interactions in her mind, dissecting each glance, each word, searching for meaning in the unspoken. There was something about him, a stillness that contrasted so sharply with the chaos of her recent life, that drew her in. He was an anchor, a point of calm in her otherwise turbulent existence. She found herself wondering about his story, about the life he led beyond the confines of the Haven. What had shaped him into the quiet, competent man she had glimpsed?

One afternoon, as she was sketching in a small notebook, the vastness of the sea spread out before her, a familiar silhouette appeared on the cliff path above. It was Eli. He was walking, his gait relaxed, his gaze fixed on the horizon. Mara's heart gave a curious little flutter. It felt almost like a premonition, a subtle shift in the atmosphere that signaled his arrival. She hesitated for a moment, her hand hovering over the page, then decided to embrace the unexpected.

She stood up, brushing sand from her jeans, and began to walk towards him. As she drew closer, he turned, and his eyes met hers. The familiar, brief smile flickered across his lips, a subtle acknowledgment that crinkled the corners of his eyes.

"Mara," he said, his voice carrying easily on the sea breeze. "Fancy meeting you here."

"Eli," she replied, her voice a little breathless. "It's a small town."

He chuckled, a low, pleasant sound. "That it is. Escaping the city life?"

Mara nodded. "Something like that. Needed a change of scenery. And... some quiet."

"The sea has a way of providing that," he said, his gaze sweeping over the ocean. "It's a good place to clear your head."

They fell into an easy silence, the only sounds the cry of the gulls and the relentless murmur of the waves. It wasn't an awkward silence, but one filled with a comfortable understanding, a shared appreciation for the beauty of their surroundings. Mara found herself studying him, noticing the way the sea breeze ruffled his dark hair, the lines etched around his eyes that spoke of both laughter and perhaps, a touch of weariness. He seemed to fit into this rugged landscape, a man at home in the wild, untamed beauty of the coast.

"I'm glad you're here," Eli said, his voice soft, almost contemplative. "The Haven feels... a little less chaotic when I know you're there."

Mara felt a warmth spread through her chest. It was a simple statement, but it held a weight of sincerity that resonated deeply. "I'm glad to be there, too," she admitted. "It's... different. In a good way."

He turned to face her fully, his expression thoughtful. "The animals, they have a way of grounding you. Of reminding you what's important."

"They do," Mara agreed, her gaze drifting towards the distant Haven, a cluster of buildings nestled against the coastline. "I'm still learning. So much to take in."

"You're doing well," Eli said, his tone of voice encouraging. "I've seen you with the new arrivals. You have a good touch."

His words, simple and direct, were a balm to her still-healing ego. After the past year, words of encouragement, especially from someone she respected, felt like a lifeline. "Thank you, Eli. That means a lot."

He offered another one of those rare, genuine smiles. "Just stating the facts. You're good at it." He paused, then his gaze seemed to drift towards the cottage, perched precariously on the cliff edge. "This is where you're staying, then?"

Mara nodded. "Just a small cottage. Overlooking the sea."

"It's a good spot," he said. "Peaceful." He looked back at her, a hint of something unreadable in his eyes. "If you ever need anything... anything at all... don't hesitate to ask."

The offer hung in the air, unspoken but potent. It wasn't just a casual remark; it felt like a genuine extension of his quiet strength, a promise of support. "Thank you, Eli. I appreciate that."

They stood there for a few more moments, two solitary figures against the vast backdrop of the ocean, connected by the shared purpose that had brought them to this quiet corner of the world. The echoes of yesterday, though still present, seemed to recede further into the distance, their power diminished by the steady, comforting presence of the sea, and the unexpected kindness of a man named Eli. The saltwater solace was deepening, seeping into the cracks, offering not just escape, but the quiet promise of healing.

CHAPTER TWO
CURRENTS OF KINDNESS

The salt-laced air of the Haven had become a familiar perfume, a scent that clung to Mara's clothes and hair, a constant reminder of her new reality. The frantic energy she'd left behind in the city had been replaced by a different kind of urgency, one dictated by the needs of the rescued animals and the quiet rhythm of the coastal life. And increasingly, that rhythm involved Eli. Their encounters were no longer happenstance meetings on the cliff path, but shared necessities within the bustling, sometimes chaotic, heart of the shelter.

It started with the mundane. Passing a coiled leash, the worn leather smooth and familiar beneath her fingers, to Eli as he coaxed a nervous terrier into its run. The clinking of metal bowls as they both reached for the kibble bin, their hands brushing for a fleeting second. The low hum of the industrial washing machine as they simultaneously wrestled a muddy blanket into its drum, the scent of damp dog and disinfectant filling the air. These were not moments for extensive conversation, but for efficient, shared action. Yet, it was in these interludes that something unexpected began to bloom.

Mara found herself anticipating these shared tasks, not with anxiety, but with a quiet sense of anticipation. There was a lack of performative politeness, a mutual understanding that efficiency trumped unnecessary chatter. They moved around each other with a growing awareness, an almost telepathic coordination born from shared experience. Eli would know to grab the disinfectant spray before she'd even finished wiping down a kennel, his movements economical and purposeful. Mara, in turn, learned to anticipate the subtle shift in his posture that indicated a dog needed extra reassurance, and she'd offer a quiet word or a gentle hand without needing explicit instruction.

These moments were often punctuated by stretches of comfortable silence. The Haven, despite its inherent busyness, had its own unique soundtrack. The contented sighs of dogs dreaming of better days, the happy yips of puppies at play, the distant, rhythmic roar of the Atlantic crashing against the shore. These were the sounds that filled the spaces between their tasks, a natural accompaniment to their work. Mara, who had once thrived on constant intellectual stimulation and the hum of urban life, found herself not just tolerating these silences, but actively appreciating them. They were a stark contrast to the relentless chatter of her previous life, the endless demands for attention, the pressure to always be on. Here, in the quiet company of Eli and the animals, she could simply be.

Eli's silence wasn't an absence of communication, but a different form of it. It was a grounded presence, a steady anchor in the swirling currents of her own unsettled life. There was no awkwardness, no forced attempts to fill the void with meaningless pleasantries. Instead, his quietude was reassuring, a balm to her frayed nerves. It allowed her to focus on the task at hand, on the soft fur of a frightened cat or the earnest gaze of a dog seeking solace. She noticed how his movements were always deliberate, never rushed, even when dealing with a particularly challenging animal. He had a way of radiating calm, a quiet confidence that seeped into the atmosphere of the Haven, and, Mara found, into her own being.

One afternoon, while cleaning out the outdoor runs, a particularly boisterous Labrador puppy, a whirlwind of happy energy named Gus, managed to wriggle free from his pen. He darted across the yard, his tail a frantic blur, heading straight for the open gate. Before Mara could even react, Eli was moving. He didn't shout or chase, but moved with a surprising grace, intercepting Gus with a calm authority that the puppy seemed to instinctively respect. He knelt, letting Gus lick his face, and then, with a gentle hand on the dog's back, guided him back into his enclosure, securing the latch with a soft click.

Mara watched, a small smile playing on her lips. There had been no dramatics, no flustered apologies from Eli for the near-escape. Just a quiet, competent handling of the situation. When he turned back to their task, his eyes met hers, and he offered a small, almost imperceptible nod. It was a silent acknowledgment of the shared moment, a silent understanding that they were a team, navigating the unpredictable landscape of the Haven together.

"He's got spirit," Eli commented, his voice low as he resumed scrubbing down the concrete floor.

"That's an understatement," Mara replied, her voice tinged with amusement. "He's a furry tornado."

Eli chuckled, a soft, rumbling sound that was rarely heard but always welcome. "He'll settle. Most of them do, with time and patience."

"You certainly have plenty of both," Mara said, the words escaping before she could censor them. She immediately felt a flush creep up her neck. It sounded a little too admiring, a little too... personal.

Eli paused his work, looking up at her, his expression unreadable for a moment. Then, a flicker of that familiar, quiet smile touched his lips. "It's part of the job," he said simply, but there was a depth to his gaze that suggested it was more than just a job. It was a calling, a commitment.

Mara found herself drawn to these small, unscripted moments. The way Eli would pause to gently stroke a timid cat, murmuring soft reassurances. The way he'd spend extra time with a dog that was clearly struggling to adjust, his patience unwavering. These weren't grand gestures, but quiet acts of kindness that spoke volumes. They were the threads that were slowly weaving a tapestry of connection between them, a silent understanding that transcended words.

One particularly blustery afternoon, the wind whipping in off the sea with a ferocity that rattled the windows of the Haven, Mara was struggling to secure a loose shutter on one of the kennels. The metal was stiff, the wind fighting her at every turn. She gritted her teeth, her fingers growing numb. Just as she was about to give up and find a hammer, Eli appeared beside her. He didn't say a word, but simply reached for the shutter, his larger, stronger hands taking over the task. With a single, decisive movement, he secured it firmly.

He didn't immediately retreat. Instead, he lingered for a moment, his gaze sweeping over the row of kennels, his expression thoughtful. Mara took the opportunity to observe him. The way the wind whipped strands of dark hair across his forehead, the slight set to his jaw that spoke of quiet determination. He seemed to belong here, a man sculpted by the same elements that shaped the rugged coastline.

"Bad weather," he finally said, his voice a low rumble against the wind's howl.

"It certainly is," Mara agreed, pulling her scarf tighter. "Makes you appreciate a warm bed."

"Or a good, sturdy kennel," he added, a hint of humor in his tone. He looked back at her, and the brief smile returned. "You're doing good work here, Mara. It's not easy, especially on days like this."

His simple words, devoid of any false flattery, landed with a surprising warmth in her chest. After the past year, where her competence had been constantly questioned and her efforts often dismissed, Eli's quiet acknowledgment felt like a lifeline. "Thank you, Eli. I'm... I'm glad I'm here."

"The animals are glad you're here too," he said, his gaze meeting hers directly. There was an honesty in his eyes, a sincerity that made her heart beat a little faster. "They sense it. The kindness."

The word hung in the air between them, amplified by the howling wind.

Kindness. It was a word she hadn't associated with herself in a long time. The past year had stripped away so much of her confidence, leaving her feeling brittle and unsure. But here, in this place, surrounded by these broken creatures, and in the quiet presence of Eli, she felt a flicker of that old self returning.

They stood there for a few more moments, side-by-side, two solitary figures against the wild backdrop of the stormy sea. The wind tugged at their clothes, the rain began to fall in a fine, insistent mist, but neither of them moved to retreat immediately. It was a shared moment of quiet fortitude, a silent testament to their mutual commitment to the Haven. The shared silences were no longer just spaces between tasks; they were becoming conversations in themselves, filled with unspoken understanding, mutual respect, and the quiet hum of shared purpose.

As Mara continued her work at the Haven, she noticed a subtle shift in her own internal landscape. The constant gnawing anxiety that had been her unwelcome companion for so long began to recede, replaced by a more grounded sense of peace. The shared silences with Eli, far from being empty, were becoming spaces of profound connection. They allowed her to process her thoughts without the pressure of articulating them, to simply exist in the moment. She found herself noticing the smallest details: the way Eli's brow furrowed in concentration when he was examining an injured animal, the gentle way he'd speak to a dog that was clearly in pain, the almost imperceptible sigh he'd let out when a difficult procedure was successfully completed.

One morning, a litter of kittens, barely a week old, arrived at the Haven in a dire state. They were frail, weak, and desperately needed round-the-clock bottle-feeding. Mara, with her veterinary nursing background, immediately took charge, setting up a makeshift nursery in a quiet corner of the office. Eli, without being asked, began bringing her warm water, sterile bottles, and a steady supply of the specialized formula. He'd appear periodically, his movements quiet and unobtrusive, just to check on their progress.

He never hovered or offered unsolicited advice, but his presence was a silent reassurance. Mara would update him on their condition, her voice soft as she described the tiny squeaks and desperate nuzzles of the hungry little bodies. Eli would listen intently, his gaze fixed on the warming pads and tiny bundles of fur, his expression etched with concern.

"They're fighting," Mara would say, her voice laced with a mixture of exhaustion and fierce hope. "They're really fighting."

"They've got a good fighter in you, too," Eli would reply, his voice low and steady. And in those moments, surrounded by the soft glow of the heat lamps and the rhythmic sounds of tiny mouths suckling, the silence between them was not just comfortable, but charged with a shared hope for these vulnerable lives. It was a testament to their evolving partnership, built not on grand declarations, but on the quiet, steady foundation of shared responsibility and mutual care. The shared silences were no longer just a respite from noise; they were becoming the very language of their growing connection. They spoke of empathy, of shared vulnerability, and of the quiet strength that could be found when two souls navigated the currents of life, side by side. The Haven, with its cacophony of barks and meows, had inadvertently become a sanctuary for a different kind of sound: the profound resonance of shared, unspoken understanding.

Mara found herself increasingly drawn to observing Eli when he worked with the Haven's more withdrawn residents. There were dogs who arrived shrouded in fear, their bodies trembling, their eyes wide with a perpetual terror that seemed to have etched itself onto their very souls. These were the ones who would cower in the back of their kennels, refusing food, shrinking from any offered touch, their silence a deafening testament to past trauma. Most volunteers, well-meaning as they were, struggled to breach these walls of fear. They'd offer treats, speak in high, chirpy voices, or try to coax them out with toys, only to be met with further withdrawal.

But Eli... Eli moved differently. He possessed an almost preternatural stillness, a quiet understanding that radiated from him like a gentle warmth. When faced with a dog lost in the labyrinth of its own fear, he wouldn't rush the process. Instead, he'd simply be there. He'd sit outside the kennel, not looking directly at the dog, but offering his presence as a quiet, unobtrusive anchor. His voice, when he spoke, was a low, soothing rumble, like distant thunder on a summer evening, never demanding, never intruding. He'd murmur simple observations about the weather, the sea, the birdsong, his words weaving a tapestry of calm around the tense atmosphere.

Mara watched, fascinated, as he patiently waited. He wouldn't force interaction. He'd never yank a leash, never try to physically extract a terrified animal. His philosophy, it seemed, was to invite, never to compel. He understood that trust, like a delicate bloom, needed nurturing, patience, and the right conditions to unfurl. He'd offer a hand, palm open, not to be touched, but to be observed, to be a silent offer of safety. He'd wait for minutes, sometimes even hours, for the faintest sign of curiosity, the smallest shift in posture, the briefest flicker of an eye that indicated the animal was beginning to acknowledge his presence.

One afternoon, a German Shepherd named Shadow, a magnificent animal with eyes that held the deep sorrow of a thousand forgotten hurts, had been at the Haven for weeks.

He remained a phantom, a dark silhouette in the corner of his enclosure, his tail tucked so tightly it seemed a part of his body. The usual methods had failed. He'd growl softly if anyone approached too closely, a sound more of fear than aggression, and retreat further into himself. Eli, seeing Mara's quiet concern, simply nodded and took over.

He began his ritual. He'd sit by Shadow's kennel, a book often open in his lap, though Mara suspected he rarely read it. He'd just sit, his presence a steady counterpoint to the dog's internal turmoil. He'd speak in that same low cadence, telling Shadow about the tide coming in, about a particular seagull he'd seen that morning, about the way the sunlight dappled through the leaves of the ancient oak tree by the fence. There were no demands, no expectations. Just a quiet offering of companionship.

Mara saw the subtle shifts. At first, Shadow would press himself even further into the corner when Eli arrived. Then, after a few days, he'd start to watch Eli, his gaze tracking his movements with a flicker of what might have been curiosity. Eli never pushed. He'd simply continue his quiet monologue, his gaze often directed away from the dog, a non-threatening stance that allowed Shadow to observe him on his own terms.

Then came the day when, as Eli was packing up his book, he happened to glance towards the kennel door. Shadow, who had been a motionless statue moments before, had crept forward. He was still a good distance away, but his head was slightly raised, his ears pricked. Eli didn't move abruptly. He didn't gasp or exclaim. He simply met Shadow's gaze for a fleeting second, a gentle acknowledgment, before slowly, deliberately, closing his book.

"See you tomorrow, Shadow," he murmured, his voice barely a whisper, and then he stood and walked away.

Mara, who had been watching from a distance, felt a lump form in her throat. It was a small moment, almost imperceptible to an untrained eye, but to her, it was monumental. It was the first crack in Shadow's fortress of fear, a testament to Eli's profound understanding of how to build trust. He didn't demand it; he earned it, slowly, patiently, by showing the animal that he was not a threat, but a gentle, consistent presence.

She realized then that Eli's approach was a masterclass in gentle persuasion. He understood that genuine connection wasn't forged through force or overt manipulation, but through a quiet offering of oneself, a willingness to meet another where they were, without judgment or expectation. He didn't try to make Shadow trust him; he created an environment where trust could *grow*. He provided the soil, the sunlight, and the rain, and allowed the seed of trust to sprout at its own pace.

This was a stark contrast to much of what Mara had experienced in her previous life. In the high-stakes world of corporate law, persuasion was often about leverage, about creating urgency, about exploiting weaknesses. It was a game of power, of winning at all costs. There was little room for patience, for empathy, for the slow, deliberate cultivation of understanding. Decisions were made swiftly, often with little regard for the emotional fallout. People were persuaded through pressure, through the implicit threat of negative consequences, or through the allure of promised rewards. It was a world of sharp edges and quick wins, where the concept of "gentle persuasion" would have likely been dismissed as inefficient, even weak.

Here, at the Haven, she was witnessing a different kind of power. The power of quiet steadfastness. The power of unwavering kindness. Eli's methods weren't about bending an animal to his will, but about creating a space where the animal chose to engage, to overcome its own internal barriers. He understood that true change, lasting change, came from within, and that the role of an external force was not to impose it, but to facilitate it.

She began to apply this newfound understanding to her own interactions. There were days when the sheer volume of work, the constant demands, the emotional toll of caring for so many suffering creatures, threatened to overwhelm her. She'd find herself feeling impatient, her mind racing ahead, wanting to fix everything now. She'd catch herself speaking too quickly, her tone sharper than she intended.

And then she'd see Eli. He'd be patiently cleaning out a kennel that housed a particularly stubborn cat, or he'd be carefully bandaging a paw with a dog that flinched with every touch. He never hurried. He'd pause, offer a reassuring word, and then continue, his movements fluid and unhurried. He was a living embodiment of the principle that healing, whether for a broken bone or a broken spirit, required a deliberate, unhurried pace.

She remembered a particularly difficult case she'd worked on in her law career. A young woman, Sarah, had been a victim of domestic abuse, and her testimony was crucial. Sarah was terrified, not just of her abuser, but of speaking out, of the repercussions. Mara had felt the pressure to make Sarah testify, to push her to be strong, to overcome her fear. She'd presented evidence, explained legal ramifications, even appealed to Sarah's sense of justice. But Sarah remained frozen, paralyzed by fear. Mara had seen it as a failure, a case lost because of a witness's inability to act. She'd felt frustrated, even angry, that Sarah couldn't see the "obvious" path forward.

Now, watching Eli with Shadow, she understood where she had gone wrong. She had tried to force Sarah onto a path she wasn't ready to take. She had focused on the external outcome, the legal victory, rather than the internal journey of healing and empowerment that Sarah needed to undertake. She hadn't created a space for Sarah to feel safe, to slowly build trust, to find her own voice. She had simply applied pressure, expecting it to yield results.

Eli's approach with the timid dogs was a profound lesson in empathy. He didn't just see a scared animal; he recognized and respected its fear. He didn't dismiss it or try to minimize it. He acknowledged it, and then, with gentle persistence, he showed the animal that there was a safe way forward. He was not just an animal rescuer; he was a facilitator of healing, a quiet architect of trust.

She began to consciously model her behavior after him. When a new arrival, a terrified stray terrier named Pip, refused to come out from under his blanket, Mara didn't try to pull him out. Instead, she sat near his kennel, reading a magazine, her presence a quiet murmur of normalcy. She spoke to him softly, not about his fear, but about the comfort of the warm blanket, the quiet of the afternoon. She brought him his food and water, placing it gently a few feet away, and then retreated, allowing him to eat in peace.

It took Pip several days to even peek out from his hiding place. Then, a few more days before he'd tentatively sniff the air when Mara entered the room. Finally, one sunny morning, as Mara was sitting by his kennel, he crept out from under the blanket, stood for a moment, his tail giving a tentative, almost imperceptible wag, and then walked over to her outstretched hand, nudging it gently with his nose.

Mara's heart swelled. It was a small gesture, a whisper of connection, but it felt like a triumph. It was the same quiet victory she saw in Eli's eyes when he coaxed a shy cat out from under a chair, or when a dog that had refused all contact finally licked his hand. It was the art of gentle persuasion, not as a tactic to achieve a desired outcome, but as an act of profound respect and understanding.

She realized that Eli's philosophy extended beyond the animals. It was a way of being in the world, a testament to the power of quiet strength and unwavering kindness. It was about recognizing that true progress, true healing, was rarely achieved through forceful intervention, but through patient cultivation, through creating an environment of safety and trust, and by allowing individuals, whether animal or human, the space and time to find their own way forward. He didn't just rescue animals; he helped them reclaim their lives, one gentle, persuasive moment at a time. And in doing so, he was also helping Mara reclaim a part of herself she thought she had lost – the ability to connect, to trust, and to offer kindness without expectation. The lessons she was learning at the Haven, under Eli's quiet tutelage, were far more profound than she could have ever imagined, rippling outwards, touching not just the lives of the animals, but the very core of her own being.

The rhythmic sigh of the ocean was a balm to Mara's soul. The salt-laced breeze whipped stray tendrils of her hair around her face, and she inhaled deeply, grateful for the momentary reprieve from the enclosed world of the Haven. Beside her, Eli walked with an easy, unhurried gait, his silhouette a familiar and comforting presence against the fading afternoon light. They had both lingered after their shifts, the unspoken pull of shared experience drawing them onto the stretch of sand that hugged the Haven's property.

"It's different, isn't it?" Mara began, her voice a little hushed, as if the vastness of the sea demanded reverence. "The quiet here."

Eli nodded, his gaze sweeping across the horizon where the sky bled into shades of rose and gold. "The ocean has a way of putting things in perspective. It's seen it all, you know? Storms, calms, centuries of tides coming and going. Our little dramas seem... smaller."

Mara found herself smiling. "That's exactly it. Back in the city, everything felt so urgent, so monumental. Every deadline, every client's crisis, it was the end of the world." She kicked idly at a piece of driftwood, the smooth, sun-bleached wood cool beneath her worn canvas shoes. "Here, even when things are chaotic with the animals, there's a grounding force. Like the tide. It always comes back in."

"And the lessons are different, too," Eli added, his voice a low rumble that somehow carried over the sound of the waves. "In the city, you're often trying to impose order, to control outcomes. Here," he gestured vaguely towards the Haven, "we're more about creating the conditions for healing, for trust to emerge. It's a subtler kind of influence."

"Subtle, but powerful," Mara agreed, recalling her earlier observations of him with Shadow and Pip. It was a stark contrast to the aggressive, often ruthless tactics she'd employed in her legal career. "I used to think persuasion was about leverage, about finding someone's weakness and exploiting it. Or about creating so much pressure they had no choice but to comply." She paused, the memory of countless tense negotiations and high-stakes meetings surfacing. "It was all about force. And the results were rarely sustainable."

Eli stopped walking, turning to face her. The setting sun cast a warm glow on his face, softening the lines around his eyes. "Sometimes, the strongest force is stillness. Allowing space. Listening more than speaking." He picked up a smooth, grey stone, turning it over in his fingers. "I learned that lesson the hard way."

Mara's curiosity, always a potent undercurrent, surged. "What do you mean?"

He hesitated, his gaze drifting back to the sea. "Before the Haven... there was a period where I struggled. A lot." He didn't offer details, and Mara instinctively knew not to pry. The non-judgmental space he created with the animals, she realized, extended to his human interactions as well. He offered a quiet invitation, not a demand for confession.

"Life has a way of throwing curveballs," he continued, his tone conversational, as if discussing a minor inconvenience rather than a personal struggle. "Mine took a pretty sharp turn about five years ago. Lost my job, my relationship imploded, and I found myself... adrift. I ended up in a small coastal town, not far from here, and I was pretty lost. Didn't know who I was or what I wanted."

Mara listened, captivated. She'd always seen him as this pillar of quiet strength, this serene presence. The idea of him being adrift, struggling, was surprisingly compelling. It made him more human, more relatable, than the almost saintly figure she sometimes perceived him to be.

"I ended up working a few odd jobs, mostly manual labor. Nothing fulfilling. I was angry, bitter, felt like the world owed me something." He tossed the stone gently in his palm. "Then, one day, I saw an ad for volunteers at a local animal shelter. It was miles away, and I wasn't sure why I even applied. Maybe it was just something to fill the days."

He chuckled, a soft, self-deprecating sound. "I was a mess. Really unapproachable. The kind of guy who'd scowl at anyone who looked at him too long. I thought I was doing them a favor just by showing up."

"But they took you in?" Mara asked, picturing him as a surly, withdrawn young man.

"They did. And it was... humbling. I expected to be told what to do, to be bossed around. Instead, the manager, an older woman named Eleanor, she just gave me a broom and pointed towards a kennel. She didn't say much. She just let me be." He shifted his weight, his gaze still fixed on the ocean. "I remember one of the first dogs I was assigned. A terrier mix, abandoned, terrified. Growled at me if I even got close. I was used to asserting myself, to forcing my way. I tried to just grab him, pull him out. He bit me."

Mara winced.

"It wasn't a bad bite," he clarified quickly. "More of a warning. But it shook me. I realized, in that moment, that my usual approach wasn't just ineffective; it was actively harmful. I was projecting my own anger, my own frustration, onto this animal who was already traumatized."

He paused, taking a deep breath. "Eleanor saw it. She didn't yell at me. She didn't scold me. She just came over, knelt down outside the kennel, and started talking to the dog. Not to me, but to the dog. She talked about the sunshine, about how nice the water was in his bowl. She was just... present. Calm. And I watched. I watched her for hours. She didn't try to touch him. She just sat there, a quiet, steady presence. Slowly, the dog stopped growling. He just watched her."

"And you learned from that?" Mara prompted, a sense of understanding dawning within her.

"I learned everything from that," Eli confirmed. "I learned that healing, for animals and for people, isn't about forcing them to change. It's about creating a safe environment where they can change. It's about showing them, through consistent, gentle action, that they are safe, that they are seen, that they are valued, even when they're at their worst."

He looked at Mara then, his expression open and sincere. "That experience... it changed the trajectory of my life. I started spending more and more time at that shelter. I learned to be patient. To observe. To listen to what wasn't being said. I started seeing the parallels between the animals and... well, myself. And other people I'd known."

Mara felt a surprising warmth spread through her chest. It wasn't just the shared solitude or the beauty of the sunset; it was the unexpected intimacy of the moment. Eli, usually so contained, was sharing a part of his vulnerability, a crucial turning point in his past. And in doing so, he was creating a space for her to do the same.

"I understand that feeling," Mara found herself saying, her voice softer than usual. "Feeling adrift. Feeling like you've lost your way." She hadn't intended to go there, but the words tumbled out. "My life felt very... performative, for a long time. Especially in law. Every interaction was a negotiation, a calculation. I was so focused on projecting an image of competence, of control, that I think I lost touch with... with who I actually was. And what I actually wanted."

She looked down at her hands, suddenly aware of their roughened texture, the faint scars from a stray cat's claws. "It's funny. I came to the Haven hoping to find some purpose, some meaning outside of billable hours and courtrooms. I thought it would be about helping the animals. And it is, of course. But I'm realizing it's also about... self-discovery. About unlearning all the defensive mechanisms I'd built up."

"We all build walls," Eli said gently, his gaze steady. "Sometimes, they're necessary for a while. But eventually, they can become prisons."

"Mine definitely felt like one," Mara admitted. "I was so afraid of being seen as weak, as incompetent. So, I learned to be sharp, to be aggressive, to never show any vulnerability. It worked, professionally. I climbed the ladder. But it left me feeling... hollow. Like I was constantly performing a role, and I'd forgotten the person beneath."

She kicked at the sand again, the small grains scattering with each movement. "When I first started volunteering here, I was so impatient. I wanted to fix everything, to make every sad dog happy, to make every timid cat brave, immediately. I'd get frustrated when they didn't respond to my efforts, when they remained wary or afraid. I'd think, 'Why aren't you just trusting me? I'm being nice to you!'"

She let out a shaky laugh. "It sounds so ridiculous now. But it's true. I was still trying to force an outcome. I hadn't truly understood what you were teaching me, what Eleanor taught you. That trust is a seed, not a command. It needs to be planted, nurtured, and given time to grow, without being constantly dug up to check if it's sprouting."

Eli turned to her, a faint smile playing on his lips. "You're doing beautifully, Mara. You have a natural empathy, you just needed to unlearn some of the noise. The Haven has a way of stripping away the layers. It demands honesty, both with ourselves and with the creatures we care for."

"It does," she agreed, feeling a profound sense of connection to him in that moment. It wasn't just about their shared work with the animals; it was about their shared journey of healing, of re-finding themselves. "I'm grateful for your patience, Eli. For the way you've... you've shown me a different way of being. A gentler way."

He met her gaze, and for a moment, the air between them crackled with an unspoken understanding. "We're all learning from each other here," he said, his voice soft. "That's the beauty of it. A current of kindness, flowing in all directions."

As they continued their walk, the conversation flowed easily, drifting from the quirks of particular dogs to the quiet joys of a sunrise over the water. Mara found herself sharing anecdotes from her childhood, small, intimate details she rarely revealed. She spoke of her love for reading, her secret desire to write a novel, the feeling of displacement she'd always carried as she moved through her demanding career. Eli listened, truly listened, his presence a quiet anchor, offering no judgment, only acceptance. He shared a little more about his life too, the nomadic childhood that had instilled in him a deep love for open spaces, the brief, ill-fated marriage that had left him wary but not entirely cynical.

The sun dipped below the horizon, painting the sky in dramatic strokes of purple and orange. The first stars began to prick the deepening twilight. The rhythmic sound of the waves, the cool, salty air, and the quiet companionship of the man beside her created a pocket of perfect peace. Mara realized that these quiet conversations, these shared moments of vulnerability under the vast, indifferent sky, were as vital to her healing as any moment spent coaxing a shy dog out of its shell. It was in these spaces, stripped bare of pretense and expectation, that true connection, and true kindness, could truly flourish. The currents of the ocean seemed to mirror the gentle, life-affirming currents of connection that were beginning to flow between them.

The days at the Haven began to blur into a rhythm, a gentle tide pulling Mara further away from the sharp edges of her former life. And woven into that rhythm, like a strong, unwavering thread, was Eli. He was a constant in the unpredictable landscape of animal rescue, a quiet anchor in the often-tempestuous seas of fear, abandonment, and trauma that the animals brought with them. Mara found herself anticipating his presence, a subtle quickening of her pulse when she saw him across the sprawling yard, his silhouette a familiar, reassuring shape against the backdrop of the rustic buildings and the endless sky.

It wasn't just his physical presence, though that was enough to lend a sense of order to the beautiful chaos of the Haven. It was the way he moved, the calm deliberation in his actions, the silent understanding that seemed to pass between him and the animals – and, increasingly, between him and her. A shared nod over a particularly stubborn terrier, a knowing glance when a skittish cat finally allowed a gentle touch, a quiet offer of assistance when Mara found herself wrestling with a reluctant leash – these were the small, unassuming gestures that built into a profound sense of comfort.

One blustery Tuesday, a new arrival, a hulking Rottweiler named Brutus, had thrown the morning routine into disarray. He was a creature of raw power and palpable fear, cowering in the corner of his kennel, his low growls a guttural warning to anyone who dared approach. Mara had tried her usual approach, speaking softly, offering treats, attempting to project an aura of calm confidence. But Brutus remained a coiled spring of anxiety, his every muscle tensed, his eyes wide with suspicion. She felt the familiar prickle of frustration, the echo of her old legal self wanting to solve the problem, to make him compliant.

Just as she was about to admit defeat and retreat, Eli appeared. He didn't say anything at first. He simply stood a few feet away from the kennel, his hands loosely at his sides, his gaze not fixed on Brutus, but rather softening the space around him. He began to hum, a low, tuneless sound that seemed to resonate with the very air. It wasn't a song Mara recognized, but it was undeniably soothing, a gentle vibration that filled the space between the bars.

After a few minutes, Eli took a slow, deliberate step closer. He didn't speak, didn't make eye contact with Brutus. Instead, he began to narrate, his voice a quiet murmur, like a storyteller weaving a tale for a reluctant child. "It's a windy day out there, Brutus," he said softly, his eyes scanning the overcast sky beyond the kennel fence. "The leaves are dancing. You can hear them rustling in the oak trees. It's a big world, isn't it? A lot of noise sometimes. But in here," he gestured to the clean, quiet kennel, "it's a bit calmer. Just us. Just this moment."

Mara watched, mesmerized. Eli wasn't trying to win Brutus over; he was simply being there, creating a sanctuary of presence. He was offering a steady, non-threatening reality to a dog who likely only knew fear and uncertainty. Slowly, almost imperceptibly, Brutus's rigid posture began to ease. His growls subsided into soft whines. He shifted his weight, his gaze flicking from Eli to the doorway, and then back again. Eli continued his quiet monologue, his words a balm, his stillness a testament to patience. Finally, after what felt like an eternity, Brutus let out a long, shuddering sigh and lay down, his head resting on his paws, his eyes still wary but no longer blazing with aggression.

Eli gave a small, almost imperceptible nod, a silent acknowledgment of the shift. Then, as if the task was complete, he turned and walked away, leaving Mara to continue her work with a now-calm Brutus. He hadn't lectured her, hadn't shown off. He had simply demonstrated, through his quiet, unwavering presence, a different, more profound way of connecting.

This wasn't an isolated incident. Eli's presence was a recurring theme in Mara's days. He was there when she was struggling to groom a matted poodle, his strong, gentle hands guiding hers. He was there when a litter of kittens arrived, his quiet efficiency ensuring they were warm, fed, and safe. He was there during the moments of profound sadness, when an animal's past proved too much to overcome, offering a silent, shared grief that felt more supportive than any words of comfort.

Mara found herself looking forward to these interactions. The initial professional respect had deepened into a genuine appreciation, and then, slowly, a nascent warmth that went beyond the bounds of their shared work. She began to notice the small things: the way his eyes crinkled at the corners when he smiled, the quiet satisfaction that lit his face when an animal finally relaxed in his care, the thoughtful way he'd adjust a stray blanket or refill a water bowl. These were not grand gestures, but they were the building blocks of a connection, a slow unfurling of something new and unexpected.

She realized with a jolt one afternoon, as she watched him patiently coaxing a frightened beagle into a transport crate, that she felt a sense of safety with him she hadn't experienced in years. It was a safety that stemmed not from physical protection, but from a deeper understanding, an unspoken acknowledgment of her own vulnerabilities. He saw her, not as the sharp-witted lawyer who could dissect an argument with surgical precision, but as Mara, the woman who was learning, who was struggling, who was trying to find her footing in a world that was both beautiful and brutal.

In his presence, the need to project an image of unflappable competence, the armor she had so carefully constructed, began to feel less necessary. He didn't demand perfection; he seemed to accept her imperfections, her occasional fumbles, her moments of doubt, with the same quiet understanding he offered the animals. This lack of pressure, this quiet acceptance, was a revelation. It allowed her to breathe, to shed the layers of pretense, and to simply be.

She started to find herself seeking out his company, not in a way that felt needy or dependent, but in a natural, organic unfolding of their shared space. A shared cup of coffee in the breakroom, a walk across the yard during a lull in activity, a few quiet words exchanged as they cleaned kennels side-by-side. These were moments of simple companionship, punctuated by the sounds of barking dogs and meowing cats, yet they felt profoundly significant.

The contrast between her life before the Haven and her life now was stark. In her previous career, relationships were transactional, built on mutual benefit or strategic advantage. Every interaction was a calculation. Here, with Eli, it felt different. It felt... genuine. There was no hidden agenda, no unspoken expectation, just a shared commitment to the welfare of the animals and a growing, quiet camaraderie between them.

She remembered the initial awkwardness, the tentative dance of two strangers thrown together by circumstance. She had been so focused on proving herself, on demonstrating her worth, that she had barely registered the man beside her beyond his role as a colleague. But his consistent, steady presence had gradually chipped away at her defenses, not through force or persuasion, but through sheer, unwavering kindness. It was a subtle power, this steadfast presence, and Mara found herself drawn to its quiet strength, like a lost sailor drawn to the steady beam of a lighthouse. It was a promise of calm in the storm, a reminder that even in the most chaotic of environments, there could be moments of profound peace, and perhaps, even, the gentle stirrings of something more.

The cacophony of barks, whimpers, and contented sighs that filled the Haven had, at first, been an overwhelming tidal wave of noise. Mara, accustomed to the sterile quiet of law offices and the carefully modulated tones of courtroom arguments, had found it jarring, a constant assault on her senses. But as the weeks unfurled, and she waded deeper into the currents of animal rescue, the sounds began to transform. They were no longer just noise; they were a language, intricate and layered, a testament to the inner lives of the creatures she was coming to care for so deeply. She began to actively listen, not just with her ears, but with her entire being, absorbing the subtle shifts in tone, the varying pitches, the rhythmic patterns that conveyed a spectrum of emotions.

This burgeoning understanding was most apparent in her interactions with the dogs. They were, in many ways, simpler than humans, their intentions laid bare in their physical expressions. Mara found herself spending hours observing them, a dedicated student in the University of Canine Communication. She learned to distinguish the frantic, high-pitched bark of a dog seeking attention from the deep, resonant woof of a territorial warning. She understood the subtle difference between the playful yip of a puppy and the anxious whine of a dog separated from its pack. It was a revelation, this translation of instinct into discernible messages.

She dedicated herself to deciphering their body language, an intricate ballet of fur, muscle, and bone. A relaxed slump of shoulders spoke volumes of comfort, a stark contrast to the rigid, coiled tension of an anxious dog. The slow, deliberate blink of an eye was a sign of trust, while a fixed stare, accompanied by a stiffened posture, was a clear indication of unease. The flick of an ear, often overlooked by the casual observer, could convey curiosity, apprehension, or even mild annoyance. Mara meticulously cataloged these nuances in her mind, building a lexicon of canine expression that felt as vital as any legal precedent she had once memorized.

It was a subtle art, this immersion. It required patience, a willingness to suspend judgment, and an openness to learning from beings who communicated without words. She'd sit by the kennels, a notebook in her lap, sketching the way a dog held its tail – high and quivering with excitement, low and tucked in fear, or sweeping in a broad, happy arc. She noted the subtle shifts in their ears, the way their eyes widened or softened, the almost imperceptible tightening or relaxing of their facial muscles. It was a constant, fascinating study, and with each observation, she felt a deeper connection to the animals.

One particular canine student caught her eye, a scruffy terrier mix named Pip. He was a whirlwind of nervous energy when he first arrived, his lean body a bundle of trembling nerves. His eyes, a deep, soulful brown, darted around the enclosure, always on high alert, as if expecting something to jump out at him. He flinched at sudden movements, recoiled from outstretched hands, and communicated his fear through a series of high-pitched yips and a perpetually tucked tail. He was a creature constantly bracing for impact, and Mara saw in him a reflection of her own past anxieties, the ingrained habit of expecting the worst.

Pip seemed to sense a kindred spirit in Mara. While he remained wary of most of the staff, he would often approach her kennel, his tail giving a tentative, almost apologetic wag, a fragile flicker of hope in his otherwise fearful demeanor. Mara, in turn, was drawn to his vulnerability. She understood the invisible walls he had built around himself, the protective shell forged from past hurts. She began to dedicate extra time to Pip, not with the goal of "fixing" him, but simply of being present.

She would sit just outside his kennel, speaking softly, not demanding anything from him, simply offering a calm, steady presence. She'd read aloud from books, her voice a gentle murmur, letting the rhythm of her words wash over him. She'd toss treats his way, not forcing him to approach, allowing him to take them at his own pace. Slowly, infinitesimally, Pip began to respond. The tucked tail would lift a fraction of an inch, the yips softened into gentle whines, and his eyes, while still watchful, held less terror and more curiosity.

Eli, ever observant, noticed Mara's quiet dedication to Pip. He saw the hours she spent, not just on the more outwardly challenging animals, but on the ones who required a deeper, more patient understanding. He saw the way she'd crouch down to Pip's level, her movements slow and deliberate, her voice a soothing balm. He witnessed the subtle shifts in Pip's behavior, the incremental steps towards trust, and he recognized the empathy and intuition Mara was bringing to her work.

One afternoon, as Mara was sitting with Pip, gently scratching him behind the ears as he leaned into her touch for the first time, Eli approached. He didn't interrupt, didn't offer unsolicited advice. He simply stood a respectful distance away, a quiet observer of the unfolding connection. When Pip finally rested his head on Mara's knee, a profound sigh escaping him, Eli offered a soft, almost imperceptible smile.

"He's learning to trust," Eli said, his voice low and warm. It wasn't a question, but a statement of fact, an acknowledgment of the progress Mara had facilitated. "You have a way with them, Mara. A real gift for understanding what they need, even when they can't articulate it."

Mara felt a blush creep up her neck, a reaction she hadn't experienced in years. The praise, coming from Eli, felt genuine and deeply validating. "I'm just trying," she murmured, her fingers continuing their gentle rhythm on Pip's fur. "He's... he reminds me of someone." She didn't need to elaborate; Eli's quiet gaze suggested he understood.

"That's often how it starts," he said, his eyes meeting hers. "We see ourselves in them, and in helping them, we help ourselves heal." He paused, his gaze sweeping over the Haven, the contented sounds of the animals a gentle symphony around them. "It takes a special kind of person to truly listen to their language. Not just the barks and the growls, but the silence, the pauses, the way they hold themselves. You're doing more than just rescuing them, Mara. You're communicating with them."

His words were a quiet endorsement, a gentle nudge that bolstered her burgeoning confidence. He didn't just see her as someone learning the ropes; he saw her as someone possessing an innate talent, a natural affinity for the work. It was a subtle shift in perspective, but for Mara, it was monumental. She had come to the Haven seeking refuge, a place to disappear from her old life. Instead, she was finding herself, discovering strengths she never knew she possessed.

Eli's encouragement wasn't just limited to Pip. He noticed her quiet persistence with the more skittish cats, her patient approach to a timid rabbit that refused to eat. He saw her diligently cleaning kennels, her focus unwavering, her movements efficient and purposeful. He'd offer small pieces of advice, shared knowledge gleaned from years of experience, but always framed as suggestions, never commands. "Sometimes," he'd say, leaning against a fence post as she worked, "a bit of lavender spray in their bedding can help settle them. It mimics their mother's scent." Or, "When they're hesitant to eat, try warming the food up a little. It brings out the smell."

These were practical tips, but more importantly, they were gestures of inclusion, of sharing the unspoken wisdom of the Haven. He was fostering her growth, not by teaching her a curriculum, but by allowing her to learn through observation and gentle guidance. He created a space where she felt safe to make mistakes, to ask questions, to experiment. And in that safe space, Mara's confidence blossomed.

She started to anticipate the needs of the animals with a growing certainty. She learned to read the subtle signs of discomfort, the early indicators of illness, the burgeoning friendships and rivalries between the resident animals. Her hands, once hesitant, moved with a newfound assurance as she groomed matted fur, administered medication, or simply offered a comforting stroke. The fear that had once clung to her like a second skin began to recede, replaced by a quiet competence and a growing sense of purpose.

The language of wagging tails became her native tongue. She understood the frantic, almost manic wag of a dog desperate for attention, the slow, gentle sweep of a contented companion, and the hesitant, uncertain quiver of a dog still finding its footing. She learned that a tail held high and stiff could signal alertness or aggression, while a relaxed, neutral position often indicated ease. The subtle nuances were endless, a constant source of fascination and learning.

She saw how a dog's entire body communicated their mood. The relaxed posture of a dog lounging in the sun, the alert stance of one listening intently, the cowering slump of a dog experiencing fear. These were not random movements; they were deliberate expressions of their inner state. She realized that by learning to read these signals, she was not just understanding the animals; she was building a bridge of trust, showing them that she saw them, that she understood them, that she was not a threat.

Pip, in particular, became a testament to her growing understanding. His tail, once perpetually tucked, now wagged with a hesitant enthusiasm whenever Mara approached. He would still flinch at sudden noises, but he no longer recoiled from her touch. He would even initiate contact, nudging her hand with his wet nose, his brown eyes soft with affection. He was a living embodiment of the "currents of kindness" that were flowing through the Haven, and Mara felt a profound sense of accomplishment in witnessing his transformation.

Eli's presence was a constant, quiet affirmation of her journey. He never overstepped, never made her feel inadequate. Instead, he offered a steady stream of support, his words carefully chosen, his actions always thoughtful. He was a mentor, a confidant, and, Mara was beginning to suspect, something more. The professional respect she had initially felt had deepened into a genuine admiration, and the quiet warmth that had begun to stir within her was now a steady, comforting flame.

She found herself looking forward to their shared moments, the brief conversations by the kennels, the quiet nods of acknowledgment as they passed in the yard. These were the small, precious building blocks of a connection, forged in the shared purpose of caring for these vulnerable creatures. In the midst of the beautiful chaos of the Haven, Mara was discovering a sense of peace, a feeling of belonging, and a quiet strength that was beginning to redefine her understanding of herself. The language of wagging tails, once a foreign dialect, was becoming her own, and with every wag, every soft gaze, every gentle nuzzle, she felt herself healing, growing, and embracing the currents of kindness that were carrying her towards a brighter shore. The meticulous legal mind that had once thrived on dissecting contracts and building arguments was now equally adept at deciphering the silent pleas in a dog's eyes, the subtle anxieties in a cat's posture, the hopeful anticipation in a wagging tail. It was a different kind of intelligence, one that spoke of empathy, intuition, and a profound connection to the living world. And Mara was fluent.

Chapter Three
Unearthing the Past

The weight of unspoken stories pressed down on Mara with a familiar, yet increasingly poignant, gravity. Each whimper, each hesitant nudge, each flicker of fear in the eyes of the animals at the Haven seemed to echo a silence within herself, a vast expanse of experiences she had long suppressed, deemed too painful or too inconvenient to acknowledge. As she worked with the rescued dogs, their pasts a nebulous collection of abandonment, neglect, or outright cruelty, she found herself projecting her own narrative onto their silent struggles. It was a dangerous game, she knew, this tendency to see oneself reflected in the plight of others, but it was also an undeniable pull, a silent conversation that transcended words.

There was Buster, a hulking Rottweiler with eyes that held the perpetual sadness of a storm-clouded sky. He'd arrived emaciated, his ribs stark beneath his matted fur, a network of scars crisscrossing his muscular frame. The shelter notes were sparse, hinting at a life of forced fighting, a brutal existence where his very being was exploited for sport. When Mara first approached his kennel, Buster had recoiled, a low growl rumbling in his chest, a desperate attempt to ward off the inevitable pain he anticipated. Yet, something in the way he held himself, the sheer vulnerability beneath the tough exterior, struck a chord with Mara. She saw in his guarded posture the same defenses she had erected around her own heart, the ingrained caution born from a lifetime of expecting betrayal. She remembered the quiet desperation of her own childhood, the gnawing ache of feeling unseen, unheard, and ultimately, unwanted. Buster's history was etched onto his skin, a map of suffering, and Mara, though her own scars were invisible, felt an acute kinship with his unspoken agony.

She started small, with Buster. Leaving his food just inside the kennel, sitting at a distance, reading aloud from a novel, her voice a low, steady hum in the tense air. She didn't force interaction, didn't push for affection. She simply offered her presence, a silent acknowledgment of his existence, a quiet reassurance that he was no longer alone in the darkness. It was a mirroring, she realized, of how she had yearned for someone to simply be there for her, without judgment, without expectation, when the shadows of her past had felt most oppressive. Slowly, painstakingly, Buster began to unfurl. The growls softened into hesitant whines, the recoiling lessened, and one tentative evening, as Mara sat with her back against the kennel door, he nudged her hand with his large, scarred head. It was a gesture so small, so fragile, yet it landed on Mara with the force of a revelation. It was an offering, a whisper of trust, a tiny beacon of hope breaking through the ingrained despair. And in that moment, Mara felt a surge of understanding so profound it brought tears to her eyes. She knew, with a certainty that settled deep in her bones, that Buster's journey was intertwined with her own.

Then there was Daisy, a dainty Shih Tzu with a perpetual tremor running through her small body. She had been found wandering, lost and terrified, her once-pristine coat matted with dirt and burrs. The story that emerged was one of neglect so profound it bordered on abandonment. Her owners, it seemed, had simply stopped caring, leaving her to fend for herself, an object of indifference. When Mara first encountered Daisy, the little dog was a quivering mass of anxiety, flinching at every sound, her eyes wide with perpetual alarm. She would press herself against the back of the kennel, as if trying to melt into the concrete, a silent plea for invisibility. Mara saw in Daisy's desperate need to disappear a reflection of her own childhood attempts to make herself small, to become so unremarkable that no one would notice her, no one would have the opportunity to hurt her. She remembered the suffocating feeling of being overlooked, the constant internal monologue of "don't make a fuss," "don't be a burden." Daisy's small, trembling form was a mirror to that deeply ingrained fear, that desperate yearning for an oblivion that offered safety.

Mara approached Daisy with the same gentle patience she'd employed with Buster, but with an added layer of tenderness that only a shared understanding of fragility could bring. She spent hours simply sitting near Daisy's kennel, speaking softly, her voice a melodic lulling, never demanding. She'd leave tiny, high-value treats within Daisy's reach, celebrating each minuscule act of bravery – the brief moment Daisy would dart out to snatch a morsel, the faint wag of her tail when Mara's voice was particularly soothing. It was a slow, arduous process, building trust one infinitesimally small step at a time. Mara understood that for Daisy, every interaction was a test, every approach a potential threat. She was carefully, deliberately, rewiring Daisy's innate fear response, replacing the association of humans with pain and neglect with the promise of kindness and safety. And as Daisy slowly, tentatively, began to inch closer, her tremors subsiding when Mara was near, Mara felt a deep resonance. She was not just healing Daisy; she was, in a way, revisiting and reinterpreting her own past, offering herself the very comfort and validation she had so desperately needed as a child.

Eli observed these quiet transformations with a seasoned eye. He saw the way Mara's hands, once hesitant and unsure, now moved with a confident grace around the most fearful animals. He noticed the subtle shifts in her demeanor, the quiet strength that had begun to emanate from her, a stark contrast to the guarded uncertainty he had first perceived. He saw her not just as an employee, but as a soul finding solace, a damaged spirit slowly mending itself through the act of mending others.

"You have a knack for the broken ones, Mara," he said one afternoon, his voice a low murmur as they watched Buster, now tentatively accepting a gentle scratch behind the ears, his tail giving a slow, hesitant thump against the ground. "You see what's beneath the surface, don't you? The hurt they carry, the stories they can't tell."

Mara flushed, a warmth spreading through her that had nothing to do with the afternoon sun. "I... I try," she stammered, her gaze fixed on Buster's contented sigh. "They remind me..." She trailed off, the unspoken words hanging in the air.

Eli nodded, a knowing look in his eyes. "We all have our ghosts, Mara. And sometimes, it takes seeing them in another's eyes to finally face our own." He paused, his gaze sweeping across the Haven, the gentle symphony of animal sounds a comforting balm. "You're not just giving them a second chance. You're giving yourself one, too. By learning to listen to their unspoken stories, you're finally learning to hear your own."

His words were a gentle affirmation, a validation of the profound, silent work she was undertaking. She realized that her connection to these animals wasn't just empathy; it was a deep, almost primal recognition. Their trauma, their resilience, their capacity for love and forgiveness after experiencing so much pain – it all resonated with a part of her that had been dormant for too long. She saw how the scars on Buster's skin were not just physical wounds, but the outward manifestations of a spirit that had been relentlessly battered, yet had not broken. And in his slow, cautious return to trust, she found a glimmer of hope for her own fractured past.

Daisy's progress was even more pronounced. The trembling had subsided to a mere flutter, and she now greeted Mara with a tentative, almost shy, wag of her tail. She would even venture out from the back of the kennel, her small body still coiled with a residual tension, but her eyes, once pools of terror, now held a soft curiosity. One morning, as Mara was cleaning Daisy's kennel, the little dog approached, nudged Mara's hand with her wet nose, and then, astonishingly, licked her fingers. It was a moment so pure, so unburdened, that it brought a fresh wave of tears to Mara's eyes. It was a complete surrender, a complete trust, a testament to the power of consistent, unwavering kindness. Mara knelt, burying her face in Daisy's soft fur, a quiet sob escaping her. She felt the weight of her own unspoken stories lifting, layer by agonizing layer, with each gentle lick, each tentative nuzzle.

The connection Mara forged with these animals was not always overt. Sometimes, it was a shared silence, a mutual understanding in a quiet gaze. She learned to read the subtle language of their bodies, the way a dog's ears would flick back in apprehension, the way a cat would slowly blink in a gesture of trust. These were the nuances that spoke volumes, the unspoken narratives that painted a vivid picture of their inner lives. She realized that their pasts, though shrouded in mystery, had undeniably shaped them, etching their experiences into their very beings. Just as her own past, a tapestry woven with threads of loss, betrayal, and self-doubt, had sculpted the person she had become.

She started journaling, not just about the animals, but about her own reactions to them. The resurfacing memories, the raw emotions that each rescued soul seemed to awaken. She wrote about the ache of abandonment that gnawed at her when she looked at Buster, the suffocating fear of insignificance that Daisy's trembling evoked. She acknowledged the invisible walls she had built, the ingrained habit of expecting the worst, the deep-seated belief that she was somehow flawed. It was a cathartic process, a way of externalizing the internal, of giving voice to the voiceless parts of herself.

Her interactions with Eli continued to deepen, evolving beyond professional courtesy into a genuine friendship. He was a steady presence, a silent confidant who seemed to understand her journey without her needing to articulate every painful detail. He would share stories of his own past, of his own encounters with broken souls, human and animal, creating a space of shared vulnerability that Mara found incredibly comforting. He never pried, never pushed, but his quiet insights and gentle encouragement were a constant source of strength.

"You know," Eli remarked one evening, as they sat on the porch of the Haven, watching the sunset paint the sky in hues of orange and purple, "animals have a remarkable ability to forgive. They don't hold grudges. They learn, they adapt, and they move forward. There's a purity in that, a lesson we humans could all learn from."

Mara nodded, her gaze fixed on a flock of birds taking flight, their wings beating in unison against the fading light. "I wish it were that simple for us," she murmured, her voice barely a whisper. "We carry our pasts like stones in our pockets, weighing us down."

"But what if," Eli countered, his voice soft and thoughtful, "what if we could learn to use those stones to build something beautiful? What if their weight could be a foundation, rather than a burden?"

His words settled over Mara like a warm blanket. She looked at the animals around her, at their resilience, their capacity for love, their quiet strength in the face of adversity. She saw how they had been broken, scarred, and abandoned, yet had found within themselves the power to heal, to trust, and to love again. And she realized that the unspoken stories of these creatures were not just tales of suffering; they were also testaments to the enduring power of hope, the incredible capacity for resilience, and the profound, transformative nature of kindness. In their silent language, she was finally beginning to understand her own. The weight of unspoken stories was still there, but it was no longer crushing her. It was becoming a part of her, a part of her history, a part of the story she was now actively, and bravely, choosing to write.

Eli found Mara by the old oak tree at the edge of the property, her gaze lost somewhere in the rolling hills that framed the horizon. The late afternoon sun cast long shadows, dappling the grass around her with a warm, golden light. He'd seen her retreat here before, a quiet observer, a silent guardian of the Haven's peace. He knew, from the subtle shifts in her posture, the way her shoulders were held just a fraction tighter than usual, that she was wrestling with something internal. The progress with Buster and Daisy was undeniable, a testament to her gentle touch, but he also sensed a deeper current beneath the surface, a reservoir of unspoken history she carried.

He approached slowly, his footsteps soft on the dry earth, not wanting to startle her. He settled onto the grass a few feet away, respecting the space she had carved out for herself. For a long moment, they sat in comfortable silence, the only sounds the distant bleating of sheep and the rustle of leaves in the gentle breeze. Eli savored these quiet interludes with Mara. He'd learned that sometimes, the most profound conversations happened without a single word exchanged, a shared understanding passing between souls like a silent current.

Finally, he spoke, his voice a low, measured rumble that didn't break the tranquility. "You seem a million miles away, Mara."

Mara started, a faint blush rising on her cheeks as she turned to him. "Just... thinking," she murmured, her eyes still holding a faraway quality.

Eli offered a small, reassuring smile. "It's a beautiful day for it. The kind that makes you want to untangle the knots." He paused, then added, his tone casual but laced with genuine interest, "I've been wondering, you know, about your journey to Port Blossom. It feels like you arrived with a whole world of experiences already packed away. Was it always this... purposeful for you? This need to mend, to care for the lost?"

He saw her hesitate, a familiar flicker of guardedness in her eyes. It was an instinct he recognized, a reflex born of self-preservation. He didn't press, didn't push. Instead, he shifted the focus, drawing on his own experiences, creating a bridge of shared vulnerability.

"I remember a dog, a scruffy terrier mix," Eli began, his gaze drifting towards the kennels, as if conjuring the memory from the air. "Came to me years ago, found wandering in a terrible state. Skin and bones, every muscle tensed like a coiled spring. Eyes that looked like they'd seen the end of the world and were just waiting for the next bad thing. He wouldn't let anyone near him. Growled at the slightest movement, flinched if you even breathed in his direction. You could practically see the fear radiating off him in waves."

He paused, letting the image settle. "The vet said he'd likely been used for fighting, trained to be aggressive, but his fear was so profound, so ingrained, it overshadowed any aggression. It was like he was terrified of his own shadow. He'd cower in the corner of his run, a pathetic, trembling heap, and you just knew he'd had a rough life, a life of constant pain and betrayal."

Eli turned back to Mara, his expression earnest. "I tried everything. Slow introductions, food rewards, quiet presence. But he was a wall. A beautiful, terrified wall. For weeks, he just stared, his amber eyes wide with suspicion, that low growl a constant warning. I started to think maybe he was just too broken, too far gone. That maybe he'd never know what it felt like to trust again, to feel safe."

He leaned back on his elbows, the setting sun painting his face with a warm glow. "But then, one afternoon, I was sitting near his run, just reading. Not looking at him, not trying to interact. Just existing. And I heard a little scrabbling sound. He'd crept out of his corner, and he was sniffing at the edge of my outstretched hand. Still tense, still ready to bolt, but... curious. Hesitant."

Eli's voice softened. "I didn't move. Didn't even breathe loud. And then, very, very gently, he nudged my fingers with his wet nose. It was the smallest thing, barely a touch. But to him, I knew it was monumental. A leap of faith across a chasm of fear. And in that moment, I saw it. Not just the fear, but the flicker of hope. The yearning for something different."

He looked at Mara, his eyes searching hers. "It took months, you know. Months of patience, of showing him, day in and day out, that my hand wouldn't hurt him, that my voice wouldn't threaten him. Slowly, he started to let his guard down. The growls became whimpers, the flinching turned into tentative tail wags. And eventually, he became the most loyal, loving companion I'd ever known. He never forgot what happened, not entirely. You could still see the scars, both inside and out. But he learned to live beyond them. He learned to love again."

Eli picked up a small stone, turning it over and over in his fingers. "That dog taught me a lot. He taught me that sometimes, the most damaged ones have the greatest capacity for healing. And that sometimes, the biggest breakthroughs come not from forcing things, but from simply offering a safe harbor, a space where they can slowly, tentatively, unfurl. Where they can start to believe that not everyone will hurt them."

He let the silence stretch again, allowing his story to resonate. He wasn't asking Mara to spill her secrets, not directly. He was simply offering a parallel, a shared experience of encountering profound brokenness and witnessing the miracle of its mending. He was showing her that he understood the delicate dance of healing, the quiet power of patience and unwavering kindness. He was, in essence, holding out a hand, not to pull her out of her thoughts, but to offer a steady anchor should she choose to step out of them.

Mara listened intently, her gaze fixed on the worn leather of Eli's hands as he spoke. His story wasn't just about a dog; it was a carefully crafted metaphor, a gentle invitation into a conversation she had long avoided. She recognized the echoes of her own internal landscape in the terrier's trembling fear, in its deep-seated distrust. She saw how Eli had navigated that minefield of apprehension with a steady, unflinching compassion, offering not judgment, but understanding.

"It sounds like... it sounds like you saw beyond the fear," Mara said softly, her voice barely a whisper. She felt a familiar tightness in her chest, a subtle ache that had been her constant companion for as long as she could remember. "Like you didn't let the immediate reaction define him."

Eli nodded, his eyes warm. "We all have layers, Mara. Sometimes, the first layer is a fortress, built to keep the world out. But beneath that fortress, there's often something beautiful, something yearning to be seen. The trick is to find a way to gently encourage them to lower the drawbridge, without making them feel threatened."

He paused, then continued, his tone more direct, though still infused with gentleness. "You have that same gift, you know. I see it in how you handle Buster, how you coax Daisy out of her shell. You have a way of seeing the hurt, the story they can't voice, and you respond to that. It's more than just training; it's... connection. Deep connection."

He looked at her, his gaze steady and unyielding, but not intrusive. "I'm curious, Mara. What brought you here? What made you choose a place like the Haven? It's not exactly a typical career path for someone with your... capabilities." He gestured vaguely, encompassing her evident intelligence and quiet strength. "Were you always drawn to the quiet places? To the ones that needed a little extra care?"

Mara looked away, her gaze sweeping across the Haven, a place that had become a sanctuary, a refuge not just for the animals, but for herself. The question hung in the air, a fragile offering that she felt both compelled and terrified to accept. Eli's story, his gentle probing, had created an opening, a space she hadn't realized she'd been waiting for. It was as if he had laid out a path, illuminated by the soft glow of his own past, and invited her to walk it with him.

"I... I didn't always know this was what I wanted," Mara admitted, her voice still soft, but with a new layer of vulnerability. "It feels like a long time ago now. Before... before I ended up here. My life was... different. Quieter, in a way, but also more... stifling." She traced the pattern of a leaf etched into the bark of the oak tree with her finger. "I grew up in a place that valued... presentation.

Appearances. Being quiet, being polite, not causing a fuss. My parents... they were very focused on maintaining a certain image. And I learned, very early on, that the best way to survive, to be accepted, was to be as invisible as possible."

She took a deep breath, the air suddenly feeling thinner. "I was a good child. Always did what I was told. Never complained. I learned to swallow my feelings, to keep my thoughts to myself. It was easier than dealing with the disappointment, the disapproval. I became very adept at reading the room, at anticipating what others wanted me to be. And in doing that, I think I lost touch with who I actually was."

Mara's voice grew quieter, a melancholic undertone weaving through her words. "There were times, in my childhood, when I felt like a ghost in my own home. I remember watching other children, loud and boisterous, so full of life, and feeling this ache, this longing to be like them. But that wasn't my role. My role was to be seen and not heard. To be pleasant, but unremarkable."

She looked at Eli, her eyes holding a deep, unexpressed sadness. "When I left home, I tried to fit into the world, but I didn't really know how. I felt... unformed. Like a piece of clay that hadn't been shaped by anything real. I drifted for a while, working jobs that required very little of me, that allowed me to remain in the background. It was safe, but it was also... empty."

"And then?" Eli prompted gently, his gaze unwavering, a silent invitation to continue. He understood the delicate nature of these confessions, the precarious balance between vulnerability and retreat.

Mara's gaze drifted back to the Haven, to the enclosures where the animals found solace and purpose. "Then I found myself here, almost by accident. I saw an ad for a kennel hand, and something about it... resonated. It was a chance to be useful, to do something tangible. And honestly, at first, I thought it would be just another job. A way to pay the bills."

She smiled faintly, a hint of self-deprecation in her eyes. "I wasn't prepared for it. Not for the animals, not for... for the way they looked at me. Like Eli's terrier. Like they had stories etched into their very beings. And as I started to work with them, to see their pain, their resilience, it felt like... like I was seeing something in them that I had suppressed in myself for so long. Their fear, their hurt, but also their capacity for hope."

She paused, gathering her thoughts, the words tumbling out with a newfound urgency. "It's like... like they were mirroring my own unspoken history. Buster's scars, his mistrust – I recognized that feeling of being marked, of expecting pain. Daisy's trembling, her desire to disappear – that was the invisibility I had cultivated for years. And then, seeing them slowly, tentatively, start to trust again, to find joy, it was like a light turned on. A realization that maybe... maybe I didn't have to stay hidden forever. Maybe I could heal too."

Mara looked down at her hands, flexing her fingers. "This place... it's more than just a job. It's become... a classroom. A place where

I'm learning to be present, to be seen. And where I'm learning, through them, that being broken doesn't mean you can't be put back together. That the scars don't define the whole story."

Eli listened with a quiet intensity, his expression one of profound understanding. He saw the raw honesty in Mara's confession, the courage it took for her to articulate the depths of her past. He recognized the familiar pattern of a soul finding its path through unexpected avenues, of a wounded spirit discovering its purpose in the act of healing others.

"That's a powerful realization, Mara," he said, his voice resonating with warmth. "And it takes an extraordinary amount of strength to even acknowledge those feelings, let alone voice them. The world often tells us to bury those things, to move on. But you're choosing to unearth them, and in doing so, you're not just healing yourself, you're becoming an incredible source of healing for others."

He gestured towards the Haven, his gaze sweeping across the grounds. "These animals... they have a way of cutting through the pretense, don't they? They don't care about how polished you are, or how well you fit into societal molds. They respond to authenticity. To genuine kindness. And you, Mara, you have that in spades."

Eli picked up another pebble, tossing it lightly in his palm. "When I first started at the Haven, I was a bit of a mess myself. Carried a lot of baggage from my own experiences. And I found that working with these animals, seeing their unwavering capacity for hope, their willingness to forgive and move forward, it started to chip away at my own defenses. It showed me that even after the worst, there's always a possibility for something good. A chance to rebuild."

He offered a gentle smile. "It's a reciprocal relationship, isn't it? We give them a safe haven, and in return, they offer us a mirror, reflecting back the best parts of ourselves, the parts we might have forgotten existed. They show us what resilience looks like, what unconditional love can be. And sometimes, they give us the courage to finally look at our own stories, to acknowledge the pain, and to begin the process of mending."

Eli stood up, brushing the dirt from his jeans. "It sounds like you've been doing a lot of that unearthing, Mara. And it's beautiful to witness. You're not just working at the Haven; you're growing here. Blooming, even. Like one of those shy wildflowers that finally finds the sun."

Mara watched him, a sense of quiet gratitude settling over her. Eli's gentle probing hadn't felt like an interrogation; it had felt like an offering. An opportunity to share a burden that had felt too heavy to carry alone. His own vulnerability, his willingness to share his own past struggles, had created a safe space for her to finally begin to speak her truth.

"Thank you, Eli," she said, her voice sincere. "For... for asking. And for sharing your story. It helps. More than you know."

He met her gaze, his eyes filled with a quiet understanding. "Anytime, Mara. We're all on our own journeys, and sometimes, it's good to know we're not walking them entirely alone." He gave a small nod, a gesture of respect and acknowledgment. "Come on, the sun's setting. Let's get the last few animals settled in for the night. And maybe, tomorrow, we can talk about that new batch of puppies that arrived this morning. They're a handful, but I think you'll do wonders with them."

As they walked back towards the main building, Mara felt a subtle shift within her. The weight of her unspoken stories hadn't vanished entirely, but it felt less like a crushing burden and more like a collection of chapters, waiting to be written, to be understood. Eli's gentle questions, like seeds planted in fertile ground, had begun to sprout, offering the promise of a future where her past, and her present, could intertwine, creating a story of resilience, healing, and quiet strength. The journey was far from over, but for the first time in a long time, Mara felt a flicker of hope, a nascent belief that she, too, could learn to live beyond her scars, just like the broken souls she cared for each day.

The sun, a molten orb sinking towards the horizon, cast long, ethereal shadows across the damp sand. The air, still warm from the day's heat, carried the faint, briny scent of the sea, a balm to Mara's senses. Beside her, Eli walked with a comfortable stride, his gaze sweeping over the vast expanse of the beach. The tide had retreated, leaving behind a glistening canvas of sand, a tapestry of fleeting impressions. Tiny, delicate footprints of shorebirds crisscrossed the surface, a testament to their morning foraging.

Delicate scours, etched by the retreating waves, formed ephemeral rivulets that snaked towards the ocean's embrace.

"Look at this," Eli said, his voice a low murmur that blended with the rhythmic whisper of the waves. He pointed to a series of intricate patterns left by a sandpiper, its quick, darting movements captured in the impressionable earth. "Each one of these is a story, isn't it? A snapshot of a moment in time. The bird was here, looking for breakfast, then it flew on. And the tide will eventually wash it all away."

Mara stooped, her fingers trailing through the cool, yielding sand. She traced the delicate imprint of a feather, its edge softened by the water's gentle caress. "It's beautiful," she agreed, her voice hushed with a sense of awe. "So temporary, yet so detailed." She understood the analogy Eli was drawing, the silent parallel to the transient nature of moments, of relationships, of life itself. Her own life, so recently reshaped by unforeseen circumstances, felt like a vast stretch of sand, imprinted with the recent passage of a life that was no longer hers.

"It makes you think about the things we leave behind," Eli continued, his eyes reflecting the fiery hues of the sunset. "Even if they're temporary, they're still a record of our presence. The choices we made, the paths we took, the people we encountered. They all leave their mark, even if it's just for a little while." He glanced at Mara, his expression open and understanding. "Sometimes, the marks are deeper than we realize."

Mara's breath hitched. The beach, so serene and vast, suddenly felt like a stage, and Eli, with his perceptive gaze, had opened a door to a part of her story she had been trying to keep locked away. The image of the footprints, ephemeral and yet so clearly present, mirrored the sudden, startling end of her previous relationship, the abrupt absence of someone who had been a constant, a defining presence in her life.

"It feels like... like I was walking along a path, and then suddenly, the ground just disappeared beneath me," Mara began, her voice softer now, tinged with a vulnerability she rarely allowed herself to show. "It was so... unexpected. One minute, everything was normal, and the next... silence. Complete silence." She remembered the day Daniel had left. It had been a Tuesday, a day like any other, filled with the mundane rhythm of their shared lives. She'd been making coffee, humming a tune, and he'd walked in, his face a mask of carefully constructed calm. He hadn't raised his voice, hadn't accused, hadn't even offered a lengthy explanation. It was a quiet pronouncement, delivered with a chilling finality that had left her reeling. "I'm leaving, Mara," he'd said, the words slicing through the morning air like a shard of ice. "I can't do this anymore."

Eli nodded, his presence a steady anchor beside her. He didn't interrupt, didn't rush her. He simply offered the quiet space for her to speak. He'd seen it before, the aftermath of relationships that ended not with a bang, but with a whimper, leaving behind a void that was far more devastating.

"He didn't... he didn't want to talk about it," Mara continued, picking up a smooth, grey stone and turning it over and over in her hand. "It was like he'd made up his mind, and anything I said, anything I felt, was irrelevant. He packed a bag, and he was gone. Just like that. It was as if the last five years had meant nothing." She remembered the emptiness that had descended upon her apartment after he'd left. The silence was deafening, punctuated only by the ticking of the clock on the wall, each second a stark reminder of his absence. His scent lingered on his pillow, a phantom presence that tormented her. His side of the closet was bare, a gaping maw that mocked her with its emptiness.

"I felt... lost," she admitted, her gaze fixed on the stone. "Utterly, completely lost. He was my future. We had plans, dreams. We were talking about moving, about starting a family. And then, in an instant, it was all gone. Like a sandcastle, meticulously built, suddenly demolished by a rogue wave." The metaphor felt all too real. Her carefully constructed life, the one she had envisioned with Daniel, had crumbled into nothingness, leaving her adrift in a sea of uncertainty.

"And your career?" Eli asked gently, sensing that this was another layer of the unexpected loss.

Mara's shoulders sagged slightly. "That was... tied up with him, too. He was a lawyer, and I was working as a paralegal in the same firm. It was a good job, stable. I enjoyed it, even though it wasn't my ultimate passion. But it was a path that we were on together. When he left, the thought of going into that office every day, of seeing him there, of pretending everything was fine... it was unbearable. And then, there was a restructuring. Layoffs. My position was... eliminated. So, it was goodbye to Daniel, and goodbye to my career, all in the same brutal sweep."

She let out a long, shaky breath, the words tumbling out now, a torrent of pent-up emotion. "It felt like the universe was conspiring against me. Like I'd done something wrong, something so fundamentally flawed that I deserved to be stripped of everything I'd known. I was suddenly alone, with no job, no partner, and this gaping hole where my future used to be. I didn't know who I was anymore, outside of being 'Daniel's girlfriend' or 'the paralegal at his firm'."

The vastness of the beach, which had initially felt peaceful, now seemed to amplify her sense of isolation. Each wave that crashed against the shore felt like a fresh assault, a reminder of the relentless march of time, and her own stalled progress. She had always prided herself on her composure, on her ability to maintain a calm exterior, but here, with Eli, under the vast, indifferent sky, the carefully constructed facade was beginning to crack.

"I remember just walking for hours," Mara continued, her voice laced with a raw pain that Eli hadn't heard before. "Just putting one foot in front of the other, not really knowing where I was going. The city felt suffocating. Every corner, every street, held a memory of him, of us. I couldn't breathe. I needed... I needed to escape. To disappear, just for a while."

Eli stopped walking and turned to face her fully. He reached out, not to touch her, but to place his hands on her shoulders, a gesture of gentle solidarity. "It sounds like you were in a really dark place, Mara. And it took immense strength to navigate that, to keep moving forward even when everything felt like it was falling apart."

Mara looked up at him, her eyes glistening with unshed tears. "I didn't feel strong, Eli. I felt broken. Like a shattered piece of glass, sharp and useless. I thought that was it. That my life, as I knew it, was over. I just drifted, working odd jobs, trying to keep my head above water, but mostly just trying to numb the pain. It felt like a punishment, a consequence for... I don't even know what."

"The Haven found you then?" Eli asked softly, his thumb gently stroking her shoulder.

Mara nodded, a faint, almost imperceptible tremor running through her. "Yes. It was a small ad, tucked away in a local paper. 'Kennel Hand Wanted'. I almost didn't apply. It seemed so far removed from everything I knew. But... there was something about it. A sense of quiet purpose. A chance to be useful again, to do something that mattered, even if it was just looking after animals." She remembered the interview, the way the previous manager, a gruff but kind woman named Eleanor, had looked at her, not with pity, but with a quiet assessment of her potential. Eleanor hadn't asked about her past, about her career aspirations, or her social life. She'd simply asked if Mara was willing to get her hands dirty, to work hard, and to show compassion.

"And I'm so glad I did," Mara confessed, a genuine warmth beginning to replace the hurt in her eyes. "This place, the animals... they've been my healing. Each one of them, with their own stories of hurt and resilience, has shown me that it's possible to overcome. Buster, with his fear and his growls, he taught me patience. Daisy, with her quiet anxiety, she reminded me of my own need for gentleness. And the new arrivals, the ones who come in so broken, so mistrustful... watching them begin to trust again, to find a spark of joy... it's like watching a sunrise. It's a reminder that even after the darkest night, there is always hope for a new day."

Eli squeezed her shoulders gently before releasing them. "That's the magic of this place, Mara. It's not just a sanctuary for them; it's a sanctuary for us too. We come here, carrying our own baggage, our own scars, and we pour ourselves into healing them. And in doing so, we find our own healing. It's a profound exchange, and you've embraced it with a remarkable grace."

He began walking again, and Mara fell into step beside him. The weight on her chest felt a little lighter. The conversation, though painful, had been cathartic. Sharing the story, the abrupt end of her relationship and the subsequent loss of her career, felt like shedding a layer of heavy skin. The footprints on the sand no longer felt like a symbol of her own dashed hopes, but a testament to the transient nature of life, a reminder that even the most significant moments eventually recede, leaving behind the potential for new impressions, new beginnings.

"It's funny," Mara mused, watching a wave recede, leaving a fresh expanse of untouched sand. "I used to think that losing Daniel, losing my job, was the end of my story. That I would just be a footnote, a lost cause. But coming here... it's like I've found a whole new chapter. A chapter I never expected, but one that feels... right. One that feels like me, for the first time in a long time."

Eli smiled, a genuine, warm smile that reached his eyes. "You were never a footnote, Mara. You were just waiting for the right story to unfold. And sometimes, the most beautiful stories are the ones that begin after the expected ending. They're the ones where we discover our own resilience, our own strength, in the most unexpected places." He gestured towards the vast, open ocean. "The tide goes out, yes, but it always comes back in. And with it, it brings new currents, new possibilities. You just have to be ready to ride them."

Mara felt a stir of something akin to hope, a fragile seedling pushing through the sandy soil of her recent past. The footprints on the shore, once a source of melancholy, now seemed to whisper a promise of new journeys, of uncharted territories waiting to be explored. She had lost a future she had meticulously planned, but in its place, something unexpected and perhaps even more fulfilling was beginning to bloom. The Haven, with its scarred and hopeful inhabitants, had become her unexpected haven, and Eli, with his quiet understanding, was helping her see that the marks left behind on the sand of her life were not scars of defeat, but etchings of experience, paving the way for a future she was just beginning to imagine.

The late afternoon sun, now a softened apricot hue, filtered through the dusty panes of the Haven's main kennel building, casting a warm, inviting glow. Mara had finished her rounds, ensuring each of the dogs had fresh water and a final scratch behind the ears. Most of them responded with wagging tails and soft whimpers, eager for attention, their individual personalities a familiar comfort. But there was one kennel, tucked away at the far end, that always held a different kind of quiet. It was Shadow's.

He was a German Shepherd, a magnificent animal with a coat the color of twilight and eyes that seemed to hold the weight of the world. But unlike the other dogs who greeted her with hopeful anticipation, Shadow remained a statue of apprehension. He'd press himself into the furthest corner of his run, his body coiled tight, a picture of silent, profound fear. Every sudden noise, the clang of a dropped bucket, the slam of a distant door, sent him flinching, his muscular frame tensing as if bracing for a blow. His gaze, when it did flick towards her, was a fleeting, sideways dart, never meeting her eyes directly, as if direct contact was an unbearable invitation to something he couldn't endure.

Mara had tried the usual methods. Gentle cooing, soft words whispered into the air, the slow, deliberate placement of high-value treats just within reach, no demand for interaction, just a silent offering. But Shadow remained resolutely withdrawn, a ghost in his own kennel. He'd snatch the treats when he thought she wasn't looking, a quick, furtive movement, and then retreat back into his shell. It was a silent testament to a past that had clearly left deep, invisible scars.

Eli had explained Shadow's story a few days ago, his voice heavy with a familiar blend of sadness and quiet determination. "He was found tied to a fence," he'd said, his gaze fixed on the dog's perpetually tense posture. "Left. Just… left. No note, no explanation. Just a rope and a silent, terrifying abandonment. Whoever owned him clearly didn't want him anymore. Didn't care enough to even bring him in." He'd paused, a rare frustration clouding his features. "He's been here for two weeks, Mara, and he's barely moved from that corner. He flinches at his own shadow, literally."

The words had landed with a heavy thud in Mara's chest. To be left, discarded, without a trace of concern – it resonated with a deep, buried chord within her. She saw not just a fearful dog, but a reflection of the profound sense of worthlessness that had plagued her in the months following Daniel's departure and the loss of her job. The feeling of being forgotten, of her existence rendered irrelevant.

"He needs more than just patience, Eli," Mara had said, her voice firm with a newfound resolve. "He needs… to know he's not invisible. That he's seen. That he matters."

Eli had nodded, a flicker of understanding in his eyes. "He's a tough one, Mara. A lot of people would have given up by now. But I have a feeling you might be the one to reach him."

And so, Mara had made Shadow her personal project, her quiet mission. She started spending extra time by his kennel, not forcing interaction, but simply existing in his space with a calm, steady presence. She'd sit on the floor a few feet away, reading aloud from a book of poetry, her voice a low, soothing melody that wove through the silence. She'd talk about her day, about the sunshine, about the funny antics of the other dogs, creating a gentle stream of normalcy that, she hoped, would eventually seep into his fear-saturated world.

"Hello, Shadow," she'd murmur, her voice barely above a whisper, each word infused with gentleness. "It's Mara. Just checking in on you, my boy. You're a handsome fellow, you know that? Such strong lines. You must have been a very loved dog once." She'd watch him from the periphery, observing the slight shift in his posture when she spoke, the almost imperceptible twitch of his ears. Small signs, perhaps, but signs nonetheless.

She'd bring him his meals, placing the bowl down carefully, then stepping back to give him space. Sometimes, she'd sit and eat her own lunch nearby, a silent companion. She'd hum softly, a tune that was neither cheerful nor mournful, just... present. She wanted him to associate her presence with quietude, with a lack of threat, with a consistent, gentle offering.

Days bled into a week, then another. The routine became a sacred ritual. The other dogs got their due attention, their boisterous greetings and happy wags a part of the daily symphony of the Haven. But Shadow's kennel remained a quiet sanctuary of slow, painstaking progress. Mara didn't expect miracles. She knew trauma wasn't erased with a single act of kindness. It was chipped away at, day by day, with unwavering dedication.

Then, one afternoon, something shifted. Mara was sitting by Shadow's kennel, a worn copy of 'Pride and Prejudice' open on her lap, though she hadn't read a word in the last ten minutes. She was simply watching Shadow, who was lying down in his usual corner, but his body seemed a fraction less rigid. His gaze was still averted, but it wasn't as sharp, as darting. He seemed to be... listening.

Mara reached into her pocket and pulled out a small, dried liver treat, her movements slow and deliberate. She held it out, her hand palm-up, keeping it low to the ground, a silent invitation. She didn't speak, didn't even breathe too loudly, her entire focus on the space between her hand and the dog.

Shadow's ears twitched. His head remained down, but his eyes, dark and liquid, flickered towards the treat. He stayed there, a statue of internal debate, the years of learned fear warring with the innate canine desire for a reward, for a connection. Mara's heart hammered a silent rhythm against her ribs. She willed him, with every fiber of her being, to trust. To take that one small step.

Minutes stretched, each one feeling like an eternity. The silence was thick with anticipation. Then, with a movement so fluid and tentative it was almost imperceptible, Shadow shifted. He uncoiled himself, not all at once, but in a series of cautious increments. He lowered his head, his nose twitching, inching closer to her outstretched hand. Mara held her breath, her muscles tense, resisting the urge to move, to speak, to break the fragile spell.

His wet nose brushed against her fingertips, a brief, cool contact. He inhaled the scent of the treat, then, with a sudden, almost startling quickness, he snatched it from her hand. His head recoiled instantly, and he retreated back to his corner, gulping down the morsel.

Mara let out a silent, shaky breath she hadn't realized she'd been holding. It wasn't a lick, not yet. It wasn't eye contact, not even close. But he had taken the treat directly from her hand. He had overcome the immediate, paralyzing fear enough to engage with her, to accept something offered directly. It was a tiny victory, a flicker of light in the deep shadow of his past, but to Mara, it felt monumental. A wave of pure, unadulterated accomplishment washed over her, a feeling she hadn't experienced in what felt like an age. It was the quiet joy of seeing progress, of knowing her persistent efforts were finally making a difference.

She didn't press her luck. She simply offered a soft, approving sigh and closed her book. "Good boy, Shadow," she whispered, her voice filled with a warmth that echoed her inner elation. "You're doing so well." She rose slowly, careful not to make any sudden movements, and gave him one last, gentle look before leaving the kennel.

As she walked away, she felt a lightness she hadn't carried before. It was more than just the satisfaction of a job well done. It was the profound sense of connection, the understanding that even the most damaged souls could begin to heal, and that she, Mara, could be a part of that healing process. She had been rescued by this place, by these animals, by their unyielding capacity for resilience. And now, with Shadow, she felt she was playing a part in rescuing him, too. The rescuer becoming, in turn, the rescued. It was a beautiful, circular affirmation of life and hope, etched not in sand that the tide would wash away, but in the quiet, persistent beating of a once-broken heart. The journey with Shadow was far from over, but for the first time, Mara felt a tangible sense of hope, a quiet certainty that they would find their way through the darkness, together. She looked back at his kennel, a small smile playing on her lips. The shadow was still there, but it was no longer absolute. A sliver of light had found its way in.

The salt-laced air of Haven clung to Mara's clothes, a comforting reminder of where she was, of who she was striving to become. But as the day wound down, a different kind of air, thick with the dust of memory, settled around her in the quiet solitude of her cottage. The soft glow of the setting sun, now painting the sky in hues of lavender and rose, cast long shadows across the worn wooden floor as she knelt before a cardboard box, a relic from her former life. It had been tucked away in the back of her small closet, a place where forgotten things went to wait, undisturbed. Today, the urge to confront what lay within had finally won.

Her fingers traced the faded tape that sealed the lid, a ritual of hesitation before she peeled it back. The scent of aged paper and something faintly floral, a ghost of perfume, wafted out. Inside, nestled amongst yellowed tissue paper, lay the fragments of a life that felt both intimately hers and impossibly distant. A small pile of photographs, their edges softened by time, lay on top. She picked one up, the glossy surface cool against her fingertips. It was Daniel. His smile, bright and unguarded, was directed at the camera, his arm slung loosely around her shoulders. They were at the beach, the sea a blurred expanse of blue behind them. A sudden ache, sharp and unexpected, pierced her chest. It wasn't a yearning to return to that moment, not exactly. It was more a profound sadness for the person she had been then, the person who had believed, so wholeheartedly, in forever. She saw the carefree sparkle in her own eyes, a reflection of a faith that had since been shattered.

She carefully placed the photograph back, her touch gentle, as if handling something fragile and precious. Beside it lay a chipped ceramic coffee mug, its once vibrant blue glaze now scuffed and faded. It had been a gift from her sister, a silly inside joke about their shared love for early morning caffeine. Mara remembered countless mornings, the warmth of the mug in her hands, the murmur of conversation with Daniel across the breakfast table. Now, the silence in her cottage was absolute, punctuated only by the distant, rhythmic sigh of the ocean. She held the mug, feeling its familiar weight, a tangible link to a past that was slowly, inexorably, slipping away. It was a ghost of comfort, a reminder of shared routines, of laughter, of a life that had been built, brick by careful brick, only to crumble into dust.

Deeper in the box, nestled beneath a bundle of old letters tied with a ribbon, she found it. A book. "The Secret History" by Donna Tartt. She'd started it years ago, captivated by the premise, the promise of dark secrets and academic intrigue. Life, however, had intervened, as it so often did, and the book had been relegated to the 'to be finished later' pile. Now, it sat in her hands, a symbol of unfinished business, of dreams deferred. She ran her thumb over the embossed title, a faint smile touching her lips. There had been so many plans, so many ambitions that had been put on hold, then ultimately abandoned, in the wake of Daniel's departure and the subsequent implosion of her career. It was more than just a book; it was a testament to her own inertia, a silent accuser of her lost momentum.

Each item she unearthed was a key, unlocking a floodgate of emotions. There was a framed picture of her and Daniel at her college graduation, his proud beaming face a stark contrast to the confusion and hurt that had followed. A collection of concert ticket stubs, faded remnants of shared experiences that now felt like whispers from another lifetime. A soft, worn scarf, the one she'd worn on their first date, a scent of his cologne still faintly clinging to it. The memories came in waves, some sweet, some sharp with regret, all of them tinged with the undeniable sorrow of what had been lost. It was a poignant inventory of a life unraveled, a tapestry torn asunder.

Mara felt the familiar pull, the insidious temptation to drown in the ocean of what-ifs and if-onlys. The ache in her chest intensified, threatening to consume her. She could feel the familiar tendrils of despair creeping in, whispering insidious lies about her own worthlessness, about her inability to move forward, to build something new. The feeling of being adrift, of being defined by her losses, was a constant, gnawing presence. She had spent so long feeling like a ghost in her own life, a pale imitation of the person she once was, that the fear of being permanently defined by that emptiness was a heavy burden.

But then, she heard it. The steady, unwavering rhythm of the waves crashing against the shore, a sound that had become the soundtrack to her new life at Haven. It was a powerful, insistent beat, a constant reminder of nature's enduring cycle, of renewal, of resilience. The ocean didn't mourn its lost tides; it simply waited for the next one, its vastness a testament to its ability to absorb and release. It was a force of nature, untamed and eternal, and in its relentless rhythm, Mara found a quiet strength.

She took a deep, cleansing breath, the cool, damp air filling her lungs. She acknowledged the pain, the raw grief that still resided within her, but she refused to let it paralyze her. These fragments of her past, while still capable of inflicting a sting, were just that – fragments. They were not the entirety of her story. She had survived. She was here. She was building something new, something meaningful, here at the Haven, surrounded by creatures who, like her, bore the scars of past hurts.

With deliberate care, Mara began to place the items back into the box, not with the haste of someone trying to bury their past, but with the gentle finality of someone acknowledging it and moving on. She stacked the photographs neatly, tucked the mug into a corner, and placed the book on top. The letters remained tied with their ribbon, a story yet to be reread, perhaps, or perhaps to remain forever sealed. She wasn't ready to discard these pieces of her history entirely, but she was no longer willing to let them dictate her present. They were memories, not shackles.

She closed the lid, the sound soft and decisive. She wouldn't seal it with tape this time. The box would remain, a physical representation of her journey, a reminder of the past she had navigated and the future she was determined to forge. The lingering sadness was still there, a dull ache beneath the surface, but it was no longer overwhelming. It was a part of her, yes, but it was not all of her. The steady rhythm of the waves outside served as a gentle, persistent whisper, urging her forward, reminding her that just as the tide recedes, so too can sorrow. The raw, jagged edges of her past were slowly being smoothed by the relentless ebb and flow of new experiences, new connections, new purpose. She stood up, her legs a little stiff, and walked to the window, gazing out at the darkening sky. The stars were beginning to prick through the twilight, distant and steady, like tiny beacons of hope. The past was a shadow, yes, but the light of the present, and the promise of the future, was growing stronger. The journey was far from over, but for the first time in a long time, Mara felt a quiet certainty that she was walking in the right direction.

Chapter Four

THE PROMISE OF DAWN

Mara found herself looking forward to the mornings. It was a subtle shift, one that had crept in almost imperceptibly, like the tide slowly reclaiming the shore. The heavy blanket of dread that had once accompanied the first hint of dawn had gradually lifted, replaced by a quiet, burgeoning anticipation. She would rise before the alarm, drawn by an unseen force, and make her way to the window of her small cottage, the cool wood floor a familiar sensation beneath her bare feet. The world outside was still hushed, a canvas of pre-dawn blues and grays, but Mara knew what was coming. She had witnessed it before, but now, she *felt* it.

The spectacle of the sunrise over Port Blossom was no longer just a pretty sight; it had become a ritual, a profound affirmation. As the first sliver of the sun began to peek over the jagged line of the horizon, it seemed to ignite the sky. Fiery oranges bled into soft, blush pinks, then deepened into vibrant reds, painting the clouds in strokes of impossible beauty. The light, initially hesitant, grew bolder, chasing away the lingering shadows and bathing the quiet harbor in a warm, golden glow. The weathered fishing boats bobbing gently in the water, the distant lighthouse standing sentinel, the very air itself – everything seemed to awaken, infused with a new vitality. It was a daily miracle, a silent promise that no matter how dark the night, the dawn would always come, bringing with it the potential for a new beginning.

This newfound appreciation for the dawn mirrored a broader shift within Mara. The relentless demands of the animal rescue at Haven, which had once felt like an overwhelming burden, had somehow settled into a manageable rhythm. The early mornings were now dedicated to the animals, their needs a tangible, immediate focus that pulled her out of her own head. The frantic energy of a sick foal needing round-the-clock care, the soft nuzzles of a rescued barn cat seeking comfort, the joyous barks of dogs eager for their morning walk – these were the anchors that tethered her to the present. There was a raw honesty in their needs, a lack of pretense that Mara found deeply grounding. They didn't care about her past, about the life she had left behind. They only cared about the kindness she offered in that moment, the safety and warmth she provided.

After the initial rush of care, there were pockets of quietude. Moments when she could sit with a cup of tea, the warmth seeping into her hands, and simply watch the activity at the rescue. She observed the volunteers, their dedication a quiet testament to the good that still existed in the world. She saw the hesitant trust slowly bloom in the eyes of an abused dog, the tentative steps of a bird with a mended wing testing its newfound strength. These were not grand pronouncements, but small, incremental victories that accumulated, like the steady work of the waves on the shore, slowly reshaping the landscape of her own heart.

The coastal air, crisp and carrying the distinct tang of salt and brine, had become a balm. It seemed to possess a unique ability to clear the cobwebs from her mind, to wash away the lingering dust of her past. When she walked along the beach, the rhythmic sound of the waves a constant, soothing presence, she felt a clarity she hadn't experienced in years. The vast expanse of the ocean, stretching out to meet the sky, no longer felt like a symbol of her own isolation, but rather a boundless horizon of possibility. It was as if the ocean's immensity had absorbed some of her own anxieties, leaving her with a lighter, more expansive view of her life.

She began to notice the subtle nuances of the changing seasons. The way the light shifted, casting longer, softer shadows in the late afternoon. The migratory birds arriving in flocks, their calls a vibrant chorus against the backdrop of the sea. The hardy coastal flowers, clinging to the windswept dunes, their resilience a quiet inspiration. These small observations, these moments of connection with the natural world, were weaving a new tapestry for her, one rich with texture and understated beauty.

Her work at Haven was demanding, physically and emotionally, but it was also deeply rewarding. She had thrown herself into it with a ferocity that surprised even herself. Learning to administer medications, to groom and exercise the animals, to patiently coax a frightened creature into accepting human touch – each new skill learned, each small success, was a brick laid in the foundation of her new life. She wasn't just surviving; she was building. She was discovering a competence, a quiet strength, that had been buried beneath the wreckage of her past.

There were still moments, of course, when the old shadows would flicker at the edges of her vision. A certain scent, a snatch of a song on the radio, a chance encounter with someone who vaguely reminded her of someone she had known – these could still trigger a pang of sadness, a fleeting sense of loss. But these moments were becoming less frequent, and their power over her was diminishing. She no longer felt the urge to recoil, to let the wave of grief wash over her. Instead, she acknowledged the feeling, breathed through it, and let it pass, like a cloud drifting across the sun.

She had started reading again, not the dense, academic tomes that had once defined her intellectual pursuits, but simpler novels, stories that offered escape and a gentle reminder of the joys of imagination. She found herself drawn to tales of resilience, of ordinary people facing extraordinary circumstances and finding their way through. It was a quiet rebellion against the narrative of her own life, a silent assertion that her story was not yet over, that it was still being written.

The community at Port Blossom, though still largely a collection of polite nods and brief exchanges, was slowly beginning to feel less like a temporary refuge and more like a nascent home. The grocer who knew her order without asking, the elderly woman who always had a friendly word to share, the other volunteers at Haven who treated her with a quiet camaraderie – these were the threads that were beginning to stitch her into the fabric of this coastal town. She was no longer an outsider looking in; she was a participant, a contributor.

One morning, as she stood by the harbor, watching the fishing boats set out, their engines a low thrum against the dawn chorus, she felt a profound sense of peace. The salt spray kissed her cheeks, the sun warmed her face, and the familiar, comforting scent of the sea filled her lungs. It was a perfect moment, simple and uncomplicated. She wasn't trying to outrun her past anymore, nor was she clinging to it. She was simply living in the present, embracing the quiet beauty of the day, and looking forward, with a gentle, hopeful certainty, to whatever the rising sun would bring. The promise of dawn wasn't just a visual spectacle; it was a promise to herself, a promise of resilience, of renewal, and of a life that was slowly, surely, finding its way back to the light. She took a deep breath, the air clean and invigorating, and turned back towards Haven, ready to meet the day, her heart lighter than it had been in a very long time. The sun, now fully risen, cast a long, bright path across the water, a golden invitation to step forward.

Mara found herself catching Eli's eye more often than she used to. It wasn't a deliberate search, but rather a gentle pull, like a compass needle finding its north. His gaze, when it met hers, wasn't the furtive, pitying glance she'd grown accustomed to from some. There was no condescension, no unspoken question of 'how are you holding up?' Instead, it was a steady, appraising look, imbued with a quiet admiration that settled deep within her. It made her feel... seen. Not as a tragedy, not as a victim, but as a person, present and capable. This simple act of being looked at without judgment was a balm, a subtle affirmation that chipped away at the lingering ice around her heart. It wasn't that she craved attention, but rather that his gaze seemed to acknowledge the effort she was putting in, the quiet rebuilding happening within the walls of Haven and within herself. It was a silent recognition, and it was surprisingly potent.

The lunch breaks, once solitary affairs spent hunched over a sandwich while catching up on paperwork, had begun to evolve. It started with an accidental crossing of paths in the small, utilitarian breakroom, a shared nod, then a hesitant question about the day's rescues. Soon, it became a comfortable ritual. Today, they found themselves drawn to the same worn picnic table overlooking the glittering expanse of Port Blossom's harbor. The salty breeze whipped Mara's hair around her face, and the cry of gulls overhead was a familiar soundtrack to their shared silence. Eli, having just finished a particularly tangled wrestling match with a stubborn knot in a fishing net, leaned back, the muscles in his arms flexing beneath his worn t-shirt. He took a long sip from his water bottle, his eyes scanning the horizon before settling back on her.

"You have a way with them, you know," he said, his voice a low rumble that seemed to blend with the rhythm of the waves.

Mara blinked, unsure if he was addressing her or the seagulls. "A way with... what?"

He gestured vaguely towards the kennels, where the distant yips and contented sighs of the animals were a constant undercurrent. "The animals. You just... connect. I've seen it with the skittish ones, the ones that flinch at every shadow. They relax around you. Even Barnaby, and that old grump rarely lets anyone near him."

A warmth, entirely unrelated to the midday sun, bloomed in Mara's chest. Barnaby was a notoriously difficult German Shepherd, rescued from a neglectful situation, who had taken months to even tolerate a gentle touch. The fact that Eli had noticed her progress with him, and more importantly, acknowledged it, felt like a significant achievement.

"I just... I try to be patient," she murmured, picking at a loose thread on her worn denim jeans. "To let them set the pace. They've been through so much, I think they just need to know they're safe."

Eli nodded slowly, his gaze unwavering. "That's it, isn't it? Safety. And you offer that. It's not just about feeding them or cleaning out their stalls. It's about earning their trust. And you do it so... naturally. Like you were born to it."

The compliment, delivered with such disarming sincerity, landed with an unexpected weight. It wasn't effusive or over-the-top. It was a simple statement of observation, grounded in what he'd witnessed firsthand. It bypassed her defenses, the layers of self-doubt and weariness she carried. This wasn't pity; it was genuine recognition of her efforts, her burgeoning competence. It made her feel a flicker of something akin to courage, a subtle rekindling of a fire she'd thought had long been extinguished. It was the quiet courage that came from being seen, from being valued for something real, something she was actively building. She found herself meeting his gaze, a small, almost shy smile touching her lips. "Thank you, Eli. That means a lot."

The quiet affirmation resonated deeper than she could have imagined. It was the gentle nudge she hadn't realized she needed, a subtle validation that her work at Haven, her new life, held a value that was perceptible to others. It wasn't about seeking external validation, but about finding external reflections that confirmed the internal shifts she was experiencing. Eli's steady gaze, his honest words, served as one such reflection, a quiet beacon in the sometimes-foggy landscape of her recovery. He saw not just the woman trying to mend broken animals, but the woman herself, piecing herself back together, one gentle touch, one quiet morning, one shared glance at a time. The promise of dawn, it seemed, was extending beyond the sunrise, subtly weaving its light into the fabric of her days, and into the quiet interactions that were slowly beginning to shape her world anew. The harbor stretched before them, a vast expanse of possibility, and for the first time in a long time, Mara felt a genuine sense of anticipation for what the next tide, the next sunrise, might bring. She looked back at Eli, and the shared moment hung in the air, unspoken but understood – a quiet acknowledgment of the strength found in simple, genuine connection, and the courage that bloomed when one felt truly seen.

The gentle hum of the generator, a constant companion to the quiet rustle of straw and the occasional soft bark from the kennels, usually provided a comforting backdrop to Mara's days at Haven. But today, a new kind of energy buzzed in the air, a tangible ripple of shared purpose that had begun to take root. It started with a simple observation, a small but persistent niggle in the back of her mind. The dogs, as much as they were cared for and loved, lacked certain stimulating outlets. Their days, while filled with walks and training, could benefit from more mental engagement, from the simple joy of a puzzle toy or the satisfying challenge of a new enrichment activity. It wasn't a complaint, not a criticism, but a quiet recognition of how even the smallest improvements could significantly impact their well-being.

She'd been sketching out a few ideas in her worn notebook during a lull in afternoon activity, doodling a prototype for a treat-dispensing ball, when Eli walked in, his usual steady presence a familiar comfort. He paused, his gaze falling on her scribbled designs, a question forming in his eyes.

"What's that you're working on, Mara?" he asked, his voice carrying the warm, grounded tone that always seemed to cut through any lingering anxieties she might have.

Mara felt a blush creep up her neck, a faint echo of the shyness that had once defined her. "Oh, nothing much," she started, then hesitated. There was no point in hiding it. He'd seen her deep in thought, his curiosity piqued. "Just... thinking about the dogs. They could use some new enrichment toys. Something to keep their minds busy, you know? Beyond the usual fetch and tug-of-war." She gestured vaguely towards a terrier mix, a bundle of boundless energy named Pippin, who was currently doing a frantic loop around his run, his tail a blur. "Pippin, for instance, he'd probably solve world hunger if it involved a treat."

Eli chuckled, a low, genuine sound that made her smile. He stepped closer, leaning over the worn wooden table, his shoulder brushing hers lightly. The scent of sea salt and something faintly earthy, like sun-baked soil, clung to him. "That's a great idea, Mara. They do get a bit... bored, sometimes. Especially the smarter ones. We get a lot of those highly intelligent breeds through here." He pointed to a sketch of a multi-layered puzzle feeder. "This looks pretty clever. How does it work?"

As Mara explained the mechanics of the feeder, her initial hesitation melted away, replaced by the familiar passion that had drawn her to animal rescue in the first place. She described how different compartments would reveal treats only when the correct sequence of actions was performed, how it would encourage problem-solving and patience. Eli listened intently, his brow furrowed in concentration, not just with polite interest, but with a genuine engagement that made her feel as though her ideas were truly valued.

"So, it's not just about getting the treat," he mused, tracing the lines of her drawing with a calloused fingertip. "It's about the process. The thinking involved. That's brilliant. It would make a huge difference for animals that need that extra mental stimulation, especially those who might be a bit anxious or destructive when left to their own devices."

A spark ignited within Mara. The possibility of actually doing something about it, of transforming these ideas from fleeting thoughts into tangible realities for the Haven's residents, suddenly felt within reach. "Exactly," she affirmed, her voice gaining a newfound strength. "But getting them made... it takes resources. And time. I've been thinking, maybe we could organize a fundraising drive specifically for this? People are always so generous when it comes to helping animals, and a project like this feels tangible. Something they can see the direct impact of."

Eli looked up from the notebook, his blue eyes meeting hers with an expression that was both encouraging and decisive. "A fundraising drive. That's a fantastic idea, Mara. And you know what? I'm in. Whatever you need, I'll help."

His immediate, unqualified offer of support was a powerful reassurance. It wasn't just a casual agreement; it was a commitment, a stepping forward to join her in this nascent endeavor. In the weeks that followed, the quiet hum of Haven was punctuated by the rhythm of their collaboration. Lunch breaks, once solitary moments of reflection, became intense planning sessions. They commandeered a corner of the office, a space usually occupied by filing cabinets and discarded adoption forms, transforming it into their makeshift command center. Papers spread across the table, sketches of toys, lists of potential donors, and draft flyers filled the surface.

Mara found herself marveling at Eli's dedication. He brought a practical, grounded perspective to her more imaginative ideas. When she envisioned elaborate, multi-tiered puzzle boxes, Eli would carefully consider the cost of materials and the feasibility of construction by volunteers. He had a knack for breaking down complex tasks into manageable steps, a skill honed by years of working with his hands.

"Okay, so these treat dispensers," he'd say, tapping a pen on a particular sketch. "They're great. But what if we started with something simpler to build a momentum? Like these durable rubber balls with holes that you can stuff with treats? Easier for volunteers to assemble, cheaper to produce in bulk, and still incredibly effective."

Mara appreciated his pragmatism. It grounded her enthusiasm and ensured that their ambitions remained within the realm of possibility. "You're right," she'd concede, already sketching out the simpler design. "We can build up to the more complex ones. Get people excited first. Build a base of support."

They worked on a shared spreadsheet, Eli meticulously entering donation amounts and tracking expenses, while Mara drafted compelling appeal letters and social media posts. He had a quiet intensity when he worked, his focus unwavering, and Mara found herself drawn to it. She'd watch him, the way his brow furrowed in concentration, the way he'd run a hand through his hair when grappling with a particularly tricky calculation. There was an unpretentious competence about him, a quiet strength that was both reassuring and, dare she admit it, attractive.

Their brainstorming sessions weren't always about logistics and budgets. Often, they'd find themselves talking about the animals, sharing anecdotes and observations. Mara would recount a particularly heartwarming interaction with a shy rescue, and Eli would share a story about a challenging rescue he'd been involved in, his voice softening with empathy. They discovered a shared philosophy about animal welfare, a deep-seated belief in the importance of patience, understanding, and giving every creature a second chance.

"Remember that Golden Retriever, Buster?" Eli said one afternoon, scrolling through photos on his phone. "The one who was surrendered because he kept chewing up furniture? Everyone thought he was just a destructive dog." He showed Mara a picture of Buster looking sheepish, a shredded cushion visible in the background. "Turns out he had severe separation anxiety. Once we got him into a foster home with someone who could be with him more and worked on positive reinforcement training, he turned into the most gentle, loving companion."

Mara nodded, a wistful smile playing on her lips. "It's always about understanding the root cause, isn't it? Not just treating the symptom. That's why these enrichment toys are so important. They address the underlying need for mental stimulation, for a sense of purpose, especially for dogs who have been through trauma."

Their shared project had become more than just a means to acquire new toys. It was a crucible, forging a connection between them that was deeper and more nuanced than their previous polite interactions. They were learning each other's strengths, recognizing their complementary skills. Mara's creativity and empathy found a practical outlet through Eli's methodical approach and unwavering support. Eli, in turn, seemed to draw energy from Mara's passion and her deep understanding of the animals' needs.

One evening, as they were packing up after a particularly long session, the sun dipping below the harbor, casting long shadows across the Haven grounds, Eli paused. He held up a prototype of a new food puzzle Mara had designed, a series of interconnected chambers that required different manipulation techniques to release kibble.

"This is going to be a hit, Mara," he said, his voice tinged with genuine admiration. "You have a real gift for this. For understanding what they need, and for finding ways to meet those needs creatively." He met her gaze, and for a moment, the usual easy camaraderie shifted, a subtle current of something more electric passing between them. "I'm really glad you decided to take this on. And that I get to be a part of it."

Mara felt her cheeks warm again, but this time, it wasn't from shyness. It was a response to the warmth in his eyes, to the sincerity in his voice. "Me too, Eli," she murmured, her own voice softer than usual. "I couldn't have done it without you." The shared purpose, the hours spent side-by-side, the quiet understanding that had developed between them, had woven a new thread into the fabric of her life at Haven. The promise of dawn, she realized, wasn't just about the light breaking over the horizon; it was also about the slow, steady unfolding of new connections, new possibilities, blooming in the quiet spaces between shared tasks and spoken words. The fundraising drive was more than just a means to an end; it was a testament to their burgeoning partnership, a tangible representation of their shared commitment to making Haven a better place, one toy, one rescued soul, at a time. The air between them, once filled with the unspoken anxieties of her past, now vibrated with the quiet hum of a shared future, a future built on mutual respect, shared purpose, and a growing, undeniable connection. The project had unearthed something profound within her, a renewed sense of capability and a quiet confidence that she hadn't felt in years, and it was inextricably linked to the steady, unwavering presence of the man working beside her.

The hum of the generator seemed to fade into the background, replaced by the soft thrum of Mara's own heartbeat. The conversation had drifted, as it often did during their late-night work sessions at Haven, from the intricacies of fundraising strategies to the more personal currents that ran beneath the surface of their shared endeavor. Eli had been talking about a particularly difficult build he'd overseen years ago, a project that had nearly bankrupted his small construction company. He spoke of sleepless nights, of the gnawing fear of failure, and of the immense pressure he'd felt to keep his team afloat.

Mara had listened, a knot tightening in her chest, recognizing the echoes of her own anxieties. Her own life, a carefully constructed edifice, had crumbled so spectacularly, leaving her adrift in its ruins. The shame of it still clung to her, a persistent phantom that whispered doubts in her ear, especially when she dared to feel proud of something, like the burgeoning success of their enrichment toy initiative.

"It felt like I was drowning," Eli admitted, his gaze fixed on the half-finished puzzle toy on the table between them. His voice was quiet, devoid of its usual confident resonance. "Every setback felt like a personal failing, a confirmation that I wasn't cut out for it. That I was just... pretending." He looked up then, his blue eyes meeting hers, and Mara saw not just empathy, but a shared weariness that ran deeper than any professional disappointment.

Mara felt a familiar prickle behind her eyes. She'd been bracing herself for this, for the moment when their shared project, their tentative connection, would inevitably brush against the raw edges of her past. "I know that feeling," she began, her voice barely above a whisper. "That constant fear that you're going to mess it all up. That you're not good enough. Since... since everything fell apart for me, it's been a daily battle. Some days, just getting out of bed feels like a victory. And then I start thinking about this, about the Haven, about you, and I wonder if I'm just going to ruin it all.

If I'm going to let everyone down. Again." The words spilled out, unbidden, raw and unfiltered. She'd rehearsed defenses, practiced nonchalance, but in the quiet intimacy of their shared space, with Eli's steady gaze upon her, the carefully constructed walls crumbled.

A wave of vulnerability washed over her, a sensation she usually fought with every fiber of her being. It was a terrifying surrender, admitting the depths of her self-doubt, the persistent specter of inadequacy that haunted her days. She braced herself for his reaction, for pity, for a hasty retreat, for anything but the quiet, understanding stillness that settled between them.

Eli didn't flinch. He didn't offer platitudes or dismiss her feelings. Instead, he leaned forward, his elbows resting on his knees, his expression one of profound attentiveness. "Mara," he said, his voice soft but firm, "what you're feeling is real. And it's okay to feel it. It doesn't make you weak. It makes you human." He paused, choosing his words carefully. "When my company almost went under, it wasn't just about the money or the reputation. It was about my identity. I'd poured everything into it. My sense of self was so tied up in its success, that its near failure felt like a reflection of my own worth."

He shifted, picking up a stray screw from the table and turning it over in his fingers. "I remember one particularly brutal day. A key supplier backed out, a major client threatened to sue, and one of my best carpenters, a guy I considered a friend, told me he was leaving because he couldn't afford to wait for things to turn around. I sat in my empty office that night, the silence deafening, and I truly believed I was a failure. That I'd dragged everyone down with me." He met her gaze again, and there was a profound sadness in his eyes, but also a glint of something else – resilience. "But then, something shifted. I realized that my worth wasn't tied to the success or failure of a single project. It was in my willingness to pick myself up, to learn from the mistakes, and to keep going."

He set the screw down, his hand coming to rest near hers on the table. His touch was light, a feather-light brush of fingertips, but it sent a jolt through her. "Admitting you're struggling, Mara, that's not a sign of weakness. It's a sign of immense strength. It means you're willing to confront the difficult parts of yourself, the parts that are scared, the parts that doubt. And that's where the real growth happens." He offered a small, reassuring smile. "You think I haven't doubted myself? Every single day since my life imploded, I've had to fight those voices telling me I'm not capable, that I'll mess it up. It's a constant battle, but the fight itself is what makes us stronger. Not the absence of fear, but the courage to act in spite of it."

Mara's breath hitched. His words landed with a quiet resonance, bypassing her defenses and settling deep within her. He wasn't just offering sympathy; he was sharing his own scars, his own battles. In his honesty, she found a reflection of her own internal turmoil, and it was strangely comforting. She wasn't alone in this silent war against self-doubt.

"It's just... it's so easy to fall back into those old patterns," she confessed, her voice still a little shaky. "To believe the lies. And when I see how much you've built, how stable and capable you seem, it's hard not to feel like I'm constantly playing catch-up. Like I'll never be able to build anything solid again."

Eli's smile widened, a genuine, warm expression that reached his eyes. "Mara, you are building something solid. Right here. With the Haven. With this project. And you're not playing catch-up; you're forging your own path. My journey, your journey – they're different. But the principles of resilience, of learning, of pushing forward? Those are universal." He reached out, his thumb gently stroking the back of her hand. The contact was electrifying, a simple gesture that spoke volumes. "What you're doing here at Haven, it's incredible. You have a vision, a deep understanding of these animals, and a passion that's infectious. Those are not the qualities of someone who will 'ruin things'."

He paused, his gaze earnest. "The fact that you're even having this conversation with me, that you're willing to be this open, tells me everything I need to know. It means you're ready to heal, to grow. And I'm honored that you feel safe enough to share that with me." His thumb continued its gentle sweep, a silent reassurance. "My past mistakes, my setbacks... they're part of me. They shaped me. But they don't define me. And your past, Mara, it doesn't define you either. It's a chapter, not the whole story."

Tears welled up, but this time, they weren't tears of shame or despair. They were tears of release, of a burden finally being acknowledged and, in that acknowledgment, beginning to lift. The weight of her past, the crushing fear of inadequacy, felt a fraction lighter. Eli's willingness to share his own vulnerabilities, to meet her own with such unwavering empathy, had created a space where she felt seen, understood, and, for the first time in a long time, truly accepted.

"Thank you, Eli," she whispered, her voice thick with emotion. "Really. Thank you."

He squeezed her hand gently, his touch grounding her. "Anytime, Mara. We're in this together, remember? Not just with the toys, but with... all of it." The unspoken implication hung in the air, a promise of continued support, of a shared journey through the complexities of healing and rebuilding.

She looked at the puzzle toy, a tangible symbol of their shared effort. It was intricate, designed to challenge and engage. Just like navigating life after trauma. But Eli was right. The complexity wasn't a sign of impending failure; it was an invitation to problem-solve, to adapt, to learn. And knowing she wasn't facing those challenges alone, that she had a quiet, steady ally beside her, made all the difference. The promise of dawn, she realized, wasn't just about the external light breaking through the darkness; it was also about the internal light, the flicker of hope and resilience that ignites when we dare to be vulnerable, when we allow ourselves to be seen, and when we find strength not in pretending to be unbreakable, but in acknowledging our humanity, our imperfections, and our shared capacity for growth. His honesty had chipped away at her self-imposed isolation, leaving her with a newfound sense of courage. The fear hadn't vanished entirely, but it no longer held the same paralyzing power. In its place, a quiet determination began to bloom, nurtured by the simple, profound act of being truly heard.

The gentle weight of Eli's hand on hers had been a revelation, a simple gesture that had rippled through Mara's carefully guarded emotional landscape. It wasn't just the physical contact; it was the unspoken understanding, the shared vulnerability that had finally cracked open the fortress she'd built around herself. For so long, her days had been a relentless internal battle against the echoes of failure, a constant vigilance against the possibility of another catastrophic misstep. But in the quiet honesty of their conversation, something fundamental had shifted. The fear that had been a suffocating shroud began to thin, allowing slivers of light to penetrate the persistent gloom.

She looked down at her hands, the same hands that had once managed a thriving business, and then, in a cascade of ruin, had been deemed insufficient, incapable. Now, those hands were busy sketching designs for enrichment toys, meticulously assembling prototypes, and gently stroking the soft fur of a rescued dog. It was a stark contrast, a testament to the resilience she'd been so quick to deny herself. Eli's words, about his own past failures not defining him, had resonated deeply. They had provided a mirror, not of her past mistakes, but of her potential for growth, for rebuilding. The very upheaval that had felt like the end of her world had, in retrospect, also been a brutal, unwanted unburdening. The dependency on external validation, the weight of expectations, the very structures that had once seemed so essential, had crumbled away, leaving behind a more fundamental, stripped-down version of herself.

This stripped-down self, she was beginning to realize, was not fragile. It was, in fact, remarkably sturdy. Like a tree that had weathered a violent storm, its roots had been forced deeper into the earth, anchoring it more firmly than before. The uprootedness, while traumatic, had cleared away the deadwood, making space for new, stronger growth. The parallel Eli had drawn between her own journey and a seedling pushing through soil felt remarkably apt. She had felt buried, suffocated, but the insistent urge to survive, to seek the light, had always been there, dormant but not extinguished. Now, with the tentative sun of Eli's understanding warming her, that urge was beginning to manifest.

It was a subtle shift, not a dramatic transformation. The anxieties didn't vanish overnight. The whispers of doubt still occasionally surfaced, especially in the quiet moments before sleep. But they no longer held the same absolute power. She found herself listening to her own instincts with a newfound attentiveness. When a nervous young Labrador, surrendered due to behavioral issues, cowered in the corner of its kennel, Mara didn't immediately second-guess her approach. Instead of panicking about doing the "wrong" thing, she sat quietly outside the kennel, speaking in a low, soothing tone, offering a soft toy. She trusted her gut feeling that patience, not force, was the key.

She trusted her growing understanding of canine body language, the subtle cues that indicated fear rather than aggression.

This burgeoning trust extended beyond the animals. It touched her interactions with the volunteers and the few potential adopters who visited Haven. Before, she'd been crippled by a fear of judgment, a constant worry that her every word and action would be scrutinized and found wanting. Now, she found herself speaking with a quiet authority, sharing her vision for Haven with a genuine passion that wasn't clouded by self-consciousness. When a volunteer asked for clarification on a new feeding schedule, Mara explained her reasoning clearly, her confidence growing with each sentence. She wasn't performing; she was simply sharing her knowledge and her commitment.

The resilience she was rediscovering felt like a muscle that had atrophied from disuse, but was now being worked and strengthened. She recalled a particularly challenging week at Haven, when a plumbing issue had threatened to flood the main building, a sick foster dog required round-the-clock care, and a crucial grant application deadline loomed. In the past, such a confluence of crises would have sent her spiraling into a vortex of panic and self-recrimination. But this time, she met each challenge with a determined pragmatism. She delegated tasks, leveraging the strengths of her volunteers. She stayed up late, not in despair, but in focused problem-solving. She allowed herself moments of exhaustion, but not defeat. She remembered Eli's words about the fight itself making one stronger. And in navigating those difficulties, she found a quiet strength, a testament to her capacity to withstand and overcome.

The fear of messing things up, once a paralyzing force, was slowly transforming into a healthy respect for the complexities of the work. She understood that mistakes were inevitable, especially in a field as unpredictable as animal rescue. But the difference now was that she viewed those mistakes not as indictments of her character, but as opportunities for learning and improvement. If a particular training method didn't yield the desired results, she wouldn't berate herself. Instead, she'd research alternative approaches, consult with experienced trainers, and adapt her strategy. This iterative process, this willingness to learn and evolve, felt far more empowering than the rigid, fear-driven perfectionism that had once defined her.

She began to notice the subtle ways in which her newfound self-assurance was impacting her relationships. Her interactions with Eli, in particular, felt more authentic, more open. The tentative threads of trust that had been woven during their late-night conversations were strengthening, forming a more robust fabric of connection. She no longer felt the need to carefully curate her words, to present a flawless facade. She could admit when she was struggling, when she was unsure, and do so without the accompanying dread of rejection or judgment. This vulnerability, once her greatest fear, was becoming her greatest strength, forging bonds built on genuine understanding rather than superficial pleasantries.

The process of rebuilding at Haven mirrored her own internal reconstruction. Each successfully rehabilitated animal, each positive adoption, each smoothly run event was not just a victory for the organization, but a personal affirmation of her own capabilities. She was no longer just *managing* Haven; she was *leading* it, infusing it with her own spirit and vision. The animals responded to this shift too. They seemed to sense the quiet confidence radiating from her, the genuine empathy that now flowed unimpeded by her internal turmoil. They approached her with less hesitation, their trust in her growing as her trust in herself deepened.

One afternoon, while observing a shy terrier mix named Pip, who had been rescued from a hoarding situation and was initially terrified of human touch, Mara felt a profound sense of peace. Pip, who had spent weeks hiding at the back of his enclosure, had slowly begun to venture closer, drawn by the consistent, gentle presence Mara offered. Today, he nudged his nose into her outstretched hand, a small but monumental act of trust. Mara's heart swelled, not with pride or a need for external validation, but with a deep, quiet joy. It was a visceral understanding that she possessed the capacity for healing, for nurturing, for building connections that mattered. This was not about proving anything to anyone else; it was about reclaiming her own inherent worth, her own ability to contribute positively to the world.

The dawn she had hoped for wasn't a sudden, blinding light, but a gradual, persistent unfolding. It was the slow, steady growth of a seed that had finally found fertile ground. The pain of her past had been the harsh winter, stripping away the superficial and forcing a reckoning. But now, with the promise of spring, the seeds of trust – in herself, in her instincts, in her ability to connect and to heal – were finally beginning to sprout, reaching towards the warmth of a new day. She was no longer defined by the rubble of what had been; she was being shaped by the burgeoning potential of what could be. The journey was far from over, but for the first time in a long time, Mara felt not just hopeful, but truly capable of embracing whatever lay ahead.

CHAPTER FIVE
WHISPERS ON THE WIND

The rhythm of the Coastal Animal Haven had begun to seep into Mara's bones, a steady pulse that was slowly but surely recalibrating her own internal clock. Mornings were no longer a descent into an abyss of self-doubt, but a gentle unfolding into a world populated by wagging tails and hopeful eyes. She found herself anticipating the soft thud of paws against concrete, the hopeful whines at the door, the symphony of barks that, once a cacophony of stress, now sounded like a choir of unique voices, each with a story to tell. Her days were structured, not by the rigid, suffocating demands of her past, but by the organic, compassionate demands of the Haven. This predictable cadence was a balm to her frayed nerves, a sturdy scaffolding upon which she was beginning to rebuild her life.

She learned them all, not just as charges, but as individuals. There was Barnaby, the gentle giant of a Newfoundland with soulful eyes that seemed to hold the weight of the world, a gentle soul surrendered when his elderly owner could no longer manage his size. Mara spent extra time with him, his quiet presence a steady anchor. She learned the nuances of his sighs, the subtle shifts in his posture that indicated contentment or unease. Then there was Luna, a whirlwind of a terrier mix, rescued from a neglectful situation, her initial distrust of human hands a painful testament to her past. Mara would sit just outside Luna's kennel, a book open in her lap, her voice a soft murmur, offering treats patiently until the tip of Luna's tail began to give the faintest of wags. Each tiny victory, each hesitant step towards trust, felt like a personal triumph, a validation of the slow, patient work she was undertaking.

Whiskey, a brindle pit bull with a perpetually optimistic outlook, arrived with a limp and a reputation for being boisterous. Mara discovered that his exuberance was a shield, a desperate attempt to connect. She worked with him on leash manners, using positive reinforcement and a firm but gentle hand, channeling his boundless energy into more controlled interactions. She learned to read the subtle tensing of his shoulders, the flicker in his eyes that signaled overstimulation. She celebrated the day he could walk calmly past another dog without lunging, a milestone that brought tears to her eyes. These weren't just training successes; they were moments of profound connection, proof that she could still make a tangible, positive difference.

She meticulously cataloged their histories, the files filled with tales of abandonment, neglect, and sometimes, heartbreaking loss. Each story, when absorbed, felt like a thread weaving itself into the fabric of her own narrative. She understood the fear in a dog that had been hit by a car and left, the anxiety of a pup whose family had moved and couldn't take him, the loneliness of an older dog whose companion had passed away. It wasn't pity she felt, but a deep, resonant empathy, a recognition of shared vulnerability. She would whisper reassurances to them, her voice a low hum against their fur, promising them that this time, they were safe, they were seen, they were loved.

The routines became a comfort. The early morning clean-up, the dispensing of breakfast, the carefully measured doses of medication for the older residents, the energetic bursts of play in the secure yard – each task was performed with a growing sense of purpose. She learned the specific barks that meant urgency, the soft whimpers that indicated a need for a cuddle, the contented sighs that spoke of a dog finally feeling at peace. She discovered a hidden talent for recognizing the subtle signs of illness, a keen eye for when a dog was just a little off, prompting a call to the vet before a minor issue could escalate. This newfound attentiveness felt like an extension of her own healing process; as she paid closer attention to the needs of these vulnerable creatures, she was inadvertently tending to her own.

Her hands, once accustomed to the sterile precision of spreadsheets and the decisive click of a keyboard, now found a different kind of fulfillment. They were busy with the gentle grooming of a matted coat, the careful administration of a pill hidden in a morsel of cheese, the firm yet loving grip on a leash as she guided a nervous dog through the bustling entrance. She discovered a surprising dexterity in her fingers as she mended torn blankets, fashioned makeshift toys from old towels, and dispensed kibble with practiced efficiency. There was a tactile satisfaction in this work, a grounding reality that cut through the ephemeral nature of her past failures.

The community at Haven, though small, was a revelation. The other volunteers, a motley crew of animal lovers united by a common cause, welcomed her with open arms. There was Sarah, a retired teacher whose quiet wisdom and vast knowledge of canine behavior were invaluable. There was Liam, a young art student who brought a vibrant energy and a knack for capturing the dogs' personalities in his photographs for the adoption profiles. And then there was Ben, a gruff but kind handyman who could fix anything, from a leaky faucet to a broken heart, with equal measure. They shared stories, laughter, and the occasional sigh of exhaustion, their camaraderie a powerful antidote to Mara's isolation.

They didn't pry into her past, but they offered support without judgment. When she stumbled over her words, unsure of how to handle a particularly anxious dog, Sarah would offer a quiet suggestion. When a potential adopter seemed hesitant, Liam would chime in with an anecdote about the dog's progress. Ben, with a gruff nod, would simply ensure that the kennels were secure and the water bowls always full, a silent testament to his dedication. This unspoken understanding, this shared commitment to the welfare of the animals, created a unique bond, a sense of belonging that Mara had long believed was lost to her forever.

One rainy afternoon, a new arrival, a timid beagle named Daisy, was brought in. She was skeletal, her eyes wide with a fear that seemed to consume her. She refused to eat, recoiling from every outstretched hand, her body trembling uncontrollably. Mara spent hours simply sitting near Daisy's kennel, not forcing interaction, just offering a silent, reassuring presence. She spoke softly, her voice a lullaby of comfort, of safety, of a future free from the horrors Daisy had undoubtedly experienced. She brought Daisy her favorite sheepskin blanket, a small offering of warmth and familiarity. Days turned into a week, and then, one morning, Mara found Daisy cautiously emerging from her hiding spot, her nose twitching towards the food bowl she had previously ignored. She tentatively licked the offered treat, a small, almost imperceptible gesture, but to Mara, it was a monumental leap of faith. The quiet joy that surged through her was pure, unadulterated. It was the reward of patience, of dedication, of a connection forged in the quiet spaces between fear and hope.

She began to see her own reflection in the eyes of these rescued animals. Their resilience, their capacity for healing, their unwavering belief in the possibility of a better tomorrow – it was a mirror to the strength she was slowly rediscovering within herself. The fear of failure, once a suffocating blanket, had transformed into a healthy respect for the complexities of life, for the messy, unpredictable nature of healing. She understood that not every dog would be adopted, not every training method would be a resounding success, but the effort, the intention, the unwavering commitment to try – that was what mattered.

The adoption days became a highlight of her week. She meticulously prepared the dogs, brushing their coats, attaching cheerful bandanas, and writing heartfelt bios that showcased their unique personalities. She would stand back, watching as potential families met their new companions, her heart swelling with a quiet pride as a nervous dog's tail began to thump against the floor, or a shy pup nudged a hand for a scratch behind the ears. These were not just adoptions; they were second chances, new beginnings, proof that love and kindness could mend even the deepest wounds. She saw the hope in the eyes of the adopters, the anticipation of a new family member, and it mirrored the hope that was beginning to bloom within her.

One evening, as the sun dipped below the horizon, casting a warm, golden glow over the kennels, Mara sat with Buster, an elderly German Shepherd who had been surrendered by his family due to financial hardship. Buster was content to simply lean against her, his breathing slow and even, his tired eyes gazing out at the fading light. Mara stroked his silver muzzle, the familiar weight of him a comforting presence. She felt a profound sense of peace, a quiet contentment that settled deep within her soul. This was not the life she had envisioned for herself, not the grand success she had once craved, but it was a life filled with purpose, with connection, and with a profound sense of belonging. She was no longer defined by her past mistakes, but by the quiet, steady work she was doing in the present, by the love she was giving and the love she was receiving. The whispers on the wind were no longer tales of failure, but the gentle murmurs of hope, of healing, and of a community built on the unwavering power of care. She was home.

Eli found himself increasingly drawn to the quiet hum of activity at the Coastal Animal Haven, a rhythm that had become as familiar to him as the ebb and flow of the tides. He wasn't a volunteer in the traditional sense; his contributions were more behind-the-scenes, assisting with repairs, ensuring the grounds were maintained, and occasionally lending a hand with larger transport tasks. But his presence was a constant, a silent observer of the dedicated souls who poured their hearts into the shelter. And lately, his observations had a singular focus: Mara.

He'd first noticed her in the blur of new arrivals, a whirlwind of nervous energy and a hesitant step. He'd seen the initial tremor in her hands as she'd approached a skittish dog, the way her eyes would dart around as if searching for an escape route. It had pained him, in a quiet, unobtrusive way, to witness someone so clearly adrift. But gradually, almost imperceptibly, a transformation had begun to unfold.

He'd catch glimpses of her during his rounds – the early mornings when the dew still clung to the grass, the late evenings when the only light came from the security lamps casting long shadows. He saw her not as the woman who had initially seemed so lost, but as someone finding her footing, her purpose. He watched the way she'd kneel beside a fearful dog, her voice a low, soothing murmur, her movements slow and deliberate. He saw the patience in her eyes as she'd sit for what felt like hours, simply offering a silent, unwavering presence to a creature overwhelmed by fear. There were no grand gestures, no performative displays of affection. It was a quiet, deep-seated empathy that emanated from her, a genuine understanding of the unspoken language of pain and the slow, arduous path to healing.

One particular evening, as the last rays of sunlight bled into a dusky purple, Eli was finishing up a repair on the outer fencing near the main kennel block. The air was filled with the usual symphony of contented sighs, the occasional playful bark, and the soft shuffling of paws. He'd seen Mara on her final rounds, her movements fluid and unhurried now, a stark contrast to the jerky uncertainty he'd first observed. She was cleaning out the last of the kennels, her movements efficient and practiced. There was a grace in her posture, a settled confidence that hadn't been there before. She'd pause to offer a gentle scratch behind an ear, a soft word of encouragement, a quiet moment of connection before moving on.

He leaned against the fence, the cool metal a familiar sensation against his back, and watched her. Her face, usually etched with a subtle weariness that spoke of past struggles, was softened by a gentle smile that occasionally touched her lips. It wasn't a broad, performative grin, but a quiet, genuine expression of peace, a subtle flicker of joy that reached her eyes. He saw the way she'd expertly administer medication, the way she'd carefully measure out food, the almost instinctive way she'd anticipate a need before it was even voiced. She was no longer just going through the motions; she was inhabiting this space, her presence becoming an integral part of the Haven's heartbeat.

As she finished with the last kennel and began to gather her cleaning supplies, she happened to glance in his direction. Her eyes met his, and for a moment, the cacophony of the Haven seemed to fade into a soft background hum. She offered a small, acknowledging nod, a gesture that was both polite and strangely intimate. It was then that Eli felt compelled to speak.

He walked over, his boots crunching softly on the gravel path. He kept his voice low, not wanting to intrude on the quiet sanctuary she seemed to have found. "You know," he began, his tone deliberately casual, "you've really found your stride here."

Mara paused, a bucket of soapy water in her hand. She blinked, a flicker of surprise crossing her features, quickly replaced by a thoughtful expression. She didn't offer a dismissive platitude or a hurried "thank you." Instead, she met his gaze, a quiet intensity in her own.

"I have?" she asked, her voice soft, a hint of curiosity in its tone.

Eli nodded, his gaze steady. "Yeah. You move differently now. More... sure of yourself. And you smile more. A lot more." He gestured vaguely with his chin. "It's good to see."

The sincerity in his words was palpable. It wasn't a casual compliment, but a genuine observation, a testament to his quiet awareness of her journey. He wasn't someone who offered praise lightly, and Mara knew that. His words weren't designed to flatter or impress, but to acknowledge a truth he had witnessed. He saw her, not just as a volunteer, but as someone undergoing a profound personal shift.

A warmth spread through Mara, a sensation entirely separate from the lingering chill of the evening air. It was the feeling of being truly seen, of having her internal landscape recognized by an external observer who hadn't been privy to the struggle, but had witnessed the outcome. Eli's understated acknowledgment was more powerful than any effusive praise could have been. It resonated because it was rooted in observation, in a quiet understanding of the subtle cues that signaled her inner change.

"I... I guess I have," she admitted, a genuine smile finally gracing her lips, a smile that reached her eyes this time. She looked down at the bucket in her hands, then back at Eli. "It's been a process. This place... it's been good for me. More than I ever expected."

"It has a way of doing that," Eli replied, his gaze sweeping over the kennels, a faint smile playing on his own lips. "It demands a lot, but it gives back even more. Especially if you're willing to give it your all." He paused, his eyes returning to Mara, a hint of something deeper in their depths. "And you, Mara, you give it everything."

His words were simple, yet they landed with a quiet force. They acknowledged not just her effort, but her dedication, her willingness to invest herself fully in the well-being of these animals. It wasn't just about cleaning kennels or filling food bowls; it was about the emotional and psychological investment she was making, the way she was allowing herself to connect and to care.

"I'm learning," she said, her voice barely above a whisper. "Learning to be present. Learning to trust myself again." She met his gaze, a flicker of vulnerability in her eyes, but also a newfound strength. "This is... this is what I needed."

Eli simply nodded, a gesture of understanding that needed no further explanation. He didn't probe, didn't ask about the "why" or the "what" of her past struggles. His acknowledgment was enough, a silent validation of her current journey. He saw the dedication in her eyes, the quiet resilience in her posture, and he understood that this was more than just a job or a volunteer position for her. It was a sanctuary, a place of healing, a stepping stone towards reclaiming herself.

As she continued with her tasks, a comfortable silence settled between them, punctuated only by the sounds of the Haven. Eli stayed for a few more minutes, his presence a grounding force. He watched as Mara's movements became more assured, her focus unwavering. He saw the way a scruffy terrier mix, who had been notoriously difficult to approach, nudged her hand gently, seeking attention, and Mara responded with a soft word and a gentle stroke, her touch confident and kind.

He'd witnessed countless individuals pass through the Haven over the years, some finding solace, others merely passing time. But there was something about Mara, a quiet determination that burned beneath the surface, a nascent strength that was slowly but surely blooming. He saw the empathy in her every interaction, the way she seemed to understand the silent plea in a dog's eyes, the subtle language of a wagging tail or a drooping ear. It was a raw, untamed compassion, and it was beautiful to witness.

Before he left for the night, he offered a final, quiet observation. "You're making a real difference here, Mara," he said, his voice low and sincere. "More than you probably know."

Mara looked up, a genuine warmth radiating from her. The earlier surprise had settled into a quiet appreciation, a profound gratitude for his insightful words. "Thank you, Eli," she said, her voice filled with a sincerity that mirrored his own. "That means a lot."

He offered a slight nod, a ghost of a smile touching his lips, and then turned to leave, melting back into the shadows as unobtrusively as he had appeared. But his words lingered, a gentle echo in the quiet space Mara had carved out for herself. Eli's observations, so quietly delivered, had provided a mirror, reflecting back to her the strength and purpose she was building, brick by patient brick, within the comforting embrace of the Coastal Animal Haven. She felt a profound sense of connection, not just to the animals, but to the quiet observer who saw her for who she was becoming.

The sun, a molten gold orb, was beginning its slow descent towards the horizon, painting the sky in hues of apricot and rose. The air, still warm from the day's embrace, carried the briny scent of the sea, a perfume of salt and possibility that always seemed to cling to Port Blossom. Mara, her heart still humming with the quiet satisfaction of a day well spent at the Coastal Animal Haven, found herself walking alongside Eli, their footsteps falling into an easy rhythm on the worn cobblestones. It was a walk born of a shared moment, a spontaneous detour from the predictable path home, a silent agreement that the day's good energy deserved to be savored just a little longer.

"It's amazing, isn't it?" Mara murmured, her voice a soft counterpoint to the distant cry of gulls. She gestured vaguely towards the harbor, where the silhouettes of fishing boats, their masts like skeletal fingers against the vibrant sky, bobbed gently on the turquoise water. "All this life, all this... movement. It feels like a whole different world from the Haven."

Eli, his gaze following hers, offered a thoughtful nod. His hands were tucked into the pockets of his worn canvas jacket, a posture of relaxed attentiveness. "It is," he agreed, his voice a low rumble that seemed to resonate with the steady pulse of the ocean. "This is where the city meets the wild. Where the work of the land meets the bounty of the sea." He turned to her then, his eyes, the color of a stormy sea, meeting hers with a warmth that felt like a gentle tide washing over her. "It's a good place to think, isn't it? To just... be."

They continued their stroll, the docks alive with the subtle symphony of a working port. The creak of wooden hulls, the low thrum of engines being prepped for an early departure, the sharp, percussive calls of fishermen mending nets, their hands moving with a practiced dexterity that spoke of generations of tradition. The air was thick with the scent of the day's catch, a pungent aroma that was both raw and invigorating, mingling with the fainter, sweeter notes of tar and damp wood. It was a scent that spoke of hard work, of sustenance, of a connection to the primal rhythms of nature.

Mara found herself drawn to the details – the weathered paint peeling from the sides of the boats, revealing layers of stories etched in salt and sun; the coils of thick rope, stout and sturdy, ready to brave any storm; the iridescent shimmer of a discarded fish scale, catching the fading light like a fallen jewel. Each element was a testament to a life lived in close proximity to the elements, a life dictated by the moon and the tides.

"I've always loved the docks," Mara confessed, a soft smile playing on her lips. "Even when I was a kid, whenever we'd pass through a coastal town, I'd beg my parents to stop, just so I could watch the boats. It felt... full of promise." She paused, her gaze drifting to a particularly sturdy-looking trawler, its name painted in bold, chipped lettering: 'The Sea Serpent'. "Like each one was setting off on an adventure, heading towards something unknown, something bigger."

Eli chuckled, a low, warm sound. "And for many of them, that's exactly what it is. Every trip out is a gamble. You're chasing something you can't always see, relying on instinct and experience. It's a different kind of reliance than what we have at the Haven, but a reliance all the same." He kicked at a loose piece of driftwood, sending it skittering across the planks. "I came here, to Port Blossom, because I was tired of the chase. Tired of the constant looking ahead. I wanted a place where I could see the results of my work, where the impact was tangible."

He gestured towards the Haven, visible in the distance, a cluster of sturdy buildings nestled against the coastline. "The Haven, it gives you that. You mend a fence, and a dog is safer. You clean a kennel, and an animal feels more comfortable. It's immediate. It's real." He looked back at Mara, his expression thoughtful. "But I suppose, in its own way, the sea offers that too, doesn't it? The fisherman brings back a catch, feeds his family, contributes to the town. It's a different kind of tangible, but it's there."

Mara nodded, absorbing his words. "I think... I think that's part of why I feel so at home at the Haven," she said softly. "After... everything... I felt so adrift. Like my own life was a ship that had lost its anchor. I was just tossed about by whatever storm came my way." She looked down at her hands, now resting on the weathered railing of a pier, her knuckles brushing against the salt-crusted wood. "The Haven, it's given me an anchor. It's given me a purpose that's bigger than myself."

A gentle breeze swept across the water, carrying with it the faint scent of salt and distant pine forests. It rustled Mara's hair, causing a few strands to escape their loose braid and dance around her face. Eli watched her, his gaze steady and kind. He didn't offer platitudes or easy reassurances. Instead, he simply listened, his presence a quiet anchor in itself.

"Port Blossom, it's a town built on resilience," Eli said, his voice low. "Look at these boats. They brave storms, they face the unpredictable. They come back, sometimes battered, sometimes empty, but they always come back. And the people who work them, they're just as resilient. They've got to be, to make a life out here." He turned to face her fully, leaning against the railing, his posture relaxed but his gaze intent. "And I've seen that same resilience in you, Mara."

His words, delivered without fanfare, landed with a gentle force. It wasn't the first time he'd acknowledged her strength, but each time, it felt like a validation, a quiet affirmation of the hard-won progress she was making. She met his eyes, a small, genuine smile gracing her lips. "I'm trying," she admitted. "It's a daily effort, isn't it? To keep rowing, even when the waves are high."

"That's all anyone can do," Eli replied. He pushed off from the railing, and they continued their walk, moving away from the immediate bustle of the fishing fleet towards a quieter stretch of the docks, where smaller pleasure crafts were moored, their sleek lines a contrast to the rugged workhorses they had just passed. "So, tell me, what were your dreams, when you were a kid staring at boats on the docks? What was Mara dreaming of then?"

Mara's laughter tinkled on the evening air, a sound of genuine amusement and nostalgia. "Oh, so many things!" she exclaimed, her eyes sparkling. "I wanted to be an explorer, discovering new lands. Or an artist, capturing the beauty of the world. Or... maybe even a marine biologist, studying all the incredible creatures in the ocean." She sighed, a wistful sound. "Life, however, has a funny way of redirecting your compass, doesn't it?"

"It does," Eli agreed, his voice carrying a hint of understanding, of shared experience. "But sometimes, those detours lead you to places you never would have found otherwise. Places, perhaps, where you're meant to be." He gestured towards the water, the deepening twilight casting a softer glow. "I ended up here, in Port Blossom, after a series of... less than ideal choices. I drifted for a while, working odd jobs, always feeling like I was on the outside looking in."

He paused, his gaze fixed on the distant, twinkling lights of the town. "Then I found the Haven. It was a place that needed hands, needed someone to fix things, to keep the wheels turning. And I discovered that I was good at it. Better than I ever thought I could be." He smiled, a slow, genuine smile that reached his eyes. "It gave me a sense of belonging, a place to put down roots, even if those roots are a little... unconventional."

"Unconventional is often the best kind," Mara mused, her gaze sweeping over the tranquil water. "It means you're not afraid to be different, to forge your own path." She turned to him, her expression open and curious. "What was it about the Haven that drew you in so strongly, Eli? Beyond just needing a place to land?"

Eli considered her question for a long moment, his brow furrowed slightly in thought. The rhythmic lapping of the waves against the pier seemed to underscore the quiet contemplation. "It was the commitment," he said finally. "The unwavering dedication of the people who worked there. They weren't doing it for recognition, or for glory. They were doing it because it was the right thing to do. Because these animals, who had no voice, deserved care and compassion. And I saw that in them. I saw that same quiet strength that I... well, that I'm starting to see in you."

A blush warmed Mara's cheeks, but she didn't shy away from his gaze. His words, so earnest and direct, felt like a balm to a part of her that had been so long neglected. "That's... that's a beautiful thing to witness," she said softly. "To see that kind of pure intention."

"It is," Eli agreed. "And it's infectious. It makes you want to be a part of it. To contribute something, however small." He gestured between them, encompassing their shared walk, their shared conversation. "This is part of that, isn't it? Finding connections in unexpected places. Finding people who see you, really see you, and acknowledge the journey you're on."

They had reached the end of a long pier, the water stretching out before them, vast and dark under the emerging stars. The sounds of the port had receded, replaced by the more intimate symphony of the sea. A lone dolphin arced gracefully out of the water in the distance, a silver flash against the deepening indigo.

"It does feel... extraordinary," Mara whispered, her voice filled with a quiet wonder. "This ordinary walk. This ordinary evening. But with you, it feels... different. Like the world has shifted, just a little."

Eli turned to her, his expression unreadable in the dim light, yet his presence radiated a steady warmth. He reached out, not to touch her, but to gesture towards the starlit expanse. "The world is always shifting, Mara. It's how we choose to see those shifts that makes all the difference. Whether we see them as threats, or as opportunities." He met her gaze again, a gentle smile playing on his lips. "And I think you're learning to see them as opportunities."

The salty air, thick with the promise of the night, seemed to wrap around them, a silent witness to their burgeoning connection. The ordinary had, indeed, become extraordinary, not through grand gestures or dramatic pronouncements, but through the quiet intimacy of shared dreams, of honest confessions, and of a walk along the docks that had led them, step by gentle step, a little closer together.

The cottage, perched on its small bluff overlooking the restless expanse of the Atlantic, became Mara's sanctuary. As dusk deepened into night, the familiar, comforting sound of the waves began its nightly serenade. It wasn't the crashing, tempestuous roar of a storm, but a consistent, rhythmic shushing, a deep sigh of the ocean exhaling against the shore. Mara would lie in her bed, the thin curtains pulled back to reveal the ink-black sky dotted with a million distant stars, and let the sound wash over her. Each ebb and flow, each whispered cascade of water over pebbles and sand, seemed to carry away a fragment of her anxieties.

In the quietude of the night, when the demands of the day, the calls of the animals, and the gentle presence of Eli receded, her mind could easily be a treacherous landscape. Ghosts of her past, of mistakes made and opportunities lost, might have begun to stir, their whispers amplified in the stillness. But the ocean's murmur was a persistent counter-melody, a powerful, grounding presence that insisted on the here and now. It was a constant, a rhythm as old as time, a reminder that while individual lives might be fleeting, the natural world endured, its cycles unbroken. She found herself listening intently, discerning the subtle variations: the soft hiss as a wave receded, the gentle tumble of stones as the tide pulled back, the deeper rumble that hinted at a larger swell approaching.

This wasn't just ambient noise; it was a deliberate, conscious seeking of solace. She began to anticipate the sound, to crave it. As she prepared for bed, the winding down of her day was marked not by the ticking of a clock, but by the increasing intensity of the ocean's voice. It was a signal that the world outside her small cottage was settling into its nocturnal rhythm, and that she, too, could find a measure of peace within its embrace. The waves became a lullaby, sung in a language of brine and motion, a melody that soothed the raw edges of her spirit.

She started to associate the sound with a sense of safety, a feeling of being protected. The vastness of the ocean, which might have once seemed daunting or even menacing, now felt like a benevolent guardian. It was a presence that was always there, unwavering, unjudgmental. Unlike the fickle nature of human relationships or the unpredictable currents of her own life, the ocean's rhythm was a constant. It was a dependable force, a testament to continuity.

There were nights when the moon, a sliver of pearl or a full, luminous orb, would cast a shimmering path across the water, transforming the dark expanse into a canvas of shifting silver. In those moments, the sound of the waves seemed to deepen, to carry a richer, more resonant tone, as if the moonlight itself infused them with a special magic. Mara would find herself mesmerized, caught in the silent, powerful dance of light and sound. It was a spectacle that dwarfed her own troubles, putting them into a perspective that felt both humbling and liberating.

She began to actively seek out that feeling. Even during the day, when the sun was high and the world bustled with activity, she would find herself drawn to her window, her gaze drifting towards the horizon, listening for the faint, distant murmur of the sea. It was a reminder that this powerful, ancient force was always present, a constant wellspring of tranquility she could tap into. The sounds of Port Blossom – the gulls' cries, the distant hum of boat engines, the chatter of townsfolk – would fade into the background, and the ocean's voice would emerge, a steadying undertone.

This reliance on the sound of the waves was a new experience for Mara. For so long, she had relied on external validation, on the approval of others, or on her own frantic efforts to control her surroundings. Now, she was discovering a different kind of strength, a resilience found not in striving, but in surrendering to something larger than herself. The ocean didn't demand anything of her. It simply existed, in all its magnificent power and perpetual motion, and in its presence, she found a quiet validation of her own existence.

She began to notice how the sound changed with the weather. On clearer nights, it was a gentle, consistent rhythm. But even a hint of an approaching storm would subtly alter its cadence, a more urgent undertow, a deeper, more resonant pulse. She learned to interpret these shifts, not with fear, but with a growing understanding of the sea's moods. It felt like learning a new language, a dialogue between herself and the natural world.

One particular evening, as the stars began to prick the darkening sky, Mara sat on the small wooden deck outside her cottage. The air was cool and carried the unmistakable scent of salt and damp earth. She closed her eyes, letting the world shrink to the confines of her immediate sensory experience. The coolness of the sea breeze on her skin, the faint scent of pine from the nearby woods, and, above all, the ceaseless rhythm of the waves. It was a sound that filled the silence, not with emptiness, but with fullness. It was the sound of life, of constant renewal, of a world that simply kept turning, regardless of individual joys or sorrows.

She thought about the animals at the Haven, their own quiet reliance on the consistent care they received. Their routines, their predictable feeding times, their safe enclosures – these were their anchors. The ocean, in its own way, provided a similar sense of stability for her. It was a constant, an unwavering presence in a world that had felt so chaotic.

There were moments, too, when the sound of the waves seemed to echo her own inner turmoil, but in a way that offered release. A particularly strong surge against the shore might mirror a fleeting surge of grief or regret, but then the inevitable ebb would follow, pulling the emotion back out to sea, leaving behind a sense of calm, of having been cleansed. It was a cathartic experience, a natural way of processing the unresolved fragments of her past without the need for conscious effort.

She started to feel a sense of deep connection to Port Blossom, a connection that transcended her work at the animal shelter. It was a connection forged by the shared element that defined the town, the vast, breathing ocean that lay just beyond their doorsteps. She realized that everyone in this town lived by its rhythm, their lives dictated by its tides, its bounty, its occasional fury. And she, too, was now part of that rhythm.

The sound of the waves at night became more than just a comforting noise; it became a symbol of hope. It represented a new beginning, a fresh start. It was the sound of a world that continued to move forward, offering new possibilities with each passing tide. It was a subtle but profound shift in her own internal landscape. Where once there had been a hollow ache of loss, there was now a growing sense of peace, a quiet assurance that even after the deepest storms, the waves would continue to break, and the dawn would always eventually arrive.

She began to dream with the sound of the ocean as her backdrop. Her dreams were no longer haunted by past failures, but filled with imagery of the sea – of vast, open waters, of graceful marine life, of a horizon that stretched endlessly towards a brighter future. The rhythm of the waves seeped into her subconscious, shaping her thoughts, her emotions, her very sense of self.

It was a slow, gradual transformation, akin to the erosion of rocks by the relentless caress of the sea. No single wave, no single night, dramatically altered her course. Instead, it was the cumulative effect of thousands upon thousands of gentle lappings, of countless sighs of the ocean, that wore away the sharp edges of her despair and smoothed the path towards healing.

She found herself looking forward to the evenings, not with dread, but with anticipation. The quiet hours, once a potential breeding ground for her anxieties, were now a time of peaceful reflection, punctuated by the reassuring, constant voice of the sea. It was a gentle reminder that she was not alone, that she was part of something ancient and enduring. The sound of the waves at night became her anchor, holding her steady as she navigated the uncharted waters of her new life in Port Blossom. It was the sound of resilience, the sound of hope, and the sound of a heart slowly, surely, beginning to mend. She realized that this constant, rhythmic presence was more than just auditory comfort; it was a profound affirmation of life's persistent, beautiful continuation. The ocean didn't just break against the shore; it rebuilt it, piece by piece, with each gentle sweep of its powerful, eternal embrace.

And in that steady, unwavering cadence, Mara found her own enduring strength.

The air, still carrying the lingering warmth of high summer, began to whisper of change. A subtle crispness, almost imperceptible at first, kissed the evenings, hinting at the turning of the season. For Mara, this shift was more than a meteorological observation; it was a palpable nudge towards a future she was only beginning to consider. The frantic energy of spring, when her arrival in Port Blossom had been a desperate flight from her past, had softened into a more measured pace. The frantic need to simply *survive* had gradually, almost imperceptibly, transformed into a nascent yearning to *live*. And with that yearning came a fragile bloom of hope, a tender sprout pushing through the hardened earth of her former despair.

It was a hope that felt precarious, like a seedling delicate enough to be crushed by a careless step. She found herself examining it, turning it over in her mind, half-expecting it to wither and die, just as so many of her previous aspirations had. But it persisted, a quiet, persistent ember glowing beneath the ashes. She caught herself smiling more often these days, a genuine, unforced curvature of her lips that reached her eyes, crinkling the corners in a way that felt both unfamiliar and deeply comforting. These weren't the polite, practiced smiles she'd once offered to deflect awkwardness or mask her true feelings. These were smiles born of quiet contentment, of moments of simple joy – a particularly sweet call from a robin at the Haven, the successful coaxing of a shy stray into her care, a shared laugh with Eli over a clumsy puppy. These smiles were proof, undeniable and profound, that her heart, so long encased in ice, was beginning to thaw, to beat with a rhythm that felt less like a frantic flutter of anxiety and more like a steady, hopeful pulse.

She still had moments, of course, when the shadows of her past would lengthen, casting a pall over her present. A particular scent, a stray phrase overheard, a fleeting glimpse of a familiar-looking car – these could still send a jolt of fear through her, a visceral reminder of the life she had escaped. But now, instead of being consumed by the ensuing panic, she found herself equipped with a new resilience, a quiet strength that seemed to have been woven into the very fabric of her being by the steady, rhythmic cadence of the ocean. The waves, her constant companions, seemed to whisper reassurances, their endless cycle of ebb and flow mirroring the natural rhythm of healing. Grief, regret, and fear were still waves that washed over her, but now they receded, leaving behind not a barren shore, but a landscape softened and prepared for new growth.

She was learning to trust this burgeoning sense of peace, this tentative optimism. It was a stark contrast to the hypervigilance that had characterized her life for so long. Before, every interaction had been a strategic assessment, every silence a potential threat. Now, she found herself able to simply *be*. She could engage in conversations without her mind racing ahead, dissecting every word for hidden meanings. She could enjoy the quiet moments, the companionship of the animals, the easy camaraderie with Eli, without the gnawing apprehension that something terrible was about to happen. This newfound ease was liberating, a freedom she hadn't realized she'd been craving until it began to manifest.

The subtle shift in the season also brought a change in her routines, a gentle redirection of her focus. The frantic urgency of spring had given way to the more established patterns of summer's end. Her days at the Haven, while still demanding, had settled into a comfortable rhythm. The animals, too, seemed to sense the coming change, their coats thickening slightly, their instincts preparing for cooler weather. Mara found a quiet satisfaction in these preparations, in the simple act of nurturing and caring. It was a tangible demonstration of her ability to contribute, to create order and well-being in a world that had once felt so irrevocably chaotic.

One afternoon, while tending to a litter of orphaned kittens, Mara paused, the tiny, purring bundles nestled in her hands. The sunlight streamed through the barn windows, illuminating dust motes dancing in the air, and a soft breeze rustled the hay. In that moment, surrounded by the gentle sounds of contented feline life and the scent of warm hay, a profound sense of belonging washed over her. It wasn't the frantic belonging of someone desperately seeking refuge, but the quiet, settled belonging of someone who had found a place to put down roots. This wasn't just a temporary stop; it was becoming home. The thought, once so terrifying, now felt like a comforting embrace.

She started to look at Port Blossom not as a place of hiding, but as a place of possibility. The quirky shops lining the harbor, the weathered faces of the fishermen mending their nets, the laughter of children playing on the beach – these elements, once viewed through a lens of suspicion, now appeared as facets of a vibrant, living community. She found herself lingering on her walks, her gaze drawn to the colorful fishing boats bobbing in the harbor, to the intricate patterns of the tide pools revealed by the receding water. She was no longer an observer on the periphery, but someone slowly, cautiously, beginning to integrate into the landscape.

The quiet evenings, once filled with the echoing silence of her solitude, were now punctuated by the comforting presence of Eli. Their conversations, initially tentative and brief, had deepened, evolving into shared stories, shared laughter, and shared silences that spoke volumes. He had a way of listening that made her feel seen, understood, without the pressure of explanation. He didn't pry, didn't demand to know the details of her past, but offered instead a steady, non-judgmental presence that allowed her to slowly, organically, reveal herself. He spoke of his own life, his connection to Port Blossom, his dreams and his quiet disappointments, and in his openness, Mara found an invitation to reciprocate.

There were evenings, as the sun dipped below the horizon, painting the sky in hues of orange and lavender, when they would sit on the bluff overlooking the ocean, the same bluff where her cottage sat. The air would be cool, carrying the scent of salt and pine, and the relentless rhythm of the waves would provide a soothing soundtrack to their quiet communion. Eli would point out constellations as they emerged, his voice a low rumble against the ceaseless murmur of the sea, and Mara would find herself sharing fragments of her own memories, stories that had once been too painful to voice, now emerging with a surprising gentleness. It was as if the vastness of the ocean, and the comforting presence of Eli, created a safe harbor for her deepest emotions.

She realized, with a jolt of surprise, that she was beginning to anticipate these evenings, to look forward to the shared quietude, the easy camaraderie. The thought of spending time with Eli no longer sparked a flicker of apprehension, but a genuine warmth, a quiet eagerness. It was a sensation that was both exhilarating and slightly terrifying. Could this be... happiness? The word felt too large, too potent, for the fragile hope she was nurturing. But the feeling was undeniable, a gentle stirring in her chest that felt remarkably like contentment.

She found herself making small, deliberate choices that reflected this growing sense of optimism. She purchased a small collection of gardening books, envisioning a more vibrant window box for her cottage. She started experimenting with new recipes, finding a quiet joy in the process of creation and the simple pleasure of a well-prepared meal. She even found herself browsing through a local craft fair, admiring the handmade pottery and knitted goods, a stark contrast to her previous tendency to avoid any situation that might require prolonged interaction or decision-making.

Each small act was a testament to her evolving mindset, a quiet assertion of her presence in this new chapter of her life.

The summer, so often associated with vibrant, fleeting energy, was now transitioning into a season of mellow beauty, of deep, rich colors and a comforting sense of ripeness. And Mara, like the land around her, was undergoing her own season of transformation. The raw edges of her past were being smoothed, not erased, but softened, like sea-worn glass. The sharp pangs of fear were giving way to a more settled awareness, a recognition of potential dangers without the paralyzing grip of panic. She was learning to navigate the complexities of her emotions, to acknowledge them without letting them dictate her every move.

There were days, on the bluffs, when she would simply stand and watch the waves, their ceaseless motion a powerful metaphor for the flow of life. She saw how they met the shore, sometimes with gentle kisses, sometimes with a more forceful embrace, but always, always returning. It was a lesson in persistence, in resilience. She saw how they carved away at the cliffs, shaping the landscape over time, a testament to the power of slow, steady change. And she realized that her own healing was not a sudden, dramatic event, but a gradual, ongoing process, much like the ocean's patient sculpting of the coastline.

She was no longer just existing; she was starting to truly live. The hesitant hopes that had begun to stir within her were no longer just whispers on the wind, easily dismissed. They were becoming a more confident melody, a gentle but insistent song of possibility, played against the eternal symphony of the sea.

And with each passing day, Mara found herself listening more closely, her heart opening to the promise of what might be. The fear hadn't vanished entirely, but it was being steadily overshadowed by a quiet, burgeoning joy. She was starting to believe that perhaps, just perhaps, she had found more than just a sanctuary in Port Blossom; she had found a home, and a future.

The possibility of building a life here, of planting roots that would take hold and flourish, was no longer a distant, impossible dream, but a tangible, exhilarating prospect. The ocean's lullaby, once a balm for her pain, was now becoming an anthem of her awakening.

Chapter Six
TIDES OF CHANGE

The first true chill of autumn arrived not with a dramatic gust, but with a subtle, insistent breath that snaked through the open windows of the Haven, rustling the hay and carrying the scent of damp earth and decaying leaves. Mara, busy mending a worn saddle blanket, paused, her fingers stilling. She inhaled deeply, the crisp air a welcome departure from the lingering, humid warmth of late summer. It was a scent that spoke of change, of nature's grand, inevitable turning. The vibrant, almost aggressive greens that had dominated the landscape for months were beginning to soften, to yield to the richer, more somber palette of gold, russet, and burnt umber. The world outside the Haven's familiar walls was slowly, deliberately, transforming, and with each shift in the light, each shortening of the day, Mara felt a corresponding shift within herself.

She watched from the barn doorway as the sun, lower in the sky now, cast long, slanted shadows across the fields. The goldenrod, a cheerful splash of yellow throughout the summer, was beginning to brown at the edges, its once vibrant blooms drooping slightly, their seed heads promising new life in the spring, but signaling the end of their current glory. The migratory birds, a constant chorus of chirps and calls, had grown quieter, their restless energy a prelude to their long journeys south. Mara felt a kinship with them, a shared sense of impending departure, though her own destination remained shrouded in a mist as thick as the morning fog that often clung to the harbor.

The Haven, with its predictable routines and the comforting presence of its animal inhabitants, had become her anchor, her sanctuary. The frantic need to simply survive, which had propelled her here, had long since faded, replaced by a quiet gratitude for the peace she had found. Yet, as the season turned, a new, more subtle anxiety began to stir. It wasn't the sharp, paralyzing fear of her past, but a more existential unease, a question mark hanging heavy in the crisp autumn air: what now? The Haven had provided refuge, but could it offer a future? Could she truly build a life here, or was she destined to remain a temporary resident, a fleeting presence in the lives of those who had shown her such unexpected kindness?

Eli, with his easygoing nature and his unwavering support, had become a constant in her life. Their shared silences on the bluff overlooking the ocean had deepened, becoming as comfortable and meaningful as their conversations. He spoke of his own dreams, of the fishing season, of the quiet rhythm of life in Port Blossom, and Mara found herself drawn into his world, her own anxieties momentarily forgotten. But even in his presence, the unspoken question lingered. He was a man rooted in this place, his life inextricably tied to the tides and seasons of the coast. Where did she fit into that landscape? Her past was a closed book, her future a blank page. The approaching autumn, with its sense of finality and transition, seemed to amplify the urgency of her internal debate.

She found herself lingering over tasks at the Haven, extending her time with the animals, as if by delaying her departure from these familiar surroundings, she could somehow hold back the tide of change. She'd groom a horse with meticulous care, checking every inch of its coat, as if the sheer thoroughness of her attention could somehow cement her place here. She'd spend extra minutes hand-feeding a timid rabbit, coaxing it closer, whispering reassurances, a silent plea for permanence. The animals, blissfully unaware of her internal turmoil, accepted her presence with simple, unconditional affection. They didn't ask about her past, didn't question her future. They simply needed her, and in that need, Mara found a temporary solace.

The autumn air, once a refreshing contrast, now seemed to carry a hint of melancholy. The leaves, in their spectacular final blaze of glory, were also a stark reminder of impermanence. They danced and swirled in the wind, a breathtaking spectacle, before succumbing to gravity, their vibrant colors fading to a muted brown as they lay scattered on the ground. Mara saw in them a reflection of her own life, a period of vibrant growth and intense emotion, now reaching a stage of inevitable decline, of falling away. It was a natural process, she knew, but it was also a painful one to witness, a visual representation of the fleeting nature of beauty and the inevitability of loss.

She remembered summers past, summers filled with a different kind of energy, a careless joy that had felt as boundless as the ocean itself. Those summers seemed a world away now, belonging to a version of herself that felt both intimately familiar and utterly alien. The woman who had reveled in the carefree abandon of youth, who had looked towards the future with an unshakeable optimism, had been irrevocably altered by the trials and tribulations she had endured. The scars, though no longer raw and bleeding, were a permanent part of her landscape, shaping her perspective, tempering her joy.

As the days grew shorter, the evenings at the Haven became longer, filled with the soft glow of lanterns and the comforting murmur of the animals settling down for the night. Mara would sit by the fireplace in her small room, a worn book open on her lap, but her gaze often drifted to the window, to the darkening sky. The stars, so much more visible now with the absence of summer haze, seemed to glitter with an indifferent brilliance, a cosmic reminder of her own smallness in the grand scheme of things. Were they watching her, she wondered, these ancient celestial bodies, bearing witness to her quiet struggle?

She knew, intellectually, that change was not inherently bad. She had embraced it, in a way, when she first fled to Port Blossom. It had been a drastic, life-altering change, a leap of faith into the unknown. But that change had been born of desperation, a flight from something terrible. This new change, the autumn of her own life, was a more introspective affair, a grappling with the desire for something more, something lasting. It was the quiet yearning for roots, for a sense of belonging that went beyond the immediate comfort of her present circumstances.

Eli would often find her like this, silhouetted against the dim light of her window, her face etched with a subtle melancholy. He never pushed, never pried. He would simply come and sit beside her, his presence a silent, steady reassurance. Sometimes he would bring her a mug of hot tea, its warmth seeping into her chilled hands, and they would sit in comfortable silence, the only sound the gentle crackling of the fire and the distant sigh of the waves. In those moments, Mara felt a flicker of hope, a belief that perhaps, just perhaps, this quiet understanding, this shared solitude, could be the foundation of something more.

The local market, usually a vibrant hub of activity, was also starting to reflect the season. The stalls, once overflowing with plump berries and sun-ripened tomatoes, now displayed the earthier bounty of autumn: pumpkins and squash, crisp apples, and baskets of late-season root vegetables. The scent of woodsmoke, previously a rarity, now mingled with the salty air, a telltale sign of hearth fires being rekindled against the encroaching chill. Mara found a strange comfort in these familiar autumnal rituals, a sense of continuity that had been absent from her life for so long. It was a reminder that even as things changed, some elements remained constant, offering a sense of stability in a world that often felt chaotic.

She overheard snippets of conversations among the townsfolk, talk of winter preparations, of fishing quotas, of the upcoming harvest festivals. They spoke of their lives with a matter-of-factness, a groundedness that Mara envied. Their futures, while perhaps uncertain, were woven into the fabric of Port Blossom, predictable in their seasonality. Her own future felt unmoored, adrift, like a small boat tossed on a restless sea.

One afternoon, while helping a local farmer deliver a cartload of hay to the Haven, Mara found herself looking at the fields, their golden hues deepening with each passing day. The farmer, a weathered man with kind eyes and a perpetual smile, noticed her gaze. "Beautiful, isn't it?" he said, his voice a low rumble. "The land gives us so much, even as it prepares to rest. It's a cycle, you see. Every ending is just a prelude to a new beginning."

His words, simple and unpretentious, resonated deeply within her. A prelude to a new beginning. Was that what this autumn represented for her? Not an end, but a transition? A time for shedding the old, the worn, the unnecessary, to make way for something new, something stronger? The thought was a fragile sprout pushing through the hardened soil of her apprehension.

She began to consciously look for these "preludes" in her own life. The way the animals at the Haven, even as they prepared for the colder months, seemed to possess a renewed vitality, a quiet confidence in their ability to endure. The way the townspeople, while acknowledging the coming winter, spoke of it with a sense of practiced preparedness, not dread. It was a subtle shift in perspective, a re-framing of the season.

The library, a quiet sanctuary she frequented on her days off, held a wealth of knowledge, and Mara found herself drawn to books on local history, on the maritime traditions of Port Blossom. She read about the families who had lived and worked here for generations, their lives intertwined with the rhythm of the ocean. She learned about the resilience of the community, their ability to weather storms, both literal and metaphorical. And as she read, a tentative sense of belonging began to take root within her. Perhaps she wasn't entirely an outsider. Perhaps, with time and effort, she could become a part of this enduring tapestry.

The encroaching autumn also brought a subtle shift in the social dynamics of Port Blossom. The summer visitors, with their boisterous energy and their fleeting presence, had departed, leaving behind a quieter, more intimate community. The focus shifted from fleeting amusements to deeper connections, from superficial interactions to genuine camaraderie. Mara found herself more comfortable in this atmosphere, her own guarded nature less conspicuous amongst the familiar faces and the established rhythms of local life.

Eli's presence continued to be a steadying force. He seemed to sense her internal struggle, offering quiet support without overt pressure. He'd invite her for walks along the deserted beach, the wind whipping her hair around her face, the roar of the waves a powerful counterpoint to the quiet anxieties swirling within her. They'd collect driftwood, their hands brushing occasionally, sending a jolt of unfamiliar warmth through her. He spoke of his family, of his father's fishing boat, of the legacy he hoped to inherit and perhaps, one day, expand. And in his openness, Mara found a mirror to her own unspoken desires for a future, for a legacy of her own.

One crisp evening, as the last rays of sunlight painted the sky in hues of amber and rose, they sat on the bluff, a shared blanket between them. The air was sharp, invigorating, and the vast expanse of the ocean stretched before them, its surface shimmering with an almost ethereal glow. "It's beautiful, isn't it?" Eli murmured, his voice soft, almost reverent. "The way the light changes this time of year. Everything glows just before it fades."

Mara nodded, her gaze fixed on the horizon. "It's like a final, magnificent flourish," she replied, her voice barely above a whisper. "A last hurrah before the quiet."

Eli turned to her, his eyes earnest. "But it's not really an end, is it?" he said, his gaze steady and reassuring. "The plants go dormant, but their roots are still strong, waiting. The animals prepare for the cold, but they know spring will come again. It's a cycle, Mara. A necessary pause, not a final stop."

His words were a balm to her restless spirit. A necessary pause. She clung to that thought, letting it seep into her consciousness. Perhaps this period of introspection, this quiet contemplation, was simply that – a necessary pause. A time to gather her strength, to consolidate her resolve, before embarking on the next phase of her journey. The uncertainty of her future still loomed, a vast and shadowy presence, but for the first time, it felt less like a terrifying abyss and more like an unwritten chapter, waiting for her to fill its pages. The approaching autumn, with its poignant beauty and its promise of renewal, was no longer just a symbol of ending, but a quiet herald of beginnings. The world outside the Haven was still beckoning, but now, instead of fear, Mara felt a tentative, burgeoning sense of anticipation. She was ready, she realized, to begin to write her own story.

The wind, a playful, insistent guest, tugged at the eaves of the Haven, its breath carrying the earthy aroma of damp soil and fallen leaves. Inside, the air was warmer, infused with the comforting scent of pine and the faintest hint of horse. Mara, her fingers still stained with the remnants of mending twine, looked up from the well-worn saddle blanket she was meticulously repairing. A subtle shift in the atmosphere, a tangible crispness that had been absent for months, permeated the space. It was the unmistakable herald of autumn, a season that always stirred a complex blend of nostalgia and a quiet, burgeoning anticipation within her. The vibrant greens of summer were yielding to a richer, more melancholic palette – golds, russets, and the deep, wine-dark hues of aging leaves. The world outside was transforming, and with each shortening day, Mara felt a corresponding, internal metamorphosis.

She found herself drawn to the wide barn doors, her gaze sweeping across the fields. The sun, already beginning its descent, cast long, dramatic shadows that stretched like inky fingers across the landscape. The goldenrod, which had blazed with a cheerful intensity for weeks, was now bowing its head, its blossoms browning, a promise of future life held within their fading forms. Even the birds, the constant, garrulous inhabitants of the Haven's skies, had grown quieter, their restless energy a hushed prelude to their long migration. Mara felt a strange kinship with them, a shared sense of impending departure, though her own destination remained as nebulous as the morning mist that often shrouded the harbor.

The Haven had become more than a refuge; it was an anchor. Its predictable routines, the quiet presence of its animal inhabitants, had provided a much-needed stability after the tempest of her past. The frantic need to simply survive had ebbed, replaced by a profound gratitude for the peace she'd found. Yet, as the season turned, a new, more subtle anxiety began to surface. It wasn't the paralyzing fear that had once defined her, but a more existential unease, a question mark hanging heavy in the crisp autumn air: what now? The Haven had offered sanctuary, but could it offer a future? Could she truly carve out a life here, or was she destined to remain a transient, a fleeting presence in the lives of those who had so generously offered her solace?

Eli, his presence a constant, gentle reassurance, had become an integral part of her new reality. Their shared silences on the bluff overlooking the ocean had deepened, evolving into a language of their own, as comfortable and meaningful as their conversations. He spoke of his dreams, of the upcoming fishing season, of the quiet, unyielding rhythm of life in Port Blossom. Mara found herself increasingly drawn into his world, her own anxieties momentarily receding in the warmth of his easygoing nature. But even in his presence, the unspoken question lingered. He was a man rooted in this place, his life intrinsically tied to the ebb and flow of the coast. Where did she fit into that landscape? Her past was a closed book; her future, a blank page. The encroaching autumn, with its potent symbolism of transition and finality, seemed to amplify the urgency of her internal debate.

She found herself lingering over her tasks at the Haven, extending the time she spent with the animals as if, by delaying her departure from these familiar surroundings, she could somehow hold back the tide of change. She'd groom a horse with an almost obsessive meticulousness, checking every inch of its coat, as if the sheer thoroughness of her attention could somehow cement her place here. She'd spend extra minutes hand-feeding a timid rabbit, whispering reassurances, a silent plea for permanence. The animals, blissfully unaware of her internal turmoil, accepted her presence with a simple, unconditional affection. They didn't question her past; they didn't demand explanations for her future. They simply needed her, and in that need, Mara found a temporary, fragile solace.

The autumn air, once a refreshing antidote to summer's languor, now carried a subtle undertone of melancholy. The leaves, in their spectacular final blaze of glory, were also a poignant reminder of impermanence. They danced and swirled in the wind, a breathtaking spectacle, before inevitably succumbing to gravity, their vibrant hues fading to muted browns as they lay scattered on the ground. Mara saw in them a reflection of her own life – a period of intense growth and emotion, now reaching a stage of inevitable decline, of falling away. It was a natural process, she knew, but it was also a painful one to witness, a visual metaphor for the fleeting nature of beauty and the inexorable march of time.

She remembered summers past, summers infused with a different kind of energy, a careless joy that had felt as boundless as the ocean itself. Those summers seemed a world away now, belonging to a version of herself that felt both intimately familiar and utterly alien. The woman who had reveled in the carefree abandon of youth, who had looked towards the future with an unshakeable optimism, had been irrevocably altered by the trials and tribulations she had endured. The scars, though no longer raw and bleeding, were a permanent part of her inner landscape, shaping her perspective, tempering her joy.

As the days grew shorter, the evenings at the Haven stretched, filled with the soft glow of lanterns and the comforting murmur of the animals settling down for the night. Mara would often find herself by the fireplace in her small room, a worn book open on her lap, her gaze invariably drifting to the window, to the darkening sky. The stars, so much more visible now with the absence of summer haze, seemed to glitter with an indifferent brilliance, a cosmic reminder of her own insignificance in the grand scheme of things. Were they watching her, she wondered, these ancient celestial bodies, bearing silent witness to her quiet struggle?

She understood, intellectually, that change was not inherently negative. She had embraced it, in a way, when she first fled to Port Blossom. It had been a drastic, life-altering change, a leap of faith into the unknown. But that change had been born of desperation, a flight from a darkness she could no longer endure. This new change, the autumn of her own life, was a more introspective affair, a grappling with the burgeoning desire for something more, something lasting. It was the quiet yearning for roots, for a sense of belonging that extended beyond the immediate comfort of her present circumstances.

Eli would often find her like this, silhouetted against the dim light of her window, her face etched with a subtle melancholy. He never pushed, never pried. He would simply come and sit beside her, his presence a silent, steady reassurance. Sometimes he would bring her a mug of steaming tea, its warmth seeping into her chilled hands, and they would sit in comfortable silence, the only sounds the gentle crackling of the fire and the distant sigh of the waves against the shore. In those moments, Mara felt a flicker of hope, a nascent belief that perhaps, just perhaps, this quiet understanding, this shared solitude, could be the foundation of something more enduring.

The local market, usually a vibrant epicenter of activity, was also beginning to reflect the shift in seasons. The stalls, once overflowing with plump berries and sun-ripened tomatoes, now displayed the earthier bounty of autumn: pumpkins and squash, crisp apples, and baskets brimming with late-season root vegetables. The scent of woodsmoke, previously a rarity, now mingled with the salty air, a telltale sign of hearth fires being rekindled against the encroaching chill. Mara found a strange comfort in these familiar autumnal rituals, a sense of continuity that had been absent from her life for so long. It was a reminder that even as things changed, certain elements remained constant, offering a semblance of stability in a world that often felt irrevocably chaotic.

She would overhear snippets of conversations among the townsfolk – talk of winter preparations, of fishing quotas, of the upcoming harvest festivals. They spoke of their lives with a matter-of-factness, a groundedness that Mara found herself envying. Their futures, while perhaps uncertain, were woven into the very fabric of Port Blossom, predictable in their seasonality. Her own future felt unmoored, adrift, like a small boat tossed on a restless, unpredictable sea.

One crisp afternoon, while helping a local farmer deliver a cartload of hay to the Haven, Mara found herself gazing at the fields, their golden hues deepening with each passing day. The farmer, a weathered man with kind eyes and a perpetual smile that seemed etched onto his face, noticed her wistful gaze. "Beautiful, isn't it?" he said, his voice a low, resonant rumble. "The land gives us so much, even as it prepares to rest. It's a cycle, you see. Every ending is just a prelude to a new beginning."

His words, simple and unpretentious, resonated deeply within her.

A prelude to a new beginning. Was that what this autumn represented for her? Not an end, but a transition? A time for shedding the old, the worn, the unnecessary, to make way for something new, something stronger? The thought was a fragile sprout pushing through the hardened soil of her apprehension, a tiny seed of hope in the fertile ground of her uncertainty.

She began to consciously look for these "preludes" in her own life. The way the animals at the Haven, even as they prepared for the colder months, seemed to possess a renewed vitality, a quiet confidence in their innate ability to endure. The way the townspeople, while acknowledging the coming winter, spoke of it with a sense of practiced preparedness, not dread. It was a subtle shift in perspective, a re-framing of the season from one of impending hardship to one of necessary preparation and quiet resilience.

The library, a quiet sanctuary she frequented on her days off, held a wealth of knowledge, and Mara found herself drawn to books on local history, on the maritime traditions of Port Blossom. She read about the families who had lived and worked here for generations, their lives inextricably intertwined with the rhythm of the ocean. She learned about the resilience of the community, their unwavering ability to weather storms, both literal and metaphorical. And as she read, a tentative sense of belonging began to take root within her. Perhaps she wasn't entirely an outsider. Perhaps, with time and genuine effort, she could become a part of this enduring tapestry.

The encroaching autumn also brought a subtle shift in the social dynamics of Port Blossom. The summer visitors, with their boisterous energy and their fleeting presence, had departed, leaving behind a quieter, more intimate community. The focus shifted from superficial amusements to deeper connections, from fleeting interactions to genuine camaraderie. Mara found herself more comfortable in this atmosphere, her own guarded nature less conspicuous amongst the familiar faces and the established rhythms of local life.

Eli's presence continued to be a steadying force, an unwavering beacon in her internal storm. He seemed to sense her unspoken struggle, offering quiet support without overt pressure, understanding her need for space and gentle encouragement in equal measure. He'd invite her for walks along the deserted beach, the wind whipping her hair around her face, the roar of the waves a powerful, primal counterpoint to the quiet anxieties swirling within her. They'd collect driftwood, their hands brushing occasionally, sending a jolt of unfamiliar warmth through her, a spark of connection that felt both startling and deeply comforting. He spoke of his family, of his father's fishing boat, of the legacy he hoped to inherit and perhaps, one day, expand. And in his openness, Mara found a mirror to her own unspoken desires for a future, for a legacy of her own, however uncertain it might seem.

One crisp evening, as the last hesitant rays of sunlight painted the sky in hues of amber and rose, they sat on the bluff, a shared, thick wool blanket spread between them. The air was sharp, invigorating, and the vast expanse of the ocean stretched before them, its surface shimmering with an almost ethereal glow. "It's beautiful, isn't it?" Eli murmured, his voice soft, almost reverent, as if speaking to something sacred. "The way the light changes this time of year. Everything glows just before it fades."

Mara nodded, her gaze fixed on the distant horizon, where the sky met the sea in a seamless blend of color. "It's like a final, magnificent flourish," she replied, her voice barely above a whisper, lost in the immensity of the moment. "A last hurrah before the quiet."

Eli turned to her then, his eyes earnest, reflecting the dying embers of the day. "But it's not really an end, is it?" he said, his gaze steady and reassuring, cutting through the twilight. "The plants go dormant, but their roots are still strong, waiting. The animals prepare for the cold, but they know spring will come again. It's a cycle, Mara. A necessary pause, not a final stop."

His words were a balm to her restless spirit, a gentle hand guiding her away from the precipice of despair.

A necessary pause. She clung to that thought, letting it seep into her consciousness, allowing it to soften the hard edges of her fear. Perhaps this period of introspection, this quiet contemplation of her future, was simply that – a necessary pause. A time to gather her strength, to consolidate her resolve, before embarking on the next, as yet unknown, phase of her journey. The uncertainty of her future still loomed, a vast and shadowy presence on the periphery of her vision, but for the first time, it felt less like a terrifying abyss and more like an unwritten chapter, waiting patiently for her to fill its pages. The approaching autumn, with its poignant beauty and its quiet promise of renewal, was no longer just a symbol of ending, but a gentle herald of beginnings. The world outside the Haven was still beckoning, but now, instead of fear, Mara felt a tentative, burgeoning sense of anticipation. She was ready, she realized, to begin to write her own story.

The demanding day at the Haven had left Mara with a pleasant weariness, a deep-seated ache in her muscles that felt earned, satisfying. The air outside had grown decidedly chill, the kind that made your breath mist in front of your face, so the small, crackling fire pit at the edge of the rescue's grounds was a welcome beacon. Eli had surprised her with two steaming mugs of rich hot chocolate, the kind that warmed your hands from the inside out. They sat on upturned crates, the flames casting dancing shadows on their faces, painting them in hues of orange and gold. The scent of woodsmoke mingled with the fainter, familiar aroma of hay and damp earth that always clung to the Haven.

"This is perfect," Mara sighed, cradling the mug, letting the warmth seep into her fingers. "Just what I needed after wrestling with that stubborn mare all afternoon."

Eli chuckled, a low, rumbling sound that seemed to vibrate in the cool night air. "She's got spirit, that one. Reminds me a bit of someone else I know." He winked, his eyes crinkling at the corners.

Mara laughed, a genuine, unrestrained sound that surprised even herself. "Oh, I don't know about that. I'm a bit more... docile."

"Are you now?" Eli's gaze was playful, but there was a hint of something deeper in his eyes, a quiet knowing. "I seem to recall a certain woman who arrived here on a whim, with nothing but a fierce determination to survive. That doesn't strike me as docile."

Mara took a slow sip of her chocolate, letting his words settle. He saw her, truly saw her, not just the façade she sometimes presented. "Well," she conceded, a small smile playing on her lips, "perhaps I have a bit more fire in me than I let on."

"I always suspected," he said softly, stirring the embers with a fallen branch. "So, what's your favorite season, Mara? If you had to pick one."

She considered it, the rhythm of the past year at the Haven flashing through her mind. "Autumn, I think," she answered finally. "It's so... dramatic. The colors, the air... it feels like a grand finale before a quiet rest. And it's so different from the endless green of summer."

Eli nodded, his gaze thoughtful. "I can see that. For me, it's probably spring. The first signs of life pushing through after the long winter. The world waking up. There's a certain hope in that, wouldn't you say?"

"Hope," Mara echoed, the word tasting sweet on her tongue. "Yes, there's definitely hope in spring. I suppose I haven't really thought about it like that for a long time. My past springs were... less about hope and more about survival."

"Port Blossom has a way of bringing out the hope," Eli said, his voice laced with a quiet pride. "It's a tough place, the coast. But it's also incredibly resilient. Like the tides. They pull away, sometimes leaving the shore barren, but they always come back, bringing life with them."

The analogy resonated with Mara. She watched the flames leap, mesmerized by their primal energy. "I used to love the beach when I was a kid," she found herself saying, the memory surfacing unbidden. "We'd go every summer. My grandmother lived near the sea. She used to tell me stories about mermaids and shipwrecks. I'd spend hours collecting shells, imagining I was a treasure hunter."

Eli leaned forward, his interest piqued. "Mermaids and shipwrecks? Sounds like a childhood straight out of a storybook."

"It felt like it sometimes," Mara admitted, a wistful smile touching her lips. "But then... things changed. The trips stopped. The stories faded. Life got a lot less... magical." She hesitated, then decided to push forward, a rare impulse. "What about you? What were your favorite childhood memories?"

He gazed into the fire, a faraway look in his eyes. "Oh, a lot of them involve fishing. My dad took me out on his boat from when I was just a little tyke. I remember the smell of the salt spray, the feeling of the deck beneath my feet, the thrill of pulling up a good catch. We'd always have a thermos of strong coffee and some of my mom's molasses cookies. Those were good days."

"Molasses cookies," Mara mused. "I can almost taste them. My grandmother used to make the best gingerbread."

"See?" Eli smiled, his gaze meeting hers. "We're not so different, you and I. We both have a soft spot for baked goods and the sea."

They fell into a comfortable silence, punctuated by the crackle of the fire and the distant murmur of the waves. The hot chocolate was gone, leaving a sweet warmth in its wake. Mara found herself feeling a sense of ease she hadn't experienced in a long time. The conversation, so simple on the surface, had revealed layers of their shared experiences, their appreciation for the quiet, often overlooked joys of life.

"It's funny," Mara said, breaking the silence, her voice soft. "I used to think that happiness was all about grand adventures, about chasing the next big thing. But lately... I've realized that sometimes, the most profound happiness comes from these small moments. Like sitting here, by a fire, with good company."

Eli reached out, his fingers brushing hers as he picked up another fallen branch to feed the fire. The contact sent a jolt of warmth through her. "I think you're right," he said, his voice low. "This place, the Haven... it's taught me that too. That the quiet moments, the simple connections, are often the most valuable." He paused, his gaze lingering on her face, illuminated by the flickering flames. "I'm glad we're sharing this moment, Mara."

His sincerity was disarming. Mara felt a blush creep up her neck, but she didn't shy away. "Me too, Eli," she whispered, her voice thick with an emotion she couldn't quite name. "Me too." The fire crackled, a warm, steady heartbeat in the quiet night, and for the first time in a long time, Mara felt a profound sense of peace, a quiet certainty that perhaps, just perhaps, she was exactly where she was meant to be.

He looked at her, his gaze traveling from her eyes down to her lips, a silent question hanging in the air between them. The way his pupils dilated, the slight parting of his lips, the way his breath seemed to hitch – it was all so subtle, so fleeting, yet Mara's heightened senses caught every nuance. It was a language spoken without words, a confession whispered in the space between heartbeats. A nervous tremor ran through her, a mixture of apprehension and a thrilling, almost unbearable anticipation. Was she reading too much into it, projecting her own burgeoning hopes onto his actions? Or was this the unspoken truth they had both been skirting around, a truth that was now, irrevocably, beginning to surface?

The gentle breeze, which had been caressing their faces moments before, seemed to hold its breath, as if the world itself was pausing, waiting for their unspoken feelings to bloom. Mara felt a strange, disorienting sensation, as if the very air around them had become thicker, charged with an invisible energy. Eli's hand, which had been resting on the rough wood of the table, was now closer to hers, his knuckles brushing against her fingertips. The contact was electrifying, sending a shiver through her entire body. She instinctively pulled her hand back, a shy, almost involuntary movement, but the memory of his touch lingered, a phantom warmth against her skin.

Eli's reaction was subtle, almost imperceptible. He didn't flinch away, nor did he press the issue. Instead, his gaze softened, a hint of a smile playing on his lips, a smile that conveyed both understanding and a touch of playful melancholy. It was as if he had recognized her hesitation, her fear of the unknown, and was offering a silent reassurance. He understood that some emotions, like the delicate seedlings of the spring he so cherished, needed time and gentle care to unfurl.

"The ocean has a way of hiding its treasures, doesn't it?" he said, his voice a low murmur, almost as if he were speaking to himself, or perhaps to the vast expanse of water stretching out before them. "Sometimes you have to dig a little, look a little closer, to find the most beautiful shells, the most intricate patterns."

Mara nodded, her heart still thrumming with an unfamiliar rhythm. His words were a veiled metaphor, she knew, a gentle way of acknowledging the hidden depths within them both, the unspoken desires that were beginning to stir. She felt a blush creep up her neck, a sure sign that her carefully constructed composure was beginning to crumble. She looked away, feigning an interest in the distant horizon, desperately trying to regain her equilibrium.

He continued, his voice laced with a quiet introspection. "It's like the tides. They can pull away, reveal the vastness of the seabed, stark and bare. But then they return, bringing with them a renewed abundance, a different kind of beauty. It's a cycle, always shifting, always changing."

His analogies, while beautiful, were also a constant reminder of the delicate balance she was trying to strike. She was drawn to the stability Eli offered, the grounding presence that had become so essential to her. Yet, the very nature of change, of the shifting tides, also filled her with a familiar apprehension. Her past was a testament to the unpredictable nature of life, to how quickly tranquil waters could turn into a raging storm.

He seemed to sense her unspoken reservations. He didn't push her to elaborate, didn't try to force an explanation from her. Instead, he simply let his words hang in the air, a gentle offering, a silent invitation to explore these deeper currents together. He picked up a smooth, grey stone from the sand, turning it over and over in his fingers. "This stone," he said, his voice thoughtful, "has been shaped by the sea for years, maybe centuries. The constant ebb and flow, the relentless waves... they've worn away its sharp edges, smoothed its surface. It's still the same stone, fundamentally, but it's been transformed."

Mara watched him, mesmerized by the way his brow furrowed in concentration, the way his thumb traced the contours of the stone. He was a man of quiet contemplation, his thoughts often as deep and vast as the ocean he navigated. She found herself wondering what it was that occupied his mind, what unspoken emotions lay beneath that calm, steady exterior. Was he, too, grappling with the implications of their growing closeness? Did he also feel the subtle shift, the electric charge that seemed to hum between them whenever they were near?

"Do you ever wonder," she began, her voice a little shaky, "what lies beneath the surface? What the sea is hiding in its deepest parts?"

Eli looked up, his eyes meeting hers, a spark of understanding in their depths. "Always," he replied, a faint smile touching his lips. "It's human nature, I suppose. To be drawn to the mystery, to the unknown. But you have to be careful, Mara. Some depths are best left undisturbed."

His words, meant to be a gentle caution, only served to heighten her curiosity. There was a vulnerability in his admission, a hint of a past he rarely spoke of. She felt a pang of empathy, a recognition of the shared weight of unspoken experiences. He, too, carried scars, she sensed, though they were likely different from her own.

He tossed the stone back towards the water, watching as it disappeared beneath the incoming waves. "Sometimes," he continued, his gaze fixed on the point where the stone had vanished, "the most beautiful things are the ones that are just out of reach. The ones that make you long for them, that inspire you to keep searching."

His gaze drifted back to her, and for a moment, Mara felt as if she were the very treasure he was searching for, the elusive prize that held his fascination. The air between them crackled with an unspoken tension, a palpable awareness of each other that transcended mere physical proximity. His eyes, usually so calm and steady, now held a restless energy, a hint of longing that mirrored her own.

She found herself wanting to reach out, to bridge the small distance that separated them, to touch his hand, to trace the lines of his palm. But she held back, her inherent caution warring with the nascent desire that was blooming within her. It was a terrifying dance, this slow, tentative approach, this exploration of uncharted emotional territory. One wrong step, one misplaced word, and the delicate balance could be shattered, the fragile connection severed.

"You're very... thoughtful, Eli," she managed to say, her voice a little breathy. "You see things in a way I never have before."

He chuckled softly, the sound a warm rumble in the quiet evening. "It's the sea, I think. It teaches you patience. It teaches you to observe. And it teaches you that even the most powerful storms eventually subside, leaving behind a sense of calm, a new beginning." He paused, his gaze unwavering. "And it teaches you that sometimes, the most important things are the ones that aren't said."

Mara's breath hitched. Was he referring to her silence, her own unspoken fears and desires? Or was he speaking of his own? The ambiguity was both frustrating and intoxicating. She wanted him to speak his truth, to lay his heart bare, yet a part of her relished the mystery, the slow unfolding of their connection. It was a testament to the depth of his character that he was willing to wait, to let her come to her own conclusions, rather than forcing her hand.

He stood up, stretching his long limbs. "The tide's coming in," he said, his voice shifting back to its more practical, grounded tone. "We should head back before we get our feet wet."

Mara rose with him, a lingering sense of unfulfillment settling over her. The moment of profound connection had passed, leaving behind a faint echo, a sweet ache in her chest. As they walked back towards the Haven, their footsteps crunching on the damp sand, she couldn't help but steal glances at him. He walked with an easy stride, his silhouette outlined against the fading twilight, a picture of quiet strength and resilience.

She wondered if he felt it too, this strange, potent pull between them. Did his heart skip a beat when their hands brushed, or when their gazes met? Did he find himself replaying their conversations in his mind, searching for hidden meanings, for unspoken invitations? She hoped so, fervently. The thought that she might be the only one experiencing this bewildering shift was a daunting one.

Later that evening, as she lay in her small room, the rhythmic sound of the waves lulling her towards sleep, Mara replayed the encounter in her mind. Eli's words, his gestures, his lingering glances – they all wove together into a tapestry of unspoken emotions. He was holding back, she knew, just as she was. They were both standing on the precipice of something new, something potentially beautiful and equally terrifying.

She thought of the stones he had described, worn smooth by the relentless tides. She felt like one of those stones herself, her sharp edges softened by the trials she had endured. But the transformation was ongoing, and she was not yet fully formed. Eli, with his quiet understanding and his gentle presence, seemed to be offering a safe harbor, a place where she could continue to evolve without fear of judgment.

She closed her eyes, the image of his earnest gaze seared into her mind. He was a man of depth and integrity, a man who understood the silent language of the heart. And in his quiet way, he was letting her know that he saw her, truly saw her, and that he was willing to wait, to explore the depths alongside her, at her own pace. The prospect was both exhilarating and daunting, but for the first time in a long time, Mara felt a flicker of hope that perhaps, just perhaps, this was the beginning of a new shore, a new tide, that would bring with it not loss, but a profound and lasting connection. His unspoken feelings, a silent symphony playing just beneath the surface, were beginning to resonate with her own, a melody that promised a future filled with possibility.

The air at the Haven, usually a tranquil balm for weary souls, was suddenly infused with a new, boisterous energy. It arrived in the form of a whirlwind of golden fur and wagging tail, a creature named Buster. He was a Labrador, all clumsy paws and boundless enthusiasm, a stark contrast to the quiet introspection that had settled over Mara and Eli in the preceding days. Buster's arrival was the spark that ignited a new phase of their shared journey, a phase marked by the exhilarating chaos of canine rehabilitation and, in turn, the subtle recalibration of their own burgeoning connection.

Buster was a rescue, his history a familiar, heartbreaking refrain of abandonment. The gentle souls at the local shelter had done their best, but the deep-seated anxieties of a dog left behind were not easily soothed. He arrived at the Haven a bundle of unchecked impulses, his every greeting a symphony of excited yips and desperate attempts to climb into any available lap. Furniture bore the brunt of his frustration, and the sound of Mara or Eli leaving the room would send him into a frenzy of mournful howls. It was clear from the outset that Buster's journey to finding his footing, his sense of belonging, would be a challenging one, demanding patience, understanding, and a united front.

Mara, with her innate empathy for creatures in distress, took to Buster immediately. She saw past the destructive chewing and the anxious barking to the wounded spirit beneath. She recognized the raw fear, the desperate plea for reassurance that fueled his every misstep. Eli, too, possessed a quiet understanding of animal behavior, honed by years of observing the wild creatures that roamed the coastline. He saw the Labrador's potential, the inherent loyalty and love waiting to be unlocked from beneath layers of ingrained insecurity. They agreed, without a word needing to be spoken, that Buster would be their shared project, a testament to the Haven's purpose of offering second chances.

Their training sessions began almost immediately, a delicate dance of positive reinforcement and gentle redirection. The first hurdle was the ubiquitous chewing. Buster saw furniture not as inert objects, but as prime targets for his gnawing instinct, a way to release pent-up energy and alleviate his distress. Mara would spend hours with him, armed with a basket of appropriate chew toys, engaging him in games of fetch and tug-of-war. When Buster's attention strayed to the leg of a well-worn armchair, Mara would calmly redirect him, offering him a rubber bone with enthusiastic praise. "Good boy, Buster! That's what we chew," she'd coo, her voice a soft melody that seemed to soothe his anxious soul. Eli, observing from a distance, would offer quiet encouragement, a nod of approval that spoke volumes.

The progress was incremental, almost imperceptible at first. There were days when Buster seemed to regress, his playful gnawing escalating into a frantic tearing of upholstery. Mara, though disheartened, never lost her patience. She understood that healing was not a linear path, especially for a soul as scarred as Buster's. Eli would often find her sitting on the floor, surrounded by a scattered array of chew toys, gently stroking Buster's head as he finally settled down for a nap, his earlier anxieties temporarily soothed. He would bring her a mug of herbal tea, his silence a comforting presence, a shared understanding that some battles were fought with quiet perseverance rather than grand gestures.

One afternoon, Mara was in the kitchen, preparing lunch, when she heard the familiar frantic barking and scratching at the door. Buster was reacting to Eli's departure for a brief trip to the village. His entire body quivered with distress, his whines escalating into a desperate plea. Mara's heart ached for him. She remembered her own feelings of abandonment, the gnawing fear that those she cared about would simply disappear, leaving her alone in a vast, indifferent world. She walked to the door, not to scold, but to offer a different kind of solace.

"It's okay, Buster," she murmured, her voice soft. "He'll be back. He's just going for a little while." She sat on the floor, cross-legged, and gently pulled Buster towards her. He shivered, his wet nose nudging her hand. She began to speak to him, her voice a low, rhythmic cadence, describing Eli's likely route, imagining his brief errands, assuring Buster of his swift return. She spoke of the predictable cycles of the tide, how it always returned to the shore, just as Eli would return to the Haven. Eli, who had unexpectedly doubled back for a forgotten item, paused in the doorway, watching the scene unfold. He saw Mara's gentle strength, her uncanny ability to connect with the most troubled of souls. He saw how she mirrored his own quiet compassion, but with an added layer of intuitive understanding that amazed him.

When Eli returned, Buster greeted him not with an explosion of frantic energy, but with a few excited barks and a wagging tail that swept across the floor. He then looked back at Mara, as if seeking her approval, before nudging Eli's hand for a gentle scratch behind the ears. It was a small victory, a testament to Mara's patient reassurance. Eli met Mara's gaze, a silent acknowledgment of their shared success. In that moment, a new thread was woven into the tapestry of their connection, a thread of mutual admiration and a deepening respect for their individual strengths, and their combined ability to nurture.

The breakthroughs, though small, began to accumulate. Buster learned to distinguish between the sofa and his designated chew toys. The frantic barking at departures slowly subsided, replaced by a resigned sigh, followed by a return to his basket of toys or a nap at Mara's feet. He still struggled with moments of anxiety, particularly when left alone for extended periods, but he was learning to cope, to find comfort in the routines they had established. Each instance of Buster's progress was a shared celebration. A quiet high-five between Mara and Eli when Buster managed to resist the allure of a dropped crumb, a shared smile when he greeted them without overwhelming enthusiasm, a contented sigh of relief when he settled down for a quiet evening.

These moments of shared accomplishment weren't confined to Buster's training. They extended, subtly but profoundly, to Mara and Eli's own interactions. The tentative conversations on the beach, filled with metaphors of the sea and its hidden treasures, began to translate into more open exchanges. Eli found himself sharing more about his life before the Haven, not in a torrent of confessions, but in gentle, carefully chosen anecdotes that painted a picture of a man who had navigated his own set of challenging tides. He spoke of the solitude of his upbringing, the quiet observation that had become his default mode, and the unexpected peace he had found in the rhythm of the ocean and the simple needs of the animals at the Haven.

Mara, in turn, found herself opening up about her past, not to dwell on the pain, but to illuminate the resilience it had fostered. She spoke of the unpredictable nature of life, the way a calm surface could conceal treacherous currents, and how that experience had made her fiercely protective of the stability she had found at the Haven, and with Eli. Their shared experiences with Buster acted as a catalyst, a safe space where vulnerability was not only accepted but encouraged. Helping Buster overcome his fear of abandonment seemed to provide a subtle, unspoken permission for them to address their own lingering anxieties.

One evening, as they sat on the porch, watching Buster chase fireflies in the twilight, Mara turned to Eli. "He's come such a long way," she said, her voice soft with pride. Buster, having finally tired himself out, lay sprawled on the grass, his breathing deep and even.

Eli nodded, a quiet smile gracing his lips. "He's a good dog, Mara. He just needed a chance to remember that. And you gave him that chance."

Mara's gaze drifted to his face, illuminated by the faint glow of the porch light. "We gave him that chance, Eli. Together."

The words hung in the air between them, simple yet loaded with unspoken meaning. It wasn't just about Buster anymore. Their collaboration had forged a stronger bond, a deeper understanding that extended far beyond the confines of canine training. They had learned to anticipate each other's needs, to offer support without intrusion, to celebrate small victories as if they were monumental achievements. Eli had learned to appreciate Mara's intuitive approach, her ability to connect with animals on an emotional level that he, with his more analytical mind, often struggled to replicate. Mara, in turn, had come to rely on Eli's steady presence, his grounded wisdom that helped anchor her when her own empathy threatened to overwhelm her.

Their shared success with Buster had become a metaphor for their own burgeoning relationship. Just as Buster was learning to trust, to overcome his ingrained anxieties, so too were they learning to trust each other, to navigate the unfamiliar terrain of their growing feelings. The impulse control they were instilling in Buster, the patience they were teaching him, were lessons they were also applying to themselves, to their own hesitant steps towards something more profound.

One afternoon, while Eli was away at a supply run, Buster had a minor relapse. A loud clap of thunder, unexpected and fierce, sent him into a panic. He barked incessantly, his body trembling, and began to chew at the doorframe in a desperate attempt to escape the perceived threat. Mara rushed to his side, her heart pounding in sympathy. She knelt beside him, murmuring soothing words, but Buster was too consumed by fear to hear her. She gently guided him towards his favorite blanket, then picked up his favorite squeaky toy, a worn-out hedgehog that had become his comfort object.

"It's just thunder, Buster," she whispered, her own voice slightly shaky. "It's loud, but it can't hurt you. Eli will be back soon. He'll make it all better." She held the hedgehog close to his nose, encouraging him to chew. Slowly, painstakingly, Buster's frantic chewing on the doorframe subsided, replaced by the familiar squeak of his toy. He still trembled, but the sheer terror in his eyes began to recede, replaced by a flicker of recognition, a desperate attempt to anchor himself in the familiar.

When Eli returned, he found Mara and Buster sitting together on the floor, the dog's head resting on her lap, his breathing gradually evening out. The chewed doorframe was a stark reminder of the setback, but the quiet scene of comfort and reassurance spoke volumes. Eli's gaze met Mara's, a silent conversation passing between them. He saw the exhaustion in her eyes, but also the unwavering determination. He understood the emotional toll it took for her to soothe such deep-seated fear, and he felt a surge of protectiveness, of admiration for her strength.

Later that evening, as they discussed Buster's progress, Eli reached out and gently took Mara's hand. His touch sent a familiar tremor through her, but this time, it was accompanied by a sense of calm assurance, rather than apprehension. "You handled that beautifully, Mara," he said, his voice low and sincere. "You were exactly what he needed."

Mara squeezed his hand, a silent acknowledgment of his words. "We're a good team, aren't we?" she replied, a shy smile playing on her lips.

Eli's thumb gently stroked the back of her hand. "The best," he confirmed, his gaze holding hers. The shared responsibility for Buster had, in a way, given them permission to be vulnerable, to lean on each other. It had stripped away some of the defenses they had both unconsciously erected, revealing a shared capacity for love, for compassion, and for a quiet, steady commitment. Buster, the boisterous, anxious Labrador, had become an unlikely architect of their shared future, a testament to the power of a second chance, not just for a dog, but for two souls learning to find their way back to each other. The tides of change, once a source of apprehension for Mara, now felt like a gentle current, carrying them both towards a shared horizon.

The gentle rhythm of Buster's contented snores filled the quiet living room, a soft counterpoint to the crackling fire. Mara watched him, a deep sense of peace settling over her. He had come so far, shedding the anxious layers of his past like a molted skin, blossoming into the confident, happy dog he was always meant to be. And in a way, she felt she had too. Eli, sitting across from her, his gaze steady and warm, was a constant, grounding presence. Their shared project, Buster, had woven them together, their lives intertwining like the vines that climbed the Haven's stone walls. Yet, as the conversation drifted from Buster's latest training success to the broader strokes of their lives, a familiar knot of apprehension tightened in Mara's chest.

Eli was recounting a story about his childhood, a memory of his father teaching him how to mend fishing nets, his voice laced with a fond nostalgia she hadn't heard before. He spoke of the patience required, the meticulous care needed to ensure each knot was secure, lest a precious catch be lost. Mara listened, captivated by the glimpse into his past, the man he was before the Haven. He paused, his eyes meeting hers, a question hanging unspoken in the air. "What about you, Mara?" he asked, his voice soft. "What lessons did your parents teach you that you carry with you?"

The question, innocent enough, landed like a stone in the placid water of her contentment. Her parents. The words felt foreign on her tongue, the memories a tangled mess of love and disappointment, of fierce independence and crushing betrayal. She found herself wanting to share, to offer him another piece of herself, but the words snagged in her throat. The fear, a shadow that had stalked her for years, crept back into the corners of her mind. It whispered insidious doubts:

What if he sees the flaws? What if he understands too much, and it scares him away? What if you're not enough?

She looked down at Buster, burying her face in his soft fur, a familiar, comforting scent. "They taught me... resilience," she managed, her voice a little hoarse. "And how to be self-sufficient." It was the truth, but it was a carefully curated truth, a polished surface that hid the jagged edges beneath. She could feel Eli's gentle gaze on her, a silent invitation to delve deeper, but the thought of unearthing the painful memories, of exposing the raw wounds of her past, felt like standing naked in a blizzard.

Eli's hand reached out, covering hers where it rested on Buster's flank. His touch was warm, steady, a quiet reassurance that didn't demand anything in return. "That's a valuable lesson," he said, his tone unhurried. "But I suspect there's more to your story than just that." He didn't press, didn't pry, but his understanding was palpable, a silent acknowledgment of the unspoken layers she guarded so fiercely. It was in that quiet space, between his gentle inquiry and her hesitant response, that Mara felt the internal tug-of-war. A part of her craved the open, honest connection Eli offered, the chance to build something real and lasting. But the other part, the deeply ingrained survival instinct, urged her to retreat, to protect the fragile peace she had so painstakingly cultivated.

She remembered the whirlwind of her teenage years, the exhilarating but ultimately devastating relationship that had left her feeling utterly adrift. He had been charming, intoxicating, a siren song that had promised everything and delivered nothing but heartache. He'd seen her vulnerabilities, her eagerness to please, and had used them to his advantage, chipping away at her confidence until she was a shadow of herself. The experience had left an indelible mark, a deep-seated distrust of easy promises and grand declarations. Opening her heart again felt like walking a tightrope over a chasm, the wind of doubt threatening to push her off balance with every step.

"It was a long time ago," she murmured, pulling her hand away from his, a subtle but deliberate withdrawal. She shifted, leaning back against the sofa, her gaze drawn back to Buster. "There are some things... best left buried." The words hung in the air, a delicate but firm boundary. She could feel the shift in the atmosphere, the subtle cooling of the warmth that had just moments before enveloped them. Eli didn't recoil, didn't push, but she saw a flicker of something in his eyes – a flicker of understanding, perhaps, but also a hint of disappointment.

He had been so open, so willing to share his own past, his own vulnerabilities. And here she was, withholding, building walls when he was offering a bridge. The self-recrimination was swift and sharp. She hated this part of herself, this ingrained tendency to protect herself by shutting others out. It felt cowardly, like a betrayal of the connection she was beginning to cherish. But the fear was a powerful adversary, a well-rehearsed habit that was difficult to break. The memory of the pain, the humiliation, the sheer loneliness of picking up the pieces of her shattered heart, was still too vivid.

"I understand," Eli said, his voice quiet, devoid of accusation. He picked up a book from the side table, his fingers tracing the spine. "But if you ever feel like sharing, I'm here to listen. Without judgment." His words were a lifeline, an offer of unwavering support, but the chasm between them felt wider than it had a moment before. She longed to take him up on his offer, to unburden herself, but the words remained lodged in her throat, choked by the fear of judgment, of rejection.

The silence that descended was heavier now, tinged with an unspoken tension. Buster, sensing the shift, stirred and let out a soft whine, nudging Mara's hand with his nose. She instinctively stroked his head, grateful for the distraction, for the simple, uncomplicated affection he offered. He didn't ask questions. He didn't demand explanations. He just offered comfort, a soft furry anchor in the turbulent waters of her emotions.

"He's a good boy," she said, her voice a little too bright, a little too forced. "He's come such a long way."

Eli smiled, a genuine, warm smile that reached his eyes. "He has. And you played a huge part in that." He set the book down and leaned forward, his elbows resting on his knees. "You have a gift, Mara. A real gift for understanding and healing."

His words were meant to be a compliment, she knew, but they also brought a fresh wave of anxiety. Was he seeing her as a healer, a caregiver, someone who existed to fix others? What if he didn't see her as a woman, as someone capable of being loved, of being *in* a relationship? The fear of being pigeonholed, of being seen only for her ability to nurture, was another layer of her apprehension. It was a subtle fear, one she rarely articulated, but it lingered nonetheless, a quiet hum beneath the surface of her interactions.

"It's just... empathy," she demurred, looking away. "I can't stand to see anyone hurting."

"It's more than that," Eli insisted gently. "It's a deep connection. The way you understood Buster's fear, the way you soothed him... it's extraordinary." He paused, his gaze thoughtful. "I think sometimes, when we've experienced pain ourselves, we're more attuned to it in others."

His observation hit closer to home than he knew. He was right, of course. Her own past, her own experiences of hurt and abandonment, had sharpened her awareness, making her hyper-vigilant to the emotional cues of others. It was a double-edged sword, allowing her to connect deeply but also leaving her exposed, vulnerable to the echoes of her own past traumas. The thought of opening herself up to Eli, to let him see those raw, exposed nerves, felt like an insurmountable challenge.

She imagined him trying to understand, his brow furrowed with concern, his words of comfort well-intentioned but ultimately falling short because he couldn't truly grasp the depth of the pain. Or worse, what if he saw her past as a weakness, a liability? The image of his face clouding over, of a subtle shift in his demeanor that signaled his withdrawal, was enough to make her instinctively pull back further.

"Sometimes, it's easier to help others than to help yourself," she said, her voice barely a whisper. It was a confession, a tiny crack in the fortress she had built around her heart.

Eli leaned closer, his eyes holding hers with an intensity that both thrilled and terrified her. "But you deserve to be helped too, Mara," he said, his voice low and earnest. "You deserve to feel safe. To feel loved."

His words were exactly what she needed to hear, a balm to the aching parts of her soul. And yet, the instinct for self-preservation, honed over years of self-reliance, was a powerful force. The idea of allowing herself to be loved, truly loved, felt almost alien. It meant letting down her guard, relinquishing control, trusting someone else with her heart. It meant accepting that she was worthy of such tenderness, a concept she still struggled to fully embrace.

"I... I'm not sure I know how," she confessed, the words tumbling out in a rush. "It feels... dangerous."

Eli reached out and gently cupped her cheek, his thumb stroking her skin. The gesture was so tender, so unexpected, that it stole her breath. "It can be," he conceded softly. "But staying guarded, staying alone, that's dangerous too, in its own way. It's a slow erosion of the spirit."

His words resonated deeply, echoing a truth she had long suspected but had been too afraid to acknowledge. She looked at him, at the genuine concern etched on his face, the quiet strength that emanates from him. He wasn't like the others. He didn't demand or push. He simply offered his presence, his understanding, his unwavering support. And in that moment, surrounded by the warmth of the fire, with Buster's soft snores a comforting presence at their feet, Mara felt a flicker of hope.

The fear was still there, a constant companion, but for the first time, it didn't feel all-consuming. The desire for connection, for genuine intimacy, was beginning to outweigh the instinct for self-protection. She understood that healing wasn't a destination, but a journey, and that sometimes, the bravest step was to allow someone else to walk alongside you, even when the path felt uncertain.

She took a deep breath, the scent of woodsmoke and dog filling her lungs. She met Eli's gaze, a silent acknowledgment of the struggle she had just revealed, and the tentative hope she was beginning to feel. "Maybe," she began, her voice still a little shaky, but with a newfound firmness, "maybe you can teach me."

The subtle tension in the room seemed to dissipate, replaced by a quiet understanding. Eli's smile widened, a look of pure relief and tenderness washing over his face. He didn't rush her, didn't press for details. He simply held her gaze, a silent promise of patience and unwavering support. And in that shared moment of vulnerability, as Buster twitched in his sleep, chasing phantom rabbits, Mara felt a new tide begin to turn, a tide of courage and a dawning acceptance of the possibility of a future, shared and perhaps, truly happy. The scars of her past were still there, a roadmap of her journey, but perhaps, just perhaps, they didn't have to define her entire landscape. Perhaps, with Eli by her side, she could learn to navigate those old wounds and find a new, open horizon.

Chapter Seven
Navigating New Waters

The air, once still and sweet with the scent of woodsmoke and contentment, began to shift. A low growl, not from Buster dozing at Mara's feet, but from the sky itself, rumbled in the distance. The gentle rhythm of Buster's snores was soon to be drowned out by a more primal, untamed symphony. A restless energy, alien to the cozy warmth of the Haven's living room, began to permeate the atmosphere. It was a subtle change at first, a prickling sensation on Mara's skin, a fleeting unease that she tried to dismiss as a lingering effect of her conversation with Eli. But then, the wind picked up, a playful gust at first, rustling the ancient oak outside the window. It grew bolder, insistent, a spectral hand rattling the panes.

Eli, who had been tracing the patterns on the worn rug with his gaze, looked up. His eyes, usually so steady and reassuring, held a new alertness. "Sounds like a squall building," he murmured, a note of concern entering his voice. He rose and walked to the window, pulling aside the heavy velvet curtain. The darkening sky was bruised with shades of purple and an ominous, bruised grey. The trees, moments ago swaying gently, were now thrashing wildly, their branches groaning under the assault.

Mara's heart gave an involuntary lurch. She knew this feeling. She'd felt it before, a primal instinct kicking in, a deep-seated awareness of nature's power to disrupt, to destroy. It was the same feeling that had always accompanied the volatile unpredictability of her own past, a constant undercurrent of vulnerability she had worked so hard to suppress. Buster, sensing the change in the air, lifted his head, his ears perked, a low rumble starting in his chest. He looked at Mara, then at Eli, his canine intuition picking up on the rising tension.

"The weather report didn't mention anything severe," Eli said, his voice thoughtful as he continued to scan the horizon. "But it's coming in fast." He turned back to Mara, a shadow of concern dimming the warmth in his eyes. "We should probably check on the animals, make sure everything is secure."

The unspoken implication hung heavy in the air. This was more than just a mild storm; it was a threat. And Mara, who had finally begun to feel a sense of stability, of safety, felt the familiar tendrils of anxiety begin to coil around her. The haven, the sanctuary she had found here, felt suddenly fragile.

They moved through the Haven with a newfound urgency, the gentle hum of domesticity replaced by a more determined, purpose-driven energy. Other volunteers, their faces etched with a similar blend of concern and resolve, were already mobilising. Sarah, her usual cheerful demeanor replaced by a focused intensity, was coordinating the movement of the smaller animals into the reinforced inner kennels. Mark, his broad shoulders a picture of quiet strength, was checking the integrity of the barn doors, securing loose roofing tiles with practiced efficiency.

Mara and Eli found themselves working side-by-side, their earlier conversation about vulnerability and trust seemingly a lifetime ago. The storm was a stark, undeniable equalizer, stripping away the delicate layers of their nascent connection and forcing them back into a more primal mode of cooperation and shared responsibility. They moved with a synchronized grace born of necessity, their hands brushing, their gazes meeting in silent understanding as they assessed the needs of each anxious animal.

"The cats," Mara said, her voice steady despite the tremor she felt deep inside. "They need to be in the dedicated cattery wing. It's the most protected." She led the way, her movements fluid and purposeful, the fear that had threatened to engulf her earlier now transmuted into a fierce protectiveness. Eli followed, his presence a silent anchor, his quiet efficiency a reassuring counterpoint to the rising crescendo of the wind.

Inside the cattery, the air was thick with the scent of fear. Hisses and frightened mews filled the small space. Mara moved among the cages, her voice a soft, soothing balm. She spoke to each cat individually, her words laced with a deep empathy that seemed to transcend their fear. "It's okay, little one," she murmured to a trembling calico, her fingers gently stroking the bars of its cage. "We're just getting you somewhere safe. This will pass."

Eli was working on the other side of the room, his approach equally gentle but with a more pragmatic focus. He was checking water bowls, ensuring each cat had access to fresh, clean water, and reinforcing the latches on the cages. He paused, watching Mara with an expression of quiet admiration. The way she moved, the way she connected with these frightened creatures, was a testament to the strength and resilience he had glimpsed in her, even when she tried to hide it. He saw not just a caregiver, but a healer, someone who understood the language of fear and offered solace without judgment.

"They can sense it," he said, his voice low, as he secured the latch on a cage housing a large, fluffy Maine Coon. "The change in the atmosphere."

"They don't understand what's happening," Mara replied, her gaze never leaving the calico. "They just feel the fear."

"And you're their calm in the storm," Eli observed, his gaze meeting hers across the room. There was a warmth in his eyes that cut through the rising anxiety, a reminder of the connection they were forging, even amidst the chaos.

As the storm intensified, the wind began to lash rain against the windows with a ferocity that threatened to shatter the glass. The lights flickered, plunging the Haven into momentary darkness before sputtering back to life, each flicker a stark reminder of their isolation. The power grid, they knew, was vulnerable.

"We need to move Buster," Mara said, her voice tight with a sudden surge of worry. "He's still in the living room. It's not reinforced."

Eli nodded, his jaw set. "I'll go. You stay here and keep an eye on the cats. Make sure they're settled."

Mara hesitated. Her instinct was to go with him, to face the storm together, but she knew he was right. Her focus was needed here. The thought of him out there, alone in the escalating tempest, sent a fresh wave of unease through her. But she trusted him. She had begun to trust him, a fragile seed of faith planted in the fertile ground of their shared experiences.

Eli moved with practiced efficiency, his movements honed by years of working with animals and dealing with unpredictable situations. He found Buster restless, pacing the living room, his whines growing more insistent. The gentle rhythm of his snores was long gone, replaced by a low, guttural growl directed at the unseen forces battering the Haven.

"Hey, boy," Eli murmured, his voice calm and reassuring. He approached Buster slowly, letting the dog acknowledge his presence. Buster's tail gave a tentative thump against the floor, a flicker of recognition in his anxious eyes. "It's okay, buddy. We're going to get you somewhere safe."

He clipped a sturdy lead onto Buster's collar, the dog leaning into him, seeking comfort. Together, they navigated the increasingly treacherous corridors, the wind howling like a banshee outside, shaking the very foundations of the building. Rain hammered against the windows, obscuring any view of the outside world. The air was charged with an electric tension, a palpable sense of nature's unleashed fury.

They reached the secure kennel block, a sturdy structure built with resilience in mind. Eli led Buster into one of the spacious, reinforced runs, the thick concrete walls offering a tangible sense of security. "You'll be alright here, boy," Eli said, giving Buster's head a reassuring pat. The dog, though still anxious, seemed to settle, his gaze following Eli as he retreated.

Returning to the main living area, Eli found Mara already engaged in another task. The storm had caused a leak in the ceiling of the main hall, a steady drip, drip, drip that threatened to escalate into a deluge. She was directing a small team of volunteers, positioning buckets and tarps with a quiet determination that belied the growing chaos.

"It's getting worse," she said, her voice tight as she looked up at Eli. Her hair was damp, clinging to her forehead, and there was a smudge of dirt on her cheek, but her eyes held a fierce resolve. "We need to reinforce that section of the roof, if we can."

The thought was daunting. Venturing out onto the roof in this gale was a dangerous proposition. But the leak was spreading, threatening to damage the historical artifacts housed in the hall. It was a risk they had to consider.

"I'll go with you," Eli said, his voice firm. He saw the worry in her eyes, the unspoken fear of being left alone to face such a daunting task. "We'll go together."

The wind snatched at them the moment they stepped outside, a furious blast that threatened to rip the door from their hands. Rain, cold and stinging, lashed at their faces, reducing visibility to mere feet. The world was a maelstrom of wind and water, the roar of the storm a deafening symphony that drowned out all other sounds. They moved with a desperate haste, clinging to the slippery roof tiles, their progress agonizingly slow. The wind tore at their clothing, threatening to pull them from their precarious perch.

Mara's breath hitched with each gust, her knuckles white as she gripped Eli's arm for stability. She could feel the tremors of the building beneath her feet, the raw power of the storm battering it from all sides. It was a primal fear, a deep-seated terror of being overwhelmed, of being swept away. She saw flashes of her past – the turbulent years, the feeling of being utterly at the mercy of forces beyond her control.

"Hold on!" Eli yelled over the din, his voice rough against the wind. He pointed towards a section of damaged flashing, where the water was pouring in most aggressively. They worked in a frantic, almost desperate rhythm, their movements dictated by the unpredictable gusts. He handed her nails and a hammer, his hands steady despite the precarious situation. Mara, her initial panic subsiding into a grim focus, began to secure the new flashing, her actions precise and efficient.

There was a moment, a brief respite between gusts, where they were able to work in relative silence, the only sound the rhythmic tap of Mara's hammer against the metal. Eli watched her, his admiration deepening with every controlled movement. She was facing her fears head-on, her resilience a testament to the strength he had sensed in her from their first meeting.

Suddenly, a particularly violent gust slammed into them, knocking Mara off balance. She cried out, her grip slipping. Eli reacted instantly, his arm shooting out, catching her before she could fall. For a heart-stopping moment, they were locked together, suspended against the raging storm, the world a blur of wind and rain.

"Got you," Eli said, his voice a low rumble against her ear, his grip firm and reassuring. He pulled her closer, shielding her body with his own. The sheer physicality of the moment, the raw dependence, was overwhelming. Mara's breath hitched, not entirely from fear anymore, but from a confusing swirl of emotions – relief, gratitude, and a nascent, undeniable spark of something more.

They clung to each other for a moment longer, the storm raging around them, a silent testament to their shared vulnerability. Then, with a renewed sense of purpose, they continued their work, their movements now more synchronized, their reliance on each other solidified. They managed to secure the flashing, a small victory against the overwhelming force of the storm, but a victory nonetheless.

Back inside, shivering and soaked but safe, they shed their dripping rain gear. The immediate crisis on the roof was averted, but the storm showed no signs of abating. The wind howled with renewed vigor, and the rain continued to lash against the windows, each drop a percussive reminder of nature's power. The power flickered again, more aggressively this time, and then, with a sickening lurch, died completely, plunging the Haven into absolute darkness.

A collective gasp went through the assembled volunteers. The only light now came from the faint, flickering embers of the dying fire in the hearth and the emergency lanterns they quickly brought out, casting long, dancing shadows that distorted familiar faces into grotesque shapes. The silence that followed the power outage was profound, amplifying the roar of the storm outside.

"Okay," Mara said, her voice remarkably steady in the sudden gloom. She took a deep breath, the scent of damp wool and fear mingling with the lingering woodsmoke. "Lanterns up. Everyone stay calm. We've got this." Her words, calm and authoritative, cut through the rising panic. She moved with a renewed sense of purpose, her earlier anxieties now a distant hum, replaced by the urgent need to keep everyone safe.

Eli watched her, a quiet pride swelling in his chest. She was a natural leader, her composure under pressure a beacon in the darkness. He saw the flicker of fear in her eyes, the subtle tension in her shoulders, but she was pushing through it, her resolve unwavering.

"The generator," Eli said, his voice carrying across the dimly lit hall. "It should kick in any minute. But until then, we'll manage." He moved towards Mara, his presence a silent offer of support.

The storm continued to rage, a relentless assault on the Haven. The wind screamed, the rain beat down, and the darkness pressed in. Yet, within the walls of the Haven, a different kind of force was at play – a quiet strength born of shared purpose, of mutual reliance, of the nascent threads of connection being woven tighter amidst the chaos. Mara and Eli, standing side-by-side in the flickering lantern light, felt the intensity of their shared experience forging a bond that was as powerful, and as enduring, as the storm itself. The storm on the horizon had arrived, and it was testing not only the resilience of the Haven, but the strength of their burgeoning relationship, pushing them to navigate these new, turbulent waters together.

The flickering emergency lanterns cast long, dancing shadows across the cramped confines of the Haven's main office. The storm outside had reached its crescendo, a relentless assault of wind and rain that battered the old building, its fury a constant, deafening roar that seeped through even the thickest walls. Inside, however, a different kind of intensity pulsed, a quiet, concentrated energy focused on a small, cardboard box nestled amongst scattered papers and files. Within it lay a litter of orphaned puppies, their tiny bodies trembling, their vulnerable cries almost lost amidst the tempest's cacophony.

Mara knelt beside the box, her movements gentle, her voice a soft murmur against the storm's din. Eli was beside her, his presence a steady anchor in the encroaching darkness. They had sought refuge in this small room, the most secure place they could find with the lights out, and it had become an impromptu nursery for the storm's unexpected casualties. The air was thick with the scent of damp wool from their storm gear, mingled with the faint, milky aroma of the puppies and the residual earthiness of the Haven's old stone walls.

"They're so small," Mara whispered, her gaze fixed on a particularly tiny, dark-furred pup that was burrowing its way deeper into its siblings. Her heart ached with a familiar pang, a deep-seated empathy for any creature in distress, especially one so utterly dependent. She reached a finger into the box, and the pup, sensing the warmth, nuzzled against it with a faint whimper.

Eli watched her, his expression a mixture of concern and a quiet admiration that had become increasingly familiar. He reached for a small, worn blanket from a corner of the office, the fabric soft and comforting, and carefully placed it over the shivering pups. "They'll be alright," he said, his voice low and steady. "We'll keep them warm. We'll keep them safe." His eyes met Mara's, and in the dim light, she saw a depth of understanding that transcended words. The storm outside was a brutal, untamed force, but here, in this small room, a different kind of connection was being forged, built on shared purpose and a quiet tenderness.

Mara nodded, a small, grateful smile touching her lips. "They don't know what's happening out there," she murmured, her gaze drifting towards the window, where the rain seemed to be actively trying to breach the glass. "They just feel the fear." Her voice held a hint of her own past anxieties, the echo of times when she too had felt overwhelmed by forces she couldn't control. But then her attention snapped back to the box, to the tangible, immediate need before her. "We need to make sure they're fed soon," she added, her tone shifting back to practical concern.

Eli had anticipated her need. From a sturdy metal cabinet, he produced a small bottle and a specially formulated puppy milk replacer. He warmed it carefully using a thermos of hot water they had brought in earlier, the simple act imbued with a sense of profound care. The ritual of preparing the milk, the careful measuring, the checking of the temperature – each step was deliberate, a counterpoint to the chaos raging beyond their sanctuary.

The first pup to be fed was the smallest, a little ball of fluff with wide, bewildered eyes. Mara held it gently, supporting its wobbly head as Eli carefully guided the nipple of the bottle to its mouth. The pup latched on with surprising vigor, its tiny tail giving a weak, rhythmic thump against Mara's hand. A sigh of relief escaped her lips, a sound lost in the howling wind.

"See?" Eli said softly, his gaze locked on the feeding pup. "They're fighters. Just need a little help."

Mara felt a warmth spread through her, a feeling that had little to do with the heated water or the comforting blankets. It was the warmth of shared experience, of witnessing this small act of survival unfold together. She looked at Eli, at the focused intensity in his eyes as he prepared to feed the next pup, and felt a profound sense of ease settle over her. The storm, which had threatened to engulf her earlier with a primal fear, now seemed less daunting. Its fury was a backdrop, a dramatic setting for this quiet act of nurturing.

As they continued to feed the litter, taking turns with each pup, a comfortable rhythm developed between them. The initial tension of the storm had given way to a shared focus, a collaborative effort that flowed with an almost instinctive grace. Their hands sometimes brushed as they reached for the bottle or adjusted a blanket, and each touch, however fleeting, sent a subtle spark through Mara. There was an intimacy in their shared vulnerability, in their common goal of protecting these fragile lives. The confined space of the office, which might have felt stifling under different circumstances, now felt like a private world, insulated from the storm's fury, a cocoon woven from mutual concern.

"Remember that time," Mara began, her voice a low murmur as she held a particularly noisy pup, "when I was trying to reintroduce the ferrets to their outdoor enclosure, and a hawk swooped down? Almost got one of them." She chuckled softly, a sound of fond remembrance. "I remember thinking, 'This is it. Nature's going to get one of us.'"

Eli smiled, a genuine, open smile that crinkled the corners of his eyes. "I remember that," he said. "You were like a lioness, yelling at the hawk, waving your arms. The ferrets were long gone, but the hawk took off, completely bewildered." He paused, his gaze softening as he looked at Mara. "You didn't hesitate. You just jumped in."

Mara felt a blush creep up her neck. "Well, they were under my care," she said, her voice a little softer now. "I felt responsible." She looked down at the pup she was holding, its small body now breathing more evenly, its frantic cries replaced by contented sighs as it nursed. "Just like these little ones. They didn't ask to be orphaned."

"And you're making sure they don't have to face the world alone," Eli added. He reached out, his fingers gently stroking the soft fur of another pup. "It's a good thing you're here, Mara. For them. For all of us."

The sincerity in his voice was disarming. Mara met his gaze, and for a long moment, the storm outside seemed to fade into insignificance. The flickering lantern light played across his face, highlighting the lines of kindness around his eyes, the quiet strength etched in his jaw. She saw in him a reflection of the very qualities she admired – resilience, compassion, and a steady presence.

"And it's a good thing you're here, Eli," she replied, her voice barely a whisper. "I don't think I could get through this without you." It was a confession, a raw admission of reliance that she had rarely allowed herself. But the storm, the darkness, and the shared responsibility for these vulnerable creatures had stripped away the carefully constructed walls she had built around her heart.

He didn't respond with words, but his gaze held hers, a silent acknowledgment of the burgeoning connection between them. It was a connection forged in the crucible of adversity, a testament to the fact that even in the midst of chaos, new growth, new hope, could emerge.

As the storm continued its relentless assault, the pups, one by one, drifted off to sleep, their tiny bellies full, their bodies nestled together for warmth. The soft, rhythmic breathing of the litter filled the small office, a peaceful counterpoint to the storm's fury. Mara and Eli sat in companionable silence, the emergency lanterns casting a warm, intimate glow around them. The shared experience, the quiet moments of reassurance, the unspoken understanding – it all coalesced into a feeling of profound connection.

Mara leaned back against the cool stone wall, her eyelids feeling heavy. The adrenaline that had fueled her earlier was starting to wane, replaced by a deep sense of contentment. She watched Eli, who was now carefully arranging the blankets to ensure the pups were undisturbed. He moved with a quiet efficiency, his every action a demonstration of his innate kindness.

"You're good at this," she murmured, the words laced with a genuine admiration. "You have a way with them."

Eli looked up, a hint of a smile playing on his lips. "I learned from the best," he said, his gaze returning to the sleeping pups. "Watching you, Mara. You have a gift."

Mara felt a warmth spread through her chest, a blush of pleasure at his words. She had always prided herself on her ability to care for animals, but to have it recognized by Eli, in this moment, felt particularly special. It was more than just competence; it was a shared understanding of the profound connection between humans and the creatures they cared for.

The storm, though still raging, seemed to have lost some of its terror. It was still a force to be reckoned with, a reminder of the wildness that lay just beyond the Haven's walls, but within this small office, a sanctuary had been created. A sanctuary of warmth, of quiet, and of a burgeoning tenderness.

Eli reached for a spare blanket and draped it over Mara's shoulders. His fingers brushed her arm as he did so, a light, electric touch that sent a shiver down her spine, not of fear, but of something entirely different, something exciting and new.

"You should rest," he said softly. "We'll need to be ready for anything when the storm breaks."

Mara nodded, her head falling back against the rough stone. She closed her eyes, the rhythmic breathing of the puppies a lullaby, the steady presence of Eli beside her a silent reassurance.

The unexpected proximity, thrust upon them by the storm, had created an intimacy that neither of them had anticipated. In the darkness, surrounded by the vulnerability of the smallest creatures, Mara felt a sense of peace she hadn't experienced in a long time. It was a peace born not just from the immediate safety of the Haven, but from the quiet certainty that she was not alone in navigating these new, turbulent waters. The storm raged on, but within the heart of the Haven, amidst the soft whimpers and the gentle breathing of orphaned puppies, a fragile, beautiful connection was taking root, as resilient and as hopeful as the dawn that would eventually break. The shared whispers, the comforting touches, the silent understanding – they were all building blocks, creating a foundation of trust and affection that would withstand whatever the coming days, or the continuing storm, might bring. The confined space, once a source of potential discomfort, had become a haven within a haven, a testament to the power of shared humanity in the face of nature's raw, untamed might.

The storm's fury had receded, leaving behind a world hushed and cleansed, painted in the muted tones of dawn. The air, once thick with the metallic tang of rain and the primal scent of fear, now carried the clean, earthy perfume of damp soil and resilient greenery. Sunlight, hesitant at first, began to filter through the tattered edges of the clouds, casting a golden benediction over the Haven. Inside, the remnants of the night's tempest – the scattered blankets, the empty puppy bottles, the lingering scent of warmth and shared vigilance – felt like the artefacts of a distant dream.

Mara stood by the office window, watching the slow, methodical repair of the storm's damage. The wind-battered trees were beginning to unfurl their sodden leaves, and the birds, silenced by the storm's roar, were tentatively reclaiming their song. A profound sense of calm had settled over her, a quiet gratitude for the shelter they had found, both within the Haven's sturdy walls and, increasingly, in each other's company. She turned, her gaze searching for Eli, a familiar comfort she had come to rely on.

He was standing a few feet away, his usual quiet demeanor amplified by the stillness of the morning. He waited until her eyes met his, and then he motioned for her to join him outside, away from the comforting clutter of the makeshift nursery. As they stepped out onto the damp earth, the quiet was profound, broken only by the drip of water from the eaves and the distant chirping of awakening birds. The world felt newly born, fresh and full of possibility.

Eli led her to a small, sheltered alcove near the back of the Haven, a place where the overgrown ivy had managed to provide a natural, verdant screen from the elements. The air here was cooler, scented with the damp moss that clung to the stone. He turned to her, his expression uncharacteristically open, his eyes, usually so guarded, now held a tender vulnerability that made Mara's breath catch in her throat.

"Mara," he began, his voice a low murmur, barely disturbing the quiet. It was a voice tinged with an emotion she hadn't heard from him before, a gentle tremor that spoke of unspoken thoughts finally finding their voice. He paused, as if gathering his courage, then continued, "The storm... it's always a stark reminder of how quickly things can change. How fragile everything is."

Mara nodded, her gaze fixed on him, sensing the weight of his words. The night had been a testament to that fragility, to the raw power of nature, and to their own resilience in the face of it.

"And through it all," he continued, his voice growing a little stronger, "seeing you... seeing how you cared for those puppies, how you instinctively knew what to do, how you didn't falter for a second... it made me realize something." He looked away for a moment, towards the distant horizon where the sun was beginning to burn away the last vestiges of mist. "It made me realize how much you mean to me."

The words hung in the air between them, simple and yet charged with a profound significance. Mara felt a warmth bloom in her chest, a feeling that was both exhilarating and a little daunting. She had felt it too, this growing connection, this quiet deepening of their bond, but to hear him articulate it so clearly, so sincerely, was a revelation.

"I've... I've been hesitant," Eli confessed, his gaze returning to her, earnest and unwavering. "You've been through so much, Mara. I've seen the scars, not just the ones on your skin, but the ones you carry inside. And I didn't want to rush anything. I wanted to be sure that you felt... ready. That you weren't just seeking refuge, but truly finding your footing." He reached out, his hand hovering for a moment before gently cupping her cheek. His touch was feather-light, yet it sent a jolt of awareness through her. "But watching you last night, seeing your strength, your compassion... it was impossible to keep it all in."

His thumb traced the curve of her cheekbone, a simple gesture that conveyed a world of tenderness. Mara leaned into his touch, her eyes closing for a brief moment, allowing the raw honesty of his confession to wash over her. It wasn't just about the storm, or the puppies, or the Haven. It was about them, about the space they were creating together, a space built on trust and understanding.

"I've admired you from the moment I first saw you," he admitted, his voice thick with emotion. "Your fierce independence, your unwavering dedication to these animals. But I've also seen the moments of doubt, the vulnerability you try to hide. And I found myself wanting to protect that vulnerability, to offer you a space where you didn't have to hide." He let out a soft sigh, a sound of release. "It's been... difficult. To feel this pull, this deep connection, and to try and keep it all contained, out of respect for your journey."

Mara opened her eyes, her gaze meeting his. She saw not just admiration or desire, but a profound respect. He hadn't pushed, hadn't demanded. He had waited, observed, and understood. That understanding was more potent than any rushed declaration.

"Eli," she whispered, her voice barely audible. The name felt different on her tongue now, imbued with a new depth of meaning. "I... I didn't realize."

He smiled, a gentle, reassuring smile. "That's the point, isn't it? For it to feel... natural. For it to grow from this shared experience, this mutual respect." He brushed a stray strand of hair from her forehead, his fingers lingering against her skin. "You've shown me a different kind of strength, Mara. Not just the strength to survive, but the strength to nurture, to care, to connect. And it's... it's breathtaking."

The words landed softly, like petals falling from a bloom. Mara felt a blush creep up her neck, a warm tide of emotion that had nothing to do with embarrassment and everything to do with a hopeful recognition. She had been so focused on her own journey, on healing and rebuilding, that she hadn't fully allowed herself to acknowledge the quiet strength of their growing bond.

"I... I was afraid," she confessed, the words tumbling out with a surprising ease. "Afraid of getting hurt again. Afraid of letting someone in. The Haven... it felt safe. Like a place where I could just... be. Without expectations."

Eli's hand moved to cup her jaw, his gaze steady and reassuring. "And I never wanted to be an expectation, Mara. I wanted to be a constant. A presence that you could rely on, whether you needed to talk, or to sit in silence, or to... well, to rescue puppies in the middle of a storm." He chuckled softly, the sound warm and genuine. "I wanted to show you that you don't have to be alone in navigating these waters. That there's someone who sees you, truly sees you, and cherishes what he sees."

The sincerity in his voice was a balm to her soul. She had spent so long feeling adrift, tossed by the waves of her past trauma, and in Eli, she had found a lighthouse. His quiet strength, his patient understanding, his unwavering presence – it was everything she hadn't known she was looking for.

"You do see me, don't you?" she asked, her voice barely a whisper, a plea for confirmation.

"Every part of you," he replied, his eyes shining with an undeniable affection. "The fierce protector, the gentle nurturer, the woman who carries her burdens with such grace. I see all of it, Mara, and I'm drawn to all of it." He leaned closer, his gaze dropping to her lips, a silent question in his eyes.

Mara's heart hammered against her ribs, a frantic bird trapped in a cage. The world around them seemed to fade away, the only reality the soft scent of moss, the gentle warmth of Eli's hand on her cheek, and the unspoken promise in his eyes. She had been so guarded, so afraid of her own heart, but with Eli, it felt different. It felt safe to let it unfurl, petal by delicate petal.

"I... I'm not sure I'm ready for all of this," she admitted, her voice trembling slightly. It was a fragile confession, born from years of self-preservation.

Eli's smile was understanding, not disappointed. "And that's okay," he said softly, his thumb stroking her cheek. "There's no timeline, Mara. No pressure. Just an honest acknowledgment of what I feel. And a willingness to be patient, to let things unfold at your pace." He paused, his gaze searching hers. "But I wanted you to know. I wanted to be honest with you, because I respect you too much not to be."

The gentle revelation. It wasn't a grand gesture, not a whirlwind of passion, but something far more profound. It was a quiet opening of his heart, a laying bare of his feelings, born from a place of deep respect and genuine affection. And in that quiet space, bathed in the soft morning light, Mara felt something shift within her. The walls she had so carefully constructed began to crumble, not with a violent crash, but with a quiet surrender.

She reached up, her fingers mirroring his touch, and gently cupped his face. His skin was warm beneath her touch, and she felt the subtle tremor of his answering emotion. "Thank you, Eli," she whispered, her voice filled with a newfound sincerity. "Thank you for being patient. For seeing me. For... for everything."

He leaned into her touch, his eyes closing for a brief moment, a silent testament to the depth of his feelings. When he opened them again, they were filled with a soft gratitude that mirrored her own. "You've made the Haven more than just a sanctuary, Mara," he said, his voice barely above a breath. "You've made it a home. And you... you've made me feel something I thought I'd lost forever."

The unspoken words hung between them – hope. The hope of healing, the hope of connection, the hope of a future that felt less like a struggle for survival and more like a journey shared. The storm had passed, but the gentle revelation had stirred something within Mara, a quiet awakening that promised new beginnings, a calm certainty that in the midst of life's unpredictable storms, she had found an anchor, a steady presence, a place where her heart could finally begin to heal, and perhaps, to love again. The dawn broke not just over the Haven, but within Mara's own soul, painting the landscape of her future with a soft, hopeful light. The tentative sunlight warmed her skin, and the quiet strength of Eli's gaze was a promise of the calm waters that lay ahead, a testament to the fact that even after the fiercest storms, new growth, new life, and new love could always emerge.

The first rays of dawn, timid yet persistent, began to pierce the bruised canvas of the sky, painting the world in hues of rose and gold. The storm, a tempestuous fury that had raged through the night, had finally retreated, leaving behind a world scrubbed clean and sparkling with residual moisture. Every leaf, every blade of grass, every weathered plank of the Haven, shimmered with a newfound brilliance, as if baptized by the very ferocity that had threatened to overwhelm them. The air, once heavy with the scent of ozone and damp earth, now carried a delicate perfume of petrichor, a sweet, clean aroma that spoke of nature's resilience and renewal.

Mara stepped out from the warm embrace of the Haven, the cool morning air a gentle caress against her skin. Eli was already there, his silhouette sharp against the soft light, his gaze sweeping across the grounds. The landscape bore the marks of the night's ordeal –

a few branches strewn across the path, a scattering of debris near the animal enclosures, and the waterlogged earth testament to the torrential downpour. Yet, there was no sense of devastation, only a quiet acknowledgment of nature's power and a shared resolve to restore order.

Together, they moved through the grounds, a silent ballet of efficiency and understanding. They worked without the need for extensive conversation, their actions guided by a shared purpose. Mara gathered fallen leaves and twigs, her movements fluid and practiced, while Eli, with his broader reach and steady hands, maneuvered larger branches, clearing pathways with practiced ease. The discarded remnants of the storm, once symbols of chaos, were now simply materials to be repurposed, removed, or set aside. Each piece of debris cleared was a small victory, a tangible step towards normalcy.

As they worked, the sunlight grew stronger, dispelling the lingering shadows and illuminating the scene with a warm, hopeful glow. The animals, sensing the shift in the atmosphere, began to stir. The puppies, nestled in their cozy bedding, whimpered softly, their tiny snores a comforting counterpoint to the gentle rustling of leaves. The older dogs, their coats still slightly damp, wagged their tails tentatively, their eyes bright with curiosity as they observed the dawn's quiet arrival.

Mara paused, leaning against the rough bark of an oak tree, its leaves still clinging precariously after the wind's assault. She watched Eli as he worked, his brow furrowed in concentration, his movements deliberate and strong. There was a quiet satisfaction in his posture, a sense of accomplishment that mirrored her own. The shared experience of the storm, the vigil they had kept together, had forged a bond that felt as sturdy and resilient as the ancient tree beside her. It was a silent acknowledgment of their collective strength, a testament to their ability to weather any storm, both literal and metaphorical.

The storm had been a trial, undoubtedly. It had tested their resolve, their resources, and their courage. But in its wake, it had also brought a clarity, a cleansing that stripped away the superficial and revealed the core of what was truly important. The Haven, though battered, stood firm. Its inhabitants, human and animal alike, were safe. And in the shared effort of restoration, a profound sense of renewal had taken root. The air itself felt lighter, as if the storm had carried away not just rain and wind, but also the lingering anxieties and unspoken doubts that had perhaps clouded their path.

Eli approached her, a stray leaf clinging to his dark hair. He offered a faint smile, a silent question in his eyes. Mara returned it, a deeper, more genuine smile this time, one that reached her eyes. "It looks like we made it through," she said, her voice soft, carrying on the still morning air.

"We did," Eli replied, his gaze sweeping over the grounds once more. "The Haven held strong. And so did everyone in it." He paused, his eyes meeting hers. "Thanks to you, mostly. Your calm through the night... it made a difference."

Mara felt a warmth spread through her, a quiet gratitude for his words. "We were a team, Eli," she countered, the simple truth of it settling comfortably between them. "I couldn't have done it alone. None of us could have."

He nodded, a flicker of something unreadable in his eyes. "That's what I've been realizing," he admitted, his voice dropping to a low murmur. "That we're better together. That this place, and what we're building here, it's more than just a shelter for animals. It's becoming a sanctuary for us too."

The words resonated deep within Mara. It was true. The Haven had become more than just a refuge for her; it had become a place where she was slowly, tentatively, finding herself again. And Eli, with his quiet strength and unwavering presence, had become an integral part of that unfolding journey. The storm, in its destructive power, had inadvertently cleared a path for something new, something hopeful, to bloom.

They continued their work, their movements now imbued with a lighter energy. The task of clearing debris felt less like a chore and more like a ritual of renewal. Each obstacle overcome, each patch of ground cleared, was a step forward, a confirmation of their resilience. The sunlight, now fully risen, bathed the Haven in a warm, golden light, erasing the last vestiges of the night's darkness. The world felt fresh, vibrant, and brimming with possibility.

As they worked side-by-side, a comfortable silence settled between them, not an awkward void, but a companionable stillness that spoke of shared understanding. Mara found herself appreciating the simple rhythm of their movements, the unspoken communication that flowed between them. It was a different kind of connection than she had ever known, one built on shared purpose and mutual respect, a quiet strength that had emerged from the heart of the storm.

Eli picked up a broken fence post, his movements efficient. "We'll need to reinforce the south fence," he said, his voice practical. "It took a beating."

Mara nodded, already mentally assessing the repair. "I'll get the lumber from the shed. And check on the roof of the dog run. I think a few shingles might have come loose."

Their collaboration was seamless, each anticipating the other's needs, their focus on the task at hand. The storm had been a formidable adversary, but it had also served as a catalyst, forcing them to confront challenges head-on and to rely on each other in ways they might not have otherwise. The aftermath was not merely about repairing physical damage; it was about rebuilding, strengthening, and solidifying the bonds that had been tested and found to be true.

As the morning wore on, other members of the community, drawn by the first signs of clear skies, began to emerge, their faces etched with relief and a shared sense of wonder at the dawn's beauty. They too, had weathered the storm, and now, in the quiet aftermath, they joined Mara and Eli in the communal effort of mending their shared world. Laughter, tentative at first, began to ripple through the air, a fragile melody of hope and resilience.

Mara watched as the community came together, a tapestry of shared experience and mutual support. The storm had been a stark reminder of their vulnerability, but it had also highlighted their collective strength. The Haven, once just a place of refuge, was evolving into a true community, a testament to the enduring power of human connection.

Eli stood beside her, his shoulder brushing hers lightly. "It's remarkable, isn't it?" he said, his voice filled with a quiet admiration. "How we can find so much strength in coming together."

Mara inclined her head, her gaze sweeping over the bustling scene. "It is," she agreed, a profound sense of peace settling over her. "The storm cleared the air, Eli. Literally and figuratively. It feels like... like we can breathe again."

He turned to her then, his eyes holding a warmth that mirrored the rising sun. "We can," he affirmed, his voice low and steady. "And we'll face whatever comes next, together."

The promise in his words was a beacon, a reassurance. The storm had passed, leaving behind not devastation, but a fertile ground for new growth. The Haven, and the lives within it, were emerging from the tempest stronger, more resilient, and more connected than ever before. The calm after the storm was not just a cessation of the wind and rain; it was a profound sense of renewal, a quiet certainty that whatever challenges lay ahead, they would navigate them, side-by-side, with a newfound strength and a shared hope for the future. The sparkling dew on the leaves, the gentle warmth of the sun, the laughter of the community – all were testaments to the enduring spirit of life, and the quiet power of connection that had emerged, unbroken, from the heart of the storm.

The aftermath of the storm had settled over the Haven like a soft blanket, a quiet stillness that spoke of resilience and renewal. The air, scrubbed clean by the torrential downpour, was now filled with the sweet scent of petrichor, a gentle reminder of nature's untamed power and its ability to restore. Mara found herself drawn to the familiar curve of the coastline, the rhythmic whisper of the waves a soothing balm to her soul. The beach, usually a place of solitary contemplation, felt different today. The lingering anxieties that had clung to her like a damp shroud seemed to have been swept away with the receding tides, leaving behind a space for something new to take root.

She walked along the water's edge, the cool sand yielding beneath her bare feet, the retreating waves leaving intricate patterns of foam that dissolved as quickly as they appeared. Each step was a quiet affirmation, a release of the past. The fear that had once held her captive, a constant companion since she'd arrived at the Haven, had begun to dissipate in the face of the storm's fury. It was a strange paradox; the very force that had threatened to overwhelm them had, in its wake, stripped away the layers of her apprehension, revealing a core of unexpected strength.

Her gaze drifted from the endless expanse of the ocean to the figure standing a little further down the shore. Eli. He stood with his back to her, his shoulders squared against the gentle breeze, his silhouette a familiar and comforting sight against the vast backdrop of sea and sky. He seemed to be lost in his own thoughts, his attention fixed on the distant horizon. A quiet understanding passed between them, a silent acknowledgment of their shared journey through the tempest. The storm had been a crucible, forging a bond between them that felt as deep and enduring as the ocean itself.

As if sensing her presence, Eli turned. His eyes, the color of warm earth, met hers, and in that instant, Mara felt a profound sense of clarity wash over her. It was a moment of truth, unvarnished and pure. The tentative hope that had begun to flicker within her during the long night of the storm now blazed with a steady flame. In Eli's steady gaze, in the gentle curve of his lips as a soft smile touched them, she saw not just a friend, but a beacon. He was the calm in her personal storm, the steady hand that had helped her navigate the treacherous currents of her own fear.

The uncertainty of her future still loomed, a vast and uncharted territory. There were still questions without answers, paths yet to be explored. But now, the prospect of facing that future no longer felt like a solitary struggle against overwhelming odds. Instead, it felt like a shared adventure, a journey she could embark upon with Eli by her side. The idea was not frightening, but exhilarating. It was a possibility, a hopeful whisper in the quiet aftermath of the storm.

He began to walk towards her, his steps unhurried, his presence radiating a quiet strength that Mara had come to rely on. She waited, her heart beating a little faster, a familiar flutter of anticipation. The wind, carrying the salty tang of the sea, tugged at her hair, a playful caress. As he drew closer, she could see the subtle lines of weariness around his eyes, a testament to the long night he had also endured, yet his smile remained, genuine and reassuring.

"The sea looks peaceful today," Eli said, his voice a low rumble that carried easily over the gentle roar of the waves.

Mara nodded, a small smile playing on her lips. "It does. It's like it's holding its breath after the storm."

"Or maybe it's just getting ready for the next one," he said, a hint of amusement in his tone. But there was no fear in his words, only a quiet acceptance of nature's cyclical nature.

"Perhaps," Mara conceded, her gaze returning to the horizon. "But for now, it's beautiful. And so is this." She gestured vaguely to the tranquil scene, the sun-drenched beach, the impossibly blue sky.

Eli followed her gaze, his eyes softening. He didn't need her to elaborate. He understood. He had been there, through the darkness, through the fear. He had witnessed her strength, her quiet resilience, and she, in turn, had seen his unwavering support, his steady presence.

"It's good to see you out here, Mara," he said, his voice losing its teasing edge, becoming more earnest. "You look... lighter."

The observation was astute. Mara hadn't realized how much she'd been carrying until it had begun to slip away. "I think the storm washed a lot of it away," she admitted, her voice softer now. "The fear, the... the hesitation." She looked at him then, her gaze steady. "I don't feel as lost as I did."

Eli's smile deepened, reaching his eyes. He understood the unspoken words, the vulnerability that lay beneath the surface. He knew the journey she had been on, the internal battles she had fought. "That's good to hear," he said simply. "You deserve to feel found, Mara. You always have."

His words settled over her like a warm embrace, a validation of her own efforts, her own quiet strength. She had been so focused on escaping her past, on finding a new beginning, that she hadn't realized she was already building one, brick by careful brick, at the Haven. And Eli had been a constant presence in that construction, a silent supporter, a steady hand.

"I'm not sure I would have gotten through the night without your calm," she confessed, the admission freeing. "Or the work we did afterwards. It felt... important. Like we were holding onto something solid."

Eli shrugged, a small gesture that held a world of meaning. "We were," he said. "And we are. This place, Mara, it's more than just shelter for animals. It's becoming... something else. For all of us." He hesitated, then added, his voice dropping slightly, "For me, too."

His honesty was disarming, and Mara felt a blush creep up her neck. The thought of Eli finding solace, a sense of purpose, at the Haven was as heartwarming as it was surprising. They had both arrived seeking refuge, but it seemed they were both finding something more profound – a sense of belonging, a renewed hope.

"I know what you mean," she said, her voice barely a whisper. "It's like... like the storm cleared the way for us to see what was really important."

"And what do you think is really important, Mara?" Eli asked, his gaze intent, a gentle curiosity in his eyes.

She looked out at the ocean, the vastness mirroring the questions that still swirled within her. But now, they didn't feel quite so overwhelming. "Connection," she said, the word feeling solid and true on her tongue. "And resilience. The ability to keep going, even when everything feels like it's falling apart. And... and knowing you're not alone in it."

Eli reached out, his fingers brushing hers as he picked up a smooth, grey stone from the sand. He turned it over in his palm, his expression thoughtful. "You're right," he said, his voice soft. "Knowing you're not alone makes all the difference. Especially when you have someone steady beside you." He looked up, his gaze locking with hers, and the unspoken implication hung in the air, potent and undeniable.

Mara's breath hitched. The warmth that spread through her was more than just the sun on her skin. It was the recognition of a shared feeling, a mutual understanding that had been building between them, subtle yet persistent. The path ahead was still uncertain, a tapestry of 'what ifs' and 'maybes'.

But for the first time in a long time, Mara felt a sense of peace, a quiet anticipation for what the future might hold, not because she had all the answers, but because she had the distinct feeling she wouldn't have to face it alone. The gentle lapping of the waves against the shore seemed to echo the new rhythm in her heart, a steady beat of hope, a melody of possibility, now intertwined with the quiet strength of Eli's presence beside her.

Chapter Eight
Harboring Feelings

The ocean exhaled, a soft, misty sigh that kissed Mara's cheeks. The sky, a canvas of bruised purple and soft rose, was a testament to the storm's departure, a gentle promise of a new day. She traced the intricate patterns the receding tide had etched into the sand, each swirl and ripple a reminder of the chaos that had just passed, and the profound quiet that had settled in its wake. It was in this profound stillness that a different kind of awareness began to bloom, a soft unfurling within her chest that had nothing to do with the salty air or the rhythmic pulse of the waves. It was a conscious acknowledgment, a deliberate turning inward to the warmth that had been steadily growing, a quiet ember fanned into a gentle flame by the shared ordeal.

Mara had spent so long guarding her heart, building walls so high they had become her own prison. The Haven had been her sanctuary, a place to lick her wounds, to find solace in the silent companionship of rescued souls. And in that quiet sanctuary, Eli had appeared, not with a fanfare or a grand pronouncement, but with a steady, unassuming presence that had gradually chipped away at her defenses. His kindness hadn't been a sudden deluge, but a persistent, gentle rain, nourishing the parched earth of her spirit. She had initially welcomed it as the balm of a fellow survivor, a shared understanding born of mutual hardship. But as the days bled into weeks, and the storm that had threatened to break them had instead forged a deeper connection, Mara could no longer deny the shift.

The storm, in its brutal honesty, had stripped away pretenses, forcing a confrontation with the raw, vulnerable core of herself. And in the aftermath, in the quiet dawn that followed, she found herself looking at Eli through a new lens. The gratitude she felt for his steadfastness, for the way he'd so effortlessly taken charge during the tempest, was still there, a solid foundation. But beneath it, something else stirred. It was the quiet joy she felt when he smiled, a genuine, crinkling of the eyes that spoke of a kindness that ran bone-deep. It was the sense of ease she found in his presence, a comfortable silence that needed no filling. It was the way her gaze would unconsciously seek him out across the bustling yard, a subtle anchor in the ebb and flow of their daily routines.

She remembered the long night of the storm, the frantic energy, the constant hum of anxiety. He had been a pillar of calm, his voice a steadying force against the howl of the wind and the terrified cries of the animals. He hadn't patronized her, hadn't treated her with kid gloves. Instead, he had seen her strength, had implicitly trusted her capabilities, and in doing so, had helped her to see them herself. He had offered a steady hand when she faltered, a reassuring word when doubt crept in, and a silent acknowledgment that they were in this together. It was that shared struggle, that mutual reliance, that had truly ignited something within her.

Today, walking on the beach, the memory felt not like a burden, but like a treasured artifact, polished smooth by the passage of time and the clarity of hindsight. The fear that had once been a suffocating shroud had receded, leaving behind a space for new emotions to take root. And among them, the most prominent was this burgeoning affection for Eli. It wasn't a sudden, overwhelming passion, but a gentle, persistent warmth that had bloomed organically, like the wildflowers that pushed their way through the sand dunes after a long winter.

She realized, with a quiet sense of wonder, that she had been actively suppressing these feelings, perhaps out of habit, out of a deeply ingrained fear of vulnerability. It was easier to categorize Eli as a friend, a comrade in arms, a fellow survivor. It was safer to keep him at a comfortable distance, to maintain the boundaries she had so carefully erected around her heart. But the storm had been a powerful force, capable of shattering even the most fortified walls. And it had done just that, not with violence, but with a gentle, insistent pressure that had finally yielded.

The tenderness she felt when she thought of him was a revelation. It was in the way he would offer a quiet word of encouragement to a skittish rescue dog, his touch infinitely gentle, his voice a soft murmur of reassurance. It was in the way he'd share a quiet moment with her during their evening chores, their conversation often meandering through the day's events, punctuated by comfortable silences that spoke volumes. These weren't the actions of a mere acquaintance; they were the gestures of someone who was beginning to see, and to appreciate, the entirety of another person.

Mara stopped, letting a wave wash over her ankles, the cool water a welcome sensation against her skin. She looked out at the horizon, where the sun was climbing higher, painting the sky in ever brighter hues of gold and cerulean. This was a new day, a new beginning, and she was no longer afraid to embrace it. The fear of being hurt, of being disappointed, was a shadow that still lingered, but it no longer held the power to dictate her choices. She was choosing to feel, to acknowledge, to allow herself the possibility of happiness.

She thought of the late nights they had spent sorting through supplies after the storm, the shared exhaustion, the quiet camaraderie. He had a way of making even the most mundane tasks feel significant, of imbuing them with a sense of purpose. He had spoken of his own past, of the restlessness that had driven him from place to place, and Mara had listened, recognizing in his words a familiar yearning for a place to belong. And she had realized, in those quiet moments, that the Haven was becoming that place for him, just as it was for her. And perhaps, she dared to hope, they were becoming that place for each other.

The simple act of acknowledging her feelings felt like a victory, a significant step forward in her own journey of healing. It was an act of self-compassion, a recognition that she deserved joy, that she was capable of giving and receiving love. The storm had been a destructive force, but it had also been a catalyst, a powerful agent of change. It had cleared away the debris, both physical and emotional, and in its wake, it had left fertile ground for new growth.

She remembered a conversation they'd had just a few days ago, while mending a tear in a sturdy canvas tarp. Her fingers had been clumsy, the needle slipping through the thick material, and Eli, working beside her, had gently taken her hand, guiding the needle with a steady, sure touch. The brief contact had sent a jolt through her, a spark that had ignited a cascade of unspoken emotions. His touch had been firm, yet tender, and in that moment, the carefully constructed walls around her heart had begun to crumble. She had pulled her hand away too quickly, flustered by the intensity of the sensation, but the memory of it lingered, a persistent echo.

He had paused then, his gaze meeting hers, and in his eyes, she had seen a flicker of something that mirrored her own surprise, her own burgeoning awareness. It was a shared moment of vulnerability, a silent understanding that passed between them, unbidden and unexpected. He hadn't pressed the issue, hadn't pushed for an explanation, but the air between them had shifted, charged with a new, subtle energy.

Now, as she walked along the water's edge, the memory of that moment returned, not with the same flustered surprise, but with a quiet certainty. The warmth in her chest expanded, a gentle blooming that was both exhilarating and deeply comforting. Eli's kindness wasn't just an act of a good person; it was a reflection of his own inner goodness, a goodness that resonated with something deep within her. His steady presence was more than just a source of comfort; it was becoming a source of joy, a gentle counterpoint to the turmoil she had endured for so long.

She thought about his easy laughter, the way it could chase away the shadows. She thought about the quiet determination in his eyes when he spoke of the Haven's future, his unwavering belief in their mission. She thought about the small gestures, the way he'd remember her favorite tea, the way he'd always ensure she had a moment to herself before the evening chores began. These were not the actions of someone indifferent; they were the quiet affirmations of someone who was paying attention, someone who was seeing her, truly seeing her.

The need to suppress these feelings had begun to feel not only futile but also foolish. Why should she deny herself the simple pleasure of this burgeoning affection? Why should she cling to the familiar comfort of solitude when the possibility of shared happiness lay before her? The storm had taught her the preciousness of life, the fragility of what we hold dear, and the importance of not letting fear dictate our choices. She had faced down her inner demons during the tempest, and now, she was ready to face the gentle unfolding of her heart.

She picked up a piece of driftwood, its surface smoothed by countless tides, and turned it over in her hands. It felt solid, resilient, much like the quiet strength she was discovering within herself. The Haven had provided a safe harbor, a place where she could begin to rebuild, to heal. And in Eli, she had found a companion, a kindred spirit who seemed to understand the quiet language of her soul.

The fear of vulnerability was still there, a faint whisper at the edges of her consciousness. What if she was mistaken? What if this was just a fleeting moment of gratitude, a temporary solace found in shared hardship? But then she would remember the genuine warmth in his eyes, the way he listened when she spoke, the quiet strength that emanated from him, and the whisper would fade, replaced by the steady beat of her own hopeful heart.

This wasn't about grand declarations or sweeping romantic gestures. It was about the quiet acknowledgment of a connection that had grown organically, a seed planted in the fertile ground of shared experience and nurtured by mutual respect and kindness. It was about allowing herself to feel the warmth, to embrace the possibility of something beautiful blooming in the aftermath of the storm. It was about recognizing that Eli's presence in her life had become more than just a comfort; it had become a joy, a quiet promise of a brighter future.

Mara continued her walk, the sand soft beneath her feet, the rhythm of the waves a soothing counterpoint to the new melody in her heart. She was no longer just surviving; she was beginning to live, to embrace the full spectrum of her emotions, to allow herself the exquisite vulnerability of hope. And as she looked towards the Haven, she felt a profound sense of peace, a quiet anticipation for the days ahead, and for the gentle unfolding of the connection she was now allowing herself to feel. The storm had passed, and in its wake, a new dawn was breaking, both in the sky above and in the quiet corners of her own heart.

The salty air, still carrying a hint of the recent storm's wildness, seemed to weave its way through the open windows of "The Salty Siren," a small, unassuming restaurant tucked away at the edge of the harbor. Mara had initially hesitated when Eli had suggested it, her mind still a jumble of protective instincts. But his invitation had been delivered with such a gentle certainty, a quiet confidence that had disarmed her usual reservations. Now, as she sat across from him at a small, linen-draped table bathed in the soft glow of a strategically placed lamp, she found herself breathing a sigh of quiet contentment.

The restaurant itself was a study in understated charm. Rough-hewn wooden beams crisscrossed the ceiling, and the walls were adorned with nautical charts and faded photographs of fishing boats. The gentle murmur of conversation from other diners, punctuated by the clinking of cutlery and the distant cries of gulls, created a warm, enveloping atmosphere. Outside, the harbor lights twinkled, mirroring the nascent stars beginning to prick the darkening sky, a soft counterpoint to the more boisterous celestial display that had been visible before the storm.

Eli had ordered for them, a decision Mara had readily accepted, trusting his instincts. He'd chosen a local white wine, crisp and refreshing, and a platter of freshly shucked oysters, their briny essence a testament to the sea that surrounded them. As he offered her the first one, his fingers brushing hers in a fleeting, almost accidental touch, Mara felt that familiar warmth bloom in her chest, a gentle unfurling that was becoming increasingly welcome.

"So," Eli began, his voice a low, pleasant rumble that seemed to vibrate in the intimate space between them, "what do you think? Is this worthy of the woman who braved the tempest?"

Mara laughed, a light, unforced sound that surprised even herself. "It's certainly a welcome respite from fighting off rogue waves and rescuing drenched seabirds. The oysters are... exquisite, Eli. Truly." She savored the cool, succulent burst of flavor, the subtle minerality that spoke of clean, cold waters.

"I'm glad," he said, his gaze steady on hers. "I wanted to find a place that felt... like us, in a way. Not too loud, not too fancy. Just honest and good."

His words resonated deeply with Mara. Honest and good. That was precisely what she was beginning to feel with him. There was an absence of pretense, a refreshing lack of artifice that made it easy to simply *be*. The walls she had so meticulously built around her heart felt less like fortifications and more like gently crumbling ramparts, their purpose no longer to keep others out, but to make space for something new to grow within.

As the evening progressed, their conversation flowed effortlessly, weaving through shared memories of the storm, the challenges of rebuilding the Haven, and the quiet joys they had found in its restorative work. Mara found herself opening up in ways she hadn't anticipated, sharing anecdotes from her childhood, dreams she had long since tucked away, and fears that had once seemed insurmountable. Eli listened with an attentiveness that made her feel truly heard, his eyes reflecting a genuine curiosity and empathy.

He spoke of his own nomadic past, of the restlessness that had once propelled him from one horizon to the next, a constant search for something he couldn't quite name. "I always thought I was looking for a place to *go*," he confessed, swirling the wine in his glass. "A new town, a different landscape. But I think, somewhere along the way, I realized I was actually looking for a place to *belong*. A place where my efforts mattered, where I could feel rooted." He looked at her then, a subtle shift in his expression, a quiet acknowledgment that the Haven, and perhaps she herself, was becoming that place.

Mara felt a surge of something akin to tenderness at his words. She understood that yearning for belonging, the deep-seated need for a connection that transcended mere acquaintance. "The Haven has a way of doing that," she murmured, her gaze drifting to the flickering lights of the boats bobbing gently in the harbor. "It draws people in, and then... it holds them. It gives them purpose."

"And you," Eli said softly, his voice cutting through the ambient sounds of the restaurant, "you are the heart of that purpose, Mara. You hold it all together."

His simple statement, delivered with such sincerity, sent a tremor through her. It was more than just a compliment; it felt like a recognition, an understanding of the quiet strength that had always been her backbone, even when she herself had doubted it. "I just... I try my best," she replied, feeling a blush creep up her neck.

"Your best is extraordinary," he countered, a genuine smile gracing his lips, the kind that reached his eyes and crinkled at the corners, softening his features.

He then shared a story about his grandfather, a fisherman who had taught him the rhythms of the sea, the respect for its power, and the quiet resilience required to navigate its unpredictable moods. Mara listened, captivated by the vivid imagery he painted, the warmth in his voice as he spoke of the man who had shaped so much of his understanding of the world. It was a glimpse into his history, a gentle unfolding of the man behind the capable hands and steady demeanor. He spoke of the camaraderie among the fishing crews, the unspoken bonds forged through shared hardship and mutual reliance. It was a narrative that mirrored, in many ways, the emerging dynamics at the Haven, and the nascent connection he and Mara were building.

As their main courses arrived – a perfectly grilled piece of local sea bass for Mara, and a hearty fisherman's stew for Eli – the conversation deepened. They talked about their aspirations for the Haven, not just as a sanctuary for animals, but as a community hub, a place that fostered connection and healing for both the creatures and the people who found their way there. Eli spoke with a passion that Mara found incredibly compelling, his ideas practical yet imbued with a genuine idealism. He envisioned workshops, educational programs, a space where people could learn new skills and find new purpose, inspired by the resilience of the animals they were helping.

"I can see it so clearly," he said, his eyes alight with enthusiasm. "A place where people can come, not just to volunteer, but to learn. To reconnect with the land, with the animals, with themselves. Imagine the ripple effect."

Mara felt a thrill of shared vision. This was more than just a shared meal; it was a shared future, a nascent blueprint for something significant. "I've always believed in that," she admitted, her voice filled with a newfound excitement. "The healing power of connection, of purpose. But sometimes, it's hard to articulate. Hard to get others to see it."

"But you see it," Eli stated, not as a question, but as a simple fact. "And I see it. And that's a powerful starting point."

There was a moment of quiet between them, filled with the unspoken understanding that their shared vision was only a part of the deeper connection that was forming. The easy laughter that had punctuated their earlier conversation had mellowed into a comfortable, companionable silence. Mara found herself studying his face in the dim light, noticing the subtle lines around his eyes that spoke of laughter and perhaps a touch of melancholy, the strong set of his jaw that hinted at an inner resolve. He was not just a kind man, or a capable one; he was a man with depth, with a rich inner world that she was only just beginning to explore.

He reached across the table, his hand covering hers for a brief, anchoring moment. His touch was warm, firm, and sent a pleasant hum through her veins. "You know, Mara," he said, his gaze earnest, "before I came to the Haven, I felt... adrift. Like a ship without a rudder. This place, this work... and honestly, being with you... it's given me a sense of direction I didn't know I was missing."

Her heart gave a little leap at his confession. It was a vulnerability that mirrored her own, a quiet acknowledgment of the impact they were having on each other. "And you, Eli," she replied, her voice a little thicker than usual, "you've brought a sense of... steadiness. A quiet strength that makes everything feel possible."

The waiter arrived to clear their plates, his presence a gentle interruption that allowed Mara a moment to collect herself. But the warmth of Eli's touch, the sincerity of his words, lingered on her skin. This wasn't just about shared work or a common vision; it was about a genuine, burgeoning affection, a mutual respect that was deepening with every shared glance, every shared word.

As they lingered over dessert – a simple, elegant lemon tart that tasted of sunshine and sweetness – the conversation shifted to more personal dreams. Eli spoke of a small cottage by the sea he'd always envisioned, a place where he could write, surrounded by the sounds of the waves. Mara confessed her long-held desire to finally learn to paint, to capture the ephemeral beauty of the natural world she so loved. They painted vivid pictures with their words, not of grand, unattainable fantasies, but of quiet, fulfilling futures that seemed, in that moment, remarkably within reach.

"Perhaps," Eli mused, a playful glint in his eye, "we could build that cottage, you and I. And you could paint the sea, and I could write about it. A partnership in every sense of the word."

Mara's breath hitched. The suggestion, offered with a lightness that belied its potential significance, hung in the air between them. It was a bold step, a clear indication of his intentions, and it sent a ripple of thrilling anticipation through her. She met his gaze, seeing the genuine hope reflected there, the quiet invitation to explore this burgeoning connection further.

"Perhaps," she echoed, her voice barely a whisper, a smile playing on her lips.

The journey back to the Haven was bathed in the soft glow of moonlight. The ocean whispered its secrets to the shore, and the air was cool and clean, carrying the scent of salt and pine. The silence in the car was no longer just comfortable; it was charged with the unspoken, with the promise of what had been shared, and what might yet be. Mara felt a profound sense of peace settle over her, a quiet joy that radiated from the warmth in her chest. The dinner had been more than just a meal; it had been an affirmation, a step forward on a path that felt both new and strangely familiar. It was the quiet beginning of something meaningful, rooted in a mutual respect that was blossoming into a genuine affection, a shared understanding that promised a future as bright and as clear as the moonlit harbor. She glanced at Eli, his profile etched against the night sky, and knew, with a certainty that settled deep in her bones, that she was no longer just guarding her heart; she was opening it, a little wider with every shared moment, to the possibility of a love that felt as natural and as essential as the rhythm of the tides.

The conversation had naturally drifted, moving from the quiet aspirations for the Haven to the more personal landscapes of their pasts. Mara had shared fragments of her own journey, the scars of past hurts that had shaped her cautious approach to life, and the deep-seated need for the Haven that mirrored her own healing. Now, it was Eli's turn, and as he began to speak, a subtle shift occurred. The easy camaraderie that had filled their conversation deepened, taking on a more intimate, reflective hue. The gentle hum of the restaurant, the distant clinking of glasses, seemed to recede, leaving them in a bubble of shared quiet.

"You know, Mara," Eli began, his gaze unfocused for a moment, as if sifting through memories, "I haven't always been this... grounded. This settled." He offered a faint smile, tinged with a hint of something Mara couldn't quite place – perhaps a touch of wistfulness, or the quiet acceptance of a chapter closed. "There was a time, quite a few years ago now, when I felt very much like that ship without a rudder I mentioned. Adrift, as you put it."

He paused, swirling the remaining wine in his glass, the amber liquid catching the soft light. "It was... a difficult period. I lost someone very important to me. My fiancée. It was sudden, unexpected, and it turned my world upside down. Everything I thought I knew, everything I planned for, vanished in an instant." He looked up then, meeting Mara's empathetic gaze. "The grief was... profound. It felt like a physical weight, a constant ache that no amount of movement, no amount of distance, could shake. I tried to outrun it, in a way. I traveled. I took on different jobs, always moving, always looking for... something. A distraction, perhaps. Or maybe a place where the memories wouldn't follow so closely."

Mara listened, her own heart aching for the pain he must have endured. She saw now the quiet strength in his eyes, the resilience that had carried him through. It wasn't a brash, overt strength, but a deep, unwavering core that had weathered storms she could only begin to imagine. "I'm so sorry, Eli," she murmured, her voice soft. "That sounds... incredibly difficult."

He offered a nod, a small, acknowledg'ment. "It was. And for a long time, I thought that was just my life now. A perpetual state of... not quite being present. Always looking over my shoulder, or yearning for a horizon that never seemed to get any closer. I became quite adept at detachment, at keeping people at arm's length. It felt safer, somehow. Less vulnerable. Less likely to experience that kind of profound loss again." He chuckled softly, a sound devoid of humor. "Irony, isn't it? Trying to avoid pain by shutting yourself off from life itself."

He set his glass down, his fingers tracing the rim. "I moved around a lot. Coast to coast, even a stint overseas. I worked in construction, managed a small bookstore, even helped out on a vineyard for a season. Each place offered a temporary reprieve, a new set of faces and scenery, but the underlying restlessness remained. The feeling that I was on the outside looking in, never truly belonging anywhere. I was always the newcomer, the transient soul. And I started to believe that was all I was capable of being."

"And then?" Mara prompted gently, sensing he was leading towards his arrival in Port Blossom.

"And then," he continued, his voice gaining a steadier tone, "I heard about the Haven. It was through a mutual contact, someone who knew I was looking for a change of pace, though they didn't know the true depth of my need for one. The description of the work, the focus on rehabilitation and sanctuary... it resonated with something deep inside me. Something that had been dormant for a long time. The idea of helping creatures who had been through their own kind of trauma, of giving them a second chance, felt... right. It felt like a purpose that extended beyond my own internal struggles."

He leaned forward slightly, his eyes now alight with a different kind of passion, the passion that stemmed from finding a place of belonging. "When I first arrived in Port Blossom, it was still with that sense of being a temporary visitor. I expected to stay for a few months, help with the rebuilding after that last big storm, and then move on. But something... unexpected happened. The work itself was incredibly demanding, physically and emotionally, but it was also incredibly rewarding. And the people... the sense of community here, the genuine care and dedication everyone showed for the Haven and its inhabitants... it was unlike anything I had ever experienced."

He met Mara's gaze directly, his expression open and sincere. "And then, of course, there was you. I'd heard about you, of course. The driving force behind the Haven, the woman who poured her heart and soul into this place. But meeting you, working alongside you... that's when the real shift happened. Your dedication, your quiet strength, your unwavering compassion... it was inspiring. You embody everything that is good and resilient about this community. And seeing the Haven through your eyes, understanding your vision for it... it made me want to be a part of it, not just as a temporary helper, but as a permanent fixture."

He paused, a soft smile playing on his lips. "It's strange, isn't it? I came here looking for a place to *recover*, to heal from my own past wounds. And in the process, I found a place to *live*. A place where I feel needed, where I feel valued. A place that feels like home." He reached across the table, his hand covering hers once more, his touch a warm, grounding presence. "And you, Mara," he said, his voice laced with a profound sincerity, "you are a significant part of that. You've made me feel... seen. Truly seen. And that's a gift I never expected to receive."

Mara felt a tremor run through her at his words. His honesty was disarming, his vulnerability a powerful testament to the connection they were building. She understood the ache of loss, the long, lonely road of grief, and the immense courage it took to emerge from its shadow and find a new path. His journey mirrored her own in so many ways, the shared experience of finding solace and purpose after profound personal upheaval.

"Eli," she began, her voice thick with emotion, "I... I feel the same way. When I first started the Haven, it was my way of finding purpose after... well, after my own difficult chapter. It was my anchor. But it was also a very solitary endeavor for a long time. I was so focused on keeping everything afloat, on protecting the animals, that I sometimes forgot about the need for... for connection. For myself." She squeezed his hand gently. "And you, with your steady presence, your willingness to dive in, your incredible ability to fix almost anything, and your... your heart. You've brought a sense of balance to the Haven, and to me. You've helped me remember that it's not just about saving these animals, but about building something sustainable, something that nourishes everyone involved. You've helped me feel... less alone in it all."

The shared confession hung in the air, a palpable manifestation of their deepening bond. It wasn't just about shared work or a common vision anymore; it was about a mutual recognition of their individual journeys, their shared resilience, and the unexpected sanctuary they had found in each other and in the Haven. The loss Eli had spoken of, the raw vulnerability he had displayed, had not created a chasm between them, but a bridge, forged from empathy and understanding. It was a testament to the fact that sometimes, it takes experiencing deep sorrow to truly appreciate the profound beauty of connection and belonging.

He looked at her, his eyes reflecting a depth of emotion that made her breath catch. "And I think," he continued, his voice a low rumble, "that is why this place, and this... this feeling between us, is so important. It's not just about rebuilding a sanctuary for animals. It's about rebuilding ourselves. About finding a place where we can finally exhale, and just... be. And knowing that I'm not the only one who understands that journey, who has walked a similar path, makes it all the more precious."

He released her hand, but his gaze remained steady, a silent promise hanging between them. "The work ahead is still significant, of course. The Haven needs constant attention, and the community still has a long way to go in fully embracing its role as a partner in our efforts. But now, it feels different. It feels... achievable. Because I'm not doing it alone anymore. And I don't think you are either."

Mara felt a warmth spread through her, a sense of profound gratitude for his presence, for his understanding. The darkness of his past, the pain he had carried, had not defined him; it had shaped him into the compassionate, resilient man he was today. And in sharing it with her, he had given her a deeper appreciation for the journey they were embarking on together. The sea air, carrying the scent of the ocean and the promise of a new dawn, seemed to whisper its assent to their shared understanding, to the quiet hope that had taken root between them in the heart of Port Blossom. This was more than just a shared meal; it was a shared understanding, a foundation built on the bedrock of shared experience and mutual healing, a testament to the enduring power of resilience and the quiet, transformative grace of finding home, and perhaps, finding love, in the most unexpected of harbors.

His journey, he explained, had been a series of determined efforts to shed the weight of his past, each move a deliberate attempt to outrun the persistent echo of what he had lost. He spoke of the initial shock, the numbing disbelief that had followed his fiancée's death. It had been a loss so profound, so shattering, that it had rendered him incapable of staying in the place that held so many shared memories. The familiar streets, the shared laughter, the very air they had breathed together – it had all become a source of unbearable pain. So, he had packed a single suitcase and left, not with a destination in mind, but with a desperate need for distance, for anonymity, for a chance to simply exist without the constant reminder of his grief.

"I was looking for a fresh start, of course," Eli continued, his voice lower now, a more reflective tone. "But I think, more than anything, I was looking for a distraction. Something to occupy my mind, to keep the memories at bay. I threw myself into work, any work that would take me. Manual labor was often the easiest. It was physically demanding, and it left me too exhausted to dwell on the emotional turmoil. I worked on construction sites, helping to build houses, bridges, anything that required strong hands and a willingness to follow orders. I learned to appreciate the tangible results of my labor, the satisfaction of seeing something concrete take shape under my hands. It was a welcome contrast to the intangible nature of my own emotional landscape, which felt like a constant state of flux."

He paused, taking a sip of his wine. "There were times when I'd find myself in small towns, places that felt a world away from where I'd started. I'd get a temporary job, live in a rented room, and for a while, it would feel almost... normal. I could almost forget. But then, inevitably, a familiar song on the radio, the smell of a particular flower, or even just a certain quality of light in the evening sky would trigger a wave of memories, and I'd be back where I started, the grief a fresh wound all over again. It was exhausting, this constant battle against my own mind."

He recalled one particular stint working in a coastal town in Maine. The relentless gray skies and the harsh, biting wind had initially mirrored his internal state. He'd found work on a fishing boat, the hardscrabble life of the fishermen appealing to his need for grueling physicality and a sense of shared hardship. "There was a certain camaraderie among those men," he said, a faint smile touching his lips. "They understood the risks, the unpredictable nature of their livelihood, and the importance of looking out for one another. I found a certain comfort in that, in being part of a crew, even if I was still keeping a part of myself hidden away. They respected the sea, and they respected each other. It was a different kind of community than I was used to, one built on necessity and mutual reliance rather than deep personal connection. I learned a lot about resilience from them, about accepting what you can't control and making the best of it."

However, even that community, as welcoming as it was in its own way, couldn't hold him. The restlessness always returned, a quiet hum of dissatisfaction that urged him onward. He spoke of a period in Colorado, working at a ski resort. The stark beauty of the mountains, the crisp, clean air, offered a different kind of solace. He learned to ski, finding a temporary exhilaration in the speed and the controlled descent down challenging slopes. "It was a different kind of escape," he admitted. "A thrill-seeking, adrenaline-fueled attempt to feel alive, to override the lingering numbness. But even then, I knew it wasn't a sustainable solution. It was just another temporary fix."

He then recounted a time he had spent working for a small, independent bookstore in a bustling city. Surrounded by stories, by the accumulated wisdom and imagination of countless authors, he had hoped for some kind of intellectual salve. "I loved being around books," he said. "The quiet reverence of the place, the smell of old paper and ink. I would lose myself for hours, reading anything and everything, trying to find answers, or at least, a different perspective. But even surrounded by all those words, my own story felt like an unfinished, unwritten manuscript. I was an observer, a reader, but not yet a participant in my own narrative."

It was during this period of extensive travel and varied experiences that he had begun to feel a deeper, more unsettling realization dawning. He wasn't just looking for a place to escape to; he was searching for a place to *be*. A place where the past didn't define his present, and where the future felt not like a looming threat, but a promising possibility. He had seen so many places, met so many people, but he had never truly felt rooted. He was always the outsider, the one who would eventually move on. This pervasive sense of transience began to wear him down, not just emotionally, but fundamentally. It chipped away at his sense of self, leaving him feeling adrift and disconnected from his own life.

"And then," Eli said, his gaze meeting Mara's with a quiet intensity, "I stumbled upon an article about the Haven. It was in a regional publication, detailing the ongoing efforts to rebuild after a particularly devastating storm. The focus on rescue, rehabilitation, and providing a safe haven for animals in need... it struck a chord. It was a mission that felt inherently good, inherently worthwhile. And the description of Port Blossom itself – a small, resilient coastal town, a community that pulled together in times of crisis – it sounded like the antithesis of the rootless existence I had been leading."

He leaned back in his chair, a thoughtful expression on his face. "I applied for a position, not really expecting much. I thought I'd come, lend a hand for a few months, and then, who knows? But from the moment I arrived, something felt different. The air here, the ocean, the sheer determination of the people who were dedicated to the Haven... it was palpable. And then, as I started to get involved, to really work and contribute, I began to feel a sense of purpose that had been missing for so long. It wasn't just about moving objects or performing tasks; it was about contributing to something meaningful, something that had a direct, positive impact."

His voice softened as he spoke of her. "And then I met you, Mara. And everything shifted again. I saw the passion you had, the unwavering dedication, the sheer force of will that you poured into this place. It wasn't just a job for you; it was a calling. And it inspired me. It made me want to be more than just a volunteer, more than just a temporary resident. It made me want to be a part of this. Of Port Blossom. Of the Haven. And, if you'd have me," he added, a hopeful note entering his voice, "of your life."

The vulnerability in his confession, the open acknowledgment of his past struggles and his present feelings, created a profound sense of connection. Mara felt a warmth spread through her, a deep understanding of his journey. She saw how the loss he had experienced had not broken him, but had instead forged him into a man of immense resilience and compassion. His quest for a place to belong had led him, perhaps unexpectedly, to the very place that offered solace and purpose, and to the woman who understood the quiet strength it took to rebuild a life, piece by piece. The shared experience of healing, of finding home after personal devastation, was a powerful and unspoken bond that now tied them together, making the burgeoning feelings between them all the more potent and real. He had not just found a job; he had found a sanctuary, and in doing so, he had opened the door for Mara to find a new kind of happiness as well.

Mara found herself contemplating the unhurried rhythm of their burgeoning relationship, a stark contrast to the frantic pace of her past. It wasn't a race, not a frantic dash towards an inevitable conclusion, but a gentle stroll through a blooming meadow. There was an unspoken agreement between them, a quiet understanding that allowed their connection to unfold naturally, like the unfurling of a delicate fern frond. No pressure, no anxious anticipation of what was to come next, only the steady, comforting presence of each other. It was a pace that suited her, a pace that allowed her to breathe, to let the walls she had so carefully constructed around her heart to slowly, almost imperceptibly, crumble.

She realized, with a profound sense of relief, that this slow, steady growth was precisely what she needed. Her previous relationships had often felt like a whirlwind, a chaotic storm that swept her off her feet before she had a chance to truly understand what was happening. There had been grand declarations, promises made under moonlit skies, and a relentless push for a future that, in hindsight, had felt premature and ultimately unsustainable. But with Eli, it was different. This connection felt safe, authentic, and deeply rooted in a shared understanding that transcended mere words. It was built on a foundation of shared values, a mutual respect for each other's pasts, and a quiet appreciation for the present moment. This gradual unfolding allowed her to let her guard down, not in a sudden, reckless surrender, but in a slow, deliberate embrace of the comfort he offered.

She remembered the initial stages of her previous serious relationship, how quickly things had escalated. The whirlwind romance, the grand gestures, the feeling of being swept off her feet – it had all been intoxicating, a heady mix of excitement and perceived destiny. But beneath the surface, there had been a disconnect, a subtle dissonance that she had, in her eagerness to believe in the fairy tale, overlooked. When the dust settled, and the initial infatuation waned, the cracks had begun to show. They had rushed into a commitment, a shared life, before they had truly known each other, before they had even begun to understand the depths of each other's souls. The pressure to conform, to fit into the expected narrative of a couple moving forward, had been immense, and she had found herself stifled, her own needs and hesitations buried beneath the weight of expectation. This time, with Eli, there was no such pressure. They were simply existing, together, their lives intertwining like vines reaching for the sun, finding nourishment and support in each other's presence.

Mara traced the rim of her teacup, the warmth seeping into her fingertips. She thought about how Eli never pushed, never rushed. When they spent time together, it was with a shared intention of simply being. Sometimes it was working side-by-side at the Haven, the comfortable silence punctuated by the sounds of their labor and the occasional shared smile. Other times, it was quiet evenings spent on her porch, watching the stars emerge, their conversation drifting from the mundane to the deeply personal, without ever feeling forced. He listened, truly listened, to her words, her silences, her unspoken thoughts. And she, in turn, found herself opening up to him in ways she hadn't thought possible. There was a gentle acceptance in his gaze, a non-judgmental presence that allowed her to be vulnerable without fear.

This sense of ease was something Mara had craved for so long. Her past experiences had left her with a lingering wariness, a fear of being hurt, of being misunderstood. She had learned to protect herself, to build emotional fortresses that were difficult to breach. But Eli, with his steady kindness and his unwavering sincerity, had found a way to gently dismantle those defenses, not by force, but by offering a safe harbor. He had shown her that vulnerability didn't have to be a weakness, but a bridge to deeper connection. The way he spoke of his own past, of his own struggles, had been a revelation. He had shared his pain without fanfare, his resilience a quiet testament to his strength. This openness had created a space for her to reciprocate, to share her own fears and insecurities, knowing that she would be met with understanding, not judgment.

She remembered a specific evening, not long ago, when they had been walking along the beach after a particularly long day at the Haven. The sun had dipped below the horizon, painting the sky in hues of orange and purple, and the air was thick with the scent of salt and kelp. Mara had been unusually quiet, lost in her own thoughts. Eli, sensing her mood, had simply taken her hand, his touch warm and reassuring. They had walked in comfortable silence for a while, the only sound the gentle lapping of waves against the shore. Then, he had stopped and turned to her, his eyes reflecting the fading light. "You know," he had said softly, "you don't have to carry it all alone." His words, so simple and yet so profound, had resonated deeply within her. It was an acknowledgment of her burdens, an offering of support without obligation. In that moment, she had felt a profound sense of peace, a quiet gratitude for his understanding, for his willingness to share her load.

This feeling of shared burden, of not having to navigate life's complexities single-handedly, was a revelation. For so long, Mara had been the one in charge, the one holding everything together. The responsibility of the Haven, the weight of its needs and the care of its animals, had often felt overwhelming. She had learned to rely solely on herself, to believe that she was the only one capable of managing it all. Eli's presence had begun to shift that perspective. He didn't try to take over, but he offered his strength, his expertise, his unwavering support. He was a partner, not a rescuer, and that made all the difference. He saw her not just as the dedicated woman running the Haven, but as a person who needed and deserved care, support, and genuine affection.

Her past relationships had often been characterized by a subtle imbalance of power, where one person felt constantly responsible for the other's happiness, or where one person's needs consistently overshadowed the other's. This often led to resentment, to a sense of being taken for granted, or to an overwhelming feeling of inadequacy. With Eli, there was a beautiful reciprocity. They gave and received in equal measure, their needs and desires acknowledged and respected. He celebrated her successes, offering genuine praise and encouragement, and he was there to offer comfort and support during her moments of doubt or frustration. It was a partnership built on mutual admiration, a rare and precious thing.

Mara found herself smiling as she thought about their shared laughter. It was a sound that had become increasingly frequent, a melody that punctuated the quiet moments of their days. They found humor in the everyday, in the quirks of the animals at the Haven, in the amusing misunderstandings that sometimes arose with the townsfolk, and even in their own shared experiences. These moments of levity were like little bursts of sunshine, warming her from the inside out. They reminded her that life, even with its challenges, was meant to be enjoyed, to be savored. And with Eli by her side, the joy felt amplified, the laughter more genuine.

The unhurried nature of their connection also meant that they were discovering each other in layers, peeling back the surface to reveal the depths beneath. They weren't rushing to define their relationship, to label it with a term that might create premature expectations. Instead, they were simply allowing it to evolve organically, guided by their feelings and their shared experiences. Mara appreciated this freedom, this ability to explore their connection without the constraints of societal norms or personal anxieties. It allowed her to be truly present, to appreciate each moment for what it was, without worrying about where it was leading.

She remembered a conversation they'd had a few weeks prior, when Eli had asked her about her dreams, not just for the Haven, but for herself. She had hesitated at first, unsure how to articulate aspirations that had long been dormant, buried beneath years of hard work and self-reliance. But Eli had waited patiently, his gaze steady and encouraging. When she had finally spoken, it had been a hesitant outpouring of forgotten desires, of quiet longings she had almost convinced herself were unattainable. He had listened intently, not interrupting, not offering solutions, but simply absorbing her words, his presence a silent affirmation of her worthiness. And when she had finished, he had simply taken her hand and said, "We'll get there." It was a promise, not of a magical fix, but of a shared journey, a commitment to working towards those dreams together.

This gentle pace, this unhurried unfolding, was not just about the absence of pressure; it was about the presence of something far more profound. It was about the cultivation of trust, the deepening of understanding, and the slow, steady building of a bond that felt both strong and fragile, precious and enduring. Mara realized that she was not just falling in love with Eli, but falling in love with the version of herself that emerged when she was with him – a version that was more open, more confident, more hopeful. He had helped her to see that healing wasn't a destination, but a process, and that sometimes, the most important step was simply finding someone with whom to walk that path. The gentle rhythm of their days together, the quiet moments of shared understanding, the comfortable silences, and the easy laughter – all of it was weaving a tapestry of connection that was far more beautiful and meaningful than any rushed, passionate whirlwind could ever be. It was a love story being written not in grand pronouncements, but in the quiet, steady beat of two hearts finding their rhythm, together, in the peaceful harbor of Port Blossom.

The familiar crunch of gravel under her worn boots was a comforting counterpoint to the swirling emotions inside Mara as she made her way home. The chill of the late evening air kissed her cheeks, a welcome sensation after the warmth of Eli's presence that had lingered long after he'd left her side. It wasn't just the physical warmth, though that had been a pleasant anchor in the fading daylight. It was an inner warmth, a radiant glow that seemed to emanate from a place deep within her, a place she'd thought long dormant. The moonlight, a soft silver wash on the deserted path, seemed to mirror the burgeoning luminescence of her own spirit. She tilted her head back, a genuine, unforced smile gracing her lips, and let the cool night air fill her lungs. For the first time in what felt like an eternity, the vast expanse of the sky didn't feel lonely; it felt like an invitation.

A peculiar giddiness had taken root, a sensation that made her stomach perform little acrobatic feats, like a troupe of tiny, delighted dancers. Butterflies. She hadn't felt this fluttery, this breathless anticipation, since she was a teenager, giddy with the thrill of a first crush. Except this wasn't the uncertain, anxious flutter of a girl trying to decipher mixed signals. This was a joyful, buoyant sensation, a feeling of pure, unadulterated hope. The prospect of a future, a shared future, with Eli, was no longer a daunting, shadowy unknown. It was a landscape painted with the vibrant hues of possibility, a landscape she found herself eager to explore. The fear that had been her constant companion for so long, the one that whispered doubts and warned of impending heartbreak, had receded, replaced by a quiet, unwavering optimism. It was a fragile hope, perhaps, like the first tentative sprout pushing through hardened earth, but it was undeniably there, and it was beautiful.

She found herself replaying moments from their earlier conversation, the easy flow of words, the shared glances that spoke volumes more than spoken sentences. Eli's quiet understanding, his ability to see beyond her guarded exterior and touch the core of her being, had chipped away at the fortress she'd so diligently built. Each interaction was like a gentle hand reaching through a gap in the stones, offering not a battering ram, but a bridge. He had a way of making her feel seen, truly seen, without the need for elaborate explanations or desperate defenses. It was a rare gift, and one she was beginning to treasure with an almost fierce protectiveness. The thought of that protection, of guarding this nascent feeling, was a new one. Her past had taught her to expect the worst, to brace for the inevitable disappointment, but this felt different. This felt like something worth holding onto, something worth nurturing.

The moon seemed to hang heavier in the sky tonight, a benevolent observer casting its ethereal glow upon her solitary walk. It was a familiar sight, one she'd seen countless times before, yet tonight it held a new significance. It was a beacon, a silent promise of continuity, of cycles that always returned, of light that always followed darkness. And in its steady radiance, Mara found a reflection of the growing light within her. She had spent so long dwelling in the shadows, tending to the wounds of her past, that she had almost forgotten how to bask in the sun. Eli, with his steady presence and unwavering kindness, had gently guided her back into its warmth. He hadn't demanded it, hadn't forced her out of the darkness, but had simply offered his hand, a silent invitation to step into the light together.

She imagined the days ahead, the ordinary moments that would undoubtedly become extraordinary because he was a part of them. A shared cup of coffee in the morning, the comfortable silence as they both worked on their respective tasks, the quiet conversations that unfolded naturally, without pretense. These were the building blocks of a life, she realized, the small, seemingly insignificant moments that, woven together, created a tapestry of belonging. Her previous relationships had been characterized by grand gestures and dramatic declarations, a frantic pursuit of a future that always felt just out of reach. They had been about fireworks and grand pronouncements, but they had lacked the quiet, steady hum of genuine connection that she was now experiencing with Eli. This was not a fleeting spark; this felt like a hearth, a steady, enduring flame that offered warmth and comfort.

A soft breeze rustled the leaves of the ancient oak trees lining the road, their branches reaching like welcoming arms towards the heavens. Mara felt a kinship with them, with their resilience, their quiet strength. They had weathered countless storms, stood tall against the fiercest winds, yet they continued to reach for the light, their leaves unfurling anew each spring. It was a powerful metaphor for her own journey, a journey that had felt like a relentless storm for so long. But now, standing under the benevolent gaze of the moon, with the scent of damp earth and pine needles filling the air, she felt a sense of peace settle over her. The storms had not broken her; they had, in their own way, forged her. And now, perhaps, it was time for the sun.

She smiled again, a broader, more confident smile this time, as she thought of the future. It wasn't a fully formed picture, not yet. There were still uncertainties, still aspects of her past that lingered like faint shadows. But the fear of those shadows was diminishing. The light that Eli brought into her life was strong enough to push them back, to make them seem less menacing, less all-consuming. He offered not a magical solution to all her problems, but a steadfast presence, a partner to walk alongside her as she navigated the complexities of her own healing and the unfolding of their relationship. It was the offer of shared journey that resonated most deeply. The idea that she didn't have to face the unknown alone, that there was someone willing to take those steps with her, was a profound comfort.

The path ahead seemed to stretch out before her, bathed in the soft, silver light of the moon. It was a path she had walked countless times before, but tonight, it felt entirely new. It was a path leading not just to her front door, but to a future brimming with possibility, a future where laughter was more frequent, where vulnerability was met with understanding, and where hope was not a fragile wish, but a quiet, steady certainty. The butterflies in her stomach, no longer a source of nervous trepidation, danced with a joyful anticipation. They were a testament to the burgeoning happiness within her, a sweet reminder that after a long, dark night, the dawn was finally breaking. And as she neared her home, Mara felt a profound sense of gratitude for the journey that had brought her to this moment, and for the gentle, steady hand that was now reaching out to guide her towards whatever lay ahead. The quiet promise of a shared future, whispered on the night air, felt more precious than any grand declaration. It was the promise of simply being, together, and for Mara, that was everything.

She embraced the lightness, the giddy flutter of her heart, and looked up at the moon, a silent acknowledgment of the beautiful, hopeful dawn that was just beginning to break. The prospect of tomorrow, and the tomorrows after that, held a sweet, exhilarating promise, a promise she was finally ready to embrace.

CHAPTER NINE
CHARTING THE FUTURE

The air in Mara's small kitchen was warm, not just from the gentle hum of the refrigerator or the lingering heat of the evening sun that had slanted through the window, but from a different kind of warmth entirely. It was the effervescence of shared possibility, the quiet hum of two hearts beating in sync, contemplating a future that, just weeks ago, had seemed an impossible dream. Eli sat across from her at the worn oak table, his gaze steady and full of an open affection that still, after all this time, made her heart give a little skip. The remnants of their shared meal, a simple pasta dish they'd whipped up together, sat between them, a testament to the comfortable domesticity that was beginning to bloom.

"So," Eli began, his voice a low rumble that always seemed to settle her. He picked up a stray noodle with his fork, twirling it thoughtfully. "We've talked about dreams, about where we want to be. But we haven't really... mapped it out. Not properly."

Mara nodded, a slow, deliberate movement. The word "mapped" resonated with her. It implied intention, planning, a deliberate charting of a course. It was a far cry from the haphazard, often painful, journey her life had been. "No, we haven't. It's all still a little... nebulous. Wonderful, but nebulous." She met his eyes, a flicker of something akin to playful challenge in her own. "Where do you see us, Eli, a year from now? Five years?"

He leaned back, a thoughtful smile playing on his lips. "Honestly? I see us here. In Port Blossom. Maybe not in this exact apartment," he gestured around the cozy, if slightly cramped, space, "but... rooted. I see us building something here. You, with your gallery – or perhaps a bigger one, one that can showcase more of the local talent you're so passionate about. And me..." He paused, his gaze drifting out the window towards the deepening twilight. "Me, still doing my work, but with more time. More freedom. Time for... us."

The unspoken "us" hung in the air, a beautiful, tangible entity. Mara felt a prickle of emotion behind her eyes. "A bigger gallery," she murmured, the words tasting sweet. "I've thought about that. About having space for workshops, for bringing in artists from further afield. And about supporting the people here, giving them a platform they deserve." Her own aspirations, long buried under layers of practicality and fear, were starting to unfurl, encouraged by his belief.

"Exactly," Eli affirmed, leaning forward again. "And for me, it's about finding that balance. I love what I do, I love the challenge, the problem-solving. But I'm also realizing that life isn't just about the next project, the next win. It's about the people you share it with. I want to be able to be here for you, Mara. For the quiet mornings, for the spontaneous adventures, for the days when the world feels a little too much." He reached across the table, his hand covering hers. His touch was warm, grounding. "I want a life that feels... lived, not just accomplished."

"Lived," Mara repeated softly, the word a balm to a soul that had felt merely endured for so long. "That resonates. I think... I think I'm finally learning what that means. It means not just surviving, but thriving. And I want to thrive with you, Eli." She squeezed his hand, her gaze unwavering. "Professionally, I envision growth, of course. I want to see the gallery flourish. But more than that, I want to feel that sense of purpose, that deep satisfaction that comes from creating something meaningful. And I want that for you too. Whatever your next step is, I want to be there, cheering you on, or just being a quiet, steady presence."

He smiled, a genuine, soul-deep smile that crinkled the corners of his eyes. "And I for you. We can be each other's loudest cheerleaders. Imagine it, Mara. You, surrounded by art, by beauty, by the buzz of creativity. And me, with the quiet satisfaction of a job well done, coming home to you. To this." He gestured between them, a silent acknowledgment of the profound connection they had forged. "Maybe we could even look at a house? Something with a bit more space. A garden, perhaps? You'd love a garden."

A garden. The idea bloomed in Mara's mind, vivid and full of life. She pictured climbing roses, herbs that filled the air with their scent, a place where they could both retreat and connect. "A garden," she breathed, a wistful smile touching her lips. "That sounds... perfect. Somewhere we can put down roots. Literally and figuratively." She traced the lines on his palm with her thumb. "And what about your work, Eli? You've achieved so much, but is there something else you've always wanted to explore, now that you're thinking about balance?"

He considered this, his brow furrowed in thought. "There are always new challenges, new innovations in my field. But lately, I've been thinking more about mentorship. About passing on what I've learned. Perhaps starting a small consultancy, or even teaching at a local college part-time, once things are more settled. It would be a different kind of fulfillment, a slower pace, but one that feels more aligned with where I am now. And it would allow me to be more present."

"Mentorship," Mara echoed, nodding. "That's wonderful, Eli. You have so much to offer. People would learn so much from you, not just about your field, but about integrity, about how to approach challenges with both intelligence and heart." She felt a surge of pride for him, a deep admiration for his evolving perspective. It wasn't just about ambition anymore; it was about impact, about leaving a positive mark. "And imagine the flexibility that would give you. More time for that garden. More time for us."

"More time for you," he corrected gently, his thumb stroking the back of her hand. "That's the most important thing. This isn't about grand pronouncements or ticking off boxes, Mara. It's about building a life that feels good, a life where we can both breathe, and grow, and be truly happy." He paused, his gaze softening. "And I want that for you more than anything. I want to see you truly shine, without any reservations, without any of the shadows that have followed you for so long."

Mara's throat tightened. The shadows. They felt so distant now, so manageable, thanks to his steady presence. "They feel so much smaller now, Eli," she confessed, her voice a little husky. "Like they're losing their power. Because you're here. And because I'm starting to believe, really believe, that I deserve this. This happiness. This future." She met his gaze, her heart full. "I want to talk about the practicalities too, though. About finances, about potential locations for a house, about how we make this work. It's not just about the dreams; it's about the doing."

"Absolutely," he agreed readily. "We need a solid foundation. I've been doing some research into the market here. There are some lovely areas around Port Blossom that are more affordable than people think, especially if we're willing to do a little renovation. And financially, I'm in a good position. We can certainly explore joint accounts, look at mortgages together. It's all part of building that shared future." He spoke with a calm practicality that reassured her. He wasn't just dreaming; he was planning.

"And for the gallery," Mara continued, her mind buzzing with possibilities. "I've been looking at spaces. There's one just off the main square, currently a vacant storefront. It's larger than my current place, and the rent is surprisingly reasonable. It would require some work, but I can see it. Walls painted a warm, inviting white, track lighting... perhaps a small café area in the corner. Imagine the possibilities." Her eyes sparkled with the vision.

"I can see it too," Eli said, his voice full of encouragement. "And I can help. Project management is my second nature, after all. We can tackle renovations together. It'll be our first big project as a team." He grinned. "And think of the satisfaction. You'll have your dream gallery, and I'll have the satisfaction of seeing you achieve it, having played a small part."

"A small part?" Mara laughed, a light, joyful sound. "You'd be the foreman, the architect, the head of operations. And the chief motivator, no doubt." She leaned forward, resting her forehead against his. The closeness was intoxicating, comforting. "This feels... real, Eli. Not just a beautiful thought, but something we can actually build. Together."

"It is real," he confirmed, his voice low and earnest. "And it's just the beginning. We'll have our challenges, of course. Life isn't always smooth sailing. But with us, facing them together, I feel like we can handle anything. We'll build our lives here, brick by brick, dream by dream. We'll create a life that's rich in experience, in love, in shared purpose." He pulled back slightly, his hands framing her face. "We'll make Port Blossom our home, not just a place we live, but a place we've actively created for ourselves."

"A place we've created," Mara repeated, the words resonating deep within her. It wasn't just about finding a place; it was about making it ours. Infusing it with their shared life, their shared dreams. "I like the sound of that. It implies intention, ownership. Not just being swept along, but steering the ship."

"Exactly," Eli said. "And the beauty of it is, we're steering it together. We'll have our individual ambitions, our personal growth, but they'll be interwoven. We'll support each other's journeys, celebrate each other's successes, and lean on each other during the tougher times. That's what partnership is, isn't it? Not just sharing space, but sharing burdens and joys, and building something stronger than either of us could alone."

Mara felt a profound sense of peace settle over her. This was it. This was the clarity she'd craved, the understanding she'd yearned for. It wasn't about grand, sweeping gestures, but about the quiet, consistent commitment to building a life, hand in hand. "It is," she agreed, her voice firm with conviction. "And I'm ready for that. I'm ready to build that life with you, Eli. To chart this course, to face the waves, to find our harbor together."

He smiled, a smile that held the promise of a thousand sunrises. "And I'm ready to navigate those waters with you, my love. We'll make our own sunshine, even on cloudy days." He paused, his gaze thoughtful. "We should set a date. Not for a wedding, not yet," he added with a wink, "but for a more serious sit-down. Perhaps next weekend? We can dedicate a whole afternoon to it. Come with spreadsheets, with wish lists, with all the practicalities and all the dreams. Let's really lay the groundwork."

Mara's heart swelled. The very idea of dedicating an afternoon to planning their future, to openly discussing finances and dreams and tangible steps, felt like a monumental leap. It was a commitment, a declaration of intent that went beyond words. "I'd love that," she said, her voice brimming with emotion. "Spreadsheets and wish lists included. We'll map out our future, chapter by chapter."

"Our story," Eli corrected softly, his thumb caressing her cheek. "Our beautiful, unfolding story. And I can't wait to see what we write next." The silence that fell between them was not empty, but pregnant with anticipation, filled with the quiet hum of shared ambition and the profound certainty of a love that was ready to build, to grow, and to endure. The kitchen, once just a functional space, now felt like the heart of their burgeoning future, a place where the first seeds of their shared life were being sown with intention and with hope. The moonlight, now a more prominent feature as the evening deepened, cast long shadows, but within their warmth, Mara and Eli saw only the promise of a bright, shared dawn.

The moonlight spilled across the worn oak table, illuminating the space where Mara and Eli had meticulously sketched out their dreams. The spreadsheets were neatly stacked, the wish lists tucked away, but the tangible sense of their shared future still hummed in the air. Yet, as Eli's hand rested on hers, a different kind of contemplation began to stir within Mara, a subtle shift in the landscape of her own aspirations. The city, with its frenetic energy and the relentless pursuit of her previous career, felt like a lifetime ago, a distant echo from a past self she barely recognized. The thought of returning, of re-engaging with that world, no longer held the same magnetic pull. It wasn't that she didn't value the experience, the skills she'd honed, but the *drive* that had fueled her then seemed to have been replaced by something softer, something more rooted in connection and purpose.

"It's strange," she mused, tracing the rim of her empty teacup. "I used to think my entire life was defined by my career in the city. It was my identity. And now..." She trailed off, her gaze drifting towards the window, where the gentle rhythm of Port Blossom's night life was a soft counterpoint to the quiet intimacy of their conversation. "Now, it feels so... irrelevant. Like a story I read once, but it wasn't really my own."

Eli's thumb brushed over her knuckles, a silent reassurance. "It was part of your story, Mara. It shaped you. But it doesn't have to be the whole book. Or even the next chapter."

"I know," she said, a sigh escaping her lips. "And I'm so grateful for that. For *us*. For this feeling of freedom to even *consider* a different path. But it's also... daunting. Because for so long, I knew exactly what I was working towards. The next promotion, the next project, the next rung on that ladder. Now, the ladder seems to have disappeared, and I'm standing in a field, with no clear direction, only possibilities stretching out before me."

She turned back to him, her brow furrowed. "I used to love the hustle, the challenge of it all. I thrived on the pressure. But here, in Port Blossom, the pace is different. The values are different.

And I find myself drawn to things I never would have considered before. Like... helping animals." She hesitated, as if the admission itself was a confession of a strange sort. "You know how I've always loved animals? And how I've found myself drawn to Mrs. Gable's cats, and helping out at the animal shelter on weekends? It's not the same as a career, I know, but there's a quiet satisfaction in it that I haven't felt in years."

Eli's expression was open and encouraging. "And what's wrong with that? Why does it have to be a 'career' in the traditional sense to be fulfilling? You have a natural empathy, a gentle touch. People notice that. Animals certainly do. And you're incredibly organized and capable, Mara. Running a gallery requires a lot of those same skills, just applied in a different context."

"But is it enough?" she whispered, the doubt creeping in. "Is it a path? Or is it just... a hobby? I'm afraid of making the wrong choice, of investing my energy in something that doesn't truly lead anywhere. The gallery is one thing. It's a concrete dream we've been building. But this... this feels more like a whisper of an idea, something that might just fade away."

"Mara," Eli said, his voice firm but gentle, taking both her hands in his. His gaze held hers, steady and unwavering. "There is no 'wrong choice' when it comes to finding something that makes your heart feel lighter, that brings you a sense of purpose. You don't have to have it all figured out today. The beauty of this point in our lives is that we can explore. We can experiment. You can spend more time at the shelter, learn more about animal care. Perhaps there are courses you could take online, or even locally, that could build on that interest. You could volunteer at a veterinary clinic, see if that sparks something deeper."

He squeezed her hands reassuringly. "And if it doesn't, that's okay too. You'll have learned something, gained experience. It won't be wasted time. The point is to follow those inklings, those quiet desires, and see where they lead. Don't put pressure on yourself to define it as a 'career' or a 'path' right now. Just call it 'exploration.' Call it 'discovery.' Call it whatever feels less intimidating."

"Exploration," Mara repeated, the word feeling lighter, less burdened. "I like that. But what about the gallery? We've talked about it so much, about the plans, the renovations..."

"And we'll still pursue the gallery," Eli assured her, his voice unwavering. "It's a significant part of our shared vision. But it doesn't have to be the only part. Imagine this, Mara: the gallery thrives, becoming the vibrant hub we envision. And alongside that, you find a way to incorporate your love for animals. Perhaps you could partner with the local shelter for fundraising events, showcase animal-themed art. Or maybe, down the line, you could even consider a smaller, more specialized gallery that focuses on nature and wildlife art, with a portion of proceeds going to conservation efforts. Or, who knows, perhaps your exploration in animal care leads you to a different opportunity entirely. Maybe a role in managing a local rescue organization, or even starting your own small, boutique pet-sitting service, focused on personalized care for animals whose owners are away."

He leaned back, a thoughtful expression on his face. "My point is, Mara, your capabilities are vast. You are intelligent, resourceful, and compassionate. You can excel in so many different arenas. This isn't about choosing one path and discarding all others. It's about seeing how different threads can weave together to create a richer, more textured life. And whatever direction you choose to explore, whatever you decide to pursue, I will be here, supporting you every step of the way. My belief in you isn't conditional on you following a specific career trajectory. It's based on who you are."

His words washed over her, a wave of warmth and validation. The pressure to have everything perfectly defined, perfectly planned, began to dissipate. It was true. She didn't have to have all the answers right now. She had the luxury of time, and more importantly, she had Eli's unwavering support.

"It's just that I've always been the one who had to be so pragmatic, so focused on survival," Mara admitted, her voice soft. "The idea of 'exploring' or 'following passions' felt like a luxury I couldn't afford. I was so afraid of making mistakes, of wasting time and resources. And now, to have the space to even consider something as seemingly 'unproductive' as spending more time with animals... it feels almost decadent."

Eli chuckled, a low, comforting sound. "Mara, your definition of 'productive' has been shaped by a very specific, and perhaps harsh, environment. But a life lived with joy, with connection, with purpose – isn't that the most productive existence of all?

What you're discovering now is that 'productivity' can take many forms. It can be the satisfaction of a well-managed business, like your gallery. It can be the quiet fulfillment of caring for a creature in need. It can be the joy of learning something new. Don't dismiss the value of what brings you happiness and a sense of contribution."

He reached out, gently tucking a stray strand of hair behind her ear. "Think about it. You've already shown incredible resilience and strength in navigating difficult circumstances. That inherent capability is what will allow you to succeed, no matter what path you choose. If you decide to pursue animal care further, you'll bring that same intelligence and drive to it. If you decide it's a fulfilling pastime, that's perfectly valid too. The most important thing is that you feel free to discover what truly resonates with you, without feeling confined by past expectations or future uncertainties."

Mara's gaze softened as she looked at him. He saw her, truly saw her, beyond the labels and the past. He saw the potential for growth, for evolving desires, and he embraced it with open arms. "You make it sound so simple," she murmured. "Just... be, and explore."

"It's not always simple," Eli conceded. "Life has its complexities. But with the right foundation, and the right partner, you have the freedom to navigate those complexities with grace and courage. We have that foundation now, Mara. We have each other. And we have the time and the resources to explore. So, yes. Be. And explore. And don't be afraid to change your mind, or to discover new interests along the way. That's what growth is."

He leaned closer, his eyes twinkling. "And who knows? Maybe your exploration into animal care will lead to a fantastic business idea. A specialized animal therapy program for children? A high-end, eco-friendly pet spa? The possibilities are endless, and they stem from genuine interest. Don't discount the power of that."

A faint smile touched Mara's lips. The idea of a "boutique pet-sitting service" or "animal therapy" hadn't even crossed her mind before, yet the thought of it, combined with her genuine affection for animals, sparked a flicker of genuine excitement. It wasn't the grand ambition of her city career, but it held a different kind of appeal – a warmth, a connection, a sense of making a tangible, positive difference in the lives of both animals and their people.

"It's just... I've spent so long focused on a certain type of success," she admitted. "A certain kind of validation. And the idea of pursuing something that might be considered less 'prestigious,' or even just different, feels like a vulnerability."

"But vulnerability is where so much of our strength lies, Mara," Eli countered gently. "It's in admitting what we don't know, what we want to learn, what brings us joy. That vulnerability is what allows us to connect, to grow, to build something real. Your past experiences have given you an incredible capacity for resilience, for determination. Those qualities will serve you, no matter what you choose to do. And if your 'exploration' leads you to a fulfilling career in animal care, or if it simply remains a source of joy and comfort in your life, both are valid and valuable. My only hope is that you feel empowered to pursue what truly lights you up, without reservation."

He paused, his gaze sweeping over her, filled with an affection that never failed to steady her. "We'll build the gallery. That's a solid plan, and I'm excited about it. But alongside that, give yourself permission to follow those other sparks. Spend more time at the shelter. Read those books on animal behavior. See where the curiosity takes you. There's no timeline, Mara. This is your life, and we're building it together, with all its different facets. Your passion for art and beauty, your love for animals, your innate drive to create and contribute – all of it is part of who you are, and all of it has a place in the future we're building."

Mara leaned her head against his shoulder, a sense of peace settling over her. The future no longer felt like a rigid blueprint, but a fluid canvas. The city's relentless demands and her former identity were fading into the background, replaced by the gentle rhythm of Port Blossom and the myriad of possibilities that lay within her reach. The gallery was a definite, tangible goal, a shared dream she was eager to bring to life. But alongside it, the quiet hum of another potential path, one woven with compassion and a love for the natural world, was beginning to resonate, and for the first time, she felt a genuine freedom to explore it, without apology or self-doubt. With Eli by her side, the uncertainty of her path felt less like a void and more like an open invitation.

The aroma of freshly baked bread and sun-ripened berries hung in the air, a fragrant symphony that greeted Mara and Eli as they ambled into the heart of Port Blossom's Saturday market. It was a weekly ritual that had quickly become one of Mara's favorite aspects of their new life – a deliberate counterpoint to the hurried, transactional interactions of her past. Here, the pace was dictated by the gentle unfolding of the morning, the murmur of conversations, and the shared appreciation for the bounty of the land and the ingenuity of its people.

Stalls, draped with colorful awnings, lined the cobblestone square, each a miniature universe of artisanal treasures. Piles of ruby-red tomatoes, their skins gleaming under the dappled sunlight, sat beside baskets overflowing with plump blueberries and tart raspberries. Golden honey, in jars of varying sizes, promised sweetness, while fragrant bundles of lavender and rosemary released their calming scents into the breeze. It wasn't just the produce that captivated Mara; it was the spirit of the place. Farmers, their hands calloused but their smiles genuine, stood proudly beside their wares, eager to share stories of their harvest and the care that went into cultivating each item. Artisans displayed their crafts with quiet pride – hand-knitted scarves in intricate patterns, pottery glazed in earthy tones, and delicate jewelry fashioned from local shells and sea glass.

Eli, his arm casually slung around Mara's shoulders, guided them through the gentle throng. He seemed as at ease here as he did on his boat, a natural connector, a man who appreciated the simple, tangible beauty of the world around him. "See that stall?" he murmured, nodding towards a display of cheeses. "Mrs. Henderson makes the most incredible goat cheese. You have to try it."

They made their way over, and a woman with kind eyes and a flour-dusted apron greeted them warmly. She offered them a sliver of creamy, tangy cheese, its flavor a revelation. Mara found herself engaging in a conversation about the local flora, how the sea air influenced the herbs, and the specific blend of pastures that contributed to the cheese's unique character. It felt less like a transaction and more like a shared exploration of taste and origin.

Further along, a stall dedicated to homemade jams and preserves caught Mara's eye. Jars of apricot, plum, and fig, their vibrant hues promising a taste of summer sunshine, were arranged artfully. The vendor, a cheerful woman named Clara, explained the recipes, passed down through generations, and offered Mara a tiny spoon laden with a glistening strawberry-rhubarb jam. The sweetness was perfectly balanced by a hint of tartness, and Mara bought a jar on the spot, already envisioning it spread on a warm scone.

"It's amazing, isn't it?" Mara said, turning to Eli, a genuine smile gracing her lips. "The sheer dedication. Every single person here has poured their heart into what they're offering. It's so different from the sterile efficiency of a supermarket, where you have no idea where anything came from or who made it."

Eli squeezed her shoulder. "Exactly. This is what community looks like. People supporting each other, sharing their talents. It's the heart of a town like Port Blossom."

They paused to admire a collection of handcrafted wooden toys at a nearby booth. A man, his hands expertly carving a small bird, explained the provenance of the wood – sustainably sourced from local forests. Mara found herself drawn to the intricate details, the smooth finish, the obvious care that had gone into each piece. She imagined a child's delight in holding one of these creations, a tangible link to the natural world and the skill of a local craftsman.

"This is beautiful," she commented, running a finger over the smooth curve of a wooden train. "It feels so... real. So unlike the disposable plastic toys you see everywhere else."

The woodworker nodded, his eyes crinkling at the corners. "That's the idea. Something that lasts, something that has a story. Something made with intention."

As they continued their wanderings, the lively atmosphere of the market seemed to wrap around them, a comforting embrace. They sampled flaky pastries dusted with cinnamon, sipped on freshly squeezed orange juice, and even debated the merits of different varieties of heirloom apples. The simple act of sharing these small pleasures, surrounded by the gentle hum of activity and the friendly faces of vendors and fellow shoppers, felt deeply grounding.

Mara found herself observing the interactions around her – the easy camaraderie between vendors, the laughter of children chasing pigeons, the quiet conversations between neighbors catching up on the week's happenings. It was a tapestry of everyday life, woven with threads of connection and shared experience. There was an authenticity here, a lack of pretense, that resonated deeply with her. The pressure to perform, to impress, to maintain a certain image – all the burdens she had carried from her previous life – seemed to melt away in the warm embrace of the Port Blossom market.

"You know," Mara mused, picking up a perfectly formed peach, its skin a blush of rose and gold, "I used to think that success was all about grand achievements, about climbing the corporate ladder, about accumulating wealth and prestige. I saw a life of quiet contentment as... well, as settling. But here..." She gestured around them, encompassing the vibrant stalls, the friendly faces, the sheer abundance of simple joys. "Here, I see a different kind of richness. A richness of connection, of craft, of appreciating the present moment."

Eli smiled, his gaze steady and understanding. "It's a lesson Port Blossom teaches us well. That fulfillment doesn't always come from the loudest applause or the highest stakes. Sometimes, it's in the quiet satisfaction of creating something beautiful, of nurturing something good, of simply being present and enjoying the journey."

They stopped at a stall that sold an array of colorful, hand-painted ceramics. Mugs adorned with whimsical sea creatures, bowls glazed in vibrant ocean blues, and small trinket dishes painted with intricate floral designs. Mara found herself drawn to a set of four mugs, each one uniquely decorated with a different local bird – a robin, a kingfisher, a wren, and a seagull. They felt personal, a reflection of the very town they were exploring.

"These are lovely," she said to the artist, a young woman with paint smudges on her cheek. "They feel like Port Blossom."

The artist beamed. "Thank you! I try to capture the spirit of the coast, the little wonders you see every day. The kingfisher fishing in the harbor, the robin in your garden..."

Mara bought the set, picturing them filled with steaming coffee on crisp mornings, a gentle reminder of their new home and the beauty that surrounded them. It was these small, tangible pieces of Port Blossom that were beginning to weave themselves into the fabric of her life, creating a sense of belonging that felt both profound and deeply comforting.

As the morning wore on, and the crowds began to thin, Mara and Eli found a quiet bench overlooking the harbor, the gentle lapping of waves a soothing soundtrack to their conversation. They unpacked the goodies they had gathered – the goat cheese, the strawberry-rhubarb jam, a loaf of crusty sourdough, and the hand-painted mugs. It was a feast, not just of food, but of shared experience.

"This," Eli said, holding up a slice of bread to the light, "is what it's all about. Simple things, enjoyed together. No agenda, no pressure, just... being."

Mara leaned her head on his shoulder, a profound sense of contentment settling over her. The grand plans for the gallery, the lingering questions about her future path, all of it felt less daunting when grounded in these moments of shared joy. The market, with its vibrant energy and its celebration of local life, had offered her more than just delicious food and beautiful crafts. It had offered her a tangible glimpse into the soul of Port Blossom, a soul that resonated with her own evolving aspirations. It was a reminder that a life rich in meaning could be built not just on grand ambitions, but on the appreciation of simple pleasures, the cultivation of connections, and the quiet celebration of community. The future, she realized, wasn't just about what she *did*, but about who she was becoming, and the shared appreciation for the small, beautiful things that made life truly worth living.

The laughter of children, a bright, uninhibited sound, echoed from the small playground adjacent to the town square as Mara and Eli strolled hand-in-hand. The aroma of salt and brine from the nearby harbor mingled with the sweet scent of honeysuckle climbing the weathered fences, a perfume that had become inextricably linked in Mara's mind with this burgeoning sense of peace. Just yesterday, they'd been lost in the vibrant tapestry of the Saturday market, a sensory feast that had offered Mara not just delicious treats and handcrafted treasures, but a profound glimpse into the heart of Port Blossom. It was a place where life unfolded with a deliberate rhythm, where connections were forged over shared meals and mutual appreciation for the land and its bounty. Eli, with his easy charm and genuine warmth, had been her compass, guiding her through its bustling lanes and introducing her to its friendly faces.

Now, as they ambled, Mara felt a new dimension unfolding in her understanding of Eli, and by extension, of the life she was beginning to envision for herself here. The market had showcased his connection to the tangible aspects of Port Blossom – the farmers, the artisans, the simple pleasures. But as they approached a cluster of weathered fishing boats bobbing gently at their moorings, Eli's gaze shifted, a subtle softening around his eyes as he pointed towards a group of figures gathered near a brightly painted shed.

"That's Liam," Eli said, his voice laced with affection. "He's been fishing these waters longer than anyone. Taught me half of what I know about reading the tides." He then gestured towards a woman meticulously mending a net, her movements practiced and economical. "And that's Sarah. Runs the little bakery down by the lighthouse. Makes the best blueberry scones you'll ever taste."

Mara's heart gave a little lurch of something akin to gratitude. It wasn't just the mention of names, but the way Eli spoke of them – as integral threads in the fabric of his life, not as mere acquaintances. As they drew closer, Liam, a man whose face was a roadmap of sun-kissed wrinkles and sea-battered resilience, looked up and his weathered features broke into a wide, welcoming grin.

"Eli! And who's this lovely lady you've finally decided to show off?" he boomed, his voice carrying a hearty, infectious warmth. Sarah, wiping her hands on her apron, echoed his sentiment with a knowing smile.

"Mara, it's so good to finally meet you properly," Sarah said, her eyes twinkling. "Eli's told us so much. Mostly good things, I promise," she added with a playful nudge to Eli's arm.

Mara felt an immediate sense of ease, a disarming lack of pretense that was becoming characteristic of Port Blossom. "It's wonderful to meet you both," she replied, her own smile genuine. "Eli's been telling me about your scones, Sarah. I'm already planning a visit."

Liam chuckled, clapping Eli on the shoulder. "He's a good kid, Eli. Smart, dependable. Always ready to lend a hand, whether it's hauling in a catch or helping a neighbor fix a leaky roof. We're all lucky to have him around."

The genuine affection in Liam's tone, the easy camaraderie between these individuals, painted a vivid picture for Mara. This wasn't just a collection of people living in the same town; it was a community, a chosen family forged by shared experiences, mutual respect, and a deep-seated understanding of what it meant to rely on one another in a place where the sea dictated the rhythm of life. Eli was clearly at the heart of it, a vital node in this intricate network of support.

They spent the next hour drifting from one conversation to another. Eli introduced Mara to a handful of other friends – a retired teacher who now curated the local historical society, a young couple who had recently opened a charming bookstore, and a gruff but kind-hearted fisherman named Old Man Hemlock, whose gruff exterior hid a wealth of knowledge about the local marine life and a surprisingly soft spot for stray cats. With each encounter, Mara witnessed Eli's deep-rooted connection to Port Blossom. He didn't just know people; he knew them. He remembered their children's names, their recent struggles, their triumphs. He offered advice, shared a joke, or simply stood by, a silent, reassuring presence.

Mara observed the way people's faces lit up when they saw him, the easy way they confided in him, the unwavering trust they placed in his judgment. It was a stark contrast to the superficial politeness and calculated interactions she had become accustomed to in her previous life. Here, connections were built on authenticity, on shared humanity, and on a collective understanding of what truly mattered. She saw him help Liam secure a loose mooring line, offer a few words of encouragement to the young booksellers about an upcoming author event, and even patiently listen to Old Man Hemlock's lengthy, rambling tale about a particularly stubborn lobster.

"He's got a good heart, that Eli," Old Man Hemlock grumbled, though his eyes held a warmth that belied his words as he watched Eli walk away after another friendly exchange. "Always has. Been that way since he was knee-high to a barnacle."

As they continued their walk, Mara felt a profound sense of hope bloom within her. Eli's deep roots in Port Blossom weren't just a testament to his character; they were a promise. They spoke of stability, of belonging, of a community that embraced its own. She had arrived in Port Blossom feeling adrift, a ship without an anchor. But seeing Eli navigate this world, seeing how he was not just in the community but truly *of* it, made the prospect of her own future here feel less like a tentative experiment and more like a deeply desired destination.

"They all think the world of you," Mara murmured, a softness in her voice.

Eli shrugged, a faint blush rising on his cheeks. "They're good people, Mara. They look out for each other. It's just how it is here."

"But it's more than that," she insisted. "It's the genuine affection. The respect. You've built something special here, Eli. A real network of support."

He stopped, turning to face her, his eyes reflecting the glint of the sunlight on the water. "It's a two-way street, Mara. They support me, and I support them. That's how you build a life, not just... exist." He gently cupped her face, his thumbs tracing the curve of her cheekbones. "And I want to help you build yours here. I want you to feel that same sense of belonging, that same security."

His words were a balm to her soul. She had been so focused on the professional aspects of her future – the gallery, the art scene, the potential for growth. But Eli was reminding her of the fundamental human need for connection, for a place to call home, for people who would see her, truly see her, and welcome her into their lives.

"I'm starting to feel it," she admitted, her voice a little husky. "This place... and you... you're making it easier."

"Good," he said, his gaze unwavering. "Because I'm not letting you go anywhere else. We'll find your place, Mara. You'll have your own connections, your own people. They'll love you just as much as they love me, maybe even more." He grinned, a flash of playful confidence.

Later that afternoon, as they sat on the worn wooden steps of Eli's boat, watching the fishing fleet return with their shimmering catches, Mara felt a profound sense of peace settle over her. Eli continued to point out the different boats, the personalities of their captains, the stories behind their day's work. He spoke of the upcoming town festival, a beloved annual event where everyone pitched in, and of his own involvement in the local maritime museum, a project he was deeply passionate about.

"It's not just about the fishing, you see," he explained, gesturing towards the bustling harbor. "It's about preserving the history, the heritage. It's about ensuring the next generation understands what this place means, what it takes to live here."

Mara listened, absorbing every word. She saw how Eli wasn't just a fisherman; he was a custodian of Port Blossom's identity, a man who invested his time and energy into the community's well-being. And he was actively, intentionally, inviting her into that world. He wasn't just offering her a place beside him; he was offering her a place within the vibrant tapestry of his life, a life deeply interwoven with the soul of this coastal town. The future, which had once seemed a nebulous and daunting landscape, was beginning to take shape, illuminated by the warmth of genuine connection and the quiet promise of belonging, all thanks to the steadfast support system Eli had so effortlessly woven around himself, and was now extending to her.

Mara found herself standing at the precipice of something new, a feeling that had been slowly brewing like a gentle tide, now cresting with an undeniable force. The lingering anxieties, the shadows of her past that had clung to her like a persistent fog, were beginning to lift, revealing a landscape painted with hues of optimism and a burgeoning sense of purpose. It wasn't an abrupt, jarring shift, but a gradual unfolding, much like the slow bloom of the wildflowers that dotted the Port Blossom hillsides. Her days at the animal rescue had been a potent catalyst for this change. Each rescued creature, each wagging tail, each soft purr had been a small testament to resilience, a living embodiment of the power of second chances. She had poured her heart and soul into caring for these abandoned souls, finding solace and a profound sense of fulfillment in their healing. In their vulnerability, she had found her own strength. In their journey back to health and happiness, she had discovered the blueprint for her own future.

The transformation wasn't solely her own doing, of course. Eli's presence had been the steady, unwavering lighthouse in her often-turbulent emotional seas. His quiet confidence, his unwavering belief in her, had been the gentle nudge she needed to step out of the shadows and into the light. He'd never pushed, never demanded, but simply offered his hand, his unwavering support, and his genuine belief that she was capable of so much more than she had allowed herself to believe. He had seen the spark within her, even when she had felt utterly extinguished, and had fanned it with a tenderness that had slowly rekindled her spirit. He'd listened patiently to her fears, acknowledged her past without judgment, and consistently painted a picture of a future where she could thrive, a future where her unique talents and compassionate heart could find a true home.

"It feels different now, doesn't it?" Eli had murmured one evening, as they sat on the porch, the scent of pine and damp earth filling the air. The stars, unmarred by city lights, were scattered across the velvet sky like a million tiny diamonds. Mara had been tracing the constellations, a quiet contemplation settling over her.

"Different how?" she'd asked, her voice soft.

He'd taken her hand, his thumb stroking the back of her palm. "Less... guarded. You're not bracing yourself for the next blow anymore. You're looking up. You're looking forward."

And he was right. The constant vigilance, the ingrained habit of anticipating disappointment, had begun to recede. It was as if she had been holding her breath for years, and now, finally, she was exhaling, filling her lungs with the clean, crisp air of possibility. The fear, that cold, persistent dread that had dictated so many of her decisions, no longer held the same power. It was still a presence, a faint echo in the corners of her mind, but it was no longer the conductor of her orchestra. Instead, it was a hesitant violist, playing a quiet, almost mournful tune in the background, while the violins of hope and anticipation took center stage.

Her work at the rescue had illuminated the kind of life she craved. It wasn't just about the animals, though they were a significant part of it. It was about the community that surrounded the rescue, the network of volunteers and staff who shared a common purpose, a collective drive to make a difference. It was about the tangible impact of their efforts, the visible transformation of each animal, from timid and broken to trusting and loved. This was the kind of purpose she yearned for – a life built on compassion, on tangible good, on the quiet satisfaction of contributing to something larger than herself.

She remembered a specific incident with a scruffy terrier mix named Buster. He'd arrived at the shelter terrified, cowering in the back of his kennel, his eyes wide with fear. He wouldn't let anyone near him, his entire being radiating a palpable distrust. Mara had spent hours just sitting outside his kennel, talking softly, offering treats that he'd eye with suspicion before snatching them when she looked away. Slowly, painstakingly, she'd built a fragile bridge of trust. One afternoon, as she was quietly reading nearby, Buster had tentatively crept to the front of his kennel, his tail giving a hesitant, almost imperceptible wag. It was a small moment, but for Mara, it was monumental. It was a breakthrough, a sign that healing was possible, that connection could overcome even the deepest wounds. Seeing Buster eventually adopted into a loving family, his tail now wagging with joyous abandon, had filled her with an elation that was both profound and deeply personal. It was a feeling that transcended any professional achievement she had ever known.

This was the essence of the life she envisioned: a life where she was actively nurturing, healing, and fostering growth, both in others and in herself. She pictured her own small studio, perhaps attached to her home, filled with canvases and the earthy scent of clay. She saw herself creating art that spoke of the beauty she was now discovering in the world, art that reflected the quiet resilience of the animals she'd cared for, the unwavering love she felt for Eli, and the newfound sense of peace she'd found in Port Blossom. It was a vision that was no longer a wistful daydream but a tangible, attainable goal.

Eli's influence wasn't just about emotional encouragement; it was about practical support, about showing her how to navigate this new path. He'd helped her research grants for animal welfare organizations, offering insights into local businesses that might be willing to sponsor her work. He'd spent hours with her, discussing her artistic aspirations, offering his own unique perspective as someone who understood the cycles of nature and the importance of observing and appreciating the subtle shifts. He'd encouraged her to experiment, to let go of the pressure to produce something perfect and instead embrace the process of creation.

"Don't think about the finished product, Mara," he'd advised, his eyes crinkling at the corners. "Think about the feeling. What do you want the viewer to feel when they look at your art? If it's the peace of the ocean, then let the colors flow like the waves. If it's the joy of a rescued dog finally feeling safe, then let the brushstrokes be bold and full of life."

His words resonated deeply. She realized that her art, like her work at the rescue, was about connection. It was about bridging the gap between her inner world and the external one, about communicating emotions and experiences that words sometimes failed to capture. She understood now that her past struggles, rather than being something to hide or forget, could be a source of profound insight and empathy, a wellspring from which to draw authentic and compelling artistic expression.

The shift in her perspective was palpable. She found herself looking at the world with a renewed sense of wonder. The rugged coastline, the whispering pines, the rhythmic crash of waves against the shore – they no longer felt like a backdrop to her life but as an integral part of it. She saw the beauty in the imperfections, the charm in the weathered facades of the old buildings, the quiet dignity of the fishermen mending their nets. Port Blossom, once a place of refuge, was slowly transforming into a place of belonging, a place where she could finally put down roots.

The thought of establishing her own art studio here, perhaps even participating in local art fairs or collaborating with the nascent bookstore Eli had mentioned, filled her with an almost electric excitement. It wasn't just about making a living; it was about weaving herself into the fabric of this community, contributing her unique talents and perspective to its rich tapestry. She envisioned a space that would not only showcase her art but also serve as a hub for creativity, a place where others could find inspiration and perhaps even discover their own artistic voices.

She recalled a conversation with Sarah, the baker, whose infectious enthusiasm for her craft had been evident from the moment Mara had tasted her blueberry scones. Sarah had spoken of the joy she found in feeding her community, in providing a small but essential comfort through her baked goods. "It's more than just flour and sugar, you know," Sarah had said, her hands dusted with flour. "It's about nourishment, for the body and the soul. It's about being a part of people's everyday lives, their morning routines, their celebrations." Mara felt a similar pull towards her art, a desire to create something that would bring joy, provoke thought, and connect with people on an emotional level.

The tentative steps she had taken towards a new beginning were solidifying, gaining momentum. The fear had receded, not vanished entirely, but diminished to a manageable hum, a reminder of the journey she had undertaken. It was a testament to her own strength, her capacity for healing, and the transformative power of love and support. Eli had been the architect of this new perspective, not by imposing his vision, but by gently unveiling her own, by reminding her of the vibrant, resilient woman she was, and always had been.

The future, once a daunting, uncharted territory, now shimmered with the promise of a new dawn, a new chapter waiting to be written, filled with purpose, passion, and the quiet, profound joy of belonging. She was ready to embrace it, not with trepidation, but with an open heart and a spirit ready to soar.

CHAPTER TEN
THE TURNING TIDE

The air in Port Blossom carried a subtle shift, a gentle sigh that whispered of summer's waning days. The sun, though still warm, cast longer shadows, and the evenings arrived with a cooler, more contemplative embrace. For Mara, this shift in season mirrored an internal turning point, a moment when the soft, diffused light of possibility began to sharpen into the stark clarity of a difficult decision. The e-mail had arrived unceremoniously, a digital missive that held the weight of her entire past within its neatly formatted lines. It was an offer from the prestigious gallery in the city, the one she'd spent years dreaming of, the one that represented the pinnacle of her artistic aspirations before life had taken its sharp, unexpected turn.

The offer was everything she had once craved: a solo exhibition, a coveted spot in their permanent collection, and the promise of a career that could finally eclipse the ghosts that had haunted her for so long. It was a return to the familiar, a path paved with the kind of professional recognition she had meticulously worked towards, a world where her talent was validated by established institutions and where the validation itself felt like a balm to old wounds. The city, with its endless opportunities and its vibrant, often relentless, energy, called to a part of her that still remembered the fierce ambition that had once driven her. She could picture it vividly: the sleek, minimalist gallery space, the hushed reverence of patrons, the satisfying click of success. It was the life she had been building before the foundation crumbled, a life that, on the surface, offered a sense of security and prestige that Port Blossom, with all its newfound charm, couldn't quite replicate.

Yet, as she reread the e-mail, her fingers tracing the embossed logo of the gallery, a strange dissonance settled within her. The excitement that should have bubbled up, the triumphant surge of accomplishment, was muted, overshadowed by a quiet ache. It was the ache of imagining that future without the present that had so unexpectedly bloomed. She thought of the animal rescue, the scent of hay and disinfectant, the chorus of barks and meows that had become the soundtrack to her healing. She thought of the small studio space she'd tentatively begun to clear out in the spare room of the cottage, the canvases leaning against the wall, waiting to be filled with the colors of her evolving soul. And she thought, most acutely, of Eli.

Eli, with his steady gaze and his hands that knew the rhythm of the earth, had become the anchor in her swirling world. He was the quiet certainty in the face of her lingering uncertainties, the gentle hand that had guided her back to herself. His belief in her, unwavering and unconditional, had been a revelation, a stark contrast to the conditional acceptance and the subtle judgments she had grown accustomed to. He didn't just see her talent; he saw her. He saw the woman who was slowly but surely shedding her protective layers, revealing a spirit that was both resilient and tender. Their evenings spent on the porch, the quiet rhythm of their shared silences, the way he looked at her as if she were the most extraordinary thing he had ever encountered – these were the moments that had woven themselves into the fabric of her new life, the threads that made it feel vibrant and real.

The decision was a tightrope walk between two vastly different futures. On one side lay the glittering allure of her past ambitions, the validation of a world that had once dismissed her, a return to a narrative that, while painful, was undeniably familiar. It represented a measure of safety, a predictable trajectory, a chance to prove to the world, and perhaps to herself, that she hadn't been broken by her past, but forged by it. There was a certain triumph in that, a hard-won victory that the city gallery represented. It was a choice that spoke of reclaiming what had been lost, of asserting her place in a world that had once felt out of reach. She could imagine the conversations, the professional networking, the return to a life that demanded a certain polished exterior, a sophisticated detachment that had once been her armor.

But then, her gaze would drift to the window, to the sun-drenched hills rolling down to the sapphire sea. She would hear the distant cry of gulls, the gentle murmur of the waves, the comforting hum of life in Port Blossom. Here, her days were filled with a different kind of fulfillment. There was the visceral satisfaction of seeing a timid rescue dog finally wag its tail, the quiet joy of creating a piece of art that captured the essence of a Port Blossom sunset, the warmth of shared laughter with Eli over a simple, home-cooked meal. This life was less about external validation and more about internal resonance. It was about building something authentic, something that nurtured her spirit rather than merely showcasing her talent. It was about love, not just the romantic kind, but the profound sense of belonging that was slowly taking root in this small, coastal town.

The "Haven," as the animal rescue was affectionately called, had become more than just a job; it was a sanctuary. It was a place where vulnerability was met with compassion, where brokenness was a starting point for healing, and where every small victory was celebrated with genuine warmth. Mara had discovered a deep well of purpose within its walls, a sense of contributing to something meaningful, of being a part of a community that valued kindness above all else. She'd found a quiet strength in caring for creatures who had known only hardship, a reflection of her own journey towards healing. To leave that behind felt like abandoning a part of herself, a crucial piece of the tapestry she was weaving.

And Eli. He was the quiet, constant hum beneath the surface of her life, the steady presence that made the uncertain feel safe. He'd never pressured her, never tried to sway her decision, but his very presence was a testament to the life that was unfolding here. He represented a future that was not defined by professional accolades, but by shared moments, by quiet understanding, by a love that felt as natural and as life-giving as the sea air. His world, rooted in the rhythms of nature and the simple beauty of the land, offered a different kind of wealth, a richness that Mara was only beginning to understand and appreciate. He understood her art, not just as a skill, but as an extension of her soul, and his encouragement had been a gentle, persistent balm. He saw the way her eyes lit up when she spoke of a new idea, the way her hands instinctively moved as if sketching an unseen form, and he celebrated those moments with a quiet joy that mirrored her own.

The gallery's offer was a siren song, a powerful echo from a life that had been, a life that promised a return to a certain kind of certainty. It was the comfort of the known, the familiar landscape of her past. But Port Blossom, and the life she was building with Eli, was the allure of the unknown, a future painted with the vibrant, unpredictable colors of genuine happiness. It was the choice between the applause of a crowd and the quiet understanding of a single soul. It was the weighing of a career built on external validation against a life built on internal peace and love.

Mara walked down to the small harbor, the salty air cool against her skin. The fishing boats bobbed gently, their weathered hulls telling stories of countless voyages. She watched as a fisherman mended his nets with practiced, patient hands, his movements a testament to years of dedication. It was a life of quiet diligence, of purposeful work, of deep connection to the sea and to the community. It was, in its own way, a form of art, a craft honed by experience and imbued with a profound sense of place.

She remembered a conversation with Sarah, the baker, her hands perpetually dusted with flour, her laughter as warm and comforting as her freshly baked bread. Sarah had spoken of the satisfaction of creating something tangible, something that brought joy to others, something that was woven into the daily lives of the townspeople. "It's not just about making a living, Mara," she'd said, her eyes twinkling. "It's about being a part of something. It's about nourishment, for the body and the soul. It's about connection." Sarah's words resonated deeply. Mara realized that her art, like Sarah's baking or the fisherman's craft, had the potential to be more than just a commodity. It could be a form of connection, a way to share her unique perspective, her healing, her newfound joy with the world in a way that felt authentic and deeply personal.

The gallery offered a stage, a spotlight. Port Blossom offered a home, a hearth. The city offered a career, a title. The small town offered a life, a love. The past, with its familiar comforts and its undeniable scars, beckoned from one direction. The future, uncertain and shimmering with promise, lay in another. The weight of the decision pressed down on her, not as a burden of obligation, but as the profound responsibility of choosing the path that would truly lead to her soul's contentment. She understood that this wasn't just about choosing between two places, but between two versions of herself. The ambitious artist, driven by external validation, or the woman who had found her voice in quiet places, in the healing of others, and in the deep, unwavering love of a man who saw her completely. The summer's end was not just a change of seasons; it was the cusp of her own personal transformation, a moment that demanded courage, clarity, and the quiet wisdom to listen to the deepest whisperings of her own heart. She knew, with a certainty that settled deep in her bones, that this choice would define not just the next chapter of her life, but the very essence of who she was becoming.

The salty breeze, carrying the scent of brine and distant pine, rustled Mara's hair as she sat beside Eli on the worn wooden planks of the dock. The sun, a molten orb sinking towards the horizon, painted the sky in hues of fiery orange and soft lavender, a breathtaking spectacle that usually calmed her. Tonight, however, the beauty felt like a poignant reminder of the approaching end of summer, and the even more significant end of a chapter in her own life. The weight of the gallery's offer, a glittering, tempting proposition, pressed down on her, a silent antagonist to the peace she'd painstakingly cultivated in Port Blossom. She had wrestled with it internally for days, the familiar pull of ambition battling the burgeoning contentment she'd found here, with Eli.

"It's just... it's everything I thought I wanted," she began, her voice barely a whisper, lost for a moment in the gentle lapping of waves against the pilings. She picked at a loose thread on her jeans, her gaze fixed on the water, unable to meet Eli's steady, understanding eyes. "A solo show. The kind of recognition I've dreamt about since I first picked up a brush. It's the validation, you know? The proof that all those years of struggle, all the doubts, weren't for nothing." She sighed, a sound heavy with conflicting emotions. "The city... it represents a life that felt so impossibly out of reach for so long. A life where my art isn't just a hobby, but a career. A real career."

Eli shifted beside her, his presence a comforting warmth against her side. He didn't interrupt, didn't rush her, simply breathed in the quiet rhythm of her words, allowing her the space to unspool the tangled threads of her dilemma. When she finally fell silent, the only sounds were the distant cry of gulls and the rhythmic sigh of the ocean. She braced herself for his reaction, for any hint of disappointment, of personal loss. But when he spoke, his voice was as calm and unwavering as the tide.

"I hear you, Mara," he said, his tone gentle, devoid of any judgment. He reached out, his calloused fingers brushing against her hand, a silent offering of support. "It's a significant opportunity, and it's completely understandable that you're wrestling with it. That ambition, that drive... it's a part of you, and it deserves to be acknowledged." He paused, his thumb stroking the back of her hand. "And you deserve all the recognition in the world for your talent. Anyone who sees your work can see the depth, the soul you pour into it. It's extraordinary."

His words, so simple, so genuine, brought a prickle of tears to her eyes. It wasn't the effusive praise she might have received in the city, but something far more profound: a quiet acknowledgement of her truth, a validation that came not from a professional critique, but from the heart of someone who saw her completely. She finally turned to him, her gaze meeting his. His eyes, the color of the sea on a clear day, held no agenda, no hint of expectation, only a deep, abiding love and acceptance.

"But..." she started, her voice catching. "But I've built something here, Eli. Something... real. The Haven, the animals... they've given me a purpose I never knew I was missing. And you..." She trailed off, the unspoken words hanging heavy in the air between them. She wanted to say, *And you, you've given me a home, a love I never thought possible.*

Eli's smile was soft, understanding. "And you, Mara," he finished for her, his gaze unwavering. "You've built something beautiful here. You've healed, you've grown, you've found a different kind of strength, a different kind of joy. And that's just as valid, just as important, as any gallery show." He squeezed her hand gently. "The art world is a demanding mistress, and that offer... it's a testament to your skill. But it's not the only path to fulfillment. It's not the only way to be seen, or to be happy."

He pulled her closer, her head resting on his shoulder. The familiar scent of earth and sea that clung to him was a comforting balm. "Whatever you decide," he murmured into her hair, his voice a low rumble that vibrated through her. "Whatever path you choose, I'll be right here. My feelings for you... they're not tied to your career, or your location, or the amount of recognition you receive. They're tied to you, Mara. To the woman you are. The woman who has faced down her past, who cares for the vulnerable, who sees the beauty in the world and translates it into something magical on canvas. That's who I fell in love with. That's who I'll always stand by."

His unwavering support was a lifeline, a steady anchor in the turbulent sea of her indecision. The fear of disappointing him, of losing this precious connection, had been a silent, paralyzing force. But hearing him articulate his unconditional love, his commitment, freed something within her. The pressure to choose the 'right' career path, the path that would impress others or secure her future in a conventional sense, began to dissipate. It wasn't about proving herself to the world anymore. It was about proving to herself that she could honor her own evolving needs, her own emerging sense of self.

"It's just... hard," she confessed, her voice thick with emotion. "To turn away from a dream, even if it's an old dream. To walk away from the possibility of that kind of success."

"Dreams change, Mara," Eli said, his voice laced with quiet wisdom. "And sometimes, the most courageous thing you can do is to let go of a dream that no longer serves you, to make space for new ones to blossom. This life here, with the Haven, with me... it's not a compromise. It's a choice. A choice to build a life that nourishes your soul, that brings you peace, that allows you to continue the healing you've already begun." He gently tilted her chin up, forcing her to meet his gaze. "And your art, Mara, it will still be there. You'll still create. Maybe it will be different, maybe it will be for a different audience, or for no audience at all, but it will still be you. And that's what matters."

He leaned in, his lips brushing against hers, a feather-light kiss that sent a tremor through her. "Don't make this decision based on what you think you should do, or what others expect. Make it based on what your heart truly wants, on what will bring you genuine happiness. I'll support you, whatever you choose. Always."

His words settled around her like a warm blanket, chasing away the chill of doubt. The fear of loss, the anxiety of making the 'wrong' choice, began to recede, replaced by a burgeoning sense of clarity and strength. She looked out at the darkening sea, at the first stars beginning to prick the velvet sky. The city lights, a distant shimmer on the horizon, seemed less alluring now, less like a beacon of hope and more like a distant echo of a life that was no longer hers. Port Blossom, with its quiet rhythms, its genuine connections, and its steady, unconditional love, felt like home. It felt like the place where her art, and her life, could truly flourish, not under the harsh glare of a spotlight, but in the gentle, nurturing warmth of a life lived authentically. Eli's reassurance was not just words; it was a profound gift, a testament to a love that saw her, accepted her, and empowered her to choose herself, unburdened and free. The tide was turning, not towards the distant city, but towards the quiet, profound shores of her own heart.

The sand, still warm from the day's sun, sifted through Mara's bare toes as she walked along the water's edge. The tide, a gentle exhalation, kissed the shore, its rhythmic ebb and flow a soothing counterpoint to the restless beat of her own heart. Each wave that retreated seemed to carry away a fragment of her lingering doubt, leaving behind a growing sense of peace. The vast, unbroken horizon of the ocean stretched before her, a canvas of endless possibility, mirroring the immensity of the choice she had been wrestling with. It was here, in the quiet grandeur of nature, that the cacophony of her inner conflict began to fade, replaced by a profound stillness.

She remembered the Mara who had arrived in Port Blossom, a ghost of her former self, haunted by the echoes of a life that had fractured. She had felt adrift, a broken vessel tossed by storms she couldn't control. The city had been a cage of her own making, gilded and desirable, but ultimately suffocating. The gallery offer, a siren's song from that former life, had initially stirred the old ambition, the desperate need for external validation. It had promised a return to a world where she believed her worth was measured by accolades and recognition. But standing here, with the salt spray on her face and the immensity of the ocean before her, that promise felt hollow.

Her journey to Port Blossom had been an act of desperation, a retreat from the wreckage. She had sought solace, a quiet corner to lick her wounds. Instead, she had found something far more profound: a haven, both for the injured animals she tended with such fierce compassion and for her own fractured spirit. The Haven wasn't just a place; it was a testament to resilience, a living, breathing embodiment of healing. And Eli. He had walked into her life like a steady, unwavering lighthouse, cutting through the fog of her despair, guiding her towards a shore she hadn't known existed.

He had seen past the carefully constructed walls she had built, past the cynicism and the fear, and had loved the raw, vulnerable woman beneath. His love was not conditional on her success, her fame, or her whereabouts. It was a quiet, constant presence, as essential and life-affirming as the air she breathed. He had shown her that true stability wasn't about clinging to the brittle remnants of a past that had failed her, but about bravely embracing the present, about building a future on the bedrock of authentic connection and personal growth.

She stopped, letting a larger wave wash over her feet, the cool water a welcome sensation. The moon, a pale sliver in the twilight sky, cast a silvery sheen on the water. This was not a retreat from her dreams, she realized, but an evolution of them. The ambition that had once driven her towards the solitary pursuit of artistic acclaim had been transmuted into a deeper, more meaningful desire: to create a life that nourished her soul, to contribute to something larger than herself, to love and be loved deeply. Her art, she understood now, was not merely a means to an end, a ladder to climb towards recognition. It was an intrinsic part of her, a language through which she expressed her deepest truths. It would continue to flow, perhaps in new directions, with new inspirations, but it would always be hers.

The gallery offer, once a heavy burden, now felt like a distant echo, a whisper from a life that no longer resonated. The choice, once agonizing, was now clear. Her heart, no longer torn between two worlds, felt a profound sense of settle. She wasn't turning her back on her dreams; she was simply choosing a different, more authentic path to their fulfillment. A path that led not to the glittering, often treacherous, streets of the city, but to the quiet, sun-drenched shores of Port Blossom, to the warmth of Eli's arms, and to the enduring promise of a life lived with purpose, with passion, and with an abundance of love. She smiled, a genuine, radiant smile that reached her eyes, and turned back towards the familiar lights of the town, towards the home she had found, not by chance, but by choosing. The tide had indeed turned, and it had brought her to a place of profound belonging.

Mara's decision wasn't a sudden, impulsive act, but rather the culmination of weeks spent listening to the whispers of her own heart, amplified by the gentle rhythm of the waves and the steady presence of Eli. The offer from the city gallery, once a shimmering mirage of her past aspirations, had faded into irrelevance, replaced by the tangible reality of Port Blossom. It wasn't just the ocean breeze that filled her lungs with a sense of freedom; it was the quiet understanding that her life's work, her true calling, was unfolding right here, amidst the salt-laced air and the grateful sighs of creatures in need of healing. The Coastal Animal Haven, a place she had initially sought as a temporary refuge, had become her anchor, her sanctuary, and the improbable birthplace of a future she was now ready to embrace with unwavering commitment.

She had arrived in Port Blossom a wounded bird, her wings clipped by disappointment and a gnawing sense of inadequacy.

The city had been a dazzling but ultimately sterile environment, one that judged worth by outward appearances and fleeting trends. Here, at the Haven, the currency was different. It was measured in the soft nuzzle of a rescued dog, the tentative chirp of a rehabilitated seabird, the quiet trust of an injured fox. It was a place where value was inherent, not earned. And in tending to these vulnerable lives, Mara found herself tending to her own. The scars that had felt so raw and exposed began to mend, not by erasure, but by integration into a richer, more resilient tapestry of self.

Her initial intention had been to offer her time, her skills as a volunteer, a way to give back while she figured out her next steps. But the more time she spent at the Haven, the more she felt its pull, its silent demand for more than just a fleeting contribution. It was the late nights spent coaxing a struggling orphaned seal pup back to health, the early mornings mending fences that had been battered by a storm, the quiet conversations with Eleanor, the Haven's founder, about the long-term vision, that had slowly, irrevocably, woven the Haven into the very fabric of her being. She saw not just animals needing care, but a community needing support, a vital organ of Port Blossom that required constant nurturing.

The idea of a more permanent role had begun as a tentative thought, a shy flicker in the back of her mind. Now, standing on the worn wooden deck of the Haven, the salty air carrying the scent of pine and the distant cries of gulls, it felt like an inevitability, a truth as solid and undeniable as the ground beneath her feet. It wasn't about a job title or a salary; it was about purpose. It was about dedicating her life to a cause that resonated with every fiber of her being, a cause that offered a profound sense of fulfillment that no gallery opening or critical acclaim ever could. She wasn't just volunteering at the Haven; she was investing in it, heart and soul.

She found Eli that evening by the small fishing pier, his silhouette outlined against the dying embers of the sunset. He was mending a fishing net, his hands moving with a practiced, unhurried grace. The rhythmic pull and knot, pull and knot, was a familiar sound, as comforting as his presence. As she approached, he looked up, his eyes, the color of the deepest sea, crinkling at the corners with a smile that always felt like coming home.

"Thinking again?" he asked, his voice a low rumble that seemed to vibrate with the gentle sway of the boats.

Mara sat beside him, the rough wood of the pier cool beneath her. "More like deciding," she corrected, a soft smile playing on her lips. "I've made my choice, Eli."

He paused his work, his gaze steady and knowing. "And what is that, Mara?"

"The Haven," she said, her voice firm, a new confidence underpinning her words. "I want to commit to it. Not just as a volunteer, but... permanently. I want to be a part of its future, to help it grow, to ensure it continues to be this haven for all the creatures, and for the people who love them." She looked at him, her heart exposed. "I want to work with Eleanor, to learn everything I can, to pour myself into this place. I think... I think this is where I belong."

Eli reached out, his calloused fingers gently tracing the line of her jaw. The touch sent a familiar warmth through her. "I knew you would," he said, his voice filled with a quiet pride that made her chest swell. "I've seen how this place has healed you, Mara. And I've seen how you heal it. You have a gift, a way with them, a deep well of compassion that this Haven needs. And Port Blossom needs it." He squeezed her hand. "I'm so proud of you."

His words, simple and sincere, were more potent than any grand declaration. They affirmed not just her decision, but her worth, her ability to contribute something meaningful. In his eyes, she saw a reflection of the woman she was becoming, a woman grounded and purposeful. Their lives, she realized, were no longer two separate paths that happened to intersect; they were becoming entwined, their futures woven together like the threads of the net he was mending. The Haven, in a way, had become a third entity in their burgeoning relationship, a shared purpose that strengthened their bond.

"It's not just about the animals, is it?" Eli mused, returning to his net. "It's about the quiet strength you've found here. The resilience. You've built something new from the pieces of what was broken."

Mara nodded, her gaze drifting towards the dark, shimmering expanse of the ocean. "I was so afraid of losing myself in the city, of becoming someone I didn't recognize. But here... here I've found myself. I've found a different kind of ambition. One that's not about proving myself, but about contributing. About nurturing. About love." She turned back to him. "And I want to build a life with you, Eli, here in Port Blossom. A life where the Haven is a part of that. A life where we, together, make a difference."

He set the net aside and turned to face her fully, taking both her hands in his. The sea air felt charged with unspoken promises. "We will, Mara. We'll build it. Together. The Haven, our home, a life filled with purpose. It's already happening." He pulled her gently closer, her head resting against his chest, listening to the steady beat of his heart, a rhythm that now felt as familiar and reassuring as her own.

The commitment wasn't just to the Haven; it was a commitment to this life, to this community, to the quiet, profound love she had found with Eli. It was a conscious choice to embrace the healing that had begun within her, to nurture it and let it bloom outwards, touching the lives of the creatures she cared for and the people who shared her world. The tide had indeed turned, not just for her, but for them, carrying them towards a future that was as boundless and full of possibility as the ocean before them. She was no longer a visitor seeking solace; she was a resident, an integral part of the tapestry of Port Blossom, her life now inextricably linked to the well-being of the Coastal Animal Haven and the man who had shown her the true meaning of home. The city's siren song had long since faded, replaced by the gentle lapping of waves against the shore and the quiet, unwavering promise of a life lived with intention, with compassion, and with a love that was as deep and vast as the sea.

The transition from volunteer to a more integrated role at the Coastal Animal Haven felt less like a job change and more like an organic unfolding. Mara found herself spending more and more time at the sprawling property, her days dictated by the needs of the animals and the ebb and flow of the Haven's operations. Eleanor, with her weathered hands and her boundless empathy, welcomed Mara's deepening involvement with a quiet satisfaction. She saw in Mara not just a capable assistant, but a kindred spirit, someone who understood the profound, often unseen, work of healing and conservation.

"You have a way with them, child," Eleanor would say, her voice raspy with age and years of shouting over the wind to coax a stubborn animal into a carrier. "They trust you. It's a rare gift. Most people see the mess, the danger, the sheer effort. You see the hope."

Mara would simply smile, her heart swelling. She remembered the initial awkwardness, the fear of not being good enough, the lingering self-doubt that had been her constant companion. But the Haven had a way of stripping away those pretenses. The raw, immediate needs of the animals demanded authenticity. There was no room for ego when a distressed fawn needed to be fed around the clock, or when a tangled pelican required delicate disentanglement from discarded fishing line. In those moments,

Mara was simply Mara, a human being dedicated to alleviating suffering.

Her art, which had once felt like a separate, almost demanding, entity in her life, began to inform her work at the Haven in unexpected ways. The keen observational skills she had honed as a painter allowed her to notice subtle changes in an animal's behavior, early indicators of distress or illness that might otherwise be missed. Her understanding of form and structure helped her design more functional and comfortable enclosures. And the patience she had cultivated during long hours spent at her easel translated into the quiet persistence needed for rehabilitation.

She started sketching again, not for exhibitions, but for the sheer joy of capturing the essence of the creatures she cared for. Her sketchbooks filled with the scruffy charm of a rescued terrier, the regal profile of a hawk, the mischievous glint in an otter's eye. These weren't just artistic exercises; they became a way for her to process her experiences, to deepen her connection to the natural world, and to articulate the beauty she found in even the most unlikely of subjects. She began to see the Haven not just as a refuge for animals, but as a living, breathing work of art, a testament to resilience and the enduring power of nature.

Eli watched her transformation with a quiet admiration that spoke volumes. He saw the way her eyes lit up when she spoke of a successful release, the way her shoulders relaxed when she was surrounded by the comforting chaos of the animal enclosures, the way her hands, once accustomed to the delicate touch of a paintbrush, now moved with confidence and efficiency in mending fences or administering medication. He knew this was not a phase, not a fleeting passion. This was Mara finding her true north.

One evening, as they sat on their porch, the scent of honeysuckle heavy in the air, Eli looked at her, a gentle smile on his face. "You're glowing, you know," he said softly. "Happier than I've ever seen you."

Mara leaned her head against his shoulder, a sigh of contentment escaping her lips. "It's the Haven," she admitted. "It's... everything. It's the purpose, the connection, the feeling of making a real difference. And it's you, Eli. Knowing I have you beside me, supporting me, believing in me." She tilted her head up to meet his gaze. "I never thought I could feel this... settled. This right."

"You are right, Mara," he affirmed, his thumb gently stroking her cheek. "You're exactly where you're meant to be. And I'm so grateful to be sharing this journey with you." He paused, his gaze thoughtful. "I've been talking to Eleanor too. About the expansion plans. About needing more dedicated staff. She mentioned you've been thinking about taking on more responsibility, perhaps even helping to manage some of the day-to-day operations. Are you ready for that?"

The question hung in the air, a tangible representation of the future they were building. Mara didn't hesitate. "Yes," she said, her voice clear and strong. "I am. I want to. I want to be a part of securing the Haven's future. I want to learn how to fundraise, how to manage volunteers, how to navigate the grant applications. I want to help Eleanor keep this place thriving for years to come." She took a deep breath, the air filled with the promise of possibility. "I want to commit to this life, Eli. To this community. To us."

Eli pulled her closer, his arms wrapping around her in a strong, secure embrace. "And I commit to you, Mara," he murmured against her hair. "To us. To this life. To this Haven. We'll build it together, brick by brick, day by day. Your passion, my strength, Eleanor's wisdom. It's a good foundation."

The decision solidified something within Mara, a sense of belonging that transcended mere physical presence. She was no longer an outsider looking in, nor a visitor seeking respite. She was a pillar, a contributor, a vital part of the fabric of Port Blossom. Her artistic sensibility had found a new canvas, her compassionate heart a new purpose, and her weary soul a new home. The turning tide had brought her not just to a place of healing, but to a life of profound meaning, a life she was ready to embrace with open arms, a life intertwined with the gentle creatures of the Haven and the steadfast love of the man who had become her anchor. The future, once a hazy uncertainty, now stretched before her, clear and bright, as boundless as the horizon she had once feared, but now embraced with a quiet, unshakeable certainty.

The air, thick with the scent of brine and the distant cry of gulls, felt different now. It wasn't just the familiar comfort of the

Port Blossom coast, but a tangible manifestation of a choice, a vibrant, living exhalation of relief. Mara stood on the weathered planks of the pier, the gentle rocking of the moored boats a subtle counterpoint to the newfound stillness within her. The city, with its clamoring demands and its sterile judgments, no longer held any sway. Its glittering allure had faded like a poorly rendered sketch, replaced by the rich, textured reality of this small coastal town, a reality that pulsed with a life far more vibrant and authentic than anything she had ever known.

Her decision, solidifying with each passing moment, wasn't a retreat from a difficult past, but a bold, unfettered stride into an uncharted future. It was the conscious selection of the unknown, not out of desperation, but out of a profound understanding of her own resilience, a resilience forged in the crucible of her own vulnerability and tenderly nurtured by the quiet strength of Eli and the unwavering purpose she had found at the Coastal Animal Haven. The whisper of the ocean breeze no longer carried the melancholic echoes of what might have been, but the encouraging hum of possibility, a gentle melody that affirmed her courageous leap. It felt like standing on the precipice of a new dawn, not with trepidation, but with a quiet, resolute anticipation.

She had spent too long chasing validation in the hollow echo chambers of galleries, seeking an elusive approval that always seemed just beyond her grasp. The art world, once her sole focus, now felt like a distant, almost alien landscape. Its critical dissections and its relentless pursuit of the next big thing seemed trivial compared to the immediate, undeniable needs of a struggling seal pup or the quiet gratitude of a rehabilitated hawk taking flight. Her hands, once trained to wield brushes with meticulous precision, now found a different kind of artistry in mending torn nets, in administering medication with a steady touch, in simply offering a calming presence to a frightened creature. This was not a compromise; it was an evolution, a redirection of her creative spirit towards a more profound and meaningful expression of her being.

Eli, she knew, was her anchor in this new sea of possibilities. His presence beside her was not a crutch, but a steadying hand, a silent testament to a shared journey. The thought of facing this future without him would have been unthinkable, a barren landscape devoid of warmth and light. But with him, the unknown wasn't a void to be feared, but a canvas waiting to be painted, a story waiting to be written, together. Their shared laughter, the comfortable silences, the way their hands found each other instinctively – these were the threads weaving their lives into an unbreakable tapestry. He saw the woman she was becoming, not just the artist or the healer, but the sum of all her experiences, fears, and newfound strengths. His unwavering belief in her was a constant, gentle reassurance, a lighthouse guiding her through any storm.

The fear that had once clung to her like a damp fog, whispering doubts and insecurities, had begun to dissipate. It hadn't vanished entirely, for courage was not the absence of fear, but the mastery of it. It was the willingness to acknowledge the tremor in her hands, the flicker of uncertainty in her mind, and still step forward, propelled by a deeper conviction. The Haven had become her sanctuary, a place where her vulnerabilities were not weaknesses to be hidden, but the very essence of her connection to the fragile lives she tended. In their eyes, she saw a reflection of her own journey, a testament to the power of healing and the enduring strength of the spirit.

She remembered the initial days, the hesitant steps onto the Haven's grounds, the overwhelming sense of responsibility. It had felt like stepping into a whirlwind of urgent needs, each one demanding immediate attention. But with each animal she helped, with each quiet success, a seed of confidence had taken root. Eleanor, with her wisdom and her gentle encouragement, had been instrumental in nurturing that growth. She had seen Mara's potential, her innate capacity for empathy, and had guided her with a knowing hand, allowing her to discover her own capabilities. It wasn't about being told what to do, but about being given the space to learn, to falter, and to ultimately, to soar.

The future at the Haven was not a neatly mapped-out plan, but a series of unfolding possibilities. There were grant proposals to be written, new volunteer programs to be developed, conservation initiatives to be explored. It was a landscape of challenges, certainly, but they were challenges that invigorated her, that called forth her intellect and her passion. The fear of failure was still a shadow that sometimes flickered at the edges of her vision, but it was no longer a paralyzing force. Instead, it was a reminder of the stakes, a spur to greater effort, a testament to how much she had come to care.

The commitment she had made was not just to the animals, but to the very essence of what the Haven represented: compassion, resilience, and the interconnectedness of all living things. It was a commitment to fostering a community where empathy was the currency, where healing was the shared goal, and where every life, no matter how small or seemingly insignificant, held inherent value. This was a different kind of ambition than she had ever known, one that was not driven by external accolades or personal gain, but by the quiet satisfaction of contributing to something larger than herself, something that resonated with the deepest parts of her soul.

She took a deep, steadying breath, the salty air filling her lungs with a sense of clarity. The vast expanse of the ocean before her no longer represented an overwhelming unknown, but a boundless horizon of opportunity. The waves, crashing and receding, mirrored the rhythm of her own journey – moments of challenge followed by periods of calm, each one shaping her, refining her, bringing her closer to the person she was meant to be. Eli's hand found hers, his thumb tracing circles on her skin, a silent reassurance that she was not alone in this grand, beautiful adventure. Together, they would navigate the currents, embrace the storms, and find their way, guided by the compass of their shared love and their unwavering commitment to a life of purpose.

The tide had turned, not just for her, but for them, carrying them towards a future as rich and as full of promise as the endless sea. The familiar scent of pine from the nearby woods mingled with the salt spray, a fragrant testament to the grounded reality of her new life, a life that felt not like an escape, but a profound homecoming.

Chapter Eleven

WHERE THE TIDES BRING US

The familiar scent of pine, usually a comforting anchor to the coastal air, now mingled with the deeper, richer aroma of damp earth and blooming honeysuckle that permeated the small cottage. It was a smell that had, in a remarkably short time, become synonymous with home. Mara found herself pausing by the open kitchen window, a half-peeled potato in one hand, listening to the gentle chorus of birdsong that had become the soundtrack to her mornings. The cottage, which had initially felt like a temporary haven, a place to simply catch her breath, had slowly, organically, transformed. Its worn wooden floors, the slightly crooked shelves, the faint scent of old books that still clung to the sitting room – they no longer whispered of transient solace, but of roots taking hold.

Her acceptance of a more formal role at the Coastal Animal Haven hadn't been a sudden, dramatic pronouncement, but a natural progression, an unfolding of responsibilities that felt less like obligations and more like destinies. The initial days, filled with a lingering uncertainty, had been a delicate dance between her past life and the nascent one she was building. But now, the rhythm had found its cadence. Her days were no longer a haphazard collection of tasks, but a structured flow of purpose. The early mornings, once dedicated to the frantic pursuit of external validation, were now spent tending to the needs of the Haven's newest arrivals. She'd rise with the sun, the cool air kissing her cheeks as she walked the short distance to the Haven, her heart already lighter, a quiet anticipation for the day ahead humming within her.

The seal pups, she discovered, were her particular fascination. Their clumsy flippers, their large, soulful eyes that seemed to hold an ancient wisdom, and their surprisingly robust cries for attention – they had captured a piece of her heart she hadn't realized was available. She'd spend hours by their tanks, a gentle hand reaching through the protective barrier, offering a soothing murmur as she prepared their meals of specialized fish. The meticulous nature of her former art had found a new outlet here, not in the precise strokes of a brush, but in the precise measurements of formula, the careful monitoring of temperature, and the patient observation of their progress. Each gain in weight, each hesitant swim, each successful gulp of food felt like a miniature triumph, a testament to the delicate balance of nature and the dedicated care she, along with the Haven's dedicated team, provided.

Eleanor, with her ever-present calm and her encyclopedic knowledge of marine rehabilitation, had taken Mara under her wing, not as a student, but as a colleague. Their interactions were a seamless blend of shared expertise and mutual respect. Mara would often find herself poring over diagnostic charts with Eleanor, her brow furrowed in concentration, her mind already racing with potential causes and solutions. Eleanor's quiet nods of affirmation, her gentle corrections, and her occasional dry wit created an environment of constant learning and growth. It was a far cry from the cutthroat critiques she'd endured in the gallery world. Here, the success of a patient was the only currency that mattered, and collaboration was the driving force, not competition.

The days at the Haven were physically demanding, a fact Mara welcomed. There were enclosures to be cleaned, supplies to be replenished, and sometimes, the arduous task of coaxing a reluctant creature to eat. Her muscles, once accustomed to the sedentary nature of studio work, now ached with a satisfying fatigue at the end of each day. She'd return to the cottage, her hands bearing the faint scent of disinfectant and animal, her mind buzzing with the day's events. But this exhaustion was different. It was a grounding fatigue, a testament to a life lived actively, a life where her efforts had tangible, immediate results.

The 'solitary refuge' aspect of the cottage had faded completely. It was now a space for shared moments, for quiet companionship. Eli's presence was woven into the fabric of her days, a constant, comforting hum. He'd often be there when she returned, the warm glow of the lamps spilling onto the porch, a smile on his face as he anticipated her arrival. Their evenings were a gentle tapestry of shared meals, quiet conversations, and the comfortable silences that only true connection can foster. Sometimes, they would sit on the porch swing, the rhythmic creak a gentle accompaniment to the murmur of the waves, simply holding hands, their thoughts a shared stream. He never pushed, never demanded, but his unwavering presence was a steadying force, a silent affirmation of her choices. He saw her, truly saw her, in a way no one else ever had.

One crisp autumn afternoon, a particularly challenging case arrived: a young fox, its leg badly injured, its eyes wide with fear and pain. The initial assessment was grim, and the prognosis uncertain. Mara found herself drawn to the small, insulated enclosure, her heart aching at the sight of the trembling creature. She sat by the bars for what felt like hours, speaking in a low, soothing tone, offering no immediate demands, just a silent presence. Eleanor watched from a distance, a knowing look in her eyes. Later, as Mara meticulously cleaned and bandaged the fox's wound, she felt a profound sense of purpose settle over her. This wasn't about artistic expression, or critical acclaim; it was about alleviating suffering, about offering a chance at recovery.

The weeks that followed were a testament to Mara's dedication and the collaborative spirit of the Haven. She became the fox's primary caregiver, her routine revolving around its needs. She'd hand-feed it, coaxing it to trust her, her patience unwavering. There were setbacks, moments of doubt, but Mara refused to give up. She'd consult with Eleanor daily, her voice filled with a quiet determination. Eli would often join her in the evenings, his presence a silent balm to her weariness. He'd listen patiently as she recounted the day's progress, offering words of encouragement and making her cups of herbal tea.

Finally, the day arrived when the fox, now named "Pip" by Mara, was able to put weight on its mended leg. It still moved with a slight limp, but the fear in its eyes had been replaced by a flicker of cautious curiosity. As Mara opened the enclosure door, Pip hesitated for a moment, then took a tentative step forward, followed by another. The sight of it moving freely, albeit imperfectly, brought tears to Mara's eyes. Eleanor, standing beside her, placed a gentle hand on her arm. "You have a gift, Mara," she said softly. "A true gift for healing."

This moment, more than any other, solidified Mara's understanding of her new life. It wasn't just about escaping her past; it was about embracing a future brimming with tangible meaning. The scent of salt air was no longer the scent of an escape, but the scent of a life she was actively building, brick by brick, act of kindness by act of kindness. The quiet hum of contentment that now permeated her days was a melody she had never expected to hear, a symphony played out in the soft rustle of leaves, the gentle lapping of waves, and the grateful eyes of the creatures she helped to heal.

Her cottage, once a symbol of solitary refuge, had become a sanctuary of a different kind. It was a place where she could shed the weight of the world, where she could recharge her spirit, and where she could share her life with the man who had become her anchor. The worn armchair by the fireplace, which she had initially envisioned as a place for quiet introspection, now often held both her and Eli, their bodies pressed close together, a shared blanket over their laps, reading or simply enjoying each other's company. The small garden patch outside, which she had initially planted with a mix of hope and trepidation, was now beginning to yield a modest harvest of herbs and vegetables, a testament to her growing connection to the land, to this place.

The transition from the bustling, demanding world of art to the quiet, demanding world of animal rehabilitation had been more profound than she could have imagined. The urgency of the Haven's work was a constant, yet it was an urgency that fueled her, rather than drained her. Each rescued animal presented a unique puzzle, a challenge that demanded her full attention, her empathy, and her growing expertise. She found a deep satisfaction in the problem-solving aspect of her work, in diagnosing ailments, in developing treatment plans, and in witnessing the slow, steady return to health. It was a creative process, she realized, just of a different order. Instead of shaping clay or pigment, she was shaping lives, guiding them back from the brink.

The fear of judgment, once a constant companion, had slowly receded. In the eyes of the animals, there was no art criticism, no societal expectation. There was only need, vulnerability, and a profound capacity for trust once that vulnerability was met with care. Mara found a liberation in this lack of pretense, a freedom to simply *be*. Her hands, once so accustomed to the delicate dance of a paintbrush, now moved with a different kind of grace, whether it was administering medication, carefully examining a wound, or gently stroking the fur of a frightened cat.

Eli, as always, was her steadfast support. He understood the toll the work sometimes took, the emotional weight of witnessing suffering. He never minimized her experiences, but he also celebrated her triumphs with a genuine joy that mirrored her own. He'd often greet her with a knowing smile, a cup of her favorite tea already brewed, and a quiet readiness to listen. Sometimes, they'd simply sit in comfortable silence, the unspoken understanding between them a language all its own. He was the steady beat beneath the rhythm of her new life, the reassuring presence that made the unknown feel less daunting and more like an adventure they were embarking on together.

Her cottage, once a stark symbol of her desire for detachment, now felt like a vibrant hub of her new existence. The scent of salt air, once a reminder of the vastness of her isolation, was now the perfume of her belonging. It was the scent of the ocean that cradled the creatures she cared for, the ocean that Eli sailed, the ocean that brought both challenges and sustenance to Port Blossom. It was a scent that now spoke of home, of purpose, and of a quiet, unfolding contentment that had taken root in the fertile ground of her own making. The days were long, the work was often difficult, but the rewards were immeasurable, a steady stream of small victories that painted her life with a richness she had never before experienced. The tides had indeed brought her here, and she was finally ready to embrace their full, transformative power.

The gentle unfolding of love with Eli wasn't a dramatic crescendo, but a melody composed of countless quiet notes, each one resonating with a profound truth. It had begun as a tentative melody, a hesitant duet in the echo of her past hurts. But as the days at the Haven grew and the rhythms of Port Blossom settled into her bones, their music had deepened, harmonizing into a rich, resonant chord. The initial awkwardness of two solitary souls finding common ground had long since dissolved, replaced by an effortless synergy that felt as natural as breathing.

Mara found herself observing them, this quiet evolution, with a sense of wonder. It wasn't the fiery passion that often dominated romance novels, the whirlwind romances that swept characters off their feet. Their love was more akin to the steady, persistent tide, its power undeniable, its presence constant, shaping the very landscape of her life with a gentle, inexorable force. There were no grand declarations shouted from rooftops, no earth-shattering proposals etched into cliff faces. Their declarations were whispered in the shared darkness of a stormy night, their promises sealed with a tender touch of hands, their future painted in the hues of a shared horizon.

He was there, always, a silent anchor in the ebb and flow of her days. When she returned from the Haven, her body weary, her mind often a jumble of rescued lives and the ongoing needs of the animal sanctuary, Eli was the calm at the center of her storm. He wouldn't pry, wouldn't demand an accounting of her day, but his quiet presence was an offering of solace. A perfectly brewed cup of tea, the worn armchair by the hearth already warmed by his earlier presence, a gentle smile that spoke volumes of understanding – these were his love languages, and Mara had learned to read them with perfect fluency.

Their shared meals were no longer a concession to practical necessity, but cherished rituals. He'd often cook, his hands moving with an easy competence in her small kitchen, the aroma of roasting vegetables or simmering fish filling the air. Mara, unwinding from her day, would often find herself leaning against the counter, watching him, a soft smile playing on her lips. He'd look up, catch her gaze, and the world would shrink to the space between them, filled with an unspoken affection. He'd tell her about his day on the water, the subtle shifts in the currents, the fleeting glimpses of marine life, and she'd listen, captivated by the passion that lit his eyes. Then, it would be her turn to share, to recount the small victories at the Haven, the tentative steps of a recovering seal pup, the feisty spirit of a rescued otter. He never diminished her work, never saw it as a lesser calling. Instead, he'd listen with genuine interest, his questions thoughtful, his admiration palpable.

The comfortable silences that punctuated their conversations were, perhaps, the most telling testament to their connection. In her past life, silence had often been fraught with unspoken tension, a void waiting to be filled with anxious chatter or defensive pronouncements. With Eli, silence was a sanctuary. It was a space where thoughts could wander freely, where emotions could simply be, without the need for articulation. They could sit on the porch swing, the rhythmic creak a gentle lullaby, and watch the sun dip below the horizon, painting the sky in shades of fire and amethyst, their hands intertwined, their hearts beating in a quiet, shared rhythm. In those moments, words felt inadequate, clumsy attempts to capture the profound peace that settled between them.

The laughter, too, was a vital thread in the tapestry of their love. It was a spontaneous, uninhibited sound that bubbled up from shared jokes, from silly observations, from the sheer joy of being in each other's company. He had a dry wit, a subtle sense of humor that Mara found endlessly endearing. She, in turn, had rediscovered a lightness of spirit that had been absent for so long, her own laughter now a more frequent and genuine sound. They'd tease each other gently, their playful banter a testament to their ease and security in their relationship. He'd mock her occasional attempts at ambitious cooking, and she'd playfully call him out on his stubbornness when it came to anything that wasn't sailing-related.

Their love wasn't built on the precarious foundation of shared past traumas, though they had certainly navigated difficult waters. Instead, it was forged in the quiet crucible of shared present moments, in the conscious decision to build a future together. Mara had never expected to find this kind of love again, certainly not here, in this seemingly remote corner of the world. She had come seeking solace, a temporary reprieve. She had found a home, a purpose, and a partner. Eli had seen past her defenses, her carefully constructed walls, and had simply offered her his steady, unwavering presence. He hadn't tried to fix her, hadn't demanded that she be anything other than who she was, in all her imperfect glory. And in that acceptance, Mara had found the freedom to truly bloom.

He respected her work at the Haven with a deep, quiet reverence. He understood the emotional toll it could take, the moments of heartbreak and frustration. He never minimized her experiences, never offered platitudes. Instead, he would simply be there, a steady hand on her shoulder, a listening ear, a silent acknowledgment of the courage and compassion it took to do what she did. When a particularly difficult case weighed on her, when the weight of responsibility felt crushing, he would often suggest a walk along the beach, their footprints disappearing into the tide, the vastness of the ocean a reminder that some things were larger than their immediate worries.

There were moments, too, when Mara felt a surge of profound gratitude for the sheer serendipity of it all. The idea that she, who had once been so consumed by the pursuit of external validation, so adrift in a sea of self-doubt, had found this quiet, profound happiness. It wasn't a fleeting happiness, tied to achievements or accolades. It was a deep, abiding sense of contentment, woven into the fabric of her everyday life. It was the warmth of Eli's hand in hers as they walked, the comforting weight of his arm around her shoulders as they sat by the fire, the shared smiles that passed between them without a single word.

She remembered a particular evening, not long after Pip, the injured fox, had been released back into the wild. The success of that rescue had been a significant moment for Mara, a validation of her choice to dedicate herself to the Haven. She had returned to the cottage that night feeling emotionally spent, yet exhilarated. Eli had met her at the door, not with questions, but with a gentle embrace and a quiet statement, "You did good, Mara." He had then simply led her to the porch, where he had set up a small telescope. They had spent the next hour gazing at the stars, a celestial map spread out above them, their bodies pressed close together. He had pointed out constellations, told her stories of sailors and their journeys, and Mara had felt a sense of awe, not just at the grandeur of the universe, but at the profound, quiet beauty of the life they were building together.

Their love story was a testament to the power of patience, to the wisdom of open hearts, and to the understanding that true connection often unfolds in the quietest of moments. It wasn't about grand pronouncements; it was about the steady, unwavering presence, the shared laughter, the comforting silences, and the profound understanding that passed between them without a single word. It was a love that felt earned, cherished, and deeply authentic, a gentle arrival that had transformed her world in the most beautiful and profound way. It was the quiet hum of contentment that now permeated her days, a melody composed of salt spray, the scent of pine, and the unwavering love of the man who had become her home.

The air at the Coastal Animal Haven hummed with a renewed energy, a vibrant symphony orchestrated by Mara and Eli's shared vision. It was more than just a sanctuary for ailing creatures; it had blossomed into a testament to what two determined hearts, united by purpose, could achieve. The initial quiet desperation that had clung to the Haven like sea mist had been systematically replaced by the cheerful cacophony of thriving life. Every wagging tail, every contented purr, every chirped greeting was a note in a melody of healing and hope.

Mara found herself constantly surveying their domain with a sense of quiet pride. The kennels, once sparse and echoing with the loneliness of their inhabitants, now boasted colorful, sturdy bedding, interactive toys, and the unmistakable scent of well-cared-for animals. Volunteers, a motley crew drawn from the surrounding towns and even from further afield, moved with practiced efficiency, their laughter mingling with the happy yips and meows. She remembered the early days, the sheer overwhelm of tasks, the constant juggling of limited resources. Now, there was a palpable sense of order, a well-oiled machine powered by passion and effective management. Eli, with his innate pragmatism and unwavering support, had been instrumental in this transformation. He'd helped Mara streamline her often-overwhelmed administrative processes, his calm demeanor a stark contrast to her sometimes-frantic pace. He'd sourced better, more affordable supplies, negotiated with local suppliers, and even lent his steady hands to minor construction projects, reinforcing enclosures and building sturdy ramps for older, arthritic residents.

One of their most significant achievements was the establishment of the 'Foster Family' initiative. Mara, drawing on her past experiences and Eli's grounding wisdom, had recognized the immense benefit of providing animals with temporary homes outside the Haven's walls. This not only freed up crucial space within the sanctuary but, more importantly, allowed the animals to experience a more natural, nurturing environment. It was a program born of compassion, meticulously crafted to ensure the safety and well-being of every foster placement. Potential foster families underwent thorough vetting, and Mara, with her innate understanding of animal behavior and human psychology, worked tirelessly to make perfect matches. She'd spend hours discussing temperaments, energy levels, and living situations, ensuring that both the animal and the family were set up for success. The success stories that emerged from this program were incredibly rewarding. She recalled the case of Barnaby, a timid Labrador mix, terrified of sudden noises and prone to anxiety. Barnaby had been placed with the elderly Mrs. Gable, a retired librarian whose quiet routine and gentle presence proved to be the perfect antidote to his fears. Watching Barnaby blossom under her care, his tail wagging with newfound confidence, was a testament to the program's profound impact. He'd shared countless emails and photos with Mara, detailing Barnaby's progress, his increasing bravery, and the undeniable bond they had formed. When Barnaby was finally ready for adoption, he went to a family that had been touched by Mrs. Gable's stories and had specifically requested a dog with similar needs. It was a beautiful, circular testament to the power of community and compassion.

Eli's influence extended beyond the practical. He possessed a unique ability to connect with the animals in a way that was both gentle and profound. While Mara was the primary caregiver, her empathy often leading her to absorb the animals' pain, Eli's presence was a calming force. He'd often take the more skittish dogs for walks along the rugged coastline, his quiet voice a soothing murmur against the roar of the waves. He understood the language of their body language, the subtle shifts in posture, the flick of an ear, the width of a pupil. He could sense their fear, their apprehension, and offer a silent reassurance that transcended words. He'd often report back to Mara, his observations incredibly insightful, helping her to better understand the nuances of an animal's recovery. He'd tell her, "That stray cat, the one that's been hiding under the workbench, she's not aggressive, Mara. She's just deeply distrustful. She watches everything. Give her time, and let her set the pace." And he'd be right. Mara, often eager to accelerate the healing process, would learn patience from Eli, allowing the animals the space and time they needed to rebuild their trust.

The 'Second Chance' adoption events, once small, sporadic affairs, had become highly anticipated community gatherings. Mara, with her flair for creating warm and inviting atmospheres, transformed the Haven's grounds into a festive marketplace of potential new beginnings. Colorful banners fluttered in the sea breeze, tables laden with homemade baked goods and crafts dotted the lawn, and the air was filled with the happy barks of dogs eager to meet their future families. Eli, never one for the spotlight, would often be seen manning the barbecue, his quiet efficiency a comforting presence amidst the cheerful chaos, his smile genuine as he served up burgers and hot dogs to eager attendees. He had a knack for striking up conversations with potential adopters, offering practical advice about animal care and sharing gentle anecdotes about some of the Haven's long-term residents. He never pushed, never pressured, but his genuine love for the animals and his quiet confidence in the Haven's mission were infectious. Mara loved watching him interact, seeing the way people were drawn to his calm sincerity. It was a partnership that flowed seamlessly, each of them bringing their unique strengths to the table, creating a synergy that was more than the sum of its parts.

The success of the Haven wasn't solely measured in adoptions or recovered animals. It was also in the growing network of volunteers who had become an integral part of their lives. Mara had implemented a robust training program, not just for animal care, but also for customer service, volunteer coordination, and even basic animal first aid. This investment in her team had paid dividends, fostering a sense of ownership and pride among the volunteers. They weren't just helping out; they were stakeholders in the Haven's mission. There was Liam, a young art student who spent hours creating intricate adoption profiles, his sketches capturing the unique personalities of each animal with astonishing accuracy. Then there was Sarah, a retired nurse who had become the Haven's unofficial 'vet tech' assistant, her gentle touch and vast knowledge invaluable in administering medications and monitoring post-operative recovery. And of course, there were the countless others, students earning community service hours, families seeking a shared activity, individuals simply wanting to contribute to a worthy cause. Mara fostered a sense of camaraderie among them, organizing potlucks and informal gatherings, creating a supportive community that extended beyond the Haven's gates. Eli, in his own quiet way, contributed to this sense of community too. He'd often share stories of the sea with the volunteers, tales of dolphins and whales, of the delicate balance of the marine ecosystem, subtly weaving in lessons about the interconnectedness of all living things.

The financial stability of the Haven had also seen a remarkable improvement. Mara, initially daunted by the prospect of fundraising, had discovered a hidden talent for it. She'd organized sponsored walks along the coast, silent auctions featuring donations from local businesses, and even a popular "Paws for a Cause" gala. Eli, always practical, had helped her set up a transparent accounting system and had advised on long-term financial planning. His knowledge of the local community and its businesses proved invaluable in securing sponsorships and in-kind donations. They had also launched a successful online donation campaign, utilizing social media to share compelling stories of rescued animals and the impact of the Haven's work. The community's response had been overwhelming, a testament to the deep well of compassion that existed in Port Blossom. Every donation, no matter how small, was acknowledged with a heartfelt thank you, fostering a sense of gratitude and encouraging continued support. Mara often found herself in awe of the generosity they had encountered, realizing that the Haven had become more than just a local charity; it had become a beloved institution, a symbol of the town's commitment to kindness.

The physical improvements to the Haven were also a source of immense satisfaction. What had once been a somewhat dilapidated structure was now a well-maintained, functional facility. Eli's practical skills had been invaluable here. He'd overseen the construction of a new, larger outdoor play area for the dogs, complete with agility equipment and a shaded seating area for visitors. He'd helped design and build a state-of-the-art cat enclosure, a multi-level paradise filled with climbing structures, scratching posts, and sun-drenched windows. He'd even tackled the leaky roof and the outdated plumbing, transforming the once-struggling sanctuary into a place of comfort and safety for its residents. Mara had sourced the best possible equipment, from specialized veterinary tools to durable, easy-to-clean flooring, ensuring that every aspect of the Haven was designed with the animals' well-being in mind. The new veterinary clinic, a project they had painstakingly planned for over a year, was finally operational. Equipped with an examination table, diagnostic tools, and a small surgical suite, it allowed them to perform minor procedures on-site, significantly reducing the cost and stress associated with transporting animals to distant veterinary hospitals. This not only saved precious funds but also meant that animals received faster, more consistent care, leading to quicker recoveries.

The very atmosphere within the Haven had shifted. The subtle scent of disinfectant, once a stark reminder of illness and injury, was now softened by the clean smell of fresh bedding and the faint, comforting aroma of kibble. The echoing emptiness had been filled by the contented sighs of sleeping dogs, the playful chirping of birds in their aviary, and the gentle murmur of volunteers tending to their charges. Mara often found herself simply standing at the entrance, taking it all in, a profound sense of peace settling over her. She saw the joy in the eyes of a newly adopted puppy nuzzling its human, the quiet dignity of an elderly cat basking in a sunbeam, the hopeful gaze of a shy dog watching the world go by. These were not just animals; they were individuals, each with a story, each deserving of a happy ending. And she, with Eli by her side, was helping to write those endings.

The Haven's success was a direct reflection of their shared journey. Mara had arrived at Port Blossom carrying the weight of past failures and the gnawing emptiness of a life unfulfilled. The Haven had offered her a lifeline, a purpose that resonated deep within her soul. Eli, with his quiet strength and unwavering belief in her, had provided the steady anchor she needed to navigate the turbulent waters of healing and self-discovery. Their collaboration was a testament to the idea that true fulfillment wasn't found in solitary pursuits, but in shared endeavors, in the messy, beautiful process of building something meaningful together. The barks and purrs, the wagging tails and contented sighs, were not just sounds of animal happiness; they were echoes of their own unfolding happiness, a symphony of second chances that played out every single day within the thriving walls of the Coastal Animal Haven. It was a place where broken things were mended, where lost souls found their way home, and where love, in its purest, most compassionate form, was the guiding force.

The morning mist, a soft, pearly veil, clung to the coastline, muffling the usual symphony of gulls and lapping waves. Mara drew her cardigan tighter, the chill seeping through the thin wool, a pleasant contrast to the warmth blooming in her chest. Her bare feet sank slightly into the damp sand as she walked along the shore, the rhythmic pull of the tide a soothing counterpoint to her thoughts. This had become her ritual, a quiet communion with the awakening day, a moment to simply *be*. The vast expanse of the ocean, stretching out to meet a sky painted in soft hues of rose and lavender, always had a way of recalibrating her perspective. It was a constant reminder of both the immensity of the world and the quiet power of small, persistent forces, like the tide, like her own healing.

Port Blossom. The name itself evoked a sense of gentle beauty, and the reality lived up to the promise. It wasn't a bustling metropolis, nor a quaint village frozen in time. It was something more organic, a place that breathed with the rhythm of the sea, its charm woven into the everyday lives of its inhabitants. Mara had arrived seeking refuge, a temporary haven from a life that felt shattered. She had expected solace, a quiet corner to lick her wounds. She had found so much more. She had found a home.

The small cottage she rented, nestled just a stone's throw from the harbor, was a testament to simple living. Its walls, painted a cheerful, sea-foam green, seemed to absorb the coastal light, making the interior feel perpetually bright. The worn wooden floors creaked a familiar welcome underfoot, and the scent of salt and old books perpetually perfumed the air. Evenings were often spent by the hearth, the crackling fire casting dancing shadows across the room, a mug of steaming chamomile tea warming her hands. She'd lose herself in novels, her mind no longer a battlefield of anxieties but a tranquil landscape of unfolding stories. Sometimes, she would simply sit, listening to the wind whistling around the eaves, a profound sense of peace settling over her. It was a peace she had long thought lost forever, a gentle quietude that whispered of resilience and renewed hope.

Her mornings began with this walk, the cool sand between her toes, the salty spray kissing her face. She'd watch the fishing boats chug out of the harbor, their engines a low rumble against the dawn chorus, their crews a familiar, hardworking presence. She knew many of them by name now, their weathered faces etched with the stories of the sea. There was old Silas, with his perpetually twinkling eyes and tales of legendary catches; young Finn, eager and ambitious, always willing to share a story about a particularly challenging tide. They'd nod, a gruff but warm acknowledgment, sometimes a wave, their presence a quiet affirmation of her belonging. These were not the superficial pleasantries of a stranger; they were the simple, genuine greetings of someone who was becoming a part of the fabric of their community.

The local bakery, 'The Salty Crumb,' had become another cherished destination. The aroma of freshly baked bread and sweet pastries spilled onto the street, a siren call she rarely resisted. Mrs. Gable, the owner, a woman whose silver hair was usually dusted with flour, greeted her with the same warm smile each day. "The usual, Mara?" she'd ask, her voice as comforting as the scent of cinnamon. "A whole wheat loaf, still warm from the oven, and perhaps a blueberry scone today?" Mara would reply, her voice soft, filled with a quiet contentment. She'd chat with Mrs. Gable for a few minutes, about the weather, about the latest community news, about the animals at the Haven, a connection forged in shared kindness and the simple act of breaking bread. It was in these small, ordinary interactions that Mara discovered the true depth of Port Blossom's charm.

The town square, a small, sun-dappled area dominated by a weathered stone fountain, was the heart of Port Blossom. On market days, it buzzed with life. Local farmers displayed their vibrant produce, artisans showcased their handcrafted wares, and the air thrummed with a cheerful energy. Mara would often wander through, her basket filling with plump tomatoes, crisp lettuces, and fragrant herbs. She'd stop to admire knitted scarves, admire hand-painted ceramics, and often find herself drawn into conversations with the vendors, their passion for their craft palpable. She remembered her initial apprehension, the fear of being an outsider, of not fitting in. But Port Blossom had a way of absorbing newcomers, of gently folding them into its welcoming embrace. Her contributions to the Coastal Animal Haven, her quiet dedication, had also earned her a certain respect, a recognition that she was not just passing through, but actively contributing to the town's well-being.

She recalled the first time she'd attended a town hall meeting, her heart pounding with a nervous flutter. It was about a proposed development that would have impacted a stretch of coastal wetlands, a vital habitat for migratory birds. Mara, usually reticent in such public forums, had found herself speaking, her voice trembling at first, but gaining strength as she spoke of the ecological importance of the wetlands, her passion for conservation overriding her shyness. Eli had stood beside her, a silent, steady presence, his quiet nod of encouragement fueling her resolve. The townspeople had listened, their faces thoughtful. The proposal was eventually amended, a compromise reached that protected the wetlands. It was a small victory, perhaps, but for Mara, it was a profound moment of empowerment, a realization that her voice, even a quiet one, could make a difference in this town.

The evenings were equally fulfilling. Sometimes, she'd join Eli and a few friends for dinner at 'The Anchor,' a cozy pub overlooking the harbor. The scent of grilled fish and ale filled the air, the murmur of conversation a comforting backdrop. Eli, his easygoing nature a stark contrast to the intensity of their work at the Haven, would share anecdotes, his laughter a low rumble. Mara found herself relaxing, shedding the last vestiges of her former anxieties. She'd listen, chime in, her contributions becoming more confident, more natural. She discovered a joy in these simple gatherings, in the shared stories, the easy camaraderie. It was a far cry from the solitary existence she had once endured.

She found a particular delight in the small, unexpected moments that punctuated her days. The sight of a lone surfer catching a wave as the sun dipped below the horizon, painting the sky in fiery strokes. The sound of children's laughter echoing from the park near the Haven. The unexpected kindness of a stranger offering to help carry her groceries. Each of these small gestures, these fleeting glimpses of shared humanity, wove themselves into the tapestry of her contentment. She learned to appreciate the quiet beauty of the changing seasons – the vibrant bloom of wildflowers in spring, the golden warmth of summer, the crisp, invigorating air of autumn, the hushed, tranquil snowfalls of winter, each offering its own unique charm.

There was a particular stretch of beach, a little further down the coast, where the sand was a soft, fine grain, and the dunes rose in gentle undulations, carpeted with sea grass. It was her sanctuary within a sanctuary, a place where she could truly escape, where the only sounds were the whisper of the wind and the distant cry of the gulls. She'd often bring a book, but more often than not, she'd simply sit, watching the waves break and recede, the endless cycle a metaphor for her own journey. She had come to understand that healing wasn't always about grand gestures or dramatic breakthroughs. It was often about the slow, steady erosion of pain, like the tide smoothing the sand, leaving behind a calmer, more peaceful shore.

The sense of belonging in Port Blossom was not a forced or manufactured feeling. It had grown organically, nurtured by shared experiences and mutual respect. When a sudden storm had damaged a section of the Haven's roof, the town had rallied. Volunteers, many of whom were already friends and neighbors, had arrived with tools and lumber, working alongside Eli and Mara to repair the damage before the next wave of rain. The local hardware store had donated materials, and Mrs. Gable had sent over trays of her famous sandwiches and thermoses of hot coffee. It was a tangible demonstration of community spirit, a testament to the fact that the Coastal Animal Haven was not just Mara and Eli's project, but a beloved institution of Port Blossom itself.

Mara had also discovered a newfound appreciation for the slower pace of life. In the city, she had been caught in a relentless current of ambition and expectation, her days a blur of meetings and deadlines. Here, the rhythm was different. Time seemed to stretch, allowing for reflection, for savoring small moments. She learned to find joy in the simple act of tending her small herb garden, in the satisfaction of a perfectly brewed cup of coffee, in the quiet companionship of a good book. These were not frivolous pursuits; they were the building blocks of a life rich in contentment, a life where happiness was not an elusive prize to be chased, but a quiet presence to be cultivated.

She found herself looking forward to the mundane, the everyday. The ritual of watering her window boxes, the weekly trip to the farmer's market, the quiet evenings spent reading by the fire. These were the anchors that held her steady, the small comforts that reminded her of the quiet joy that could be found in ordinary life. She had once believed that fulfillment lay in grand achievements, in external validation. Now, she understood that true contentment often resided in the quiet corners, in the unpretentious beauty of everyday moments, in the deep, abiding peace of knowing that you are exactly where you are meant to be. Port Blossom, with its gentle tides and its warm, welcoming heart, had become more than just a place of refuge. It had become her home, a place where her own quiet strength had finally found fertile ground to bloom. The charm of Port Blossom wasn't in its grand vistas or its bustling energy; it was in the subtle, persistent melody of everyday life, a song that Mara now hummed with a joy that was as deep and as vast as the ocean stretching before her. She realized that sometimes, the quietest places hold the greatest capacity for joy and profound change.

The horizon, a soft, blurred line where the cerulean sky melted into the deep sapphire of the ocean, was a canvas of endless possibility. Mara stood on the weathered, salt-bleached planks of the pier, the rhythmic creak of the wood beneath her bare feet a familiar lullaby. The salty breeze, usually a brisk caress, felt softer today, almost as if the sea itself was whispering secrets of contentment. She inhaled deeply, the air a potent blend of brine, kelp, and the fainter, sweeter scent of the wildflowers that dotted the cliffs above. It was a scent that had, in its own quiet way, become the perfume of her peace.

A profound sense of gratitude washed over her, as warm and all-encompassing as the midday sun beginning to climb higher in the sky. It was a feeling that settled deep within her bones, a quiet hum of thankfulness for the winding, often unexpected, path that had brought her to this very moment, to this very place. Port Blossom. The name, once just a geographical marker on a map, now resonated with the resonance of home, of belonging, of a life rebuilt, stone by patient stone. She remembered the Mara who had arrived here, a fragile vessel tossed by storms, her spirit bruised and battered. The journey from that brokenness to this present state of serene fulfillment had been a long one, marked by quiet persistence and the gentle, unwavering support of those who had become her anchor.

Eli. The mere thought of him sent a ripple of warmth through her. He was standing a few feet away, his silhouette etched against the bright expanse of the sea, his gaze fixed on the distant horizon, much like hers. He turned, a slow smile spreading across his face, a smile that held the quiet understanding of shared journeys, of unspoken promises. He walked towards her, his footsteps sure and steady on the wooden planks, and took her hand. His touch was a familiar comfort, a silent testament to the strength and depth of their bond. "Thinking?" he asked, his voice a low rumble that seemed to harmonize with the ocean's murmur.

Mara squeezed his hand. "Just... grateful," she replied, her voice barely a whisper against the vastness. "Grateful for all of it. The good, the bad, the messy, the unexpected. It all led here." She gestured to the sparkling water, the distant sails of a fishing boat, the sleepy charm of the town nestled against the coast. "This place, this life. I never thought it was possible."

Eli's thumb brushed over her knuckles, a small gesture that spoke volumes. "You did the work, Mara. You opened yourself up to it. And it opened up to you." He paused, his gaze drifting back to the ocean. "Life has a way of surprising you, doesn't it? Just when you think you have it all figured out, it throws you a curveball. Or, in our case," he chuckled softly, "it brings you to Port Blossom."

She leaned her head against his shoulder, the familiar scent of his worn leather jacket a comforting presence. "I used to fear those curveballs," she confessed. "I used to dread the unknown. Now... I don't. Not as much, anyway." She watched a flock of gulls circle overhead, their cries a wild, untamed song. "There will always be uncertainties. That's just the nature of things, isn't it? The tides will always shift, the weather will always change. But I know now that I can weather those changes. I've learned how to find my balance, even when the ground beneath me feels unsteady."

Eli nodded, his arm wrapping around her waist, pulling her closer. "That's the beauty of it, isn't it? It's not about avoiding the storms, but about learning to navigate them. About trusting that you have the strength within you to find your way back to shore, or to discover a new shore altogether." He looked down at her, his eyes, the color of a stormy sea, filled with a warmth that melted away any lingering shadows. "And it's about not having to navigate them alone. Knowing that someone is standing beside you, through every ebb and flow."

The future, once a looming specter of anxiety, now felt like an open sea, vast and inviting. It wasn't a naive optimism, nor a blind faith in destiny. It was a hard-won confidence, forged in the crucible of her past experiences, tempered by the quiet strength she had discovered within herself. She had learned that resilience wasn't about being unbreakable, but about the ability to mend, to adapt, to find beauty even in the scars. And love, the kind of love she shared with Eli, was not a fragile flower to be protected from every breeze, but a deep-rooted tree, its branches reaching towards the sky, its roots firmly anchored in the earth.

"Remember when we first met?" Mara mused, her gaze following a distant trawler as it chugged towards the harbor. "It feels like a lifetime ago. I was so guarded, so afraid to let anyone in. And you... you were so patient. You saw something in me that I couldn't even see in myself."

Eli's hand tightened around hers. "I saw a fire," he said, his voice low and sincere. "A spark that just needed a little tending. You had been through so much, but the core of you, Mara, was always strong. You just needed a safe harbor to find your way back to yourself." He smiled. "And I was lucky enough to be the one who found you drifting in."

She laughed, a light, happy sound that was carried away by the wind. "Lucky indeed. I think I'm the lucky one, though. You showed me what it meant to truly live, not just exist. To embrace the messy, imperfect beauty of it all." She tilted her head back, looking up at the endless blue. "I used to think happiness was a destination, something you arrived at after ticking off all the right boxes. Now I know it's more like the journey itself. It's in the quiet mornings on the pier, the taste of Mrs. Gable's blueberry scones, the laughter shared with friends at 'The Anchor,' the furry faces of the animals at the Haven."

"It's in the little things," Eli agreed. "The things you can almost miss if you're not paying attention. The way the light hits the water at sunset, the sound of the waves crashing on the shore, the warmth of a shared silence." He brought her hand to his lips, pressing a gentle kiss to her knuckles. "It's in the knowledge that whatever tomorrow brings, we'll face it together."

The vastness of the ocean no longer felt intimidating, but exhilarating. It was a symbol of the infinite possibilities that lay ahead. The currents might pull them in unexpected directions, but they had each other, a compass of love and trust that would guide them through any storm. The unknown was no longer a source of dread, but an invitation to explore, to discover, to continue growing, both individually and as a couple.

"I don't have a five-year plan anymore," Mara confessed with a smile. "No grand ambitions that consume my every thought.

It's freeing, in a way. I'm just... open. Open to what's next. To wherever the tides may bring us."

Eli's gaze met hers, a profound understanding passing between them. "And that's exactly where you're meant to be," he said, his voice filled with a quiet conviction. "Open. Ready. With a heart that knows its own strength and a love that can weather any sea." He pulled her into a warm embrace, the scent of salt and sea filling her senses. The rhythmic pulse of his heart against hers was a steady, comforting beat, a promise of the life they were building together, day by quiet, beautiful day. The horizon stretched before them, a boundless expanse, and for the first time in a long time, Mara felt utterly, completely at peace, ready to embrace whatever adventures the tide might bring.